BY ROSALIND LAUER

LANCASTER CROSSROADS
A Simple Faith
A Simple Crossroads (novella)

SEASONS OF LANCASTER
A Simple Winter
A Simple Spring
A Simple Autumn

A Simple Faith

A Simple Faith

A LANCASTER CROSSROADS NOVEL

Rosalind Lauer

BALLANTINE BOOKS TRADE PAPERBACKS
NEW YORK

Copyright © 2013 by Rosalind Lauer
Excerpt from *A Simple Hope* by Rosalind Lauer
copyright © 2013 by Rosalind Lauer

Published in the United States by Ballantine Books, an imprint of The Random House Publishing Group, a division of Random House LLC, New York, a Penguin Random House Company.

BALLANTINE and the HOUSE colophon are registered trademarks of Random House LLC.

All scripture taken from *The Zondervan KJV Study Bible*. Copyright © 2002 by Zondervan. Used by permission of Zondervan Publishing House.

This book contains an excerpt from the forthcoming book *A Simple Hope* by Rosalind Lauer. The excerpt has been set for this edition only, and may not reflect the final content of the forthcoming edition.

LIBRARY OF CONGRESS CATALOGING-IN-PUBLICATION DATA
Lauer, Rosalind.
A Simple Faith : A Lancaster Crossroads Novel / Rosalind Lauer.
pages cm. — (A Lancaster Crossroads Novel)
ISBN 978-0-345-54326-4 (paperback) —
ISBN 978-0-345-54327-1 (eBook)
1. Amish—Fiction. 2. Accidents—Fiction.
3. Lancaster County (Pa.)—Fiction. I. Title.
PS3612.A94276S535 2013
813'.6—dc23
2013023867

Printed in the United States of America on acid-free paper

www.ballantinebooks.com

2 4 6 8 9 7 5 3 1

First Edition

Book design by Karin Batten

This one is for the nurses,
sister Maureen, cousin Rachel,
and my good friends from Wagner College,
Champions of Service,
Love, and Compassion.
God bless!

PART ONE

The
Good Samaritan

Thou shalt love the Lord thy God with all thy heart,
And with all thy soul,
And with all thy strength,
And with all thy mind;
And thy neighbour as thyself.
—LUKE 10:27

ᴏɢ 1 ᴏɢ

"*D*on't leave me." The woman lifted a withered hand from the white bedsheets, reaching for Haley. "You're the only one who listens."

Haley Donovan held the patient's hand yet again, gently stroking the mottled skin on her wrist. "Mrs. Pendergrass, I would love to stay, but you know I have other patients to take care of."

"I know that, but you can't say no to an old woman who needs you. Now, be a doll and get me my handbag from the closet."

As Haley reached for the purse, her nail caught on a sharp edge of the small cubby, snagging it. She winced as she handed over the bag, her supervisor's voice haunting her.

Keep your nails trimmed and short. Don't let your vanity get in the way of patient care.

"What's the matter, princess?" the old woman asked.

"Nothing." Haley looked away quickly, not sure what bothered her more—tearing her nail or being called a princess. Was it because of her blond hair? Her long legs? Too much makeup?

People were so quick to stereotype her as a dumb blonde, and the princess thing . . . that just rubbed her the wrong way. Graham had called her princess, and he'd fully intended to take care of her as if she were a queen.

A queen trapped in a castle.

If she had stayed with him, she wouldn't have to be here now, emptying bedpans, breaking nails, and ducking her supervisor. She would be well rested, well dressed, and well manicured. A fair princess, destined to follow her husband's decisions and dream his dreams.

No . . . that wasn't the life Haley wanted. But sometimes she wondered if she was really cut out for hospital work. Patients like Mrs. Pendergrass made Haley wonder if she was doing the right thing, trying to be a nurse. She didn't mind giving the woman a sponge bath and brushing her hair and listening to her stories of how things used to be. But the woman, who seemed fit as a fiddle, was monopolizing her time. Haley couldn't do anything to help Mrs. Pendergrass, and with two other patients waiting for care, Haley felt tension mounting.

She wasn't cut out for this. Already she was a failure in her profession, and she wasn't even out of nursing school yet.

It seemed to be a pattern in her life now. Failure in love. Failure in school. Failure in life.

No, that wasn't entirely fair. She was giving it all another try, with some major changes. She'd returned to school and she was trying to make a positive difference in the world.

She tuned in to what her patient was saying, another story about her daughter and grandchildren who had moved to Pittsburgh. Her heart ached for this woman's loneliness, but if Dr. Swanson found out that Haley had already spent so much time with one patient, she would be in big trouble.

"You won't want me chattering in here when your show is on. It starts in ten minutes." Haley showed Mrs. Pendergrass the TV remote and the call button, and then reminded her to drink some water.

"But you'll come back?" the woman asked, her face awash with worry.

"Definitely."

Haley sank her teeth into her lower lip as she noticed the clock over the nurses' station. Two hours of her shift had already passed, and they'd been monopolized by Mrs. Pendergrass. It wasn't fair to the other patients who legitimately needed care, and Haley knew she was going to be in a pickle if she didn't get started on her clinical assessments. She hadn't taken any notes, and if she didn't get something down soon she would be lost when it came time to start her reports. "It's clear that, as a nursing student, writing is your weakness," Dr. Swanson, her clinical advisor, had told her. "You need to work on time management, and your patient notes need to be more concise."

It was true—Haley knew it—but these were issues she had wrestled with all her life. A simple report became a challenge when letters jumped around the page and turned sideways.

"Stop biting your lip; it's not a good look for you." Aeesha didn't even look up from the computer, where she was updating charts. Aeesha Wilkins, a fellow nursing student, always managed to keep her sense of humor, even during tense moments. "What's stressing you, sweet pea?"

"Mrs. Pendergrass in 312."

"The whiner?"

Haley blew back her bangs, nodding. "She's sweet, but nothing I do satisfies her, and she just doesn't understand that I can't spend my entire shift doting on her. I have two other patients."

"And charts to do. And Swanson breathing down our necks." Aeesha clicked the mouse, then typed in some notes. "How about I trade you my Amish man for your whiner?"

Haley looked up at the board. "Mr. Yoder in 320? I wish." Yoder had mangled a hand in a farming accident—a dramatic injury that had made the local news. Although she was still a nursing student, Haley knew she was drawn to patients who required more intensive care. "At least Mr. Yoder has a real injury," Haley said. "He needs medical attention. Unlike Mrs. Pendergrass, who complains of phantom pain that comes and goes."

"The old phantom pain story." Aeesha shook her head. "So many of them just come in for drugs. It's sad, but I don't mind doting. I figure TLC is nonaddicting, and I'm good with the old ones. The Amish—that's another story. Did you see all the visitors he has? His room is packed with Amish men. All those men, talking a mile a minute with their long beards and black fedoras. It's way out of my comfort zone to march in and start a sponge bath. Telling an Amish man to get naked, that just seems wrong."

Haley grinned. "He's a patient, like any other. And he needs real nursing care, not just sympathy and back rubs. Believe me, I'd switch with you if Swanson wouldn't blow a gasket over it."

"At least you're considering my gaskets before you make an arbitrary change." The clipped voice made Haley and Aeesha look up from the counter. Dr. Sonia Swanson, their clinical supervisor, stood there beside a young man in a navy suit with the bluest eyes Haley had ever seen.

"Dr. Swanson . . ." Haley stammered. "We were just—"

"Comparing notes? Broadcasting patients' personal details? Displaying blatant unprofessionalism?" She glared at Haley and Aeesha as if they'd been dancing down the hall in bikinis.

"Sorry." Haley wasn't sure how much their instructor had heard, but she couldn't let this incident impact her grade. With her test anxiety, she was counting on a high clinical evaluation to bring up her overall grade. Her scholarship would dry up if she didn't maintain a B average, and she couldn't afford to continue nursing school without that stipend. "We were just wondering if our patients might be better off if we made a switch."

"We're just trying to work things out so that we can play to our strengths," Aeesha added. "No disrespect intended."

"None taken." Swanson pinched a button on her crisp white jacket with her name monogrammed over the pocket. "But before you go trading patients like stocks, you need to know that I don't sling out assignments randomly. When you're certified staff nurses, you'll need to work with patients who do not play to your strengths, and you might as well learn to do it now."

"I get your point," Aeesha said, "but does it really matter if Haley changes a dressing while I help Mrs. Pendergrass onto the toilet?"

"It does." Swanson cocked her head to the side, as if she needed to see Aeesha from a new angle. "You need to review your class notes on assessing patient needs. Mr. Yoder is showing signs of posttraumatic stress, and just because Mrs. Pendergrass isn't diagnosed yet doesn't mean she doesn't deserve your time and attention."

"We treat the body and the mind," the young man said. "At least, we try to."

When the man spoke up, Haley was glad to have a chance to ease away from the glare of her professor. He wasn't from around here—she could tell by the smooth suit and the crisp-collared shirt. Plenty of doctors wore suits, but they weren't quite so designer perfect. Or was he too young to be a doctor? Haley couldn't tell, but she liked his vibe. She would have smiled and chatted him up if she weren't still facing the wrath of Swanson.

"Are you a doctor?" asked Aeesha.

Swanson gestured toward the young man and introduced Aeesha and Haley. "Meet Dr. Dylan Monroe. He just joined our staff as a psychologist."

"I'll be coordinating the community outreach program."

So he was here to stay. That was good news. "Welcome to LanCo General, Dr. Monroe," Haley said, trying to smooth over the shaky introduction. He probably thought she was a slacker, trying to dump Mrs. Pendergrass on another nursing student.

"Please . . . call me Dylan. If I'm going to blend with the community, I can't stand on formality."

As Dr. Monroe shook her hand, Haley wanted to tell him that there was no way he would blend in here wearing a suit like that. Lancaster County was the land of Amish and rolling hills, apple butter and quilts. But for once she kept her mouth shut and smiled up into his bedazzling eyes. The new doctor was one good-looking guy, but he didn't seem to know it. By the end of the week, he'd be the talk of the nursing staff, students and RNs alike.

No wedding ring, Haley noticed. Of course, she was just curious, not looking for herself. After the disastrous results of a wedding called off at the last minute in June, she was taking a break from relationships and commitments. Her mind spun to the image of the gold band she'd purchased for Graham, which had been returned to the jeweler for a partial refund.

"Back to our patients." Swanson looked up at the scheduling board, squinting in calculation. "Dylan, perhaps you can assist Haley in her assessment of Mrs. Pendergrass."

He nodded. "I'd be happy to."

Swanson turned to Aeesha. "As for our Amish patient, I will show you how to direct visitors out of the room so that you can care for Mr. Yoder."

"It's not that simple, Dr. Swanson," Aeesha objected. "Believe me, I've tried."

"Plain folk are very big on rules," Dr. Swanson said, leading the way down the hall. "You just have to look them in the eye and communicate, same as with anyone else." She motioned Aeesha away from the nurses' station. "Come on. Let me show you how we do it."

"So . . ." Dylan turned to Haley, showering her with the full force of his blue eyes. "Where is Mrs. Pendergrass?"

"In 312." She pointed down the hall, reminding herself to breathe. What was this stupid, silly giddiness brought on by this man? It was more than the embarrassment over the bad first impression she must have made. She hadn't felt this way since . . . well, since her parents had given her a puppy for her thirteenth birthday.

"You're new here?" she asked cordially.

"This is my first day."

"Where did you come from?"

"St. Xavier in Philadelphia."

"What brought you here? You don't look like the type to be lured by Amish quilts and jams."

"Really?" The corner of his mouth curved a bit. "So I guess you're not interested in my quilt collection."

"I'm just saying, most city people who head out this way are looking for a quaint country weekend. They don't come to stay."

"City life doesn't hold much appeal for me anymore," he said as they walked side by side down the corridor. "And I am interested in the Amish, but not for their quilts. I'd like to develop a community outreach program for the Amish. A program that really works."

"But they keep to themselves." Haley considered her personal experiences, growing up side by side with the Amish here in Lancaster County. "I've lived here all my life, and I've barely exchanged a dozen words with Amish people. Mostly I notice them when I'm passing their horse-drawn buggies on the road or waiting in line behind them at Walmart or the ice-cream parlor."

"Even Old Order Amish are allowed to be treated by medical doctors," Dylan pointed out.

"But you're a psychologist. You think they're going to turn to you with their problems?"

"That's the way the psych thing works."

"I don't think they'll go for that. They've got lots of family and ministers to help them work things out. You won't find an Amish person in therapy or anything."

He turned to her, rubbing his knuckles over his chin. "Do you like seeing rain ruin a parade? Ice-cream scoops drop from cones? Babies cry?"

"I'm not that way. I'm just telling you—"

"Someday we'll have the conversation about the glass being half full or half empty. For now, tell me about the patient."

Haley swallowed back the defense of her cheerful disposition and reeled off Mrs. Pendergrass's profile. "She's eighty-two and lives alone. No significant medical history, but came to the ER with complaints of abdominal pain. Nothing showed up in her film or blood work."

"So far there's no diagnosis?"

"Right, but she's very cranky. She's worried that the pain will return once she's home alone."

"And do you think her pain is real?" he asked.

"I know it's real," she said carefully. "I just don't know if there's a medical explanation for it."

"Excellent answer, Haley. Do you think she'll mind if I ask her some questions?"

"I think she'll like it." *I would definitely like it,* she thought.

Outside the patient's door, he reached for Mrs. Pendergrass's chart. His hand brushed hers as she gave him the clipboard, a casual contact that seemed so personal. It was personal. This was a guy who lived in the moment, not like the other doctors who seemed to have their minds on a thousand different things.

"Mrs. P is a talker."

"That works. I'm a listener."

Looking up at him, she suspected Dylan Monroe was an excellent listener.

Later that day, before her shift ended, she checked the schedule and changed her hours to coincide with Dr. Monroe's. Sometimes destiny brought people together. And sometimes destiny needed a slight schedule change.

2

*E*lsie Lapp stepped onto a stool so that she could open the curtains to the warm glow of the sun rising over the trees. Orange and pink chased away the purple and sapphire of the night sky, promising another glorious day. Cold air seeped in, and she traced her fingers along the sill to a gap at the base of the windowpane.

Another repair for Dat and Caleb. She would put it on their list, but she didn't expect them to get to it anytime soon. Lately their days had been full of work, trying to get the old carriage house into shape.

She could hear them now, putting new shingles on the roof in the chilly air of early morning. The sound of hammering was music to her ears.

Dat planned to start a business in the old building, a wheelwright or harness shop. Folks were always asking Tom Lapp's advice on how to fix their buggies, and it made good sense for Dat to make a living doing what he knew best.

And leave me to run the Country Store, Elsie thought with a little smile as she smoothed down the last quilt. Although she was only seventeen, Elsie managed the store these days, with a little help from her father and her older brother, Caleb, and it was a task that brought her great pleasure. The store that had been in Mamm's family for three generations had begun to fail in the past few years. Mamm's death had plunged Thomas Lapp into a business he didn't know or understand.

It wasn't Dat's fault that the merchandise had crossed the line. A few years back, Bishop Samuel had ordered Dat to stop selling plaques that depicted Amish folk. The bishop had been emphatic that the carved statues violated the Ordnung, the strict rules that the Amish lived by. Graven images were forbidden by the Bible, and the bishop deemed that the images of Amish children violated that rule. Dat had gone and pulled all the Amish crafts from the shelves of their shop—including homemade jams and quilts, trivets and birdhouses.

Just like that, the Country Store, once a popular stop for tourists in Lancaster County, had withered into nothing more than a corner convenience store providing folks with bottled water and candy bars.

Such a sad, dusty store it had become.

Not at all what Mamm would have wanted.

Elsie had been just six years old when her mother died. A child, ya, but old enough to recognize her father's heartbreak and his unease at running the shop. At the age of eight she'd started helping out in the store after school and on weekends. As soon as she'd finished her schooling, she'd become the full-time face of the Country Store, greeting tourists and Amish alike, creating decorative displays in the shop windows and bringing back Amish crafts like homemade soaps, heather, honey, and sock dolls.

With each new product, Elsie had seen sales and profits increase, bringing in enough income to support their family. The Country

Store was on its way back, and Elsie was ready to take the next step—selling to vendors in Philadelphia.

For that move, she needed to talk to Dat.

She grabbed the broom and hurried down the stairs, eager to talk to her father at breakfast. If he could spare a day away from the work here, they could go to Philadelphia together and work everything out.

The kitchen was warm and animated with the chatter from the gathering family . . . her loving family. After Mamm died it had been just the four of them—Dat, Caleb, Emma, and Elsie. Then, when Elsie was still a girl, Dat married Fanny Yoder, and now they were a family of seven. Amish families were usually large like that—lots of siblings and lots of love. But for Elsie, family mattered even more because of her lack of social life. To the rest of the world, she was an oddity—a tiny person with wide-spaced, pebbled teeth and misshapen ears. But here, she was just Elsie, a true helper, a caring sister and daughter.

Heat from the woodstove cut through the chill that lingered in the rest of the house, reminding Elsie of the reason why the kitchen was her favorite place in the house. Food to feed the body and conversation to feed the soul.

At the stove, her older sister, Emma, slid warm slices of ham onto a platter. Dear Emma took such good care of them all now that Fanny had to stay off her feet. Not a single strand of her brown hair was out of place, and her dress and apron were spotless—a good example for her young scholars at the schoolhouse. Emma taught the Amish children in Halfway, and Elsie admired her sister's steady patience with the children who sometimes got out of hand.

Dat sat down at the table opposite his wife, Fanny, who had her head bent over a bit of mending. Little Beth perched on her knees on a chair beside Dat, who was teaching her how to cut ham with a fork and knife.

"The beds are made and the upstairs swept," Elsie said, touching Fanny's shoulder. Every day Elsie thanked Gott for bringing this good woman into their lives. There was no denying the under-current of excitement in the house, with Fanny expecting a little one soon. Pregnancy wasn't something Amish folk talked about, especially not in public, but with Fanny's high blood pressure, they'd had to take some measures to keep her resting.

"Good." Fanny tied off a knot and broke the thread with her hands. "After breakfast I'm going to have Beth help me. She needs to practice her stitches."

"And we're going to have Will help us with the roof," Dat said. "Caleb's outside with him now."

"I'm here," Caleb called from the mud porch. A moment later he lumbered in, all six feet of him. Elsie sometimes marveled that this young man who towered over her—a full three feet taller than she was—could be her brother. "Big miracles come in small packages," Caleb used to reassure her when, at the age of nine, she realized she would always be a little person.

The door popped open again, and young Will stepped in. "I'm here, too, and I'm hungry. What's for breakfast?"

Fanny looked over at her son and pointed toward the porch. "Boots off."

Will's eyes opened wide as he looked down at his feet. "Oops."

"We'll take care of that," Caleb said, sweeping the younger boy off his feet. "There you go." He held the five-year-old aloft. "You don't mind hanging on my shoulder while I eat my breakfast, do you?"

"But I'm hungry!"

"I'm sure there'll be leftovers," Caleb answered.

Everyone laughed as Caleb teased the boy in his arms.

"Let me down!" Will squirmed in protest. "I'm not a baby."

"Thank the Almighty for that." Fanny passed a tray of toast down the table.

Elsie smiled. Will would be taking on more responsibility once there was a new baby in the house. But for now, he was the little one in Caleb's arms.

"Let me down! Let me down!" Will insisted, grinning through his protests.

"Only because my breakfast is getting cold," Caleb teased, carrying the boy to a safe landing out on the mud porch.

A moment later, Elsie was still smiling at her brothers' antics as everyone settled at the table, their heads bowed in silent prayer.

Thank you for this meal. Thank you for my wonderful good family, Elsie prayed. There were times when she still missed her mother, but Fanny had brought love and tenderness into their home again. "A woman's touch," Dat always said. It had proved to be just what their family needed. From their many conversations, Elsie knew that Fanny understood the need for the shop to change . . . but would Dat?

As Elsie sipped her coffee, Dat talked about the progress on the roof and the plans to rebuild the carriage house. "There's more rotten wood in there than I thought at first," he said. "We might have to replace some studs and maybe that main beam."

"We'll need to get some help if we go that far," Caleb said, holding a triangle of toast aloft.

"The King brothers would be a big help," Elsie suggested, knowing that her sister Emma would be happy to have her beau, Gabe, come around to help with the work. "Gabe is handy, and Adam used to be a carpenter."

Emma's silver eyes caught Elsie with a glimmer of amusement. Of course, Emma wanted Gabe here, but she wasn't ready to admit that in front of Dat.

"That's a good idea," Dat said. "I'll ask them next time I see them at church."

When conversation turned to the weather, and how the lack of ice and snowstorms was bringing a good amount of customers to the Country Store, Elsie saw her chance.

"I've been wanting to talk to you about some new ideas for the store, Dat." Nerves fluttered in Elsie's chest, a trembling butterfly, but she tried to keep her voice steady. "There are some vendors in the city who would like to carry some of our products. The soaps and heather, and there's a lot of folks interested in honey and jams put up by Amish women."

"Englishers in the city?" Dat lifted his coffee mug. "How do they know about our little store?"

"Word travels when you've got something good. I've been writing letters to them, but they want to meet us—you and me. It would only take one trip to Philadelphia. We could go next week in George Dornbecker's van."

Dat's dark brows jutted together. "A day trip to the city is the waste of a day."

"Not a whole day," Elsie insisted. "We could leave after lunch and be home in time for dinner. The vendors will meet us at the marketplace, so we won't have to traipse all around the city."

Tom looked at his wife. "And how will this help sales at our store?"

"We would get a good commission on most sales," Fanny said. "Elsie explained it all to me, and there's a chance for a profitable side business. She's got a good head on her shoulders, this one."

Hope fluttered in Elsie's chest as she twisted her small hands together under the table. *Please say yes, Dat.* It would make a world of difference for their little shop.

"And what about Bishop Samuel? I don't want to take any chances and sign a contract that would have us selling graven images."

"This is a very different matter," Elsie explained. "We would be selling approved items to vendors in the city."

"And I've already spoken with the bishop, just to be sure." Fanny lifted her gaze from the table, her soft eyes on her husband. "Samuel says it doesn't violate the Ordnung."

"Then there's no reason not to give it a try." Tom turned to Elsie. "You've been pushing me on the shop, I know that, but I have to say, you've taken it in a good direction. More folks are stopping in now, a lot more customers. We've been turning a good profit for the past few months."

Joy welled up inside Elsie. Dat had noticed.

"We'll go into the city in the next week or two, in the afternoon," Dat said. "Caleb and I need to finish the roof first. You'll get us a spot in George's van?"

Elsie nodded, pleased to have Dat's approval. She would call George today, from the shop. *"Denki,"* she said, knowing her father would not regret this. Already the shop was the family's major source of income. With a little more sprucing up and a chance to sell to countless people in Philadelphia, the shop would make them a very comfortable living, with enough profits to get Dat's business on its feet.

At last, Elsie's hard work and planning were beginning to pay off.

၆၉

After breakfast, Elsie and Emma shared the cleanup. They moved quickly and efficiently, scouring the cast-iron skillet and drying dishes, mindful of the time limit. Emma had to get to the schoolhouse in time to greet her students, and Elsie had the shop to open in Halfway.

"Was that a bit of matchmaking?" Emma asked as she wiped a bowl.

Elsie smiled. "I knew someone in the community would help out. It might as well be Gabe."

"Denki. It would be nice to see more of him." Emma's relationship with the tall, blond Gabe King had been a secret until recently. Now every young person in the community knew she was Gabe's girl, though word hadn't yet spread to their father.

Elsie wondered what their dat would think about his oldest daughter choosing the man she wanted to spend the rest of her life with. A glimmer of longing flickered through her at the thought of falling in love. It was every girl's lifetime wish, but Elsie could never attach herself to that dream. Anyone looking at her knew from the start that she was not an ordinary girl.

"Church is at Gideon Yoder's this Sunday," Emma said, bringing Elsie's thoughts back to the bubbles floating between them. "There'll be a bonfire at the singing, and it's bound to be a good time. Won't you come along, Elsie?"

"We'll see," Elsie said, warding her sister off gently. Since she'd turned old enough to attend youth events, Elsie had learned that it was better to waffle about going than to downright refuse. Emma just didn't understand why Elsie felt uncomfortable at social gatherings.

"Something tells me you have no intention of going."

"How do you know?" Elsie looked down at the suds, a thousand bubbles with a thousand iridescent reflections. A village of bubbles in different sizes, though all of them were shiny and bright. "I didn't say that."

"But I can read between the lines. When you teach thirty pupils in a one-room schoolhouse, you begin to know what they're thinking. As if there were thought balloons over their heads, like in a comic. Jeremiah Miller can't wait until recess. Rose Beiler would like to sit all day practicing the curly loops in her handwriting. And you? Your balloon says that there's no way you're coming to the singing."

"I've got a lot going on right now, fixing up the store. Did you hear Dat? We're going to Philadelphia next week to meet with vendors. Once we get the distribution set up, I'm going to work on a website. Well, I won't work on it myself, but Nancy Briggs knows a Mennonite woman who will do it for a small fee. She'll even manage orders and billing for us, all over the Internet." Nancy Briggs, Halfway's mayor, was a great help to both Amish and Englisher folks.

Emma tossed the dish towel over one shoulder and waggled her fingers in the air. "The Internet is a little strange, don't you think? Words and thoughts floating through the air?"

"You're the one who sees thought balloons," Elsie teased.

They both chuckled.

"Dear Elsie, all I'm saying is, don't pour your heart into the business. You need a social life, too. Friends outside the family. And what about a beau? How will you meet the right fella if you're stuck in the Country Store day and night?"

"I'm not stuck there. You know I like working in the shop." Although Elsie felt very comfortable "hosting" people in the store, she had never gotten into the habit of attending singings, and she had no desire to change that. The Country Store was easy for her. The way she perched on her stool at the register or hustled up and down the aisles seemed very natural. It was what Gott intended. But outside the safe confines of the shop, she felt awash with self-consciousness. When Elsie was in public, she tethered her smile to hide her unusual teeth and she didn't like making people uncomfortable with her small size.

"You know what I mean." Elsie felt Emma's hands on her shoulders, firm but gentle. "Why do you stay away from folks outside the family?" Emma asked. "If I didn't see you bouncing around the store and talking with customers, I would think you were shy."

"It's not shyness." Elsie felt her resolve weaken under her sister's massaging hands. "But sometimes I do feel awkward about these teeth."

"So you keep your lips pressed closed when you smile."

"Ya. And though I'm used to being shorter than one of your first graders, I hate it when people stare at me."

"But it's the Almighty Father who made you different. He made you special."

"I know that." But it was little reassurance when Englisher folks narrowed their eyes and stared at her. "I pray that Gott's will be done, but sometimes . . . sometimes I long to be normal."

"Oh, Elsie." Emma slipped her arms around her waist, and Elsie felt her sister's cheek pressed to hers. "Do you remember how Dat used to rock you in his lap and sing to you? How he used to call you his button-nose girl?"

Elsie's resolve softened. She felt likely to melt in her sister's arms as poignant memories embraced her. "Button nose . . . I do remember that."

"It was right around the time that Mamm died, and I used to be jealous. Silly, I know, but I wanted Dat to hold me in his arms, too."

"Poor Emma. You were always the responsible one. You still are."

"Ya. That's why I'm going to make sure you go to a singing, or a quilting bee or a frolic—anything to get you out and about."

"Maybe a quilting bee," Elsie conceded, knowing that sort of gathering wouldn't involve courting.

That was her deepest, darkest secret . . . a terrible sin she wouldn't share with anyone—not even Emma.

Elsie had vowed never to marry.

She could not take the chance of having a child who looked like her, and Dr. Trueherz had told her that this condition was genetic. Something she could pass on if she had children. And Elsie couldn't bear to subject a child to the cold eye of the world.

"A quilting bee," Emma said. "Mary King was talking about having one real soon. It would be fun to go together, wouldn't it?"

"Anywhere we go together is fun," Elsie responded as her sister's arms slid away.

"Look at the time! Here I am chattering away and the schoolhouse is filling up with students."

"You'll make it in plenty of time," Elsie said, knowing her sister's sense of order would not allow her to be late. "Mind you don't forget your lunch."

As she finished up the dishes, Elsie watched her sister climb into the buggy Caleb had hitched up for her. Her brother and sister supported her in every way, and it hurt her to think of the disappointment they would feel if they knew of her plans to stay single for the rest of her life.

Such a complicated web she was weaving.

As a young Amish woman, Elsie was expected to find a husband and marry. But Elsie figured that Gott had made her different for a reason, and accepting that was the same as accepting that no man would ever want to court her.

Not that she'd had to fend any fellas off, anyway. Elsie tried to maintain a sense of humor about it, but inside it hurt to think that she would always be alone.

An *Alt Maedel*—the Amish name for an old maid.

Old Elsie Lapp, a jolly little lady on the outside. A sad, heavy heart on the inside.

ҩҩ 3 ҩҩ

Dylan followed the country doctor up the street with a sense of purpose and amusement. It was the first Monday in recent memory that he hadn't lost the entire morning to meetings and bureaucratic reports. Dylan was shadowing Dr. Henry Trueherz with the intention of accompanying him on house calls, but so far they had spent nearly an hour shopping in the little town of Halfway and chatting up the Amish merchants there.

At Ye Olde Tea Shop, Lovina Stoltzfus had given them an update on her husband, Aaron, who was recovering at home from heart surgery. "We're going to stop in and see him this morning," Henry had told the middle-aged Amish woman, who had wiped down a table and served them tea in record time. "But how are you doing? It can't be easy running this shop and taking care of your husband and keeping the sheep business going."

"It would be overwhelming if it were all on my shoulders," Lovina had answered. "But the Heavenly Father helps us when we need it most. I've got some good girls like Susie here to help me run the shop, and we got some good men pitching in at the farm. You know Jonah King? I think he's sweet on our Annie, but he's a right good worker, keeping everything going."

Dr. Trueherz seemed to know all the Amish in Halfway by name. He cajoled all the young women working in the tea shop, asking about their families, whom he also knew by name. He reassured Lovina that her husband would be more active in the coming months, and he told a girl named Susie that he would be visiting her little sister Katie today to see if he could give her something to stop that fever.

At Molly's Roadside Restaurant, the doctor had purchased breakfast for the two of them while Molly updated him on recent developments in Halfway. A loaf of bread from the Sweet 'N' Simple Bakery came with news of the Fisher family, who owned the bakery. And now, Doc Trueherz wanted to stop in at the Country Store.

"I like your methodology," Dylan told the country doctor.

Henry raised his chin as he paused, his hand on the knob of the Country Store. "And what's that?"

"Personal attention. You're one of the few doctors I know who is happy to leave the clinic. You've stepped out of the crisp white coat, and you've built relationships with the community."

Henry pushed his glasses up on his nose, barely hiding a grin. "You noticed."

"It's not just that you remember all these faces and names, as well as their medical histories. These people seem to like you; they trust you."

"And I'm a good customer. Did you notice that, too?"

"I did. Are you going to stop in the Amish furniture store and pick up an armoire?"

Henry laughed. "Don't be silly. I leave the large purchases to my wife."

Dylan liked Henry Trueherz more by the minute. Staff at Lancaster General seemed to think of him as some legendary folk hero, and now Dylan was ready to sing along with their praises. "Seriously, how did you gain their trust?"

"Time and patience." He looked back at Dylan, his eyes twinkling. "Give it twenty years and they'll trust you, too." The bell jingled as Henry opened the door.

"Something to look forward to," Dylan said under his breath.

"Good morning, Elsie." Henry greeted the teenage girl seated behind the counter as he made a beeline down one of the aisles.

Dylan paused between a display of birdhouses and a handmade cradle to smile at the young woman.

"This young man is Dylan Monroe," Henry called. "He's a psychologist interested in working with the good people of Halfway."

"Another doctor?" Her smile lit up the room, though from the rue in her brown eyes Dylan sensed that there was more to Elsie than a cute button nose and rosy lips. "It'll be so nice to have two doctors helping folks."

"But he's a therapist," Henry called from behind an aisle of candles and sock dolls. "He doesn't look at sore throats. He treats problems we can't cure with an antibiotic."

"I see." When Elsie spoke, Dylan got a flash of her jagged, unevenly spaced teeth. "Well, there must be some very sad folks who need you. I just don't know who they might be."

"I realize the Amish don't usually go outside the church community for counseling," Dylan said. "But I want to let people know that my services are free and readily available. I'll be working at Lancaster County General, but I'm hoping to set up a counseling center here in Halfway."

"That's nice of you, trying to help folks that way." Elsie wore the same clothing as other Amish women—a violet dress, black apron, and cape. Her dark hair was parted in the center and pulled back into a knot under her white prayer *Kapp.*

But despite her manner of clothing, Elsie was different. Even seated on a high stool, it was obvious that she was extremely short. Dwarfism, dental abnormality, malformation of the wrist bones . . .

Of course, it was Ellis-van Creveld syndrome, a mutation of the EVC gene. He had read that this rare disorder was more common among Old Order Amish, a genetic abnormality traced back to one ancestor named Samuel King.

He felt a bit foolish for not detecting it right away, but Dylan tended to pick up the vibe of a person—their aura or tone—before the details of their physical features registered. He liked to equate himself with a musician who could compose a beautiful song but became lost when it was time to write down the notes on stark white paper. For Dylan, the flowing wellspring was lost when you stopped to collect the small puddles of detail.

"My wife loves this soap." Henry placed two bars of lavender soap on the counter. "Last Christmas, she sent it to all the out-of-state relatives."

"Mary Zook makes it," Elsie said. "The lavender grows like a weed on the back acres of their land."

Dylan lifted one of the bars and sniffed. A relaxing scent. Some therapists used scents and white noise to enhance guided imagery, and lavender was a classic, used since ancient times to heal everything from headaches to blemishes. "Do you have lavender oil?"

"We do." Elsie slid from her stool and disappeared down one aisle. Dylan followed.

"Planning to do some aromatherapy?" Dr. Trueherz asked.

"Maybe," Dylan said as he chose the larger bottle from the selection on the shelf. *Or maybe I'll just rub it into my temples and pray for a clean slate.*

"How's everything at home, Elsie?" asked Henry. "Fanny's doing well?"

"Ya, she's fine."

"The baby must be due soon. Anna's checking in on Fanny? Taking her vitals? She's got to watch her blood pressure."

They were talking about preeclampsia. Dylan recognized the symptoms from when his wife, Kris, had been pregnant, but when he turned to say something, he noticed Elsie looking down, her cheeks flushing. The conversation embarrassed her. Of course it did. He had read that Amish women did not discuss pregnancies in public; sort of a throwback to the days when babies were delivered by storks.

"Anna visits a few times a week. And Sarah comes along."

"Good." As Henry opened his wallet and paid for his purchase, Dylan handed a ten to Elsie Lapp and exited the store, wanting to escape the memory of Kris that had crept up on him.

Climbing into the Jeep, Dylan asked about Elsie Lapp's small stature, and Henry confirmed that it was EVC.

"I've come across some unusual cases here," Henry said. "Maple syrup disease and hemophilia. And glutaric aciduria, a metabolic disorder that requires a fairly complex treatment. Remember Susie King, back at the tea shop? She has GA, but her family has worked with me and she's navigated through it. It's her family we're visiting first, the Kings."

"The Kings . . ." Dylan found his list. "And who is Susie's father?"

"That was Levi King, but he's dead now. Both parents are gone. Her brother Adam is now the head of the household, alongside his wife, Remy."

Dylan made the notes. "What happened to the parents?"

"A double murder, around two years ago. It was a tragedy."

The details were vaguely familiar. "I think I read a few news stories about it."

Henry nodded. "Levi and Esther King. You can imagine the trauma suffered by their family."

"I can." He could imagine it, feel it, taste it. He'd lived trauma, though Dr. Trueherz was probably not aware of his history.

Dylan wrote down names, trying to piece together families as the Jeep traveled on the road dividing broad expanses of open fields. Stoltzfus . . . Zook . . . Lapp . . . King . . . Not so many surnames, but lots of people.

"When did you decide to make it your specialty, studying ailments specific to the Amish?" Dylan inquired.

"I saw myself as a country doctor at first. A few months out here, I began seeing cases among the Old Order Amish that doctors back in the city weren't encountering."

"And you've made some real progress in helping these people." Henry Trueherz's dedication to helping the Amish was an inspiration to Dylan. In many ways, Dylan wanted to model his outreach program after Henry's clinic in Paradise. He would have told Henry that, but the doctor was not a man who enjoyed praise.

"I don't suppose you've ever made a house call before?" Henry asked.

"Can't say that I have."

"Have you ever been inside an Amish home?"

Dylan shook his head. "I did my research, but this is my first clinical experience. Actually, this is a first for me in many ways."

Henry grunted. "You don't look nervous at all. Nerves of steel?"

After what I've been through, I don't have any nerves left at all, Dylan thought. "Not that." The expanse of winter blue skies and rolling purple hills that surrounded them reminded him of passages from the Bible. The land of milk and honey. Canaan. Or Paradise, as the nearby town was aptly named. "I've learned that people are people. Inside, we all have the same essential needs. Shelter, food, drink . . . love."

"For a young man, that's downright philosophical." The Jeep slowed as Henry turned into a lane at the top of a hill. "But then again, you are a psychologist."

"I'm not that young. Pushing thirty. And though you think of yourself as a general practitioner, I see that you haven't forgotten Psych 101," Dylan teased as the silos and outbuildings of the King dairy farm came into view.

"The human being is a complex thing, a marriage of body and mind," Henry said. "I treat the body, but I respect what you're doing, Doctor. I just hope you're not disappointed when the Amish decline your services. They've got a complicated social system that provides a certain therapy of its own."

"So I've heard." Dylan knew that community outreach would not be easy here, but then anything worthwhile was generally not easy. "But I've also come across a few cases where outsiders have provided therapy for Amish clients. I think their ministers prefer to call it counseling, which would be fine with me. Right now, I just want the Amish community to know that I'm here if the need arises."

"Fair enough."

The group of buildings that comprised the King dairy farm gave way to hills and valleys of golden fields punctuated by dark cows.

No, you're not in Philly anymore, Dylan told himself. Which was a good thing . . . exactly what he'd needed.

"Get away from here . . . far and fast," Patrick had advised. "Every day you spend in your apartment, in your neighborhood, on these streets . . . your surroundings are making you miserable. Why are you torturing yourself here?"

A good question.

So he'd taken his therapist's advice and left the city, and here he was in Lancaster County, land of sprawling farms and horse-drawn buggies. Sometimes he fantasized that he had not just changed locations but gone back to a simpler time where you couldn't be in a rush because your horse didn't move so fast. A time when your day ended at sundown because there were no electrical inventions to keep the mind churning against sleep.

Of course, he had a car and electricity; still, the notion of simplicity helped to clear some of the cobwebs from his mind, and it seemed like good karma to be living among the peace-loving Amish people. He had the best of both worlds, with an apartment overlooking an Amish farm and a job at LanCo General, where he'd been able to work outside the shadow of grief.

The farmhouse door flew open when the Jeep pulled up, and a woman in her twenties waved them in. "Dr. Trueherz, thank you for coming. I've been so worried. Her fever's so high, and you know me. No experience with kids."

"Remy, don't undersell yourself. You've got all the tools these kids need. Where's our little patient?"

Henry made quick introductions as Remy directed them into the kitchen, where a little wisp of a girl, two, maybe three years old, was curled up on a daybed. Her little face, barely visible for the cloth doll wedged under her chin, seemed aglow, with two patches of red dotting her cheeks.

"Well, hello there, Katie. What's going on with you today?"

The little girl's mouth puckered as she looked up at the doctor.

"Too sick to talk? Well, we'll see what we can do about that."

Henry washed up at the kitchen sink, and then opened his black satchel. He scanned her forehead with a thermometer and whistled softly. "A hundred and two. Have you given her Tylenol?"

"Children's Tylenol, but the last dose was last night."

Henry placed his hands around the child's neck, checking her glands. "I'll do a quick test, but I'm fairly certain she's got strep throat."

"I should have known." Remy sat beside the girl and rubbed her back. "I used to get strep all the time when I was a kid."

Dylan noticed that her speech pattern didn't have the same rapid-fire cadence as other Amish people he'd met. And something about her demeanor—or maybe it was her flaming red hair—struck him as distinctly un-Amish. Englisher, as the locals called it.

The door off the kitchen opened, and a tall man in a wide-brimmed black hat looked in from a side porch.

"How is she, Doc?"

"I don't like this fever, but from the looks of this throat I'd say it's strep."

"Could it be the GA, like Susie has?"

"I wouldn't worry about that. We've been testing her since she was born, and it's been negative."

"Okay, good. Then I'll get back to work." The man turned to Dylan and nodded.

"Adam, this is Dylan Monroe. He's a psychologist shadowing Dr. Trueherz," Remy said, looking up from the sick little girl.

Adam nodded again. "I'll get back to it, then." He turned away, the door closing, along with an opportunity.

"Excuse me," Dylan said before following the man out through an enclosed porch to a path to the barn. "Adam? Do you have a minute to talk?"

"Come, and you can talk."

"This is quite a farm. Dexters and Jerseys?"

Adam turned to face him, his stern face softening. "You know dairy farming?"

Dylan had been to a farm once in his life, but he'd done his research. "Just a bit. But I've never milked a cow. I can't imagine the man-hours it takes to keep this place running."

"This farm has been in my dat's family for years. We got some new milking machines in the last year. That made things easier, but now we're down a set of hands, with my brother Jonah helping out a neighbor."

"If you ever need some temporary help, I'm your man." The words flew out before Dylan had really processed them, but he had no regrets. A little hard work would do him good while it got him involved in the community.

Adam grunted. "Thanks. We can manage, but you can help me now. Two make work much lighter."

They had arrived at the red barn, where Adam led the way through wide-open doors.

Stepping into the darkness ripe with the smell of hay and manure, Dylan sensed that he truly had entered another world.

"Here." Adam tossed something from the shadows.

He caught the ball of soft leather—a pair of gloves. A few bales of hay needed to be transferred from the floor of the barn to an open cart.

"You take one end; I'll take the other," Adam said, and they lifted together.

"I wanted to talk to you about a program I'm starting here in Halfway." The hay bale was heavier than Dylan had expected. "Counseling services, open to everyone. We've got funding, so the treatment will be free."

"Mmm. There might be some Englishers who would do it. I can't speak for them, but Amish? Probably not."

"I'm just trying to get the word out. I figure that if the help is available and it's free, people might take advantage of it."

Adam did not waver. "We work out problems on our own. The family takes care of things, or else we take serious matters to our ministers."

"I hear you." Dylan braced his muscles as they lifted another bale. "But I'm committed to this program. Everyone needs help at some time in their lives."

Dylan had needed therapy, and he suspected that Adam could have used some counseling when he lost his parents . . . and by such violent means.

Adam grunted, and Dylan wasn't sure whether it was an answer or a reaction to lifting the heavy weight.

"Don't get me wrong. I respect your traditions and rules." He admired the culture's complex social system, designed to deal with matters within the community. "But there's no rule against getting help from an outsider, right? You wouldn't get in trouble for getting counseling?"

"No trouble. Folks just wouldn't do it."

Dylan was not surprised by Adam King's mild rejection. Maybe the closed Amish community was part of the reason he'd accepted the position here. He liked a challenge, and he'd been getting burned out on the city.

"You know, back in the city, people would have jumped at the offer of free therapy. I used to do counseling there, and some of my clients couldn't choose a flavor of ice cream without calling for a consult."

Adam's lips twitched, then he smiled. "I lived in the city for a few years. Providence. People had so many problems, so much to talk about."

"But you came back home."

"I came back, and I don't miss the life I had out there. This here—tending cows, working the land. This is how a man should live. Close to the land, close to God, surrounded by family. Not that I'm criticizing what you do. It's a good thing, being a doctor and caring for others."

"No offense taken. I've only been here a few weeks, and I don't miss what I left behind." He thought of his old apartment, his familiar neighborhood with the kids on the playground across the street where he used to take Angela. The landscape had become a source of pain for him.

And he thought of his friends, always concerned, always trying to ease the pain that would never go away.

He had needed a break.

The last hay bale hit the cart with a thud. "Thanks for the help. I hope you can find some Englisher folk who need your counseling."

Dylan nodded. "I'm sure I will. And I meant what I said about pitching in. Get in touch if you need some help around here."

He handed Adam a card and headed back to the house, undaunted by Adam King's attitude. When the time came that someone in this community needed help, he would be here. Right now, Dylan just needed patience.

What had Dr. Trueherz said? Just give it twenty years. Looking ahead, Dylan could see himself spending the next few decades here in Lancaster County. The solitude, the rolling hills, the pastoral charm . . . it was a world apart from the life he'd lost. The perfect escape.

ᛘ 4 ᛘ

*I*n the hospital break room, the usual forum for talk of catheters and sponge baths, Twizzlers and vitamin water, there was one topic on everyone's mind.

Dylan Monroe.

Haley had plenty to say about the new psychologist, but she didn't want to put it out there.

"I think he's waiting for Ms. Right to come along," Caitlin said as she stirred creamer into her coffee.

"And you think that's you?" Danica asked, leafing through a chart on the table.

"Haven't you guys noticed that he's all about me?" Madison tucked a fat blond curl behind one ear. "Did you not see? Yesterday, he spent the whole day with me."

"Because you landed the patient who decided to practice his tai chi on the double yellow line of the highway," Danica said. "Of course he's going to stick with you if you've got the only psych patient on the floor."

"Cat fight!" Haley teased, and she made a noise that sounded like an angry cat's meow for emphasis.

"Y'all don't have to get all fanatical about it," Aeesha said. "He's just a therapist. Not even a real doctor."

"But he's so nice." Caitlin took a sip of coffee and cocked her head to one side. "He cares about your problems. He can tell when you're having a bad day. I've never met a doctor who was that sweet."

"Forget about a doctor; I've never met a man who was that sweet," Danica said. With a son in school, Danica was the oldest nursing student and the most focused on the doctors at LanCo General. She knew who was married, who was divorced, who was looking for marriage, and who was looking for fun. "There's something about him, some secret he's holding back. I don't know what it is, but he sure is buttoned up about it."

"It's that mystery that makes him so irresistible," Madison said.

"That and the fact that he's gorgeous," added Caitlin.

Aeesha tapped a lacquered nail on the table. "He sure is eye candy."

"And those designer suits don't hurt." Danica closed the chart and sighed. "Like he stepped out of the pages of a magazine."

"Did you notice how he stopped wearing the suit jacket?" Caitlin asked. "Just a shirt and tie now. Crisp shirt and designer tie. I think he didn't want to make the other doctors look bad."

"Maybe he just wanted to fit in," Aeesha suggested. "No one's really fancy around here."

In the week or so since he'd joined the hospital, Dr. Monroe had softened his style a bit. Haley had noticed every little nuance. Gone were the immaculate suit jackets. Instead, he wore a crisp white clinical jacket over his shirt and tie. It was a step toward a more casual look, though the pants were so well pressed that Haley was sure you could cut butter with the crease.

Reluctant to add a comment, Haley wiggled her toes in her clogs as images of Dylan played through her mind like a romantic slide show. Working with him over the past week, she'd been struck by his kindness, his compassion, his sense of humor. The way he held a patient's hand as she cried. The way he listened. The way he made everyone feel better after being around him. The way he made tedious tasks enjoyable.

The way the air sizzled between them whenever he was around.

Oh, she had it bad, and she knew it. But right now, she didn't want the other nursing students to know. Admitting that she had a crush on Dr. Monroe would be like tossing chum off the boat before a swim. She didn't want to be shark bait.

Fortunately, break time was winding down and the women began to file out of the room.

"Have you noticed that he rarely smiles?" Danica asked. "Almost never. Somehow, he communicates compassion without smiling. But it makes you wonder what happened to make him so serious."

"There is something about a man with sadness in his eyes." Aeesha gave a sigh. "Makes you just want to snuggle him up and make him all better."

Aeesha was right; Haley had felt the same urge to reassure Dr. Monroe. As if she had the power to make him feel better with a hug. She frowned. This hen session was ridiculous. All of them really needed to leave Dylan Monroe alone.

"He may be a man of mystery," Madison said as she tossed away her coffee cup, "but Dylan Monroe sure keeps things interesting around here."

Haley smiled, knowing Madison was right. Since Dylan had joined the staff, Haley looked forward to coming to the hospital for clinicals.

"You're awfully quiet today." Aeesha stopped Haley with a hand on her arm. They were the last two in the break room. "You didn't chime in on the Dylan fest. What is it? He's not your type?"

"I don't know." Haley wiped a napkin over the table, hoping her friend wouldn't pursue the question.

"What are you talking about? Girl, I've never seen you stumped by a question. What's the matter? You got on a crush on Dr. Monroe?"

Haley looked around to be sure the others were out of range. "Maybe." She gathered up a sandwich wrapper from the table and tossed it into the trash. "That's the problem."

Hands on her hips, Aeesha gaped at her. "I thought you were taking a break? It hasn't even been six months since you left your fiancé crying at the altar."

"Don't make it more dramatic than it was," Haley said. "I called it off the week before the wedding, and to be honest, I think he was relieved. I didn't fit his image of a good wife. He thought that would change, but it wasn't going to happen."

"I hear you. But I do like the idea of the man crying at the altar."

"Graham didn't shed any tears. In fact, when I broke it off, he was more upset about canceling the wedding than about canceling our lives together."

"I wish I'd known you then." Aeesha patted her arm. "Sounds like you needed someone to cheer you on."

"I still do. My parents think I made a huge mistake. They really liked Graham, and they want to see me married and squared away like my sisters. More than that, I think they were happy that I would be financially secure after I married him."

"Do you ever look back and wonder if you made a mistake, letting him go?"

"No. Never. He's a nice enough guy, but we wanted different

things. Graham wanted to spend our vacation on a cruise ship, and I wanted to go along on a church mission that was sending medical aid to Africa. He liked to eat out at trendy restaurants, and I was always campaigning to have a picnic in the park."

"Did you really quit nursing school because he wanted you all to himself?" Aeesha asked, adding, "I heard that through the grapevine."

"It's true." Haley pressed her palms to her face, wondering what she had been thinking back then. "I can't believe I thought I could be happy as Graham's wife. That would have been disastrous. I get so antsy when I'm cooped up at home."

"I hear ya."

"Graham always talked about how good we looked together, and that struck me as odd. I mean, you can be a gorgeous couple, but it's not going to work unless you enjoy each other. The chemistry has to be there."

"And it wasn't?"

"I had fun with him, but it wasn't anything special. I think I was in love with falling in love. Then one night, I got annoyed with him. He had a tantrum about how they'd changed the menu at his favorite restaurant. Then, while I was trying to talk to him, he kept checking his text messages. I felt invisible. I decided to go home, but that hurt his feelings. He pointed out that once we were married, we'd be together forever and always."

"And you felt smothered."

Haley nodded. "That was it. That night I told him I needed breathing room. He told me there was no time, that we were getting married in a week. That ended it for me. I wished him the best and called the catering hall to cancel."

Everyone loved wedding planning, but no one ever talked about the awkwardness of calling off the event. Although Haley's mom had been disappointed, she had helped Haley call their side of the guest list to explain. Seventy-two personal phone calls, most of them to relatives, Mom's friends, and Dad's business associates.

Graham's mother had refused to make a single call. "How can you do this to me? I'm going to be the laughingstock of all my friends."

Graham's side of the list had been more than ninety phone calls. Haley had said a prayer of thanks every time she got someone's voice mail. It was so much easier to leave a message than to open yourself up for a barrage of questions.

Is someone sick?

Who called it off?

Will the gifts be returned?

Are you planning to postpone until next year?

Sometime amid all the phone calls Haley had realized that this had not been her wedding at all. With nearly two hundred names on the guest list, only a handful of them were her friends.

How had it gotten so far out of control? She still wondered about that.

"So that's how that all went down?" Aeesha narrowed her eyes. "Then I take back what I said. Not that I'm judging you or anything, but you should go for Dr. Dylan."

"You heard what they said. He's aloof and mysterious."

"Please." Aeesha waved her off. "A curvaceous blonde like yourself should not have a problem with aloof and mysterious."

"I've talked to him, and I don't think he's that easy."

"I didn't say it was easy." Aeesha arched one eyebrow. "I just said you should go for it."

5

On Tuesday morning, there were extra passengers in the Lapp buggy as the horse trotted down the road into Halfway. While Caleb ran some errands, Elsie would show Fanny and the children around the shop so that they could handle it tomorrow, while she and Dat took their trip to the city.

As Caleb helped Fanny out of the buggy, Elsie put her arms on the shoulders of her younger brother and sister and guided them down Halfway's Main Street.

"It's good to have some helpers this morning," Elsie told the children. "Many hands lighten the load."

"Something smells very good," Will said, pushing back the brim of his black hat to look around.

"There's nothing like fresh-baked bread," Elsie said. With the mouthwatering scent in the air, getting past the Sweet 'N' Simple Bakery was always a practice in fighting temptation, more so today with a three-year-old and a five-year-old in tow.

Will eyed the bakery. "I would like a cinnamon bun right about now."

"Me, too. Can we go to the bakery, Elsie?" Beth detached herself from Elsie to turn toward her mother, who moved slowly but steadily, the bulk of her belly barely noticeable under her black wool shawl. "Mamm, can we buy some treats?"

"Maybe later, honey girl," Fanny said. "Right now Elsie has to open the shop, and we need to learn the routine. We're going to manage the store while Elsie and Dat go into the city tomorrow, and you're going to be my helper, right?"

Beth nodded as Will added, "I'm going to help, too."

"Of course you are," Elsie said. "There'll be plenty of errands to run."

"I like to run." Beth raced ahead, her small boots pattering on the walkway, before she pivoted back. "See? I'll run for you, Mamm."

"It's good to know I can count on you," Fanny said as they moved past the steamy windows of the bakery. "It's been a while since I've made it here to Main Street, and I must say, it feels good to be out of the house."

"I don't know what it is about Halfway, but I always look forward to opening the shop each morning." Elsie found the Main Street of the little town comforting. Maybe because she was surrounded by Amish here in town. So many businesses owned by Plain folk. The Fishers had the bakery and the Mast family had run Molly's Roadside Restaurant since Molly Mast started serving soup and sandwiches back in the 1950s. Lovina Stoltzfus had opened Ye Olde Tea Shop as a side business, and it had become a popular spot. There was the Amish furniture store, the ice-cream shop, the candy shop, and just down the road, Zook's barn hosted a marketplace for farmers and crafts.

Now more than ever, Amish were giving up farming to start other businesses. Many folk in the Old Order saw that as a bad thing—especially the elders who believed that working the land brought a person closer to Gott. Elsie understood their concern. No one wanted their community to change, and folks sure didn't want to step away from the Almighty Father! But farmland had become scarce for the growing Amish population in Lancaster County. For her own family, Elsie knew that the income from the Country Store was the one thing that earned them money to pay for groceries and gas to make it through the winter months. She was glad that the store had made enough profit to get Dat and Caleb started in their new business.

But for her, the Country Store had become more than a business. It was a second home, a place where she felt confident moving about as the little person that she was. Amid these four walls, folks seemed to accept that she looked different from them. Oh, there was still the occasional squint of curiosity, usually when people realized she was not a child but a young woman of a child's height. But given the chance to assist a customer, share a story, or evoke a smile, Elsie could demonstrate that she belonged here as much as water belonged in a riverbed.

Elsie turned the key in the lock as her stepmother cooed beside her.

"Look at that!" Fanny steered her daughter around to face the shop window, where Elsie had hung a colorful blue, purple, red, and orange Sunshine and Shadow quilt as a backdrop for the display. "The last time I looked in this window, there was a stack of soda pop cans. Now it's like taking a peek inside a rainbow."

"Sure is different," Will said, his breath a white puff in the air.

Beth nodded. "A winter rainbow. And look, Mamm. A treasure chest."

Biting her lips against a grin, Elsie couldn't deny a surge of pleasure at Fanny's compliment. "I hung up one of Mary King's quilts. That's for sale. The box is just for display. It's been in our family for years. There's a little message painted inside that says it was a gift from Elizabeth Lapp to Sammy Lapp in 1933."

"And the other items?" Fanny asked.

"The dolls and embroidered linens are for sale. All made by local Plain folk." Elsie's step was a little lighter as she pushed through the door and slid off her coat. In the past year, she had begun to take an interest in the details of the shop, restocking specialty items made by local craftspeople in lieu of the standard drinks and snacks that had drained the character from their little store. She was glad that Fanny was noticing the improvements. She wanted their little store to reflect the skill and hard work of Halfway's Amish community, even as it helped the local women make some money on the side.

"Such a welcoming sight." Fanny sent the children to the back room to hang up their coats and sat down on a bench by the door. "Elsie, if I didn't see you open the door, I'd think we came into the wrong store. You've made this place downright pleasant."

"I've just tried to bring back the unique things that tourists want to buy. Of course, we'll always carry fabric and sewing notions for Amish women." In their community, women bought fabric and sewed dresses, aprons, shirts, and pants on treadle machines at home, so it was handy to have a place to buy sewing materials in town. "I know Dat didn't want to go back to carrying Amish crafts after that business with the bishop, and I understand that."

"Bishop Samuel is a good friend of ours, and of course, we had to hold to his decision. Your dat couldn't take a chance of breaking the rules."

"I know that. But I thought there was a way that we could sell Amish crafts without going against the Ordnung."

"So you talked to Bishop Samuel about it."

Elsie nodded, picking up a faceless doll made of cloth and stuffing. This one was a girl, with a purple dress, blue apron, and matching blue bonnet. "I brought a few crafts over to the bishop. Some pincushions and soaps. Placemats and pillows. And as I was showing him, trying to get his okay, I saw his granddaughter Sallie holding a doll like this. Turned out Lois makes a hobby of sewing these dolls, which a lot of customers had been asking for."

Fanny lowered her shawl with a smile. "And Samuel had to say yes, with his wife pushing on him."

Elsie gave the doll an affectionate squeeze and placed it back on the shelf. "I'll admit, it didn't hurt to have the bishop's wife on my side. But I believe his decision was based on a lot of thought and a close, careful look at the Bible."

"You've got a head for business," Fanny said.

"I like running the shop. I'm grateful that Dat held on to it." Elsie ran a feather duster over some merchandise and paused. "And you've been a big help, Fanny. You've always encouraged Dat to let me make decisions here."

Fanny waved off the gesture. "You're the life of this store, Elsie. It's always been you. Your dat tried his best to keep the store going, but I don't think his heart was ever in it. But now, look around you. What fine displays you've made. And the new merchandise you've brought in makes the Country Store a special place. Handmade crafts, needlepoint pictures and pincushions. Homegrown lavender and honey."

Elsie felt a glow of pleasure as she gazed over the shelves of homemade merchandise. The store had come a long way since the days of dusty fabric and soda pop. "Mostly I wanted to bring the store back to the way Mamm used to have it."

"And you did. So much merchandise from folks here in Halfway, things made by Plain folk. It's no wonder the Country Store is making money again. I'm smiling just sitting here beside the bright placemats that Rose Miller wove. Did you ever see such colors? Like Christmas."

"Customers have been asking for Amish crafts. Some of the handmade items sold out over Christmas. And wait until Dat and I meet with the vendors in the city. It's a great chance to increase our sales. Talking to one of the vendors, I learned that we might even double them."

"Well, we won't count those chickens before they hatch." Fanny folded her shawl and placed it on the bench beside her. "But every day I thank Gott for keeping us fed and warm and clothed. And a lot of that is happening because this shop has been doing so well. I know your dat is grateful, too, even if he doesn't talk about it much. You've seen him, hammering away on the carriage house. He's happy to be starting a business of his own, something he and Caleb can do together."

"I know his heart wasn't in this shop after Mamm died." As she talked, Elsie moved through the aisles, swiping at the merchandise with a dust cloth. "I'm grateful he let me have a crack at it."

The bell on the door jingled, and both women looked over to see a young Amish woman burst in. Her black coat hung open and there were rose swatches on her cheeks from the cold. "Good morning to you," called Rachel King. She was the artist who had painted the big watercolors that covered one wall of the Country Store.

Although Rachel looked like every other Amish girl Elsie knew, she had a special eye for painting small, ordinary objects from Amish life in a way that warmed the heart. Her canvases were filled with quilts lifting in the breeze and flowers lining the drives to Amish homes. A kerosene lantern on a table. A potbellied stove. A buggy moving through golden hills. The sun setting over a clothesline of black pants and colorful dresses. So much color and light! Rachel's beautiful paintings were among the most expensive items at the Country Store and worth every penny, as far as Elsie was concerned. Although Rachel never showed Plain folk in her scenes, she managed to capture the true heart of Amish life.

"Rachel." Fanny nodded, rising from the bench. "How's the painting going?"

"It's good when I can find time to do it. Mamm and Dat still need my help to run the dairy farm."

"I wish you could paint all the time," Elsie said.

"Ya, and I would if I could get out of milking the cows. But tomorrow, I'm free of the farm. At least for one day."

"It's nice to have a little break," Fanny called as she went to the back room to check on the children.

"So you talked to your dat," Elsie asked. "Will he let you go to the city to meet with Claudia?"

Rachel nodded, her eyes bright with enthusiasm. "As long as I combine it with my turn to help out at the cheese shop at the market. It's all arranged. I'm going tomorrow."

Elsie clapped her hands together in delight. "So I'll see you in George's van?"

"On the way home. But I still wish you would meet with the Englisher lady instead of me. I'm not good when it comes to talking and socializing with folks I don't know."

Elsie pressed one hand to her mouth to hold back a laugh. "And you think I'm better at that?" Apparently Elsie's insecurities about dealing with the world beyond the shop were not as obvious as she'd thought.

"Everybody is charmed by you, Elsie. Why don't you just do it for me and take the fifteen-percent commission out of anything that sells? I don't mind paying you. You've done so much for me already. I wouldn't have my painting on the side if it weren't for you. I wouldn't even have enough money to buy new watercolors, let alone special paper and frames."

"But Claudia wants to meet you. She's an art dealer, and if she takes you on, she'll be taking a percentage out of the money you earn. You don't need two people doing that, when you do all the painting."

Rachel let her fingers fall over one of the dolls on the shelf. "I don't mind, Elsie. Really I don't."

"Just call Claudia Stein and tell her you're coming to Philadelphia tomorrow. And no need to be nervous. She told me your artwork is wonderful good. I'm sure she'll like you, too."

"I don't know. . . ." Rachel plucked at one of her thumbnails, a nervous habit.

"I'm not going to let you be a crabapple about this." Elsie fished through an envelope and came up with what she was looking for. "Here's Claudia's card. Call her. And I'll see you in the van for the ride home."

As Rachel plodded out on her mission, Elsie thought of a Bible passage she had always liked. She had memorized it when she was little. "Neither do men light a candle, and put it under a bushel, but on a candlestick; and it giveth light unto all that are in the house. Let your light so shine before men, that they may see your good works and glorify your Father, which is in heaven."

She liked to think that she was helping Rachel let her light shine.

Singing a little song as she dusted, Elsie smiled and prayed that Gott's happy light inside her would shine to make someone else smile today.

6

*D*espite her friend's advice, Haley resolved to keep things with Dylan Monroe strictly professional. Right now, she had her hands full trying to get through nursing school.

There was also the unknown factor of whether or not Dylan was interested in a relationship. The prevailing attitude among female staff members was that some lucky woman was going to snatch up the new psychologist, as if he were the last chocolate in the box.

But Haley didn't think anyone would be catching Dylan anytime soon. She couldn't put her finger on the reason why. There was just something about him—a flicker of regret in his eyes, a hesitancy that she didn't see in guys in the market for a girlfriend. He was giving out a very solitary message.

Single and staying that way.

For Haley, Dylan's attitude was refreshing and a little disturbing. Relating to a male peer on a strictly professional level was a new thing for her. At the same time, it bothered her that he didn't seem to notice that she was a young woman who was showing signs of attraction to him.

This was also a new thing for Haley.

Am I losing my touch? she wondered that Wednesday afternoon as she stared at herself in the ladies' room mirror. Same amber eyes, rimmed with a light touch of eyeliner. Her lashes were naturally thick and dark, so she never bothered with mascara. She turned her head this way and that, checking the golden highlights woven through her honey-blond hair. She had done them herself to save money, and it wasn't a bad job at all.

She had her father's high cheekbones and her mother's heart-shaped face. Long legs and a runner's spare frame, with just the right amount of curves. As a teenager she had done some modeling for local flyers and catalogs, so she knew God had blessed her with the right stuff.

At least on the outside.

The inside, well, she was working on her issues, trying to patch things over with her parents, trying to get herself out of debt.

But the turmoil swirling inside her wasn't reflected in her honey-eyed hair and amber eyes. So why didn't Dylan Monroe take notice? Why didn't he realize how much he enjoyed her company and suggest that they get to know each other better?

Enough time wasted. She swung open the restroom door, determined to rid her mind of Dylan Monroe. Unfortunately, he chose that moment to come walking down the hospital corridor.

"Haley . . . just the person I wanted to see. Can you spare a minute?"

"Sure." *Be still, my fluttering heart.* Why did she always have such an extreme reaction when he was near? "What's up?"

He gestured down the hall. "There's a twelve-year-old girl in exam bay three, minor burns from a fire. It sounds like she was heroic, but I can't get anything out of her."

"And you think she'll talk to me?" Haley felt a mixture of pride and trepidation. Although she had taught fourth-grade Sunday school one year, her experience with kids was limited.

"How old are you?" Dylan asked.

"Twenty-two."

"You're six years closer to twelve than I am. Plus you're female. That can make a big difference when it comes to getting a patient that age to feel at ease."

"I'm game," she said as he directed her down the hall. "But did you try guided imagery with her?" she asked. Dylan had briefed the staff on a type of therapy he'd had success with in private practice.

"It's not really appropriate in an emergency room setting."

"I thought you used it on patients suffering post-traumatic stress?"

"That's true. But it's more of a long-term therapy. A step-by-step program. It's something an ER patient might consider after discharge."

He paused by the curtain. "Knock, knock." A calm smile warmed his face when he peered in at the girl sitting on the bed. "Charlotte, can we come in? I brought Haley with me. She's a lot younger and cooler than I am."

Haley stepped in and rolled her eyes. "I am way cooler than this guy."

Scared eyes studied Haley from beneath a strip of white gauze. "Hi." Patches of Charlotte's hair were gone—burned away, Haley assumed—and the skin of her neck and the right side of her face were red and slick with ointment. "My mom went to the gift shop to buy me a scarf to . . . to cover this."

"Okay, we'll wait with you until she gets back," Dylan said. "So is she getting you a cool bandana or something more decorative?"

Charlotte said she had asked for something purple, and Dylan launched into an explanation of why purple was the color chosen by creative people. When that got Charlotte talking about how she liked to sketch things, Dylan found her paper and pencil and engaged her in a discussion of graphic novels that Haley knew nothing about.

And he said he wasn't cool, Haley thought, filling the girl's water pitcher while they talked. It seemed to Haley that they were just chatting, and she wondered what clinical details Dylan extracted from a conversation about comic books. How did he assess Charlotte's psychological health by talking with her about anime?

Soon, the girl's mother returned with a zebra print scarf in purple and black that pleased Charlotte.

"I'm glad you like it, honey." Irene Metcalf collapsed in the visitor's chair, looking frazzled and stressed. "Sorry it took me so long, but the scarves downstairs were way too expensive and way too ugly, and I had to drive a few miles to find a shopping center."

"It's nice, Mom. Thanks." Charlotte folded the scarf in half and held it up to her head. "How do you put these things on?"

"Well, you have a few options. There's Hollywood-starlet style, turban style, and what we used to call hobo chic," Haley piped up.

Charlotte grinned, warming to Haley. "Can you show me?"

While Dylan talked with Irene, Haley demonstrated different styles. She showed Charlotte how to twist and fold the fabric as Dylan mentioned some breaks that had come up on Charlotte's X-rays. Broken bones in her arm from a previous injury.

Although Haley kept working with Charlotte, she couldn't help but listen in.

"I know exactly when that happened, and I still feel terrible about it," Irene said, her voice thick with emotion. "She fell off the play structure in the park and her arm hurt something awful. But, Doctor, I didn't have medical coverage and there was no money for all of this."

Dylan sympathized, saying he knew how expensive medical coverage could be.

"Please don't take my girl away from me," Irene begged. "I brought her here today because I was so worried about the burns and her hair and everything. And we have medical coverage now, through my new job." Irene talked about saving money for a new heating system so that they wouldn't have to use the kerosene heater anymore. She talked about the stress and pressure of being a single parent. "My only saving grace is that Charlotte is such a good girl. Did you know she got burned today 'cause she was trying to keep my nephew away from the heater?"

"Charlotte is a brave girl. I'm glad her wounds will heal, but sometimes a trauma like that can cause wounds inside that also need treatment." Dylan went on to describe his outreach program in the community, and his healing therapy. He gave Irene a card, and asked her to call and set up an appointment. "There would be no charge for patients like you and Charlotte."

"Me? Why would I need treatment?"

"Don't you suffer from stress and anxiety?"

Irene let out a deep sigh, then chuckled. "I do. Indeed, I do."

When they looked over at Charlotte, she had tied the scarf under her chin, Hollywood-style.

"If I had some big dark sunglasses, people might think I'm Lady Gaga," she said.

"I bet they would," Haley agreed. "But honestly, you're a lot cuter."

When Charlotte looked up at her and smiled, it was all worthwhile. Let Swanson make her rewrite her clinical reports. Let Mrs. Pendergrass monopolize her time. If Haley could actually help someone in the course of her day, she could put up with the petty problems.

By the time they finished with Charlotte and Irene, it was nearing the end of Haley's shift.

"Thank you for that," Haley told Dylan as they approached the nurses' station. "It's nice to feel like I've made a difference, and I think I learned a lot from listening to you."

"Really. What did you learn?"

"You didn't need my help getting through to Charlotte. You wanted me to be there to distract the patient so that you could get her mother to open up."

He crossed his arms in a defensive gesture. "So . . . you've been studying my methodology."

"I've been studying, all right. That's about all I do these days. My grades are just so-so, and if I lose this scholarship, I'll be out of nursing school."

"That would be a shame." There was real compassion in his eyes. "You've got a wonderful way with patients, Haley. You've got the potential to be a fine nurse."

"Would you tell Dr. Swanson that?"

One side of his mouth turned up in half a grin. "I just might."

"And I have another question for you." Since she was on a roll, Haley figured she would go for it. "Some of us are going out to Snyder's after the shift. Appetizers are half-price today. Do you want to come along?"

"I'd better not."

"Come on," she persisted. "Everyone wants a chance to talk with the elusive Dr. Monroe."

"Really." He rubbed his square jaw. "Is that the scuttlebutt?"

She nodded. "Yup. And I think it's time to cut loose a little. Take off your tie and unbutton that collar. Talk to people and eat some spicy wings. Go wild."

He almost grinned. Almost. "I like you, Haley. I appreciate your candor. But . . . not tonight."

"Okay." She folded her arms. "Some other time? Or should I back off?"

"Some other time," he said.

That was the first time he'd smiled at her.

This was progress. Most of all, he had given her hope. He liked her. Haley waited until he disappeared into the elevator before she broke into a happy dance. He liked her!

7

"It was a good thing, coming here," Dat told Elsie Wednesday afternoon when their meetings with the Englisher vendors had finished. They waited under the red awning near the bright sign for Reading Terminal Market. This was the drop-off and pick-up point, probably because the market was a popular spot for Amish folks to sell their wares in the city.

He tapped the satchel of paperwork that Elsie had brought along. "I see now how our store will make much more profit by letting these businessmen sell our merchandise outside of Halfway."

"And at the same time, we'll be helping Plain folk sell their crafts," Elsie said. "It's a deal that could benefit many people."

"A smart business deal. I'm glad you're using the brain that Gott gave you, Elsie. I'm going to put you in charge of the store, make it official. That way I can spend more time at home, fixing up the old house and setting up the carriage house for the new business."

Dat's words warmed her inside—a very good thing on this chilly

January day. "I'm so very happy it all worked out." She knew she was grinning from ear to ear, and if she wasn't in such a public place, she would have skipped out of the market. She had worked many hours to expand their little Country Store through outside vendors.

Tom touched his beard as he eyed the small white box in her hands. "What's that you got? A snack for the way home?"

"I bought some cupcakes for the little ones. The one for Will is decorated with a green frog. The other one, a purple horse."

"Who ever heard of a purple horse?"

"I know. I laughed when I saw it, but something told me Beth would like it."

"She'll certainly like eating it. Those two have quite a sweet tooth."

"Most children do," Elsie said, "but I don't think I ever grew out of mine."

Dat's eyes were thoughtful as he glanced down at her; how rare it was for the two of them to be alone like this. From the way he cleared his throat, Elsie sensed that he had something important to say.

"Maybe you'll grow out of it when you have children of your own," he said. "But I don't mean to put the cart before the horse. You need to find a good Amish man and marry first. If you just give it a chance, some young fella is going to come courting. Give the young men a chance to know you. No one can resist your sunny disposition. Of all my children, you're the one who can turn any frown upside down."

"Dat . . ." Elsie looked around awkwardly. Some of the other passengers were nearby. Cousin James, just a few years older than Elsie, was talking with Ruben Zook, a large young man who hunkered into his coat against the cold. Three older Amish men waited inside the lobby, watching through the window. Elsie knew them all, and she didn't want to share such a personal matter with members of their church. Gossip was frowned upon, but that didn't keep people from indulging. "Someone might hear."

Her father held up one hand, stopping her objections. "It's something I've been meaning to ask you about. Fanny tells me to leave it be, but now that the horse is out, we might as well plow the whole field. Your *Rumspringa* has been a very quiet time, and here you're already seventeen."

"I am," she said, forcing cheerfulness in her voice that belied her wariness. She could see where this was heading, and if she wasn't careful she would paint herself into a corner.

"The thing is . . . well, I never had to push your brother or sister into rumspringa. Emma would have dragged a team of horses behind her to get to a singing. But I've noticed you don't go. And the youth gatherings . . . the volleyball games and bonfires. How is it that you're always going to bed early when those events come around?"

She tipped her head to the side, glancing over at some passing shoppers to avoid looking in her father's eyes. "Just tired, I guess."

"Is that so? Every time?" He stroked his beard. "Something tells me you're a late bloomer. There's no shame in that. To everything there is a season, that's what the Bible says. Your season will come, Elsie."

She bit her lower lip, touched by her father's loving words. Her dat loved her so much, he truly believed that she could have a life like other girls, that a bit of socializing at a singing would lead her to find a young man. He thought she would be able to fall in love and marry and have a family like other Amish girls.

Dear Dat! His love for his daughter made him blind to who she really was.

The white van that pulled up was a welcome distraction from their conversation.

"There's George." Elsie was relieved to end their conversation, to see George Dornbecker, their driver, jump out of the van and open the rear doors for cargo. She knew Dat wouldn't talk about personal things inside the confines of the van.

"And it's a good thing," said Dat. "January weather wasn't meant for standing around."

Alvin Yoder peered through the glass of the marketplace. A moment later the door popped open and the three older men emerged, John Beiler talking all the way. Jacob Fisher plodded along slowly. A great-grandfather, he was probably seventy or eighty for all Elsie knew, but he liked working on the business end of the family bakery.

Ruben and James waited respectfully for the older men to climb into the van.

"Hold on there, Elsie," George said, appearing with a plastic footstool in hand. He placed it on the pavement in front of the door. "There you go."

"Thank you, George." She cradled her white box carefully as she stepped into the van and took a seat at the window, right behind the driver. It wasn't often that Elsie got to ride in an automobile, and she enjoyed peering forward to watch the world race toward her at a remarkable speed. So much faster than the fastest horse!

Dat decided to take the seat in front, beside George, and Elsie watched the others board, hoping her friend Rachel would get to sit beside her for the trip home.

Lizzy King went to the seats in the very back row, and her husband, "Market Joe," followed. They rode in George's van nearly every day so that they could run the King family's cheese concession at the Reading Terminal Market. Today, their helper was Rachel King, who took the empty seat beside Elsie.

"Did you have a chance to meet with Claudia?" Elsie asked quietly.

"I did." Rachel's eyes glimmered. "I'll tell you all about it when we get going." She fastened her seat belt and watched as Zed Miller took a seat in the back row, behind the older men. A handsome man in his late twenties, Zed had just returned to Halfway after years of being shunned.

"Mmm." Rachel's eyebrows lifted. "Two more empty seats, and one beside me. What are the chances that James will be sitting with me?"

Elsie smiled. Her cousin James had been courting Rachel for a few months, and the chance to sit beside him for a van ride was an unexpected treat. "I think your chances are good."

Just then the door was blocked by the bulk of Ruben Zook. He paused in the opening, and then lowered himself into the seat beside Rachel. "This seat is just fine for me," he said. His eyes were lazy slivers as he watched Rachel react with uneasiness.

Ruben had a reputation as a joker, though Elsie didn't always find his pranks to be so funny.

"Ruben." Elsie leaned across Rachel, getting his attention. "I think there's a lot more room for your long legs in the back row."

"Ach, but the view of Rachel squirming is so much better from here."

Rachel frowned, crossing her arms as James appeared in the doorway. He took in the situation quickly, and smiled. "Looks like I'll be sitting on your lap, Ruben. Unless you want to move."

Ruben heaved a sigh. "Some people just can't take a joke." He rose, careful not to bump his head on the padded ceiling as he moved back.

"That's better." James settled in, buckling his seat belt. "I don't like to get that close without at least going on a buggy ride first."

Rachel and Elsie chuckled as James beamed. "How was your day in the city? I can tell you, I spent a lot of time riding in cars on crowded streets, just to pick up a part for the tractor. I'll be happy to get back to Halfway, back to my horse and buggy."

Elsie smiled and readjusted her hands on the bakery box. George had closed up the doors and turned up the heat, and though the warmth seeping into the van felt good, she didn't want her cupcakes to melt or get smashed. She would hold them close, right in her lap for the ride.

"Everyone have a seat belt on?" George called back through the van.

"All buckled," John Beiler answered. "We're good to go, George."

"Okay, then. We're on our way to Halfway." George turned the steering wheel and the van eased through the parking lot. "Anyone not wanting to go to Halfway . . . well, you'll just have to take the next van to Hawaii."

Everyone chuckled, and Elsie felt that a delicate ribbon bound all the folks in the van together. Tired travelers, grateful for a warm, cozy seat and a congenial driver.

"That's the thing about Halfway," George added. "It's the only town where, when you arrive there, you're still Halfway there."

Another murmur of laughter rose from the passengers.

"All right, I'll let you folks get some rest. We've got clear, dry roads this afternoon, so traffic permitting, we should be back in Halfway in an hour and a half."

The gusty conversation of the men in the back row made Elsie more comfortable talking with the friend beside her. "How did it go with Claudia? I want to hear everything."

"You were right about her," Rachel said. "She's a right good woman. Younger than I expected, with little plates through her ears, big as candy mints. Do you think that hurts?"

"I couldn't say. But she favors your paintings, of course. Is she going to sell your work in the gallery?"

Rachel's head bobbed and the grin on her face could have lit a kerosene lamp.

Elsie gave Rachel's hand a squeeze. "I'm so excited for you!"

"Claudia said my paintings were soothing and full of peace. A throwback to a simpler time."

Elsie nodded. Although Rachel was not allowed to paint portraits, she brought the color and simplicity of Amish life alive in her paintings. The contrast of summer flowers against a gray barn. A pristine white quilt with a deep green and blue Double Wedding Ring pattern hanging in the yard. A cloth doll sitting before a Sunshine and Shadow quilt.

"And what do you think about having your paintings in an Englisher art gallery?" James asked.

"I like the idea of bringing Gott's peace to Englishers, even if it's just in a painting. Claudia wants to have a dozen in the gallery to start," Rachel said. "And I've barely got eight right now."

"You'd best get painting," Elsie teased.

Rachel sighed. "I reckon so."

"Ach, don't say that," James chimed in. "She won't have a free moment for courting. I barely get to see her as it is."

"Oh, I'll always find time to see you, James," Rachel said. "If I never saw another cow, I'd be fine. But you . . . I can't give you up."

"Well, that's good to know," he said wryly. "Though I have to admit, I'd miss my cows if I had to give them up. There's nothing like a good herd of milk cows to keep a man company."

The girls chuckled, but James simply shook his head. "I wasn't kidding."

Elsie chatted with Rachel and James for the first half hour or so, watching as the crowded streets and traffic lights of the city gave way to shorter buildings and smooth highway. The blue of the clear winter sky was getting bolder now as purple dusk approached. Elsie shifted so that she could peer over George's shoulder to watch the world zoom toward them. Funny how the land seemed to split and wash around the vehicle when you moved at this speed.

The highway in this spot was straight and narrow, down to one lane, and the lights of cars heading east toward the city reminded her of ants returning to the nest as they meandered down the hill and whooshed past. Elsie moved the pastry box to the side of her seat, thinking of how Will had stepped up last summer to protect his little sister from the frogs down at the pond.

On a hot summer night, Elsie had strolled down to the water's edge with the children in search of some relief from the heat. As the sun began to set, a chorus of croaks filled the air.

"Froggies?" Beth had pressed her palms to her cheeks in a panic. "The froggies are mad! What if they chase me?"

Elsie had tried to console the little girl, but to no avail.

Then Will had stepped in. He'd placed a hand on his sister's shoulder. "Don't worry about them frogs. I'll eat the froggies!"

"You will?" For some reason, Beth had believed him. And Will spent the rest of the night repeating that promise, a phrase that had become part of family history. Whenever someone worried that things might go wrong, Elsie would joke that Will could "eat the froggies," and everyone felt a bit better.

That was why the frog cupcake would get a chuckle out of everyone. She crossed her legs and fixed her gaze on the windshield again.

Just ahead, a pair of headlights zigzagged on the road, sending a little quiver of fear up Elsie's backbone.

No . . . it was just her imagination. Or maybe it was a crooked road.

But the approaching car wobbled again, and this time Elsie could see that it had crossed the double yellow line.

Just then, the van began to slow as George pressed the brakes . . . but it was too late.

The vehicle loomed closer. As if in slow motion, it floated toward them like a bee moving to a flower.

Only these white lights were rushing toward them at a sickening speed.

Oh, good Gott in heaven, it's going to hit us!

Elsie wanted to make it stop, but all she could do was stare, horrified and helpless.

Tires squealed against the pavement.

The seat belt cut into Elsie's flesh, a choking yoke across her neck. But that discomfort was forgotten when the world exploded.

Bam!

A gunshot? A crack of thunder?

What was going on?

The dark mass had smashed into them, sending the van into a tailspin.

Screams and cries and low groans rose, as if the van itself were moaning against the large, dark beast that was attacking it. Elsie felt something rip from her throat, but her cry blended into the horrible sound of scraping metal, searing tires, and panicked voices.

The whole world spun around and around, like a child's spinning top.

Elsie would have reached for something to hold on to, but she could not lift her arms. Her entire body was pinned against the seat and window.

Spinning and whirling, round and round.

Another explosion stopped the spinning motion, as the right side of the van smacked into something hard. Solid. Brutal. Unforgiving.

The impact rattled Elsie's teeth and bones. In rapid motion, her body was jostled right and left, flung like a cloth doll. She banged into the van's wall, then back to the right, her head hitting Rachel's upper arm.

Then, the vehicle shivered into silence. An eerie calm.

The terrible spinning motion had ended, but Elsie could do nothing more than close her eyes and welcome blessed stillness.

8

The impact had knocked him out of a dream.

When the first jolt had hit the van, Ruben Zook had been asleep. The fierce noise did not belong in the pleasant dream of a singing where he was the only young man who had attended, and plenty of young girls were going out of their way to let him know they fancied him.

That dream had quickly given way to a nightmare of shrieking steel and desperate voices.

A living, breathing nightmare.

Now the van had stopped spinning, he sat upright in his seat, his nerves tingling with adrenaline. What was that dust that filled the van? Many of the windows were shattered and he couldn't see beyond the windshield through the pillowed air bags that had puffed up in front of George and Tom Lapp. The van seemed to be intact. Dented in a few spots, but still in one piece.

Someone had to move . . . make sure everyone was okay . . . and

from the cries and murmurs in the smoky van, he knew that someone was him.

Beside him, Zed Miller rubbed his eyes, getting his bearings, and
Market Joe tended to his wife, who was crying. They seemed okay.
All shook up, but okay.

As the dust began to clear, Ruben noticed a dark mound blocking the aisle down beneath his feet. What was that? He winced to
realize it was a man's body slumped in the aisle. His dark coat was
covered with slivered glass.

One of the older men had been tossed out of his seat.

Blocking out the murmurs and groans of the other passengers,
Ruben unbuckled his own seat belt and nearly fell on the man
when his legs gave way.

Gott, give me the strength to do thy will, he prayed as he gained his
balance and moved over the elderly man. "Jacob?"

Jacob Fisher, who had been sitting in the aisle seat of the second
row, now lay on his side on the van's floor, in a very bad way. The
arm beneath him was angled in an unnatural position, but when
Ruben leaned down to see his face, his eyes were moving.

Ruben moved his face close so that the old man could see him.
"All right, there? Looks like you hurt your arm."

"Can't breathe," Jacob gasped, desperation in his flinty gray
eyes.

The sight of the man's pale face brought Ruben back to a memory of long ago, a tragedy long buried in his mind.

"Take it easy, Jacob." Tenderly, Ruben placed his palm against
the man's cheek and found that his skin was cold and clammy.

Jacob reached up and squeezed Ruben's wrist, a surprising gesture considering that he barely knew the man. Even more unexpected, Ruben squeezed back.

"I'll get you help. A doctor . . . and an ambulance. Just keep
breathing, okay?"

The dry gasp that came in answer tore at Ruben's sense of calm and order, propelling him forward. Jacob needed help.

Go, go, go. Each heavy thud of his heart urged him to move.

Still crouching under the van's ceiling, Ruben carefully shifted toward the damaged double doors, a twisted mass of metal. The square panels of the windows were warped and bent, and most of the glass had been blown out, save for one drape of shattered glass in one corner. Shiny and cracked, like ice on the frozen pond.

Ruben seized the latch and pulled. The door wouldn't budge, and as he gave it another tug, pain flared through Ruben's hands. He pulled back and looked at his palms, dashed with blood. The shattered glass was cutting into his hands.

He winced as he pulled out a large chunk of glass. The smaller pieces would have to wait; he couldn't waste precious time. Jacob needed help.

Go, man. His heart thudded. *He said he couldn't breathe. Get help now!*

Bracing against the pain, he tried the door again and realized that it was locked, and there was no mechanism on the door to undo it. Frustration tore at him as he turned toward the front seat. Amid the cacophony of voices, he could make out George talking briskly to Thomas Lapp.

"George! George, listen to me," Ruben shouted, praying to Gott Almighty that his voice would be heard.

Over James's moaning and Lizzy's sobs, George somehow heard him. Hands in the air, he pushed at the puffy air bag and turned around. "What is it, Ruben?"

"Can you unlock the door back here? We need to get out and go for help. Jacob needs help."

"Right." George turned away for a moment and Ruben heard a satisfying click in the door.

One tug on the handle, and the battered door popped open. "Got it!" he shouted.

"Go get us help, then." George waved him on. "Such a hard hit. I saw it coming, but ... ah ... Is everyone okay back there?"

Despite the groans and murmurs, no one answered the driver's call.

Too much confusion, Ruben thought as he tried to work the second door open. Everyone was dazed. Stuck in a waking dream.

A nightmare.

Ruben had to hunker down to squeeze through the single door. His feet stung when his boots hit the ground, but he thanked Gott that his legs felt solid beneath him. Ready to run.

9

*H*aley sat staring from the side of the highway, her car idling as she reeled from the horrible collision that had just taken place before her eyes. The purr of a ringing line in her ear amplified her panic. She'd dialed 911, right? Why weren't they answering?

When someone came on the line, she reported the accident, giving the nearest mile marker. "There were two cars involved. A dark-colored SUV just came right across the double line from the other direction."

She could still see the searing pair of headlights carving an unnatural path across the yellow line. It was the oddest sight, especially on a clear, bone-dry day like today. At first, she had thought her eyes were going buggy, but then the SUV hit the van, catching the front end with such force that both cars had spun in a cloud of dust and sparks.

"I can't believe a car would just cross the line like that," she said, her voice trembling at the thought of a random universe in which one stray turn could cause so much damage.

"Is there visible damage to both vehicles?"

"Yes, well, I think so." She twisted around, looking for the dark SUV. "The passenger van is definitely damaged, but I can't see the SUV. It seems to have vanished."

"A possible hit-and-run," the woman said in a very even tone.

"I don't know." Haley cut the engine and threw open the door. She was okay. She had been spared. But that van had taken a terrible hit. "I'm going to see if there's anything I can do to help the passengers in the van."

"Ma'am, please take caution if you leave your vehicle."

"Yes, yes, I will. Just get an ambulance here, please."

"They're on their way."

Haley was already running along the shoulder of the road, grateful for her clogs and for dry pavement, when she slid the cell phone into her pocket. A car passed, moving slowly but coming within inches of the van. She had hoped that the emergency flashers on her car would warn drivers to slow down.

A door on the side of the van opened and a large man jumped to the road bed. He was a young man dressed all in black with a sort of Dutch boy haircut just at the ears. An Amish man. His gait was a bit uneven as he ran toward her.

"Do you have a cell phone?" he called to her. "We need help. Ambulances and doctors."

"I called them already. I'm a nurse," she said, realizing that wasn't entirely true, but . . . whatever.

He stopped running and gestured toward the van. "A blessing from Gott. Please, come help Jacob."

Already, people were spilling out from the van behind him. Two older men. A man bolstering a crying woman. A tall young man in his late twenties. When a small girl jumped out, Haley thanked God that a child had survived; a moment later she realized the young woman was older than she thought—a teenager—but a little person.

"He's in here, on the floor of the van," the large man said, directing her to the open side door. "He's having trouble breathing."

It occurred to Haley that she had no stethoscope—no tools in hand, not even a first-aid kit—but when she looked down at the man struggling to breathe on the floor of the van, the basic protocol came to her.

ABC. Clear the Airway. Make sure he's Breathing. Support Circulation.

She leaned over the man, noting his white beard and wrinkled skin. He had to be seventy or so. "My name is Haley and I'm going to try and help you. Can you answer some questions?"

"Yes," he gasped.

He was conscious; that was a good sign.

"Is there something in your throat? Something blocking the airway?" she asked.

"Nay. It's down lower." He patted his chest with one withered hand.

"Okay." She turned back to the young man who had summoned her and asked his name.

"Ruben Zook."

"I'm Haley. Ruben, can you go back to my car and get my medical bag? It's just a black backpack in the backseat."

"I'll bring it," he said, backing away.

Haley took the injured man's pulse, which was rapid, but that was no surprise. His labored breathing was a huge concern, and she worried about a punctured lung or even a lung collapse.

And internal injuries.

Her mind raced back through her medical training as she reached for ideas on how to help him. But nursing school wasn't focused on this type of emergency care. She had no real tools beyond her stethoscope. There was no doctor, no sterile equipment . . . no Dr. Swanson barking orders.

But this was a random universe, where a shiny dark mass of metal haphazardly smashed up a van full of people.

She turned back to the elderly man, leaning down low so that she could see his face as she pressed a hand to his cheek. "I know you're in pain, Jacob. Just keep breathing as best you can, okay? You're doing great. You're doing great."

10

*I*t was a miracle.

To be able to open her eyes, unbuckle her seat belt, and slide out of her seat. To walk and talk and see the beautiful orange and purple flame of sky beyond the smoking wreck of the front of George's van. Gott had blessed her in this terrible moment.

Sure, she couldn't stop shaking like a leaf in the wind, but that didn't stop her from breathing the crisp air of twilight as she went to the passenger door of the van to try to help Dat open it.

George was already there, tugging and probing the dented metal. "Would you look at that? It's a wonder your father wasn't hurt with a hit like that."

"Can you get it open?" Elsie asked.

"Looks like the latch is all gummed up."

"It's bashed in," Elsie called to Dat, not sure how clearly he could hear through the smashed window that had stayed in place, a crinkled, crackled panel that caught the fading light.

There came another thump from inside the door.

Hands in his pockets, George grimaced at the crumpled door. "It's not going to budge. Go tell your dat to climb around over my seat."

"You stay there. I'll come around," she hollered, then hurried around the battered van.

George had left the driver's side door open, and she peered into the front seat. "Dat? You need to climb out this way."

She waited, but there was no answer.

Buzzing with adrenaline, she struggled to get a handhold to make the steep climb up into the driver's seat. It was covered with powder from the big bags that now draped, half deflated, over the steering wheel. Air bags.

Her father sat there calmly, knocking on the passenger door.

"Dat! I guess you didn't hear me. The door won't open. George says to climb out this way."

"Is that right?" Thomas squinted at her, as if recognizing her for the first time. "Elsie girl! Are you all right?"

"Ya . . ." she said hesitantly. Her father had asked the same question when she'd leaned forward to check on him, just before she'd hopped out of the van. "I'm a little shook up, but praise Gott, I'm alive."

"I can't get my door open," he told her. "Can you help me? Tell George."

Alarm made the hairs on the back of her neck tingle. They'd had this conversation. Maybe Dat was in shock.

"Dat, George can't get the door open. Come out this way. Just climb over the console here."

He frowned down at the barrier between the seats, glanced up at her and smiled. A big, wholehearted smile, the likes of which she hadn't seen since the day he announced that he was marrying Fanny Yoder after missing Mamm for so many years.

"Elsie girl! Are you all right?"

The air around her seemed to crackle with a warning. "I'm fine, Dat. But I'm worried about you." She leaned closer, moving her hand along his arm and up his shoulder. "You look like you're in one piece, but are you okay?"

"Fit as a fiddle." His usual answer.

That was reassuring.

Until he turned to the glittering smashed window and tried the door handle. "Hmm. I can't get the door open."

"It's okay, Dat." She rubbed his shoulder as her throat grew tight with fear. "Dat, I think you should stay right where you are."

He turned back to her and this time she noticed his eyes were so round and wide, the dark centers big as dimes. Something was wrong with her father.

"An ambulance," she whispered under her breath. He needed to see a doctor. And this door . . . she hoped that the emergency team would be able to get it open.

"Elsie girl." Dat smiled as he reached over and patted her cheek. "When did you get here?"

She bit her lower lip, fighting back tears.

Something was very wrong.

11

*B*reathe. Swallow. Breathe. Haley had to suppress the loud thumping of her own racing pulse so that she could listen to Jacob's heart and raw breath sounds with her stethoscope.

"How is he?" Ruben asked.

"I'm afraid to move him. It could make things worse. I wish there was more I could do, but the paramedics will have oxygen . . . and a backboard. His arm seems to be dislocated." As she spoke, she slid off her coat and placed it over the old man. "But we can try to keep him warm. He's in shock." She could tell from his pale, clammy skin. "Honestly, you might all be in shock. We need to make sure no one wanders into the highway."

"That's right," said the tall, handsome Amish man. "I got these flares from George, and I'm going to go back a few feet to set them up."

"Good idea." Haley nodded. "And that's my car, the blue Geo. Maybe some of you folks should go back there and sit inside. The heater works pretty well, and you'll be off the road."

"Let's go, Lizzy," one of the men said. "Alvin and John . . . we'll get out of the way so the ambulance can help those who need it."

"You go, John. I'm going to stay with Jacob," said one of the older men.

"Me, too." The man named John brushed past Haley to climb around his friend and reclaim a seat in the van. "We're not leaving you alone, Jacob."

The other man climbed back in, and the couple headed back toward Haley's car.

With a deep breath, Haley lifted her gaze from the prone man and noticed a young man and woman sitting in the second row seat. The young man's eyes were closed, and the young woman—a girl, really—had tears streaming down her cheeks. Haley hadn't thought to ask about other injuries, but now she realized that this young man was unconscious.

"Are you okay?"

The girl shook her head, and that was when Haley noticed that she was holding very tightly to the young man beside her, as if propping him up. "It's James. Something was wrong with his seat belt and . . . when we crashed, he doubled forward and . . . I don't know if he hit his head or what happened but he won't wake up. Can you help him wake up?"

"And Dat, too," the other young girl called from the front of the van. "He's nodded off here and something's not quite right."

Triage, Haley thought. She had to prioritize, based on level of injury. She probably should have asked about other injuries when she first arrived at the scene, but she'd never done this before.

"I'll be right there," she called toward the front of the van. "Just let me know if he stops breathing, okay?"

"I will," the girl's voice called back.

Haley climbed into the side door of the van, stepping carefully around Jacob so that she could examine James. She moved her stethoscope over his chest. "Healthy breath sounds," she told the worried young woman. "And that's a good thing."

A sob slipped from the girl's throat as she watched Haley open his closed eyelids and take his pulse.

"What's your name?" Haley asked, mostly to distract the distraught girl.

"Rachel, and this is James."

"Is he your brother, or a friend?"

"A friend. A good friend."

"He's lucky to have a friend like you holding on tight to him," Haley said, listening to his heartbeat. It was slow and steady. A good heartbeat. But as she touched his coat she realized that there was a problem with his seat belt. James had been wearing only a lap belt during the collision. It was possible that he had suffered some sort of spinal injury, but diagnostics like that were way beyond her knowledge and experience.

"I keep praying that he'll be all right," Rachel said. "That he'll just wake up and . . . and tell me he's had a good rest and . . . and ask if we're back in Halfway yet."

"You never know," Haley said, praying herself for this unlikely scenario to be true. The whooping sound of a siren in the distance gave her a modicum of relief.

Finally . . . some relief for Jacob.

"Do you hear that, Rachel?" Haley asked. She removed the earpieces of the stethoscope and let it rest around her neck. "The paramedics are on their way. They're going to put James on a backboard, and they'll probably put a neck brace on him. Just so you know when you see it. You won't be afraid of it if you understand it, right?"

Another tear rolled down Rachel's cheek. "And what should I do? What can I do to help him?"

"Keep praying," Haley said. "Just keep praying."

∞ 12 ∞

"Dat? Won't you wake up and talk to me? It's me, Elsie."

Most of her body was shaking, whether from cold or panic, Elsie wasn't sure. But she tried not to let her father feel her fear as she squeezed his hand and stroked his arm, feeling the bone and muscle padded by the sleeve of his coat. Everything seemed fine. From her spot, kneeling on the driver's seat, Dat looked fit as a fiddle, just as he said. Not a scratch on him that she could see.

But he hadn't acted right before, and now he wouldn't wake up.

Elsie kept searching her mind, trying to come up with a prayer for hope or healing, but she kept drawing a blank.

What was wrong with her?

She tried to make up her own, but her words seemed pale and limp.

Heavenly Father, please awaken Dat. And help Jacob breathe again. And James . . .

So much to pray for on a day that had begun with so much hope and excitement. The sorrow and pain pressed down on her, but she couldn't give in to them. She had to stay strong now, for Dat and James and Jacob, and that other driver, whoever he was.

She rubbed Dat's large hand between her small ones, trying to press warmth and life into him.

Open his eyes, she prayed. *Bring the spark of your love back into his smile.*

She longed to see the eyes that had watched her so carefully back at the marketplace, showering her with concern and gauging her reaction. Elsie felt sure that if Dat would open his eyes, the rest of him would awaken, too. All back to normal.

His chest seemed to still, and her whole body quivered in alarm. Had he stopped breathing?

She leaned close, her ear to his nose.

There it was: the soft rush of air. He was still breathing, thank the Lord.

Elsie let her head slide down to Dat's chest. There, pressed gently against his coat, she could hear his heart beating. Or maybe that was her heartbeat ... or maybe it was the whoosh of passing traffic. She couldn't be sure, but for now it was the only thing she could cling to, and she reasoned that she was keeping her father warm, nestled against his chest.

"How's it going?" A woman's voice, and the gentle pressure of a hand on her back.

Elsie pulled away from Dat and twisted around to see the young woman who had stopped to help ... the nurse. She had pretty golden hair and warm brown eyes, and right now she was wearing only thin green cotton scrubs, having given her coat to Jacob.

"How's your father?"

"He's still breathing," Elsie said, turning toward the young woman. "He was talking with me before he fainted, but to tell the truth, he didn't make a lot of sense. Do you want to switch places with me so that you can examine him?"

"Sure." The young woman introduced herself as Haley, and asked Elsie her name.

"I'm Elsie, and this is my dat, Thomas."

"Did he recognize you?" Haley asked as Elsie climbed down to the pavement.

"Ya, but he kept saying the same thing, over and over again. What does that mean?"

"Maybe a head injury." Elsie could only see Haley's back as she knelt over Elsie's father. "Thomas? Tom, can you hear me? Maybe it's just shock. I'm doing my best here, Elsie, but I'm out of my league. I'm just a nursing student."

"You've been wonderful good, helping everyone here." Elsie was grateful that the young Englisher woman had stopped to help.

"There's an ambulance back there, tending to Jacob right now," Haley said as she leaned over the console to examine Thomas. "The paramedic told me he's got two more on the way. And the fire truck should have some way to get this door open. The jaws of life, they call it."

The jaws of life. Something about the expression made Elsie shiver. "Maybe they'll have something to wake Dat up?"

"I'm not sure it will be that simple," Haley said over her shoulder. "But they'll get him to the hospital fast. And LanCo General is an excellent hospital. That's where I work."

Elsie had always disliked hospitals. Their local doctor, Henry Trueherz, had always treated her with respect and understanding. But she remembered a time as a child when Mamm had taken her to a hospital in the city to have surgery on her legs. The images of pain had never faded. Never again did Elsie want to see one of those cold rooms with shiny equipment and needles and bars on the beds.

"I've never been fond of hospitals," Elsie said, "but right now, I would take Dat there myself if I had a horse and buggy."

Watching from the ground, Elsie noticed the care Haley was taking with Dat. A gentle touch, this one had. "I couldn't find a mark on him," Elsie said. "Why do you think he passed out like that?"

Haley gripped Thomas's chin and moved his head slightly. "I see some swelling on the right side of his head. It's called a contusion. He probably hit his head against the door frame."

Elsie felt the earth opening up beneath her feet. "A contusion. Is that serious?"

"I'm afraid it might be." Haley gently touched one palm to Dat's forehead. "We need to get him to the hospital." Then she climbed out of the van. "I'm going to update the paramedics. The thing with a head injury is that, if there's brain swelling, they need to treat it in the first hour. The golden hour, they call it."

Brain swelling . . . Elsie's heart began to thump loudly, a thudding pulse in her ears that overshadowed the trembling in her limbs.

Haley's mouth dropped open and she reached forward to grasp Elsie's shoulder. "I'm so sorry. Did I just give you too much information?"

"No." Elsie pressed a hand to her cheek and the iciness of her own palm brought her back to reality. "I just . . . I don't even know how long we've been here by the side of the road."

Haley checked her watch. "More than twenty minutes now."

Twenty minutes . . . It seemed like so much longer. A terrible month. A very sad year.

"Elsie, I don't mean to scare you. I could be wrong about this, but it's best to be careful. Better safe than sorry."

"I'll be fine. It's Dat I'm worried about." Elsie lifted her dress so that she could climb back into the seat beside her father. Tears stung her eyes, but she swallowed hard, holding them back. She couldn't cry now. She couldn't let Dat hear her crying. "I'm going to stay with him. And I want to go to the hospital with him."

"Of course." Haley pivoted to go, then paused. "Keep talking to him, Elsie. He might be able to hear you, and I'm sure your words are comforting to him."

Elsie nodded, swallowing over the lump of emotion growing in her throat.

"I'm here again, Dat. Your little daughter, Elsie." She took his hand, and this time she lifted it and pressed a kiss there, just below his knuckles. Dat's hands were strong and tough, calloused from working with tools, as both a farmhand and a carpenter. Good, strong hands of a workingman who loved Gott.

She closed her eyes as a swell of fear for him overwhelmed her. When she looked at his hand again, a teardrop had landed on his palm. She massaged it away and took a deep breath, preparing for a long conversation with her dat.

"Dear Dat, I never told you how happy I was when you married Fanny. There was so much going on at the time, and I know you didn't need the approval of your children, but just so you know, that was a good thing to do. Fanny's a good woman, and look at the way she's turned our house around! We've all come to love her, Dat. And now that there's Will and Beth in the family and another little one on the way. . . ."

Her voice cracked at the thought of the baby. Dat had to get better so that he could raise his newest child. Every child needed a father.

Outside the van the sun was setting and an inky blue light soaked the air.

"You just rest now, Dat. Rest now so you can be all better for the baby. And, Dat, just remember that I love you. And Emma and

Caleb, Fanny and the little ones. We all love you, Dat, and we'll be by your side to help you get better."

Just then he drew a deep breath in, as if he was telling her that he heard her.

"We love you, Dat. Just remember that."

❦ 13 ❦

$\mathcal{H}$aley walked away from the third and final ambulance that would take Thomas Lapp and his daughter Elsie to the hospital. The accident scene had been intense and heartbreaking, unlike any challenge she'd ever encountered, but she was grateful for the way the Amish passengers had banded together, helping each other.

Haley had learned their names quickly by necessity. Jacob Fisher was the oldest man, with difficulty breathing and a dislocated arm. The other two older men, Alvin and John, had ridden off with him in the first ambulance. James Lapp had gone off in the second ambulance with his girlfriend Rachel. Lizzy and Market Joe were the married couple waiting patiently in Haley's car.

Ruben had run back to her car many times, fetching her medical bag and water from her stash in the trunk. Zed had set up flares to slow traffic. Then he'd stationed himself alongside the van and waved passing vehicles on like a traffic cop. It was a task she would not have expected from an Amish man, but Haley was glad to have Zed enforcing their safe zone around the van.

And the driver, George . . . what a sweetheart. He was still crestfallen and distraught, despite the fact that his passengers insisted that he was not to blame. Haley herself had witnessed the dark SUV crossing the center line, and she would give her statement to the police.

But right now, she wanted to make sure the rest of the passengers made it to the hospital to get checked out. She had told them she insisted on it, even if she had to drive them herself.

She approached Zed, who was now helping the crew from the fire truck direct eastbound traffic onto the shoulder of the highway.

"Have you seen Ruben?" she asked. "I think we're about ready to head to the hospital, and he needs to come in my car. You, too."

"I saw him walk up the road a ways."

"What?" She squinted into the gathering darkness. "He's not trying to walk home, is he?" Having grown up in Lancaster County, she knew that the sight of an Amish person walking or scootering down the local roads was not unusual—even after dark.

"Nah. I'm sure he wants to go to the hospital with you. We all want to go. It's what the Amish do—gather around the sick and injured. None of us wants to get examined by an expensive doc for no reason, but one way or another, we'll all wind up at the hospital."

"Good." Behind Zed, the van driver stood off to the side of the road in the sizzling light of flares, going over details with a female police officer. George Dornbecker had assured Haley that his wife would take him to his doctor to get checked out.

"Miss?" One of the paramedics waved her over to the ambulance. "We've got a complication here. This man wants his wife to get to the hospital right away, but I can only take two passengers besides the patient."

Haley glanced over at Lizzy King, who was still visibly shaken. "Lizzy, you can go in the ambulance. You can ride in the front seat and Elsie can go in the back with her father."

"I can't go without Joe. I just can't do it after everything that's happened."

"I can see you're upset," Haley said. "And that's to be expected after everything you've gone through."

"It's more than that," Joe said. He looked to see who was listening, then lowered his voice. "We're expectin' a baby, only no one knows yet. Not even our families."

Lizzy's lower lip trembled as tears streamed down her cheeks. "What if something happened to our baby?"

Haley touched the woman's arm, reminding herself to be patient despite the urgent need to get Thomas to the hospital. "Your baby is well-cushioned in there," she said reassuringly. "But they can do a sonogram at the hospital and check the fetal heartbeat. Please get in the ambulance."

"But I can't go without my Joe. We'll go later, in your car."

"Okay." Haley held her hand up. "This ambulance needs to leave now, so I'll take you."

"Hold on." Elsie peeked out from the back of the ambulance. "You'd better go now, both of you." She scooted to the edge of the tailgate and hopped down to the pavement. "Everyone knows they'll take care of you faster if you arrive in an ambulance."

The paramedic held up his hands, as if in surrender. "All I know is, whoever is going needs to be in the bus now. We need to get Mr. Lapp to the hospital."

"Go," Elsie urged the couple. With an arm around Lizzy's waist, she ushered her toward the passenger door of the vehicle. "You need to do everything you can for your little one."

Seconds later, Joe was beside them, helping his wife into the truck and buckling her seat belt.

"And, Joe." Elsie looked up at the man, her eyes shining. "Please talk to Dat during the ride. He needs to know someone is here for him."

"Sure, Elsie. And I'll pray for him, too."

She nodded, watching as the doors were slammed. The flashing red and blue lights washed over them one last time as the engine started and the ambulance pulled away.

"That was very kind of you," Haley said as the siren began to fade.

"It made good sense for them to go. I just . . . it was hard to leave my dat alone." The tears that had sparkled in Elsie's eyes now flowed down her cheeks.

Haley bit her lower lip, trying to stay objective and professional. "I'll take you to the hospital. We'll go right now."

"I know but . . ." A sob caught her voice. "He shouldn't be alone."

The young woman was so distraught; Haley couldn't resist folding her arms around her. She held her close, wishing she could transmit love and support to Elsie. "He's not alone. God is with him." Haley didn't know where the words had come from. Of course, she believed in God, but it was not something she had been taught to talk about with a patient. Her faith wasn't even something she discussed with her friends or family, beyond deciding which church service to attend on Sunday.

"I know that Gott is with him." Elsie drew in a deep breath. "And I'm ever so grateful for all your help."

Haley had been patting Elsie's shoulder, and now the younger woman was patting Haley's back, too. It warmed Haley's heart to think of Elsie's thoughtfulness and care, but Haley knew she couldn't relax yet. She was afraid that if she started to think about all the things that had happened today, she would crumble to pieces.

"But, you know, Dat's family should be there, too. I've got to get a message to Fanny and Emma and Caleb. They'll want to come to the hospital."

"You can use my cell phone on the way there," Haley promised. "Now . . . let's find Ruben and Zed, and we can get going."

Unfortunately, that was easier said than done. As they headed down the road, they found that the fire truck was pulling out and a lone police car was staying behind. Deputy Granger from Halfway was going to guard the accident scene until the state highway patrol could arrive to investigate.

"Where did Ruben go?" Haley asked Zed, who stood beside the patrol car, talking with Keith Granger.

"I was beginning to wonder the same thing." Zed turned on a flashlight that the emergency crew had given him and pointed the beam down the road. "Let's go find him."

᠖᠖ 14 ᠖᠖

$\mathcal{B}$racing himself, Ruben got a grip on the side of the vehicle and pushed with all his might. His muscles quivered and the pressure rose up his neck into his head, but it was no use. Despite his effort, the SUV barely budged.

Dear Gott in heaven, what am I to do?

If the force that had pushed him down into this ditch to find the vehicle was some kind of angel, or even the Heavenly Father, then he trusted that Gott would show him the next step.

Ruben stamped his feet together and tucked his hands under his armpits for warmth. He'd found the dark SUV flipped onto its roof and buried in ivy and bushes in this ravine off the side of the road. He knew that someone was inside. At least the driver—maybe a passenger or two—but he couldn't get inside. One side of the SUV was pressed into the embankment, and the other side had been smashed flat as a pancake.

"Hallo?" he called once again, hoping for an answer. "Can you hear me in there?"

But the cold air was still and silent . . . and dark. When had the sun set? He'd been so preoccupied with the overturned car that he'd lost track of time.

"Hello?" came an answer, jolting Ruben to awareness. The sound didn't come from inside the vehicle, but up on the ridge by the highway. The red tip of a light caught his eye, and a white beam of light streamed down over the ivy. "Ruben? Is that you?"

"Ya! Down here!" he shouted, moving away from the brush. He could just make out three figures by the side of the highway. When a car flashed past, the light revealed two taller people and the little person, Elsie Lapp. "*Kumm!* I need your help."

"Do you need help getting up to the highway?" called the Englisher girl, Haley.

"No, no. There's a little path to come down here. It starts back there. Go back by that sign."

"You need to kumm, Ruben," Zed shouted. "We need to get to the hospital, and Haley's driving us."

"But there's someone down here that needs help!" Ruben hollered. "The other car! I found the car that hit us."

There was a clamor of reaction, with many questions all at once as the three of them made their way down into the ravine.

"How did you ever find this in the dark?" Zed asked, shining the beam of the flashlight over the wreck.

"It was still light when I first saw it, and I could smell the gasoline. I tried to get inside, but there's no getting in through the smashed windows. We need to flip it over."

"We'll never be able to do that, and it might be bad for the driver to roll the car over," Haley said, and a beeping sound told Ruben that she had her cell phone out. "I'm calling 911. They'll send another emergency crew out. They have clamps and blow-torches and things to cut through metal."

"There's no need to wait for them when we can do it," Ruben said. The same determination that had pushed him to find this vehicle now urged him to rescue its passengers. "If we put two of us on each side, we can push it away from the hill."

Haley was lost to her phone call, but Zed was circling the over-turned vehicle, outlining it with his flashlight. "You're right, Ruben. We should give it a try."

"You take that end with Haley," Ruben instructed. "Elsie, do you think you can do this?"

"Ya," she said. "I'm short, but I'm very strong."

"Good. You take this end, beside me."

Elsie got into position, wedging her boots into the hill, and he showed her what direction she would be pushing, while Zed and Haley figured out the best place to hold on to the vehicle.

"Ready? We'll go on the count of three." Ruben counted down, and everyone pushed. The vehicle budged, but it didn't get far. "We'll go again," he said.

After three tries, the hunk of metal finally flipped onto its side. While it was still teetering there, they gave another push, and it shifted down, bouncing slightly on its tires.

As Zed and Haley went to the nearest window and flashed the light into the vehicle, Ruben waited beside Elsie with a strange pressure in his gut. It was good that he'd found the car, but now, seeing the battered metal amid the smells of raw, scraped dirt and gasoline . . . now the impact of the crash weighed him down like a bushel of potatoes on his shoulders.

No one wanted to say it, but the fact floated over them all like a dark cloud. The passengers were probably dead.

"Looks like it's just a driver inside," Zed said. He moved to the next window and held the light while Haley reached inside.

"A woman," Haley reported. "She's got her seat belt on, and the air bag deployed." Everyone waited as the big question hung in the air.

"I think I'm getting a pulse," Haley said. "Yes! It's slow, but steady. She's alive."

"Praise be to Gott," Elsie said. "But how do we get her to the hospital?"

"An ambulance should be here soon," Haley said.

It was decided that Ruben and Elsie would climb up to the highway to point the way for the EMS workers, while Haley and Zed stayed with the driver.

"It was a good thing, what you did, Ruben," Elsie said as they climbed the steep path up the ravine. "How did you ever find that SUV, covered in the bushes and all?"

"I really don't know," he said. "It just bothered me that everyone saw the dark SUV but no one could find it. I know the police were thinking it was a hit-and-run accident, but with the way the van was damaged, I didn't think the other vehicle would get too far."

"Maybe it was Gott that led you there," Elsie said.

Ruben had been thinking the same thing, but he didn't respond. He couldn't have Elsie or anyone else thinking that he heard voices from nowhere. He wasn't well liked by many of the young people in their community. Some thought he was lazy because his father ran a business instead of a farm. Others thought he was heavy because he sat around doing nothing all day.

Neither was true, but because of his reputation Ruben had developed a thick skin. He had stopped looking most young women in the eye because he didn't want to see their looks of disapproval, and he had taken to playing jokes and pranks on the other men his age, mostly to keep them on their toes and at a distance.

They reached the top of the path, and he turned to offer Elsie a hand up.

"Denki," she said as they paused to look down the highway at the police car.

"Anyway, it's something good to come out of such a terrible thing." In the light from the streetlamps along the highway, her breath formed small puffs of steam that hung in the air. It was probably the first time Ruben had really looked at her face, and he was struck by her wide mouth and big brown eyes. She had a pretty face, mostly because Elsie Lapp wore her peace like a cape.

This was a girl with inner grace, a beautiful thing if you could catch sight of it.

"Look at that," she said.

Ruben's eyes scanned the inky blue sky until he realized she was staring down at the asphalt.

"No snow or ice. Not even a drop of rain. What do you think happened? Why did that car come across the line and send us spinning around?"

"I don't know." Ruben kicked at a stone on the side of the road. "Should we tell the deputy that we found her?"

"That's a good idea," Elsie said, "but one of us needs to stay here, so the ambulance can find her."

"I'll go. I can run fast. You stay here, and mind you keep off the road."

"You, too." There was a light in her eyes, an earnestness as bold as a lightning bolt. Elsie Lapp really cared about him . . . about everyone, he was sure of that.

He ran to the police car, his boots flying through the dark, heavy night.

❧ 15 ❧

*I*ntensive Care.

Even the name of the hospital unit sounded serious. So dramatic for a man who had a small bump on his head. A small bump that grew bigger until the doctors decided they might have to do surgery. If the drugs they were using didn't do their job, they would take Dat into the operating room and remove a piece of his skull so that his brain would have room to swell.

"A very common procedure for traumatic brain injury," the surgeon had told their family. "We do it all the time."

All the time, they cut off a piece of someone's head. . . . Elsie marveled at that. It was amazing medicine; she just hoped and prayed that they would not need to do it to her dat.

Seated in the hospital waiting room, Elsie stretched her hands and refolded them on her lap, in prayer position.

Dear Heavenly Father, bless Dat and make him better. Please . . . please.

She felt like an old washrag that had been wrung out and

squeezed and wrung out again, but of course, she had to keep praying. For Dat and James and Jacob. And for the driver of the dark blue SUV, too. They didn't know that woman's name, but surely the Heavenly Father knew her well.

Although the waiting room was bursting with Amish folk from her community, Elsie felt very alone right now. Fanny and Emma were in Dat's room in the ICU, where children were forbidden and only two family members were permitted. Caleb had taken the little ones across the street to get them a snack and a bit of escape from the chaos of a waiting room packed with so many Plain folk.

Tonight there was only a handful of Englishers in the intensive care waiting room. At first Elsie had stared at them, wondering if the driver of the dark SUV belonged to someone sitting right in this room. But then, on the way to LanCo General, Haley had told them that the driver might end up at a different hospital. Sometimes the paramedics did that so that they wouldn't overwhelm one emergency room.

And as it was, this hospital was getting overwhelmed with Amish people. The Fishers, such a big group of them, took up half the waiting room. Ruben Zook's father, Joseph, paced in the aisle at Elsie's feet. Preacher Dave talked with Ira and Rose Miller in one corner, and word had got around that the bishop was on his way. James's parents and sisters, family relations on Elsie's father's side, were now huddled in the hallway, talking with a team of doctors. Rachel stood with them, her mamm, Betsy, by her side, holding her close. Such a lovely thing, a mother's love.

Sometimes when Elsie closed her eyes she could see her mother's bright smile. It was a smile that said *I love you, darling girl, no matter how short or how tall you are, or the shape of your teeth. I love you from now till the end of time.*

Elsie closed her eyes and tried to remember her mamm, but instead, the sight of those fierce headlights cut through her mind.

She saw the crazy loop of the lights across the double line. She heard the sickening noise of glass exploding and metal scraping.

When she opened her eyes, her heart was pounding. She gasped, taking heated air into her raw throat. So much heat in this room, from the hospital furnace and the body heat of too many people. She couldn't take it.

She rose and removed her coat and wondered how she could have sat here all this time with her winter coat on. Her mind wasn't quite right, she knew that. She folded her coat and sat down with it on her lap, feeling that something was missing. What was it?

The pastry box. Whatever had happened to the cupcakes?

A knot grew in her throat as she imagined the green froggy and the purple horse smashed to crumbs. She sniffed. What a silly thing to cry about when so many folk were suffering tonight. But she'd been so pleased to give the cupcakes to the children. A few hours ago, it had mattered.

Just then Will and Beth darted in, roses on their cheeks from the cold outside. Elsie sniffed back her tears and pulled little Beth into her arms and held her close until Beth squirmed away to announce that Caleb had bought doughnuts for everyone.

"And this is for you," Will said, handing Elsie a pint of milk.

"Denki." There was no way she could eat, but the milk would help to soothe her throat.

"Any news?" Caleb asked as he offered her a doughnut.

She shook her head and watched as he made the rounds with the giant box.

"Two dozen doughnuts," Caleb told everyone. "I got a discount because the shop was closing for the night." He passed the box around to everyone, including the Englishers.

Elsie sipped her milk and watched the hallway, hoping for a doctor to appear and tell them that Dat was going to be just fine. But when a young doctor in navy blue scrubs arrived, he asked for the family of Jacob Fisher.

Half the waiting room gathered round him.

The news of Jacob was good. A few broken ribs and a punctured lung. A dislocated arm. "He's in excellent shape for a man in his eighties," the doctor said. "And it was wise of that young nurse not to move him at the scene. Her caution may have saved Jacob's life." The announcement that Jacob was being moved to a room on the third floor prompted the Fisher clan to rise and head for the elevators.

The empty seats beside Elsie prompted some of the other people to shift away from folding chairs that had been set up in the hall near the snack machines. A solitary woman with jet black hair streaked with silver took the chair beside Elsie.

"So many people," she said with a quiet smile. "Did I hear someone say there was an accident with a large van?"

"Ya," Elsie spoke softly. "A terrible thing. My father got hit on the head. We're waiting for him to awaken."

"My daughter is in surgery for a ruptured spleen. She was in a fender bender, but I'm guessing it was a different accident. Someone told me that the van was hit on Route 30 outside Halfway, but that's way out of Clara's stomping grounds. She's not allowed to drive that far from home, and she's such a good girl. I never have to worry about her that way."

Elsie nodded. "That must be a very good feeling, to have a good daughter."

"She's a good girl. This is the first time anything like this has ever happened to her, so I'm doing my best to keep calm." The woman blinked back tears and nodded. "I'm Graciana Estevez."

"Elsie Lapp."

"You know, you and Clara are around the same age. She's seventeen."

"Me, too."

Just then Rachel came over and sat on the other side of Elsie. "How's James?" Elsie asked her friend.

"He's sleeping now. They gave him something to help him sleep." Rachel explained that he had been talking with his parents and with doctors in the emergency room. "He told them he couldn't feel his legs." Rachel twisted a handkerchief around one hand. "They did some tests, and they think he has a spinal injury."

Elsie closed her eyes. Dear Gott, how could she bear more terrible news?

"Is he having surgery?" Graciana asked, joining the conversation.

"Not yet. They're going to wait and see how it looks when the swelling goes down." Rachel sighed, her lower lip quivering. "So I'll be waiting, too. For as long as it takes, till James comes home."

Elsie clasped her friend's hand. "I've been praying for James. You know there's a reason the Heavenly Father had us all on that van today."

Rachel frowned. "What reason? Nothing good will come of this. I never should have gone to the city today. If there'd been more seats, James wouldn't have used that bad seat belt. He would be fine right now."

"You don't know that," Elsie said. "We have to trust in Gott's plan and keep praying for James and Dat."

Rachel didn't respond, but the older woman warmed to Elsie's words.

"I've been praying, too, ever since I got that call from the police," said Graciana. "I keep praying that God will guide the surgeon's hands, and I'm hoping for a quick recovery. Clara is in her last semester of high school and these final classes are so important. Not to mention the prom and all those fun things for seniors. I don't want this to ruin her senior year for her."

"I'll add Clara to my prayers," Elsie promised. Although her head was already swimming with sorrow and fear, she reached to find the love and patience this woman needed. "Did you get a doughnut, Graciana? My brother brought them for everyone." She pushed out of the chair and brought the box to the older woman, who helped herself and thanked Elsie. "Rachel?"

Her friend waved her off. No appetite—Elsie understood that.

🙙🙜

Without windows, time didn't seem to pass in the hospital waiting room. The only thing that changed was the occasional arrival of a doctor with news, or another family waiting for a loved one.

A huge fish tank in a wooden case against one wall kept capturing Elsie's attention, luring her to a place underwater where food floated down to you and you could swim through the weeds and castle and back in less than a minute. Those fish were lucky in there. No giant steel demons to smash into them out of nowhere.

Sandwiched between Rachel and Graciana, Elsie kept quiet as the women talked. She was wondering if she would ever forget the icy sliver of fear that stabbed at her as the headlights came toward them. The terrible explosion of metal as the two vehicles collided.

The sound of footsteps in the corridor made Elsie look up expectantly. With relief, she saw that it was Haley Donovan, her new Englisher friend.

"How's everything going?" Haley asked, bringing a swirl of energy into the room. "How's your father, Elsie?"

"Still unconscious. They're giving him medicine to reduce the pressure in his brain," Elsie reported, knowing Haley would understand.

Haley nodded. "Trying to avoid a craniectomy. And how's James?" she asked Rachel, who gave her the latest update.

"I saw Kate Fisher in the hall, and she filled me in on Jacob. Sounds like he's going to be fine."

Elsie wished she could smile, but she could only manage a weary sigh. "Ya. That's a good thing."

"Excuse me." Graciana stood up. "I'm just going to call my boss and leave a message at work, and I know they don't want us to use cell phones here. If the doctor comes looking for me, would you tell him I'll be right back? My daughter is Clara . . . Clara Estevez."

"Sure." Elsie nodded. "And we'll save your spot, right here."

The Englisher woman thanked her and headed out of the waiting room.

"I'm sorry I missed so much," Haley went on, "but the police had a gazillion questions about the accident scene. It sounds like I'm the only witness outside the van who saw the whole incident."

Elsie nodded. Although she appreciated Haley's willingness to help the police, the Amish would have nothing to do with testifying or filing a lawsuit. "I saw everything," Elsie said. "The lights of that dark SUV crossing the double lines . . . I will never forget it."

"I know what you mean. It's kind of burned in my memory." Haley rubbed the plastic handles of the chair. "The police think the driver was texting; they found a cell phone in the car, and I guess they pulled up a message from the time of the crash."

"What is this, texting?" Rachel asked.

Haley explained how a person could type in and read messages on a cell phone.

"And they type and read while they're driving?" Rachel asked. "I would never think to read a book while driving a horse and buggy."

"Exactly," Haley said. "Well, at least I'm through with the interviewing for now." She looked up as two Amish men entered the waiting room. "It's our long-lost friends. What's up, guys?"

Zed Miller and Ruben Zook stepped in.

"We heard there were free doughnuts," Ruben said quietly. "So we came right away."

Elsie almost smiled despite the turmoil roiling inside her. "Have a seat and a doughnut."

Ruben held up his hands, both wrapped in white gauze and tape. "I'm not supposed to get crumbs on these."

"You'll have to use your fingertips," Haley said, handing over the large box as the young men sat down across from Elsie.

"We heard that Jacob is doing good, thanks to you, Haley." Zed gestured at Haley with a doughnut. "The doctor said that it was good we didn't move him."

"And I saw Market Joe and Lizzy leaving the ER when I got my hands bandaged," Ruben said. "Joe told me everything is fine."

"That's good," Haley said wistfully. "What happened to your hands, Ruben?"

He explained that he had cut them on glass when he first opened the van door, and so many small pieces had been embedded in his palms.

"And you didn't say anything?" Haley shook her head. "Shame on me for not noticing."

"You're just one person with two eyes," Ruben said.

"But you never said a word about it," Elsie pointed out. She had never talked much with Ruben before, and somehow she had not expected to find humility. "And everything you did—running around and finding the SUV and flipping it over. You did it all with glass in your hands?"

"Very heroic," Haley said.

Ruben shrugged. "Those things had to be done."

"And I was pretty impressed by the way you moved the traffic along, Zed," Haley said. "How did you know to set out flares?"

Zed frowned. "I spent eight years driving a truck."

"But I thought the Amish weren't allowed to drive."

Elsie knew Zed's long story. Everyone in Halfway knew about his long rumspringa and the job he'd gotten as a truck driver and the Jeep he'd left behind that had caused a bit of trouble for his parents. But she didn't think it was her place to say.

"I left home during my rumspringa," Zed said. "Do you know what that is?"

Haley nodded. "A time of freedom for Amish youth?"

"Something like that. I learned to drive an eighteen-wheeler. I took a class and everything, and for a long time driving was how I made a living."

"But you're back. Visiting Lancaster County, or are you back for good?"

Funny, how Zed didn't meet a person's eyes very often. Elsie wondered what heavy burden kept him looking down at the ground.

"Ya, I'm back."

Just then Graciana returned, navigating around legs in the aisle.

"I saved your spot." Elsie patted the seat. When the woman thanked her, Elsie introduced her, mentioning that the others had been in the van, and that Haley was a nurse who had fortunately been driving on the same highway.

"Actually, I'm just a nursing student," Haley corrected. "I was driving home on Route 30 when . . . when everything happened. I had just finished up my clinical class here."

"And you were the first car on the scene?" Graciana rubbed her arms. "That just gives me goose bumps. It was meant to be."

"Seeing how you helped everyone after the accident last night, I think you'll be a right good nurse," Elsie said.

"Tell that to my clinical instructor. I'm not so good with the class work and reports."

"But Gott blessed you in the things that really matter," Rachel said.

Haley pressed a hand to her heart. "Thank you for saying that." She turned to the older woman. "I don't think we met. I'm Haley."

"Graciana Estevez."

"Graciana's daughter was in an accident near Lancaster," Elsie explained.

"That's right. We live in Lancaster, and Clara was on her way to work," Graciana said. "She's been working at the Shopmart every afternoon and evening, trying to save money. Clara has always wanted to go to Disney World, and as a graduation present, I'm paying for our trip. She's got to save up the money to pay for our admission to the parks."

"I like Mickey Mouse," Elsie said without thinking.

"How do you know Mickey Mouse?" Zed asked.

She shrugged. "I see him on signs and advertisements. His round black ears."

"Not in *The Budget*," Ruben said, mentioning the newspaper read by Amish people.

That actually brought a chuckle from the group. Even Elsie felt herself smiling. "Not in *The Budget*. But I like the way Mickey is always cheerful."

"Even if he is a mouse," Rachel said. "With Graybeard the cat, he wouldn't last in our barn for ten minutes."

"Sometimes I forget he's a mouse," Elsie said.

"Clara likes Pooh Bear," Graciana said.

"Now there's a bear with a bad name," said Ruben. "I wouldn't like to have a name that makes folks think of manure."

Again, there was a murmur of laughter.

"But I can't believe we're laughing about this in such a terrible moment."

"Laughter is a great de-stresser," Haley said. "I know. Mickey told me."

Maybe it was good to laugh in the face of fear. Elsie had to admit that her mind had been free of the memory of the crash, at least for a second or two. Maybe she would be rid of it eventually. Her dat always said nothing lasts forever, not even your troubles.

16

*H*aley felt such a strong emotional connection to the group assembled in the waiting room, she couldn't even think about heading home yet. She had called her parents to fill them in about the accident. After Haley had assured her mother that she was still in one piece, Wendy Donovan had started in on the worries of having a single daughter out on the road.

"This was exactly the sort of thing I was looking forward to being finished with," Mom had told her. "If you were married and settled now, I wouldn't have to worry about you coming across a terrible accident on the highway at night. You think you're independent because you're in your twenties, but, honey, your father and I still worry."

"Ma, are you saying you would have stopped worrying if I'd married Graham? I still could have encountered the same accident. How would it be any different?"

"It just would be. You don't understand and you probably won't until you have children of your own. Which may not be until the next millennium, at the rate you're going."

Mom didn't get it, but that was nothing new. Still, Haley wished she could get her parents to understand a fraction of the last few hours of her life. The joy of helping someone. The incredible fulfillment that came with reaching a person who needed help, connecting with someone at one of the most vulnerable, desperate crossroads in his or her life.

An Elsie . . . a Rachel . . . a Graciana.

Right now Elsie Lapp was explaining why she and her father had traveled to Philadelphia for the afternoon. They had met with some vendors in Philadelphia who were interested in carrying the local products they sold. Things like honey, lavender, homemade soaps and jams and popcorn, and Amish crafts like cloth dolls, quilts, embroidery, and pincushions. Her loving description made Haley curious about the Country Store in Halfway. She'd never even noticed it.

"With a little love and care, our shop will be a true Country Store again," Elsie said. "The way it was when Mamm used to run it."

"Your shop sounds charming," Graciana said. "Clara and I will have to stop in, after all this is over." Her phone buzzed in her pocket, and she took it out to check the message.

"Your boss again?" Ruben asked. He was a quick study and a quick wit. Haley was grateful for his ability to lighten up a difficult situation, though she knew that under every comic's veneer there was an acute awareness of pain.

"Yes. He wants to know if I'll be at work in the morning. And I don't know the answer to that." She raked the silver streak of hair back with one hand. "I want to be here for Clara tomorrow, but if she's going to be drugged up and sleeping all day, I hate to lose a whole sick day. Especially with our vacation coming up."

"What kind of boss contacts you at ten o'clock at night?" Haley asked.

"A pesky mosquito who will not let you sleep," Ruben added.

Graciana pointed to him. "That's exactly the way Charles Showalter the third is. Have you met him?"

Dark blue uniforms passed by the waiting room—not a color that belonged here at the hospital. It was two police officers, the ones from the state highway patrol who had taken Haley's statement for their accident report.

"Officer Wood," Haley called after them.

The men stopped, nodding in recognition.

"Haley?" Larry Wood checked his watch. "You back at work already?"

"Just keeping these folks company," she said. It sounded so silly when it was really so much more than that.

"Maybe you can help us. We're looking for . . ." He looked down at his clipboard. "Graciana Estevez."

"Oh." Haley turned to find Graciana on her feet. "That's me, Officer. Are you the ones who towed my daughter's car away? I've been trying to get information on the extent of the damage."

The cops exchanged an uncomfortable look. "Didn't you talk to the sheriff?" Wood asked. When she shook her head, he went on. "Ma'am, I'm sorry if there's been a miscommunication. Your daughter's car was totaled. It crossed the median strip, hit a van full of people, and went down into a ravine on the side of the road. She might still be hidden there if it weren't for the diligence of these folks here."

"What? What do you mean?" Graciana blinked in confusion.

"Hold on," Haley said. "You mean the driver we found in the ditch at the side of the road was her daughter? Clara Estevez?"

Regret shadowed Wood's face. "That's right."

"No, no, no. That can't be right." Graciana tapped two fingers against her lips. "Their van crashed on Route 30, near Halfway, and my daughter isn't permitted to drive so far from home. It couldn't have been her."

"Ma'am, does your daughter drive a dark blue Ford Explorer?" the second cop asked.

"Yes, but—"

"Is that her vehicle?" Wood turned the screen of his cell phone toward Graciana.

Haley moved closer to Graciana and slid an arm around the woman's waist, bracing her for the worst.

A moment later, when they both viewed the smashed vehicle shining in the ghastly light, a wail peeled from the older woman's throat. Haley felt the woman begin to tremble beside her.

"Oh, no, no, no! It can't be!" She pushed the screen away, then made the sign of the cross. "That's her car, yes, it is. Such a terrible crash! It's a wonder my Clara survived, thank the Lord."

"Mrs. Estevez, why don't you sit down." Officer Wood's voice was quiet now, conciliatory. He helped Haley guide Graciana to a chair, where she collapsed, sobbing helplessly.

Haley sat beside her, trying to lend support. She shot a look over at her Amish friends, expecting to see horror and disdain on their faces.

Instead, their eyes burned with concern. Rachel pressed a hand to her mouth as if she were going to be sick. Elsie and Ruben exchanged a look of disbelief. Zed stared with a hard-bitten look, his arms crossed over his chest.

"I know this must be hard for you to hear, but we have reason to believe your daughter was texting when her car collided with the van. We found her cell phone and there's part of a message. We're still conducting interviews and compiling our report, but when it's finished, everything goes to the district attorney's office. For now,

Clara Estevez will be charged with reckless driving. The DA will decide if there will be other charges."

"But she's a good girl. She never hurt anyone in her life."

"That's the shame of it." Wood tucked his clipboard under his arm and tilted his head. "These kids don't understand the dangers of what they're doing. Sometimes I wish that cell phones had never been invented. I'm sorry to be the bearer of bad news, Mrs. Estevez."

Haley was grateful for the cop's attempt at sympathy, but Graciana was so upset she didn't seem to notice.

"I didn't realize the accident was this serious," the woman said, staring at the floor. "No one told me that . . . I just didn't know."

"No one's blaming you," Haley said, shooting a look at the cops. It didn't seem fair that this woman had to face such terrible news while her daughter was in surgery.

"Are you saying it was her fault . . . all this pain and suffering? My Clara is responsible for this?"

"Graciana . . ." Haley took the older woman's hand. "There are no official charges yet. Take a breath and wait and see how things develop. The police investigation isn't even finished yet."

"But I know it's true." Graciana took a deep breath, her shoulders still quivering. "I'm very good at denial, but this—the cell phone and texting . . ." She shook her head, wincing. "It's one of Clara's obsessions. I can't get that phone out of her hands."

Haley was at a loss for words, and the heavy atmosphere in the room made it hard to think.

The drama had penetrated to all the visitors now. Conversations had ceased. Everyone was watching, save a handful of children who were playing some sort of hopscotch game on the tile floor.

Everyone remained respectfully quiet as Graciana pushed out of the chair, turned, and, with deliberate steps, moved back toward the circle of Amish. Haley remained near the doorway with the cops. From here, she could see the faces of the Amish people, their curiosity and interest.

"I'm sure you heard." Graciana took a shaky breath, straightening her shoulders.

All eyes were on Graciana.

"I'm so sorry," she whispered, pressing her hands into prayer position at her breast. "I'm sorry for all the pain and suffering my daughter has caused you and . . . and your families."

The room was suddenly silent, save for the rumble of the heating system and the noise of a cart down the hall.

In that moment, Haley saw through a window to the compassion in the hearts and minds of the Amish. From the oldest wizened man to the mother with a sleeping infant to the middle-aged woman crocheting a blanket, they were simply people who recognized another person in crisis.

Elsie went to Graciana and squeezed her hand, her eyes shiny with tears. "You don't have to worry about what we're thinking. All is forgiven." Her voice was soft, but firm, like a mother soothing a child to sleep. "Gott our Father forgives us, and we follow in His footsteps."

Ruben rose and extended a hand to Graciana. She gripped his hand and he looked her in the eye. "Tell your daughter we forgive her."

Rachel nodded, touching Graciana's arm. "God bless Clara."

Behind her came Zed, who said he was praying for Clara. And behind him came another Amish man, and an Amish woman holding the hand of a toddler, and another Amish man. . . .

The quiet procession continued, people rising and filing past Graciana until every Amish person in the room had shared the same reassuring message.

All is forgiven.

17

"I'm just here to let you know that help is available to anyone who needs it." Crouched down in the waiting room so that he could be eye-level with Ada Fisher and Bishop Samuel Mast, Dylan was grateful that he'd worn jeans and a soft sweater. Casual was more approachable and a heck of a lot more comfortable for the late hours stretching until after midnight. Besides, he didn't think his reputation as "Dr. Fashion" would earn too many points in the Amish community, where basic black broadcloth was the standard for men's attire.

In the past three hours he had played on the floor with different groups of Amish children. He had knelt beside and paced with people who were ready to spend the night in the hospital, waiting on their loved ones. He had handed out the three pizzas he'd picked up on the way to the hospital. And he'd exhausted his knowledge of marine life, trying to make small talk about the fish in the tanks that decorated the larger waiting rooms.

At the moment, he was trying to win over the bishop of Half-way's religious community; it was a challenge that would apparently take some time.

"And did I mention that there's no charge for the counseling?" Dylan asked. "We have a grant to set up a program in the community."

"That's right kind of you," Ada said, flipping Dylan's card around to see the sunset over a farmhouse printed on the back. "Now, that's a pretty picture, isn't it?" She showed it to the bishop, who was not so impressed. "I'll give this to Jacob when he's feeling better."

Although Dylan knew that her husband, Jacob, had been injured in the collision, he wanted to make it clear that his services were not only for accident victims. "And you might want to come to a meeting yourself, Ada. Sometimes it puts a strain on the loved ones, caring for someone who's been through a trauma."

"Oh, I don't know about that." The elderly woman clucked her tongue as she glanced at the bishop, who seemed to be soaking up every word. "I'm fine. I've been taking care of Jacob for nigh sixty years. It won't break my back to change a few bandages or bring him a meal in bed."

"I hear you," Dylan said. "No one knows a man like his wife of sixty years. But keep my card and feel free to pass my number on to anyone. Even if they just need someone to talk to."

"Plain folk talk to each other." The bishop's eyes seemed huge, magnified by his eyeglasses. Dylan was reminded of the Wizard of Oz—a man whose reputation was amplified beyond his true powers. "Folks help their own families and friends. And when they need advice beyond that, they turn to a preacher or bishop, like me. Family, faith, and community. That's how it goes."

As he listened, Dylan tried to squash all his intellectual learning about community models and hierarchy so that he could speak to Bishop Samuel realistically. "From what I've seen, your community works very well together. I don't want to change anything there. I'm just wondering, if an Amish person wanted to get counseling— if he or she wanted to join in a group counseling session or participate in a meeting—would that violate any of your rules? Would they be going against the Ordnung?"

"Hmm." Samuel hitched his glasses up with the knuckles of one hand. "From what you describe, no laws would be broken. It's not a sin to talk to someone who isn't Amish, but then, you know that 'cause we're talking to you now."

Dylan nodded. "That's good to know. Thank you, Bishop."

"Call me Samuel. Everyone does."

"Samuel. My plan is to have some group meetings in Halfway. It would give people a chance to talk about the accident and get support from others who have had a similar experience."

"You could do that." Samuel grunted. "But I don't reckon anyone will come. Folks have work to do. Children to mind. Farms to run. Not time to sit around and talk about their feelings."

"I figure I'll give it a try," Dylan said, "as long as it wouldn't break any rules."

"Sure. You can try it."

Dylan straightened and stretched his arms out as he surveyed the waiting room. He'd reached out and made contact with everyone here. That was all he could do right now, in the early stage of the trauma.

As he pressed the elevator button to go down to ICU and reach out to the other Amish families, Dylan felt that he was exactly where he belonged. A new venue had done wonders for his state of mind, and the fact that he'd arrived here before this tragedy had struck the community, well, that had to be Divine Intervention.

And Haley Donovan . . . if she hadn't called him on his cell to let him know about the accident, he'd still be home in bed, sleeping through the chance to reach out and serve his new community. Yes,

Haley was brilliant. Beautiful and caring. Every morning, he counted his developing relationship with her among his blessings.

The elevator doors opened, and the subject of his musings stood before him.

"Haley!"

"Dylan! Just who I was looking for." She waved him off the elevator. "Quick, quick. Someone told me you were upstairs, and I paged you but there was no answer. Aren't doctors supposed to answer pages?"

"I'm not on duty." He got off the elevator and fell into step beside her. Haley was moving fast, a woman on a mission. "Besides, electronics are disruptive when you're trying to work with people. Especially the Amish. What did you want me for?"

"Remember the woman I told you about? The mother of the driver who crashed into the van?"

He nodded, urging her on.

"She's on her way out of the hospital, but she stopped in the waiting room to tell us that her daughter died. During the surgery they found that there was too much internal damage. They kept her on life support, and Graciana had a chance to say good-bye, but she's gone now."

He slowed his pace as that familiar dread tugged at his gut. A parent's love. A parent's failure to protect a child.

The tragedy that defied the natural order of things: a parent burying her child.

He knew that pain. He owned it, lived with it, hated it.

She paused and wheeled around. "Are you okay?"

He hadn't realized that he'd stopped walking. "I'm trying to put myself in this woman's position." *Which is easier than you might think.*

She motioned him toward the waiting room and pointed out a Hispanic woman with dark hair streaked with silver. "That's her. Talking with Elsie."

As Dylan joined the two women, he realized that he'd met Elsie Lapp in Halfway at the Country Store. She'd given him no false hope about his outreach program, but she'd been kind about her lack of support. From the list Haley had given him, he knew Elsie had been one of the passengers in the van, but when he'd been down in this waiting room earlier, he had missed her.

"Sorry to interrupt," Haley said, making quick introductions. "Graciana, I just wanted to make sure you connected with Dr. Monroe before you left."

"We have an outreach program in Halfway." Dylan was learning that if it sounded real, people would have confidence in the program. "I wanted to make sure you knew about the services available to you. But right now . . ." He paused.

Graciana's eyes were red and puffy. Her skin was pale and her expression was vacant. Numb with pain. In the morning, she would not remember meeting him.

"Right now, I suspect you need to be with your loved ones, and get some sleep, if you can."

At that, Graciana lifted her gaze to really look at him. "That's right."

"Here's my card. I'm on staff here, so you can always reach me through the hospital directory."

She tucked the card in a pocket and nodded. "Thank you." She leaned down to hug Elsie, and then kissed Haley on the cheek. "You're good girls, good people, but I need to go. My brother is picking me up."

"Would you like me to walk you to the door and help you find him?" Dylan offered.

"No." She shook her head. "You stay with these girls, Doctor. Help these girls feel better. They deserve it." Graciana kissed her fingertips, reached for Haley and Elsie once more, then headed down the corridor.

Elsie and Haley stared at each other, a tint of sadness in their eyes. Then Elsie opened her arms and they shared a hug.

"I can't believe it," Haley said. "Graciana is donating Clara's organs. What kind of grace does it take to make that decision for your own daughter?"

"She was only seventeen," Elsie murmured. "That's what Graciana told me. Such a sad thing."

Haley looked up at Dylan. "Do you think Graciana heard you? Do you think she'll get some counseling? She's definitely going to need it."

"She's overwhelmed right now." He noticed the genuine weariness that weighed Elsie down as she fished coins out of a satchel. "We're all feeling the stress, and I imagine you both must be exhausted. It's well after midnight."

"I don't remember the last time I was up this late." Elsie fed the coins into the machine and pressed a button for a sandwich. "Fanny needs to eat something. I told her she's got to keep up her strength."

Dylan searched his memory but did not remember a Fanny on the list. "Where is Fanny now?"

"In the room with Dat. She won't leave his side. Emma and Caleb took the little ones home for the night. Emma wants to teach her class tomorrow—trying to keep things as normal as possible. But Fanny won't leave Dat's side."

He remembered Fanny was Thomas Lapp's wife. "Can I meet her?"

"If you come to the room with me. But there's only two visitors at a time."

"That's okay." He tapped the hospital ID card hanging around his neck. "I've got a pass."

Dylan spent a quiet half hour with Elsie Lapp; her stepmother, Fanny; and her father, Thomas. Fanny was obviously pregnant, and Elsie explained that the hospital had given Thomas a room with an empty bed because Fanny needed to stay off her feet.

Although Thomas was on a breathing apparatus that moved his chest up and down with each whoosh of air, Fanny and Elsie spoke to him as if he were quietly watching from beneath the crisp white sheets and medical lines and tubes. They talked of repairs on the old carriage house, and their plans to start a wheelwright business or a harness shop. Fanny talked about the little ones, who had gone home with Emma and Caleb, and Elsie assured Thomas that the children would be back to visit in the morning.

Dylan knew nothing of the man's medical prognosis, but the atmosphere in the room was warm and homey. This was a place of profound love, and any man would consider himself blessed to have such a family.

When he saw that Fanny was dozing off, he waved good-bye to Elsie and slipped out the door. Elsie followed him into the hall.

"Thank you for visiting," she told him. "I'm a little worried about Fanny. Her first husband died, and now to face this terrible thing. All this stress and she's already sick with preeclampsia. What do you think?"

"She's doing as well as anyone would expect. It's good that she's getting rest. I'll be happy to stop in tomorrow. Once she's gotten some rest, she might want to talk."

"Good." With a sigh, Elsie smoothed down the hair at her forehead. "I know it's a sin to worry, but my heart is so heavy right now. I hope you're looking after Haley, too. She's an angel. Smart and a caring person, too. But she's been through a lot, coming up on our smashed-up van like that."

"I'll keep an eye on Haley, but how about you?" Dylan asked. "You were actually in the van. That must have been frightening."

"Ya. I keep seeing it, every time I close my eyes." Her face puckered for just a moment, then it smoothed out again.

Dylan knew it wasn't unusual for a victim to keep flashing back to a moment of crisis. "Sometimes that happens to people in your situation. It helps to talk about it, and there are other therapies that—"

"I'm fine, thank Gott in heaven. It's the others . . . I think they're going to need your help."

"I'm on it," he assured her. "And don't hesitate to give me a call. I'm here for you, or anyone else in your family. Anyone else in your community."

"Thank you." She nodded, then returned to the room.

Dylan returned to the waiting room on the third floor and found most of the people asleep or hunkered down for quiet time. It was late, and he had probably done enough for now. He would check in with these folks in the morning.

He headed out of the hospital, noticing that the place had a very different face at night when the elevators were nearly empty and most of the traffic in the corridors came from janitors and their carts. So much happened within the confines of this building—life and death and pain—but he was glad to see the old girl at a calm moment.

Downstairs in the main lobby, he came upon Haley, who had said she was leaving half an hour ago.

For some reason, she stood, a statue in the lobby, staring out at the lights of the parking lot through tinted glass. She wore her coat and hat—gloves, too—but she didn't seem to have any intention of stepping outside.

"Haley?"

She flinched, startled.

"I thought you'd be well on your way home by now."

"Oh . . . Yeah. I'm on my way."

"Want me to walk you out to the parking lot?"

"Okay." The bewilderment in her eyes was hard to read, but he sensed her distress.

The doors whooshed open, they walked out, and Haley burst into tears.

"I can't . . . I can't do this." She turned to Dylan and clung to his shoulder. "Please take me home."

Aching for her, he put his arms around her and gave her a big bear hug. He should have expected this. She'd been through a major trauma. "You're exhausted. Overwrought . . ."

"And I can't drive. I can't get on Route 30 and go past that stretch where . . . the SUV just cut right across the center and . . . It was so violent. The sound of the impact and . . . the randomness of it. One car crossed the line and look what happened. Someone is dead now. Lives are changed, forever."

He patted her back, maintaining a therapeutic touch despite the depth of emotion that crossed the line of patient-therapist. "You're right."

"Clara Estevez is dead." She pulled away, and though he let his arms slip away he wanted to hold on. "She made a stupid mistake and it killed her. And do you know what her mother said? That . . . that she was in heaven now. That the angels had taken her away. But you and I know she's just . . . dead. Gone. Flatline."

It was unusual for a medical professional to hit this wall so early in her career, but Dylan had seen it before. "It's good that Graciana can find solace in her faith. Many people in crisis turn to their faith. It can be a valuable source of support."

A tear slipped down Haley's cheek as she sniffed. "I wish the angels did take her away. It would be so much better than what really happened. I saw her, you know. She was covered in blood and . . ." She shook her head. "It was horrible."

"And you've held it in all this time, haven't you? You kept your emotional response tamped down so that you could be professional."

"I had to. I had to keep moving and try to make the best decisions for everyone out there. Everyone needed attention in one way or another."

"And you gave them what they needed. A spectacular job, from what I've heard around here. You did everything you could, Haley. You're a hero, sweetheart. But you're going to have an emotional reaction to the trauma, too. We need to talk about it, probably more than you will want. We'll schedule some sessions. And you might want to try guided imagery therapy, too."

She swiped at the tears on her cheeks. "Can I come to the group therapy sessions with the Amish victims?"

"Sure." Right now, he wasn't so sure there were going to be any sessions, since the Amish response so far had been a resounding no. But if he and Haley got things going, some Amish people might drop in.

She took a deep, ragged breath, her eyes sweeping over the parking lot. "I guess I can drive soon. I mean, aren't you supposed to get back up onto the horse that throws you?"

"Not necessarily." He wanted to kick himself for not reading the signs of her distress earlier. "I'll drive you home tonight. We can use my GPS to find a way to your house that doesn't include Route 30."

Obviously relieved, she let out a breath and looked back at him. "Okay."

Her eyes, wide and trusting and full of pain, evoked something deep inside him, something that had been buried for years.

Buried forever, or so he'd thought.

18

*R*uben Zook leaned against the hitching post outside the candy shop and watched as her hands turned the OPEN sign on the door to CLOSED.

Now was the time.

He intended to pay Elsie a visit, but when he'd first arrived on this busy part of Main Street, he didn't expect to see all the customers filling the aisles of the Lapps' store. Such a business they had now. That was not how he had imagined his visit with Elsie, and he'd been thinking about it these past days, waiting for the shop to open so that he could see her.

For three days, the Country Store had been closed, on account of Elsie and her family spending as much time as they could at the hospital. The little ones were staying with a friend now, as they weren't allowed in to see their dat, who was still in a coma, still sleeping.

Since the accident, Ruben had tried to get to the hospital to see

Elsie and pay respects to her family, but carfare was expensive, and his dat didn't see the need to trade a day of work for a day spent sitting in a hospital. "No need to pay your respects now," his father had told him. "You'll see these folk soon enough when they return. Maybe even at church next week."

He couldn't tell his father that next week was not soon enough … that ever since the accident, he thought of Elsie Lapp constantly, and he needed to check on her and make sure there wasn't anything she needed. Because Elsie was one of those people who didn't take things for herself. She made sure everyone else was all right first. A heart of gold, that girl, and somehow, since that cold day on the highway, Ruben felt that Gott was making it his job to protect that good heart.

He crossed the street, and then quickly shifted his hat down to cover his face from the reporters who had stood outside the shop all afternoon. Usually, as a courtesy, most media folks didn't photograph an Amish person without permission, knowing that it went against their beliefs to be cast in a "graven image." But Ruben shielded his face from their view. You never knew when one of those photographers was going to break the unspoken rule.

They had been hanging around Halfway ever since the accident, looking for people to interview. It seemed like an odd way to spend the day, waiting for someone to talk to you about a terrible thing. If Ruben was going to wait around, he'd want to be hunting or fishing, waiting for something that would make a good dinner, at least.

A little bell jingled as he opened the door and stepped in, his hat in his hand.

"We're about to close, but if I can help you—" Elsie peeked out from one of the aisles, blinking up at Ruben. "It's you. I was just closing. Got to get to the hospital. But you can come in."

He went around a small village of birdhouses and paused at a display of baby items. The store had changed a lot since the last time he'd been in here as a boy, buying a soda pop on a hot day. "I noticed the store's been closed until today."

"Caleb and I have been at the hospital, almost day and night, so we've had no one to cover the store. Emma comes, too, as soon as school is over." She finished restocking the display of candles. "I have half a mind to keep the store closed, but it's this shop that pays our bills." She shrugged. "What can you do?"

"And how is your dat?" Although he knew the answer, he sensed that she wanted to talk about Thomas.

"Still sleeping. Unconscious." She took the cash box out of the old register and began to count bills, busying herself. "The doctors say they're not seeing any brain activity. You know those special machines and X-rays they got to see what's going on inside a person's body? Those machines are telling them that Dat isn't going to wake up. But they said we can give it time. Anything is possible." She stopped counting and looked up. Her sweet face reflected a wide pond of worries. "Do you believe in miracles, Ruben?"

"I do. I think it's a miracle we're both alive." He'd seen his share of miracles. Tragedies, too.

"Then can you help me pray for a miracle? Because everyone else is walking around with a sad face. No one's talking about it, but I think they've given up. But I won't. I'm not giving up on Dat. Will you pray for him?"

"I already am."

"Denki." She continued counting out the register drawer.

He looked around the shop, which was much improved from the last time he'd been in here, but that was years ago. So, this was where Elsie spent her days.

"Are you going to the funeral tomorrow?" he asked.

She nodded. "I'm getting a ride with the Kings."

Ruben planned to go with Zed, though he dreaded it. Funerals were difficult to get through, and a funeral for a teenage girl was a terrible thing to endure. "It's so hard to understand Gott's plan," he said. "When I found her car, I thought Gott intended to spare her life." He shook his head. "I was wrong."

"I don't think our brains are able to understand what Gott intends."

He picked up a delicate puff of a pincushion with a heart pattern in the center. Many of the items here—the quilts and honey, jams and lavender—were items that vendors sold in his father's market-place, but not these pincushions.

"I've never seen the likes of these before," he said, holding it out in the palm of his bandaged hand.

"That was made by Hannah Ebersol. Very nice stitching."

He placed it on the counter. "I'll take it, if it's not too late."

"Sure. But what would a fella like you want with a pincushion?"

"My mamm sews. She needs a place for her pins."

"Then this will brighten her day."

"I reckon it will." In truth, his mother didn't favor sewing, but he wanted to make a purchase that might help bring along the Lapps' profits after two days of being closed. He understood how a house-hold could rely on a retail business. His family lived on the money made at Zook's barn.

She wrapped his purchase in a small piece of cloth—a remnant from the fabrics they sold—and tied it off with a ribbon to make a dainty package that would melt his mother's heart.

"That looks so nice; now I'll have to save it for her birthday," he said.

There was no hint of a smile on Elsie's face. She seemed tired and worn down, and he wished that there was something to do to relieve the heavy burden on her shoulders.

"I guess you'll be getting back to the hospital?" he asked.

"As soon as I close up here. There's a driver coming to pick up me and Emma. Don Goldbright. Do you know him?"

"We've used him before." But mostly, his family hired George Dornbecker when they needed a driver. George was reliable and always good for a few laughs. "Did you hear that George got burns on his arms from the air bags?" Somehow, talking about the people in the van reminded Ruben of the bond they shared.

Elsie nodded. "He's been to visit with Dat at the hospital. I wish he didn't blame himself. I saw that car coming and there was nothing he could do to stop it."

"He came to check on me, too. I hear he's been to see everyone who was in the van. George is a good driver and a good man. I hope he gets another van."

"Ya." She closed the register and took a pouch of money to the back room. "I've just got to get my coat. I want to be ready when Don gets here."

He knew he had to let her go, but the prospect of not seeing her for another few days made him hungry for conversation. "I'll let you go. I just wanted to let you know, if there's anything you need, just get word to me," he called toward the back room. "Anything your family needs, too. I want to help."

"Denki. You've already helped a lot, Ruben."

He moved toward the door, catching sight of the back of a sign in the window that said: NO SUNDAY SALES. That was a rule among the Amish, since Sunday was a day of rest, meant for church every other Sunday, and for family time.

"You're closed tomorrow," he said, thinking aloud. "But Monday . . ." He turned to Elsie, who now stood in her coat. "How about if I run the shop for you on Monday? That way you can spend the day with your dat."

The veil of worry lifted as she looked up at him. "That would be ever so kind, but you've never run the shop before."

"Ya, but I've managed the marketplace at the barn. Two dozen vendors, and hundreds of folks coming and going. I may not have your eye for detail, but I can handle some customers."

"I'm sure you can." She looked at the key in her hand and held it out to him. "I hope you mean it, because I'm going to take you up on it. Ya, I will, and I'd be ever so grateful. It would ease my load to be able to be with Dat and know that the shop is being tended to."

He took the key from her. "I'll be here Monday morning." He looked at the sign, checking the hours. "The store will be open by nine."

"We're open nine until sunset," she said. "I'll come check on you, just in case you have any questions."

"That would be good."

"Thank you, Ruben." She wrapped a wool scarf around her neck—a small one that a child would wear—and let out a deep sigh. "You've eased my heavy heart."

That was exactly what he'd been hoping to do. He pressed the key into his palm, looking forward to Monday.

19

$\mathcal{A}$ bitterly cold wind stirred the air, bringing tears to Haley's eyes as she made her way up around the block to the front of the church. *Good thing for sunglasses,* she thought. Otherwise, people would know she'd been crying.

Which she had been, at the most unexpected times.

Every morning in the shower and every night in bed, her eyes filled with tears. She let the warm spray wash down the sorrow and pressed her face to her pillow to drown out the sobs, but even if someone heard, what could they do?

No one could stop the rush of panic that overwhelmed her . . . the racing heartbeat and tightness in her chest. No one could remove the jagged knife of fear that lodged in her ribs, reminding her that life could end in a nanosecond, and that the ending might be unexpected and fraught with pain.

At the hospital, she was treated like an Olympic gold medalist. People regarded her with awe and respect, when the truth was that she had only acted as any decent human being would have, with a few semesters of nursing classes under her belt. Her parents had softened toward her, too, and suddenly Haley seemed to have the life she had craved, minus the happiness.

Yesterday she had completed her clinical shift at the hospital with barely a blink, but then when she went to the hospital cafeteria for a cup of coffee, the realization that she had forgotten to bring money caused her to burst into tears and gasp for air.

That had frightened her—losing control in public. She was afraid it would happen again, and honestly, she had no idea how to prevent a public breakdown.

And if her panic jags weren't bad enough, there was also the fact that she was too frightened to drive now. Dylan had told her that it was a normal reaction, and at least her father understood. He had rearranged his schedule so that he could drive her to the hospital and school. And he'd left his easy chair in front of a televised football game so that he could drive her here, to Clara Estevez's funeral.

The bell of the old church was ringing. *Calling Clara to heaven,* Haley thought. She still clung to Graciana's words about her daughter being taken by the angels. It was such a beautiful image, even if Haley had trouble believing it. Of course, she believed in God, but sometimes she wondered if the rules and stories set forth in the Bible had any place in the real world these days. Somehow it was easier to believe that angels existed back in the old days, before filmmakers could make transparent angels seem real, before people could actually fly through the skies on commercial jets.

As she reached the church steps, the soft patter of horses' hooves sounded from a distance. Lifting her gaze, she saw the procession of horses pulling carriages in the street. Haley didn't know much about horses, but these creatures were large—taller than any man—and each pulled a boxy gray buggy. Although she'd grown up seeing

Amish people traveling this way, she was now struck by the charm of their lifestyle, a world nearly free of cars and cell phones, of televisions and mesmerizing computer screens.

She waited for the carriages to unload and greeted her friends quietly outside the church. Inside, seated between Rachel and Elsie, she felt a certain peace wash over her as the service began. Dressed in black, her face hidden behind a dark veil, Graciana seemed distant. She was supported by a man and a woman on either side of her, and they entered the church together, followed by other mourners. The organ music, the white coffin moving up the aisle, the grieving family, many of whom had flown in from the Dominican Republic—all of it stirred a certain sadness deep inside Haley.

But there was also a barb of anger for the girl who had been killed.

Clara, I did not know you, but I'm suffering from your bad choice. And all around me I see good people suffering because of you.

Harsh words for a dead girl, Haley knew that, and she was ashamed of herself. Especially when she saw the forgiveness of her Amish friends, whose calm faces radiated peace in the hollow chamber of the church.

I'm just an unforgiving person, she thought as the congregation bowed their heads to receive God's blessing. *Cold and unforgiving, that's me.*

When the service had ended, Elsie told her that they were driving to Graciana's house to deliver some food and baked goods.

"But you've been at the hospital every day . . . all day," Haley said. "How did you find time to bake?"

Elsie shrugged. "It didn't take much time. And to tell the truth, I've been having trouble falling asleep."

Haley put a hand on Elsie's shoulder. "It's the accident."

Elsie nodded. "I can't get it out of my head."

"Talk to Dylan. He's right over there." Haley had noticed Dr. Monroe in the back of the church when the service ended. "He wants to help. That's why he's here."

"Some other time," Elsie said. "We have to get going." She patted Haley's wrist. "You talk to him today. Let him help you."

Haley squinted. "What do you mean?"

"Do you know the expression about the pot calling the kettle black?"

"Can I get a translation?"

Elsie tilted her head in that way that made her seem wise for her years. "You wore your sunglasses through the whole funeral. I don't know why you're hiding in there. I just know that sometimes we hold the hurt inside and hope that no one else will see it."

Reflexively, Haley touched the corner of her sunglasses. "I forgot that I had them on. That must have seemed rude."

"The sunglasses are not the problem, honey girl," Elsie said sweetly.

Before Haley could object, Rachel came to fetch Elsie, and after a quick round of good-byes the Amish visitors were streaming toward their buggies.

Haley stood on the church steps, watching as a plastic milk crate was placed on the ground for Elsie, to accommodate her shorter legs climbing into the buggy. She liked the way the Amish took care of each other.

It was time to call her father for a ride home, but Haley felt as if her feet were too heavy to move, stuck in invisible muck. Her whole body felt weary, though she had been getting sleep with the help of some blue pills, an over-the-counter sleep aid that left her groggy in the mornings.

"How's it going, Haley?" Dylan was suddenly beside her, looking down the road at the horses and buggies.

"Okay, I guess." She tried to sound positive, but her voice was thick with emotion. She felt a storm approaching, and she was powerless to get out of the rain.

"I'd like to schedule a group session this week and see who will attend," Dylan said. He went on to describe his conversations with Rachel King, and Samuel Mast, the bishop, and some other Amish people, but Haley couldn't listen over the roar of turmoil rising inside her. It bubbled up like a boiling pot, spitting at the air and sloshing over the rim.

Suddenly, Dylan touched her shoulder. "Haley? What's going on?"

"I can't stop crying," she sobbed.

"Okay. It's okay to cry. Your pain is real, and crying is one way of expressing it."

"But I can't stop. I cry all the time now, at the drop of a hat. And my heart races and sometimes my chest gets so tight I can barely breathe."

"Sounds to me like you're having panic attacks. Has this ever happened to you before? I mean, before the accident."

"No." Her breath was trapped in her lungs, and she had to make an effort to push it out. "I feel like I'm dying." She grabbed his arm, desperate for relief. "Help me, please. Help me."

20

"And then the dark SUV swerved across the yellow lines. The lights seemed so bright, and the direction of the car was so wrong."

"What was your reaction at that moment?" Dylan asked.

"Fear. Panic. I know I hit the brakes, hard." Haley sat back, her hands gripping the armrests as if the chair itself might spin out of control and she needed to hold on for dear life.

So far she had been an exemplary patient. Her story of the accident was clear and cohesive, and she didn't seem to mind repeating it three times. In fact, the repetition of the story often helped patients see it from a new angle. Reducing the events to a story often helped extract the sting from the memory.

"And then what happened?"

"Then Clara's vehicle hit the van and, like in slow motion, there was this explosion of glass and the loudest noise you'd ever want to hear. The SUV sort of got caught on the van, and the two vehicles spun around together. There were sparks underneath where the metal hit the highway, and I remember thinking it would have been a spectacle if it weren't so awful. Then the van shot around toward my car and groaned to a stop. And the SUV shot off in another direction and disappeared."

Dylan noted that Haley's skin was no longer flushed with fear, and her frozen posture had softened. She was improving already, and he wanted to sag with relief. He was way too vested in this patient. He was falling in love with Haley Donovan, and he knew that could mean trouble.

"What did you learn from the accident?" he asked, drawing her away from the crash scene momentarily.

"I learned that anything can happen, at any time, and . . . we're all just flesh and bone. Our bodies are really so fragile. They're not built to last and . . . and we're all going to die."

"Our time here is temporary, that's true. I think part of the human psyche denies that as a way to keep going and take chances."

She nodded, her face calmer now. "Am I ruined for nursing? I mean, now I look at people and see their anatomy, as if they're some plastic model you could take apart and put back together."

"Some healthcare workers experience what you're going through. In some ways, a medical professional needs to reduce things to flesh-and-blood components—the mechanics of science. But that's forgetting the one thing that makes human beings unique in the animal kingdom. Each person has a unique personality, a certain energy. The spiritual self. Do you get what I'm saying?"

"When you label it personality, I definitely see it. But spirituality sounds hokey to me. Next you'll want to hold my hand and sing 'Kumbaya.'"

He grinned. "We can leave that for another session." He went to a cabinet in the back of the small conference room and removed a light strip that he had stowed there just yesterday. "I hope you're not losing patience, because I'm going to ask you to recall the incident one more time."

"I don't mind talking about it," she said. "Every time I go there, it's a little less painful."

"That's what we're aiming for." He propped the horizontal bar of lights on the table and plugged it into the wall. "Now, can you follow these lights with your eyes as they move back and forth?" He turned the switch, and the row of lights blinked from right to left.

Haley watched cautiously. "Is that it? They're not going to explode or pop or anything?"

"No. They'll keep blinking in the same direction." He sat down, glad to see that she was getting more relaxed, her breathing slow and steady. "This time when you recall the event, I want you to keep following the movement of these lights."

"Okay. So . . . starting from the beginning. I was driving home on Route 30 when a dark SUV began to stray out of its lane. It swerved across the double yellow lines, and the headlights—they seemed so bright. . . ."

Dylan coached her along, watching to be sure that she kept her gaze on the movement of the lights. At this point, Haley recited the sequence of events by rote. That simple familiarity was another way to give the random event order in her mind and make it easier to put it behind her.

He leaned back in the upholstered chair. This room was perfect. Thankfully, he had secured this space in the back of the library just two days ago, after meeting with the head librarian and the mayor of Halfway. To effectively serve the people of Halfway, it was essential that he have a place right here in town to hold sessions and meetings, and the library was about as centrally located as you could get.

"The room is set up for conferences," the librarian, Crystal

Lenowski, had told him. "But aside from the weekly book club meetings, we don't have much use for it."

"Our people are hurting from that accident," Nancy Briggs, the town mayor, had said. "I'd like to get behind any program that's going to offer them assistance."

And in the blink of an eye, he had a venue for therapy sessions in Halfway. After so many years of requisition forms and board meetings, Dylan was impressed by how things worked out here in the country. Crystal had given him a copy of the key right then and there. A good thing, because he'd needed someplace to take Haley when she began to break down at the church. He had known she was struggling with post-traumatic stress the other night when she'd been unable to drive home from the hospital, but at the time, he hadn't realized the extent of her distress.

"And then the van stopped spinning and I stayed in the car, sort of frozen with fear. That's when I called 911," Haley finished.

"Okay. You're doing great. Keep watching the light bar and tell me about the moment when you realized that you were safe."

She paused, her eyes moving with the flickering lights. "I think it was when I threw open the door of the car. The dispatcher on the phone was asking me something, and all I could think about was that I was fine—still in one piece—but those people needed help."

"So you did have a moment when it dawned on you that, although death can come in an instant, you were spared."

"I did."

"But you didn't linger to celebrate your narrow escape. You threw open the door of the car and went to help the passengers in the van. You tried to restore life."

"I did my best."

"That's all anyone can do, Haley."

He turned off the light bar and studied her. Her color was back to normal and her stance in the chair was relaxed. Crisis averted.

"Are we done?" she asked.

"We can be. Or we can repeat the exercise one more time with the light bar on." He sat back in the chair, not wanting her to feel rushed. "How do you feel?"

"Better. Much better. You're a really great doctor!"

"O ye of little faith." He smiled. "You're an excellent patient. You followed all my instructions."

"Of course I did. I was so desperate for some relief, I would have run naked through the streets of Halfway if you'd told me it would take that horrible knife out of my gut."

"Wow. I've never come across the research on running-naked-through-the-streets therapy."

"I can't believe how much better I feel," she said.

"We'll want to do another session or two. Just to make sure that you remain asymptomatic."

"I think it's a miracle. Two miracles. One that the SUV didn't knock the van into me, too. The other that you saved me from a total meltdown."

Her smile seemed to cast a light through the shadowed room. Dylan believed in miracles, but he wasn't sure that Haley was on the same page.

"Your breathing seems to have evened out," he observed. "Do you still feel that pressure on your chest? The dagger in your ribs?"

She took a deep, steady breath, then relaxed as she exhaled. "It's gone. That awful feeling is gone and I feel this new energy. It's like the pain has been replaced with these awesome fuel cells. I feel like I could lift a building and run a marathon."

"Maybe tomorrow. For today, see if you can get some rest." There was still more healing to be done, but Haley had made some real progress today. "You did good, kid. If you're ready, I'll drive you home."

She pushed out of the chair and found her coat. "You'd better put your magic lights away. You'll definitely want to hold on to those suckers."

"You're right."

"Where did you get those, anyway?" she asked as she wrapped a striped muffler around her neck.

He had purchased them online, but that sounded too boring. "Some kid traded them to me for a handful of magic beans."

When she laughed, it was a joyous, refreshing sound. "Okay, then. Let's hit the road, Jack."

21

Thursday morning dawned bright, with a smudge of pink glowing over the roof of the carriage house that Dat and Caleb had been working to repair.

Such a beautiful sunset. If only Dat could see it.

Although Elsie's father had opened his eyes from time to time in the week or so since the accident, the nurses and aides told her that he could not see her. It was a reflex, they said. Elsie sensed that they were right, because when she searched for the love and care and concern that had always shined there, she found only a blank stare.

Dat's spark was gone.

But that didn't mean it wouldn't come back. Gott could heal him.

She closed the curtains on the window and looked down at herself. "Look at me, still in my nightgown." Normally she would be dressed by now with beds made instead of mooning over a sunrise. But she was moving slow these days. Making mistakes and forgetting things. Her thoughts were scattered like seeds in the wind, mostly from lack of sleep and worry about Dat.

And maybe she was dragging her feet because she dreaded the big meeting at the hospital. It had been more than one week since the accident, and since Dat's condition was unchanged, the doctors thought it was time to discuss a "treatment plan for Thomas Lapp." All the doctors who worked with Dat would be there, and they had asked that the family be present. Fanny had sent Caleb round to invite Bishop Samuel and Dave Zook, the preacher. Such good thinking on Fanny's part. Elsie didn't know how poor Fanny kept a clear head through all this, with her blood pressure going crazy and her husband unconscious in the hospital. Gott bless her.

And Dat . . . she needed to pray for Dat. As she began to get dressed Elsie searched her mind for the words, but she felt like she was groping in a dark hole. Had she used up all the words she knew to beg Gott for Dat's safe recovery?

She would have to rely on a prayer she knew by rote. The Our Father.

With a heavy sigh, she began. *"Unser Vater in dem Himmel! Dein Name werde geheiligt . . ."*

∞

The hospital conference room was brimming over with people, both Amish and Englisher. Elsie recognized the medical staff who sat on one side of the table. The younger doctor, Dr. Pohawalla, checked on Dat a few times a day, and he always asked Fanny how she was doing. At one point, they had even joked that they were getting two visits for the price of one doctor. Two of the nurses, Jenny and Courtney, were there. The graying, bespectacled Dr. Stransky reminded Elsie of Bishop Samuel, with his slow, thoughtful movements and crackly voice. And the other very familiar face on that side of the table was Dylan Monroe, who had spent a lot of time in Dat's room, talking and waiting with the family.

Dr. Benton was speaking quietly with Fanny, his head bent down to meet her eyes when the meeting started.

"So many family members here!" Dr. Stransky threw his arms open wide in a boisterous gesture as he took in Elsie and her siblings Caleb and Emma. Even Will and Beth had been allowed to come to this meeting. Will sat straight as a stick beside Caleb, and Beth sat on Elsie's lap due to the shortage of chairs and a touch of insecurity at all the strange faces. "It's good to see family support," Dr. Stransky added.

"This is small for an Amish family," Preacher Dave pointed out. "But then, Thomas and Fanny are still working on theirs."

Dat's brother Jimmy and his wife, Edna, were there. Their son James was still in the hospital, and their other children had been left at home to run the orchard.

"I'm glad you all could be here." Dr. Stransky raised his voice, demanding the attention of everyone in the room. Conversation ceased as he went on. "But I'm sorry to say, this is not an easy meeting for any of us." He turned to Fanny. "I hope you know that, since your husband arrived here, we've done everything we could to help him."

"I know that," Fanny said. "Everyone has been good to him."

"Thomas suffered a traumatic brain injury in last week's auto accident," Dr. Stransky continued. "We had hoped that when the swelling in the brain was reduced, we might see a return of function. Unfortunately, that hasn't happened."

"So his brain isn't functioning anymore?" Fanny asked.

Dr. Benton put his hands in prayer position and rested his chin on his fingertips. "Our neurological tests show that he has lost both voluntary and involuntary function. He will never speak or walk again, and his body systems are beginning to shut down."

"But he looks good and healthy," Emma said. "I was just holding his hand, and it's soft and warm. I think he's far from dead."

"Right now he looks pink and feels warm because his blood is still artificially being circulated throughout his body," explained Dr. Benton. "But the 'command and control' center in the brain has shut down."

"He's dying?" Fanny said, her brows arched in disbelief.

"Yes." Dr. Benton's word hissed through the room like a snake.

Elsie felt her lower lip jut out in defiance. Dr. Benton was a kind man, but she didn't like this negative side of him. Elsie shifted in her chair, surprised at how still Beth was keeping. Like a little angel.

In the odd silence, Emma began to cry. Will patted her shoulder, looking like a big man, and Emma reached an arm around him to hold him close. One of the nurses pushed a box of tissues over, and both Fanny and Emma grabbed a few.

The men were frowning, so stern, as if they disapproved of this whole thing.

Maybe they're like me, Elsie thought. *Maybe they know the doctors are wrong.*

"Thomas is in the final chapter of his life," Dr. Stransky said. "In his condition, our goal shifts to giving him comfort and allowing him to die in a peaceful state, surrounded by family."

Caleb tipped his hat back and faced the doctors. "How do you know this?" He pointed to his head, rotating his hand in a circle. "How do you know there are no thoughts and dreams in his head?"

"We've run numerous tests, Caleb." Dr. Benton's pale eyes were sympathetic. "Brain waves are electrical impulses that are easily detected. In your father's case, we are not seeing any brain activity, upper or lower."

"What if you're wrong?" Elsie cried. "I've heard stories of folks in a coma who woke up weeks, even months later and they were just fine. How do you know he won't wake up today or tomorrow . . . or in two weeks and . . ." A sob wracked her voice, but she knew she had to fight for Dat. How could they sit here and talk about Dat as if he were already gone? How could they give up on him?

"Elsie, I understand your concern for your father." Dr. Benton's voice was soft now, more comforting than scientific. "If Thomas were my father, I'd be asking the exact same questions. But Thomas is not in a coma. He's not going to wake up."

"But, Doctor, I was there." Elsie was not one to argue, but she could not make sense of any of this. "He was talking to me and he seemed just fine. It was just a bump on the head. Not even a drop of blood."

"Brain trauma isn't always apparent from the outside." Dr. Benton held her gaze, and the sorrow she saw in his eyes frightened her. This was real. Impossible, terrible, but real. "You're lucky that you got to speak to him before he was gone."

She bit her lower lip and shook her head. She wasn't lucky at all, and she didn't believe in luck. She believed in blessings and miracles.

Fanny pressed her palms against the table, as if searching for a solid foundation. "What can we do?" she asked.

Dr. Stransky flipped open the file on the table. "I don't suppose he had a DNR . . . a Do Not Resuscitate order?"

Fanny shook her head, her eyes glistening.

"I've never seen one in the Amish community," Dr. Benton said. "But, in his state, we don't need one to turn off the machine."

"Can we do that? Turn everything off. All the electric things." Fanny looked from the doctors to the bishop, who nodded.

"Then we'll turn everything off and take him home," Fanny said, firmly. "I think that's what he would have wanted."

"You are free to do that," Dr. Stransky said. "But at this point he's being kept alive by machines. Once we disconnect the breathing apparatus, there's a good chance he'll stop breathing. He'll be gone before you can get him home."

Fanny buried her face in her hands. "Oh, dear Gott in heaven, I don't know what to do."

"I think I speak for the entire staff when I say that it's the right thing to turn off the machines." Dr. Benton paused, taking a moment to make eye contact with every Amish person in the room. "But I just want to be sure you understand that Thomas is dying. Even if you leave him on the machines, his organs will begin to fail. If you turn the machines off, well, it will happen sooner. I see that as a more dignified death."

But Elsie didn't want any death at all. "Samuel." She turned to the bishop. "Is this Gott's way? To turn off the machines and let my father die?"

Samuel's big nose was red, his eyes glassy, and Elsie realized that he was struggling to hold in his own sadness. "It's Gott's plan, Elsie. We can't understand why the Heavenly Father calls men to Him when he does. It's something we must accept."

Her lower lip began to wobble as tears filled her eyes. She could not argue with the bishop. She could not stop Dat from dying.

Her life was like those bright headlights. Blinding. *Verhuddelt.* Veering out of control.

She tried to remember her mother's loving arms, her father's warm voice. She needed someone to catch her, to stop her from falling.

But there was no one.

22

$\mathcal{H}$aley leaned away from the nurses' station to check the door of the conference room.

Still closed.

"They're taking a long time," she said, clicking a pen rapidly.

"It's not something you'd want to rush." Aeesha jotted a few things in her notebook, then closed a chart. "Would you stop that clicking and find something to do? I hate people who finish before me."

"Your patients were more challenging than mine today." Haley was finished with her clinical work, but she had decided to hang around in case Elsie wanted to talk after the meeting.

She clicked and clicked as she thought of what Elsie and her family must be going through. Although she wasn't privy to Thomas Lapp's chart, she had heard that the repeated screenings had found no brain activity at all. Today's meeting would be difficult for everyone involved.

Poor Elsie. When Haley had spoken with her earlier today, Elsie still maintained hope that her father would recover. Not being a doctor, Haley had kept mum on the subject. She knew the experts would communicate with the family in today's meeting. Besides, over the past week they had gone over the science of brain function a few times.

"Did they tell you about the two parts of the brain?" Haley asked. She had boned up on her knowledge of brain function, anticipating that the family would have some questions and worries. "The brain is very complex, but sometimes doctors separate the upper and lower regions because they have very different functions. You might think of it as upstairs and downstairs. Upstairs is where the higher functions of the central nervous system take place. The ability to see, hear, taste, and smell. And our personality and intellect. Our reasoning skills."

"It's a wonder, the way Gott made us," Fanny had said, grateful for Haley's information.

Now Haley clicked the pen, curious about the conversation in that meeting.

"Would you stop?" Aeesha reached up and swiped the pen out of Haley's hand. "Enough!"

"Sorry. Nervous habit, and I hate waiting around."

"If you've got nothing to do, look up the treatment protocol for postsurgical appendectomy for me."

"Okay." Haley was clicking on a website when she heard a shuffle in the corridor. She shot a look down the hall and saw the dark dresses and suits of the Amish people emerging from the conference room. "They're out. Gotta go."

Haley stepped into the corridor, then paused when she realized the group was headed this way. She held her breath, trying to get a beat on the group's mood. The medical personnel were unfathomable; Thomas's family seemed sad but reconciled to their loss.

Most eyes were red and puffy, but there were no dramatic tears or sobs.

Elsie came down the hall, holding hands with her little sister, Beth.

"Hey." Haley swiped a strand of blond hair out of her eyes.

Elsie looked up, her eyes pleading. "They've given up on Dat."

It wasn't that simple—Haley knew that—but this wasn't a conversation for a crowded hospital corridor. "Do you want to talk about it?"

Elsie nodded. "Can you come with us to Dat's room?"

"Sure."

"But I'm getting a candy bar from the machine first." Beth looked up at Elsie. "Right?"

Elsie gave a playful tug on the little girl's braid. "Ya, you can have a candy bar."

Room 303 had become familiar to Haley over the past week, with its small window overlooking the parking lot, the second bed used by Fanny Lapp, and the dozen folding chairs that had been brought in for Tom's visitors, a group that had sometimes swelled to large numbers over the past week.

Haley helped Jenny open up chairs once again, making sure that everyone had a comfortable place to sit with Thomas. When Beth appeared with a giant Snickers bar, she told Haley that Elsie was waiting for her outside.

She found Elsie leaning against a wall by the snack machines, staring off into space.

"What's the matter? Can't decide between Snickers and Three Musketeers?" Haley asked.

"It would be nice if that was my worst problem." When Elsie looked up at her, Haley noticed the dark smudges under her eyes. "They're going to let my dat die. I've been praying for a miracle, but instead, everyone is giving up."

"Have you considered the fact that no one has a choice here?" Haley glanced at the shiny linoleum floor beneath them. "Let's pull up a seat," she said, sliding down against the wall until she was sitting on the floor. Side by side with Elsie, with knees pulled up to the chest, they were eye to eye.

"I can only imagine the way you're feeling right now," Haley said. "But I want you to know that the doctors here don't give up on a patient. If they think there's a chance of recovery, they're all over it. The thing is, I don't think they're giving up on your father. I think they're looking at the medical facts, and the reality is that he is dying. You and I can't stop it, and neither can the doctors."

"Only Gott in heaven has the power over life and death."

"That's right. And we can cry and scream and shut down." *The way I did, until Dylan helped me.* "But in the end, we can't control these things."

"I know that." With a heavy sigh, Elsie let her head drop back against the tile wall. "My head knows that it's true. It's my heart that won't let Dat go."

Haley felt the sting of tears in her eyes at the thought of losing a loved one. Elsie articulated her feelings so well. "I know you've been praying for him."

Elsie nodded. "I can't be disappointed with Gott. I keep telling myself that I don't understand His plan. But I'm going to miss Dat."

"I'm sure you will. Do you want to be with him now? A chance to say good-bye?"

Elsie closed her eyes for a moment, fraught with weariness. Haley thought she might be falling asleep until she spoke. "Ya. I want to be with him. And Fanny needs looking after . . . the little ones, too."

"I think Beth is all set for now." Haley stood up and reached down to help Elsie. "She's got her Snickers bar."

Elsie didn't smile—she didn't respond at all—and Haley wondered if she should stop trying to cheer her friend up. Sometimes, people needed space to grieve.

Back in Thomas's room, the mood was quiet but social as folks chatted and a nurse hovered near the patient. Elsie and Haley took a seat.

Over the past week she'd witnessed the Amish custom of bringing the entire family to the hospital whenever possible. Unlike many Englisher people who were uncomfortable around sick or dying patients, the Amish seemed at ease keeping vigil beside a dying friend.

Caleb's tall silhouette filled the door frame. He entered and came over to crouch near Elsie. "It's done then. Fanny signed the papers with the doctors."

Elsie pressed a hand to her mouth and nodded.

Emma appeared with Dr. Benton, who spoke with some of the visitors about the weather and the "marvelous" cookies one of the women had brought for the nursing staff.

"I know they were meant for the nurses," Dr. Benton said, "but occasionally they feed me if I'm good."

To Haley, the lack of solemnity seemed a bit odd for the room of a dying man, but the relaxed atmosphere definitely made the situation easier to tolerate. Death seemed to be yet one more aspect of living that the Amish had learned to cope with.

When Fanny entered with Dylan, Haley breathed a little easier, knowing that he would be nearby to support Elsie's family and friends. After the successful treatment of her own problem, Haley was an advocate of guided imagery therapy, and she sensed that the Amish would be equally interested in a treatment that didn't involve drugs or surgery.

Fanny stood by her husband, touching his face fondly. When she bent down and kissed him, Haley had to look away. It seemed like such a private moment.

"We need to say our good-byes," Fanny said, cutting through the chatter. "Then Dr. Benton is going to turn off the machines."

Elsie rose and went to her father's bedside. She climbed the stool that had been placed there, kissed his cheek, and whispered a few words.

Emma and Caleb followed, and then Fanny brought the two small children over. Beth leaned out of Caleb's arms to give her dat a kiss, and Will climbed up on the stepstool and gave him a hug.

Will and Beth seemed to understand what was happening, and no one sought to take them from the room. The children weren't being shielded from the truth; they were being taught that death was a fact of life.

Without ceremony, Dr. Benton turned the breathing apparatus off, then unclamped the tubing that went into Thomas's mouth. From his chair in the back of the room, the bishop began singing something. It was really just a round "O," but everyone joined him, their voices rising and blending in. Each graceful, gliding note was held for so long, Haley was reminded of a yoga chant. The sound was sweet and sad at the same time; a hopeful lament that made goose bumps rise on the back of Haley's neck.

Whether it was a prayer or a hymn, the doleful sound that filled the room made Haley think of a soul rising to the skies. She thought of what Graciana had said about the angels carrying her daughter off to heaven, and she tried to imagine the same happening for Thomas Lapp.

Thomas's chest was no longer rising and falling. There would be no more pain for him, but no more sunrises, either.

Summoning her sliver of faith, Haley silently said a prayer for the soul of Thomas Lapp, and the comfort of his family here on earth.

23

"*Y*oung man, will you add this to my purchases?" The old woman, who was swallowed up in the large coat, pointed to a birdhouse with a roof of copper-colored tiles.

Ruben came around the counter and lifted the hefty house from its pillar. He placed it on the counter and brushed his hands together. "There you go."

"I could use a big, strong man like you around the house. Ever since my knees went out, I don't trust myself to balance and lift."

"Can I get you anything else?"

"No, but I'm going to need some help getting these things to the car." She peered up at him over her reading glasses. "Now I know you ride only in horse-drawn buggies. Are you allowed to deliver things to a car? As long as you don't ride in it?"

"We can ride in automobiles," he said. "But we can't drive 'em or own 'em."

"Really? Well, that explains a lot of things. So I guess you could ride in an ambulance or on a fire truck if you needed to. That's a good thing."

Her words reminded Ruben of the accident, and his mouth went sour. It had been a little more than a week since that awful day, but time hadn't buffered the memory yet. How could the pain fade, when they'd just lost Thomas last night?

It's his store I'm running, Ruben had told himself all day as he went through the motions of making sales for the Lapp family.

"You can just leave the package here for a bit," the woman said. "I'm waiting on my sister, who's deliberating the merits of cherry versus peach pie filling."

Ruben leaned back on Elsie's high stool and focused on the customer. Conversation helped keep his mind off things. "I take it this is your first visit to Lancaster County."

"Can you tell? I live in Massachusetts, and I'm visiting my sister in Delaware. She's never been here, either, but we're loving the handmade crafts. I love anything that's organic and homemade, and your store has a wonderful assortment of things. It's a treasure. I'm so glad we found it. I'm Doris, by the way."

"I'm Ruben." He was about to explain that this wasn't actually his store, then he thought better of it and kept his mouth shut. He didn't mean to trick Doris in any way, but he didn't want to get to the point of explaining why Elsie couldn't run the store herself right now.

The accident was something that Ruben did not discuss with anyone, and he wasn't going to change now and blather on to a total stranger.

"Oh, that's lovely," Doris said as he began to wrap her smaller purchases in cloth and ribbon, the way he'd seen Elsie do. "But I have another question for you. Why is it that you don't have a beard like the other Amish men we've seen driving their rigs?"

"Because I'm not married." He took out a bolt of the cheapest fabric and cut off a large piece of cloth—big enough to wrap the birdhouse. "A man starts to let his beard grow after he gets married."

"Oh, I see. Did you hear that, Meryl?" she called to another woman who had now moved on to the quilt section. "He's not married." She turned back to Ruben. "Do you have a girlfriend?"

He felt his cheeks warm with embarrassment. "I hope I will soon."

Doris chuckled; it was the harsh caw of a cackling crow, but a merry laugh nonetheless. "I've given up hoping for that."

"Hope is a funny thing," he said without looking up. "Just when you give up trying to catch it, it lands right in the palm of your hand."

Doris sighed. "That's a beautiful saying."

He gave her the total for her purchase, and she wrote out a check in flowery handwriting. Another big sale. And five minutes later, when her sister purchased the quilt she'd been deliberating over, he saw that the sales total for the day was the highest since he'd started minding the shop on Monday.

It was good knowing that Elsie's family would keep getting the income they needed, especially with the hospital expenses for Thomas. And part of him was relieved that he hadn't scared her customers away—being a man who was all thumbs and not too good with dainty things.

Ya, they were going to need money for the hospital and doctors and now the funeral expenses, too. He'd heard that Caleb was working with Adam King, a good carpenter, to build his father a coffin. Maybe it was a way to save money, or maybe he just wanted to do one last thing for his dat. Ruben didn't know for sure, but he knew that these were sad days for the Lapp family.

He'd had a taste of that kind of sorrow himself, and he knew it was a hard boulder to move.

Ruben was just finishing up with the last customers of the day, some ladies who'd come on a minibus, all of them with red hats, when the door bells jingled and in walked Elsie.

Her skin was pale and ashen, her eyes shadowed with gray, and yet, to Ruben, she was the most beautiful sight he'd ever seen.

He blinked. "I wasn't expecting to see you at all today. Not here, at least. I thought I might stop over to your house when the shop closed, just to sit with you."

"I didn't want to leave you carrying this load on your own. You've been so good and kind." She went to the shelf of dolls, picked one up, then put it back absently. "But I wasn't even sure you'd be here. Ira said he was sending someone to handle every-thing."

"Ya. He sent Zed over." Ruben knew that Ira and Rose Miller had stepped in to run the Lapp household so that the family could be free for some quiet time together. "He helped sweep up and such, but I told him I knew the ropes, having managed the store for the past few days. I figured it was best that I stay on. I hope you don't mind."

"Mind? Oh, no, Ruben. I'm most grateful. And you did the right thing." She pressed her fingertips to one temple. "At least, I think so. Some folks say we should have shut down. Do you think we should have closed the store out of respect to Dat?"

"When a farmer dies, his family and friends have to keep the animals fed and the crops going," Ruben pointed out. "The way I see it, you need to keep your family business going, too."

"I reckon. I wanted to ask Fanny but . . . it sort of slipped my mind."

She looked lost, like a kitten left out in the cold. The sight of Elsie in such sorrow tugged at something deep inside him. "I hope you don't mind my saying it, but you don't look so good. Your pretty eyes are sinking away, and your skin is pale as snow."

"I'm in a bad way." She turned away from him and went to the window. The last light of day lingered, like a flame flickering in the wind. "I can't sleep. I can barely eat. I can't think right, and my mind keeps playing tricks on me."

"I could tell something was wrong." He went around the counter but didn't want to get too close. Elsie was so shaky; he thought she was likely to flee like a deer in the woods if he pressed her. "Did you talk to the bishop? Tell him what's going on?"

"I spoke with him yesterday, and he was right kind. He said he'd pray for me and told me to be strong. Told me to look to Gott for strength."

"Are you doing that, Elsie?"

"I'm trying. Really I am. I reckon I'm just too weak, because I just can't clear my mind. Every time I close my eyes, I see those lights coming toward us. Two angry eyes, with a big hunk of car behind them. Those lights keep me up at night, and when I do fall asleep, I see the headlights in my dreams." She turned to him. "Don't you see them, too?"

"I never saw them that day. I was sleeping when the SUV hit us the first time."

"Oh." Her voice fell as she looked down at the floor.

"But you're not alone in your worries," he said. "I know how you're feeling on account of something bad that happened when I was younger."

Her fingers smoothed over the edges of her apron as she paused. "The plow accident?"

He didn't think she would know about that. It had happened so long ago, when he was only six and Elsie was even younger, but of course everyone in Halfway would have heard about it. In their community, every story was shared, whether it was tragic or wondrous. "That's right."

"What really happened there?" she asked.

"The plow hit a bees' nest," he said, regret bitter on his tongue. For Ruben, the judgment had been harsh. Folks didn't understand that his burly look and uneven gait were a result of the accident. While the Amish had plenty of compassion for the little people made by Gott, there was a stigma for other folks beyond the norm. Especially when folks thought an accident was your fault. That was the problem with an old bit of gossip. People only remembered the juicier parts.

"When that happened, I couldn't sleep. I thought I would never sleep again. Every time I closed my eyes, I saw the accident happening all over again. The bees. Paul slapping at his arms, scratching them away." The image still made his throat grow thick, but the panic wasn't there. He had learned how to let the good things chip away at the bad. He had found protection in Gott's loving arms.

"Such a heartbreak." Elsie's cute lips puckered. "Whatever did you do to get that out of your mind?"

"I prayed to Gott and . . ." Ruben faltered, at a loss for what to tell her. Although he knew that Elsie was a sweet girl with a good and kind heart, he couldn't tell her about the angels. He'd never told anyone about them, and if word got out, he'd be the laughing-stock of Halfway. Already he knew that tongues wagged about him, working in an easy business with his father. Once, at a singing, he'd heard someone call him "Fat Ruben" and "Lazy Man" behind his back. Talking about this would only make things worse.

"But I've been praying," Elsie said, tears shining in her eyes. "I know Gott is the only one with the power to help me. I'll just have to pray some more and wait on the Heavenly Father." Her words seemed far more hopeful than the mournful expression on her face.

"Gott's surely watching over you, Elsie. You know how the song goes. There are angels watching over us. They're there all night and all day."

"That's what I need. A guardian angel."

He thought of the folks who'd stopped into the store with messages of faith and hope for her. "So many folks have been in here to wish you well," he said. "Preacher Dave and Nancy Briggs and Dr. Monroe."

"So many kind people." She sniffed. "It makes me feel ashamed that I don't appreciate their care and kindness."

"You know, Dr. Monroe offered to give you counseling for free," he said. "And me, too. He thinks that all the passengers in the van need some kind of counseling."

"He's a nice man, but talking about it won't help. I've talked and talked so much, my mind is full of that accident. The glass and that thundering noise. Those lights, coming right at us."

"Haley said that he helped her."

"Ya, she told me all about it. I'm glad for her, but . . . this is different." She turned to the window and heaved a tender sigh. "The sunset. It always reminds me! Every day at this time, it happens all over again in my head. One minute the sky was washed with pink and purple, like one of Rachel's paintings. The next thing, we were spinning and spinning round. . . ." She squeezed her eyes shut and sobbed into one hand.

"Elsie . . ." He closed the distance between them and put his hands on her shoulders. Her body trembled beneath his touch, rocking with grief.

How he longed to take her into his arms and hold her tight and share his angels with her. Surely Gott's love would light the shadows in her heart.

He squeezed her small shoulders, but he couldn't allow himself any more than that soothing touch. It was not the way of Plain folk to hold a girl that way outside the bounds of courtship. If people saw them, they would jump to the wrong conclusion. They wouldn't understand that Ruben shared her pain.

"I can't stop seeing it, Ruben. I can't make it stop."

"I wish I could make it stop for you, Elsie." He patted her back, floundering for a way to help her. "All I can tell you is to pray and think of Gott's angels. You know they're surrounding you with love right now."

"I don't think so. I feel so . . . so alone."

"But the angels are here. Take a breath and try to picture them in your mind. Maybe one is your mamm, watching over you. You can see her if you try, Elsie. You know she would be here to take you in her arms if she could."

Elsie sniffed, opened her eyes, and looked around her. "I don't see her."

"Then close your eyes and look in your mind, and a memory will come. A memory of your mamm cooking in the kitchen, or hanging the wash."

"Hanging the wash—I remember that. I always wanted to help her, but I was too short to reach the clothesline, so Mamm had me hand the clothes to her."

"Ya."

Elsie took a deep breath, the tension on her face softening. "Do you really think there are angels guarding us?"

"I know there are."

"Do you think they can help me stop these terrible pictures in my head?"

"I think it's your faith in Gott that's going to help you get over this," he said. "Gott and His angels."

That night, as Elsie lay huddled under the covers in bed, she softened her gaze on the moonbeams at her window and retraced the steps she had taken with Ruben that evening. He had closed the store, his capable hands turning the lock. He had calmed her fears for the moment and made sure she got home safe and sound. Sitting in his buggy, Elsie had found herself studying the young man who had brought her so much comfort of late. Ruben Zook, once a prankster who never seemed to have a kind word, was becoming Elsie's best friend. He'd been quick to lend a hand with the store. He'd given her a shoulder to cry on and so many kind words. He'd talked of Gott Almighty and His angels with the voice of a wise man.

He was a wonderful good man, Ruben Zook. Which got her to wondering why she used to avoid him. Well, everyone steered clear of a prankster, and that had been Ruben. He used to be quick to spring a trick, always looking for the laugh, but at someone else's expense.

What had happened to the joker? It only showed that you never knew a person until you got a chance to peel through the outer layers, like an onion. Dat used to say that.

Oh, Dat . . .

Would this heavy weight of sorrow ever lift from her soul?

Ruben had told her that it would. He had said that Gott's angels were surrounding her, watching over her. She imagined them hovering in the moonbeams, shining silver like corn silk.

Ruben's angels.

She closed her eyes and took a deep breath, imagining a gentle hand on her forehead, pushing back her hair. And for the first time in many days, she fell into a restful sleep.

24

*A*lthough Haley's stomach was in knots over the prospect of visiting an Amish house in the midst of a wake, her desire to support her new Amish friend helped her push past her nervousness as she parked her car opposite three buggies with their horses tied to a hitching post beside the front porch. Hers was the only car in sight, which meant she would probably be the only Englisher person here.

You can do this, she thought as she got out of the car and tugged her jacket down over her slim black pencil skirt. *You can do it for Elsie.*

The door was answered by an older woman who introduced herself as Rose. With a courteous nod, she invited Haley inside the house, and Haley was grateful to step in out of the cold. The circle of people talking quietly in the main room didn't seem to notice Haley's arrival, and she had a moment to get her bearings and take in the home.

In the room off the kitchen, family and friends sat on rockers and benches near a potbellied stove. A handful of children sat at the kitchen table playing a card game.

"Go fish!" Will announced jubilantly as Beth's cards fluttered to the floor.

"Oops!" She set her cloth doll on the table and climbed down to get the cards.

There was a second room off the kitchen—a fairly empty room, but for a few rows of chairs facing a tall counter. Haley recognized Emma sitting in the front row. Then her gaze caught on the object all the chairs were facing.

It wasn't a counter; it was Thomas Lapp's body, at rest in a wood coffin.

Whoa. Dylan had warned her that the body was being waked right in the home. He'd explained that it was customary among some Old Order Amish. Still, it was a bit of a shock to see that in her friend's living room. She turned away to study the rest of the house.

A hutch in the corner held at least a dozen coffee cups hanging from hooks. The sofa in the living area was covered with a crocheted throw in vibrant shades of blue. Over the sofa was a clock with a calendar on either side. The only art on the walls were the calendars, one showing a mountain range, the other a rocky coastline.

The older woman returned with a pretty brunette dressed in black, and Haley recognized Fanny. She was a picture of grace in a black dress that hung loose around her prominent belly. The dark fabric of her dress made her skin appear pale as bone china, stark, but pretty.

"Thank you for coming," she said. "It's kind of you." She took Haley's hand and turned to the group. "If you didn't meet her at the hospital, this is Haley Donovan, the Good Samaritan who stopped to help at the scene of the accident."

Haley felt her mouth drop open; she hadn't expected this sort of attention.

There were quiet murmurs of approval, and a few people came forward to tell her that they appreciated what she had done. She nodded, trying to appear friendly but really wanting nothing more than to escape to a quiet room to talk with Elsie.

When a woman named Rebecca finished talking, Haley turned to Fanny. "How is Elsie doing?"

"Mmm." Fanny looked toward the kitchen door. "I sent Rose to find her for you. I don't know why, but I think she's out back."

"I'll go look for her, if that's okay." When Fanny nodded, Haley headed out through the kitchen door, bracing against the cold once again.

Dusk was falling, painting the sky with lavender, purple, and indigo. It was a sad sunset, Haley thought, but then maybe her view was colored by the sorrow that hung over this house right now.

Crossing the side yard, she saw the dark profile of the old carriage house that Elsie had mentioned. Thomas and Caleb had been renovating it themselves, working to make a suitable space for some sort of repair shop.

With Thomas's death, their plans had been derailed.

"Who's that?" a frightened voice called.

Haley turned to see a small form clinging to a post-and-rail fence. "Elsie? It's me, Haley."

"Oh."

There was an awkward silence for a moment. *Am I intruding?* Haley wondered.

"I can't talk right now." Elsie's voice was flat and withdrawn.

"Is this a bad time?" Haley peered into the gray dusk, trying to glimpse a clue that would help her understand Elsie's mindset. "Wait. That's a stupid question. I know it's a terrible time, and I'm sorry for your loss." She took a step closer, but Elsie turned away.

"I'm sorry." Elsie stood her ground. "Please, just go."

Suddenly, Haley felt awkward. She shouldn't have come here. She didn't belong here. Why had she thought that a few bonding moments in crisis could dissolve a cultural divide that had existed for generations?

She turned away and headed back, her boots clunky on the frozen earth. The light of the kitchen loomed closer, and she turned and circled round the back of the house. With this knot in her throat, she couldn't bear to make nice with the visitors in the house.

It was time to get in the car and get out of here.

Her hands were cold, and tears were beginning to sting in her eyes as she reached into her coat pockets and fumbled for the keys.

Why had she locked it? *You big dummy.* The last place her car was going to be stolen was outside an Amish home in Lancaster County.

At last, she ripped the door open, slid into the driver's seat, and slammed the door. She gathered the keys and jammed one into the ignition. But when she turned the key, the engine didn't rumble to life.

There was just a choking sound, then quiet.

Have the mechanic check your battery, her father had warned her. *If it's low, this cold weather will make it die.*

The swell of pain inside her rose up and splashed over all her intentions. Pain gave voice to doubt. Doubt to malice.

You're hardly a hero.

Think you'll make it through nursing school?

You failed again. Just like everyone expected.

The keys fell from her hand as she slumped forward and cried. She cried for all the mistakes she'd made in her life. For the ruse her life had become, with these people thinking she was a hero. For the wrong man who wanted to own her, and the right man who didn't love her back.

She cried because she was in the heart of Amish country with a dead battery, both in her car and in her soul.

25

*E*lsie turned away from the shadow of the old carriage house and tried to shake the image of those twin lights veering toward her.

Imagine an angel . . . that was what Ruben had told her.

Mamm.

Dat.

Woody. She smiled at the memory of the little brown dog who used to love to follow at her heels, but then the minute she opened her eyes and felt the heavy night sky falling upon her, those lights were back.

Cutting across the line of the highway.

Grunting toward her.

The blast of the horn jolted Elsie from her reverie. A car horn?

Haley.

She gathered the skirts of her dress and raced around the house. Cold air burned her lungs as she paused, spotting the little car, still and quiet in the gathering darkness. Why had it made that noise?

Her eyes adjusted again, and she saw that Haley was sitting in the car, her hands pressed into her face.

"Haley?" She knocked on the window. "Are you all right?" There were no lights on in the car, so it was hard to see her friend's face.

A moment later, the door opened and Haley peered out. "My car isn't starting. Do you think I can come inside for a few minutes?"

"Kumm." The word was out before Elsie remembered that she had been trying to keep to herself, trying to keep from sharing her torment with everyone. And privacy was not something that was easy to find in an Amish house—especially when friends and family had gathered to mourn the dead.

"Come inside, and we'll get you something to eat," Elsie said, knowing that a good hot meal could cure many a trouble. Just not everything.

◈◈

They sat together at the kitchen table, talking quietly, while Haley ate a bowl of the venison stew that Mary Beiler had brought. Haley was very upset about her car, and though Elsie sensed there was more going on, she didn't probe. She knew that Haley didn't want to talk about personal things in front of all these people, either.

Haley needed her father to come and pick her up, but her phone wasn't "getting service." Elsie went outside with her and waited as she tried to get a phone connection, but the milky white sky didn't let Haley get through.

"We have a neighbor who has a phone," Elsie suggested. "Marta is a Mennonite, and her family has electricity and a phone. Cars, too."

"Can we walk there?" Haley asked.

"Sure. It's just around the bend."

Now that the sun had set, Elsie's anxiety had drained, leaving her tired. This was the pattern of her days now. An unpleasant edginess leading up to the terrifying minutes of sunset. She yawned, noticing the wisp of white steam around her mouth.

"You're tired." Haley sighed. "I'm so sorry to do this to you now, with your whole family mourning your father."

"You're not to blame, and I'm happy to be out for fresh air. You can only sit around for so much time, talking and eating pie."

"You always find the good in things, Elsie. I wish I could be that way. Sometimes I feel like everything I touch turns to dust."

Elsie looked up at the beautiful girl. Even in the dim light, she could see the imprint of sorrow on Haley's face. "Why do you think that? You do so many good things for so many people."

Haley blinked back tears. "But I can't even hold my own life together. Do you know my father has been reminding me about that car battery? It's just a big example—a symbol—of how I'm still not being a responsible adult."

"Mmm. From down here, you seem very responsible. But no one except Gott can see what's truly in our hearts."

"Ain't that the truth." Haley's breath came out in a puff of white. "Maybe I should live Plain. It would be nice to live a simpler life. Less complicated."

"Plain is good, but Gott has called you to something different." *And Plain lives aren't free from pain,* Elsie thought as they turned down the Kraybills' lane.

They walked in silence for a bit before Haley spoke. "Elsie Lapp, there's something you're not telling me. I can feel your tension. No, more than that. Something has got you on edge, and I know you just lost your father, but this is something else. Tell me what it is. Because if you don't talk about it, no one can help you."

Elsie stepped onto the frozen mulch under the Kraybills' big, bare oak and unburdened her heart. She told Haley about the terrible feelings that came every day at sundown. The horrifying memories. The sureness that darkness was crashing down over the world with each setting sun.

"That's why I couldn't talk to you before. It's such a bad time for me," Elsie finished. "I can barely breathe."

"My heart aches for you. And you say it's every day?"

"Ya. I thought it would go away. Emma said to give it time, and Ruben . . ." She paused, not wanting to share Ruben's advice about the angels all around them. "Ruben tried to help, but it still hits me every day. Every day at sunset."

"And it's wearing you down," Haley said. "I can see that."

Elsie twisted her hands in the tips of her woolen scarf, searching for warmth she couldn't find. "I don't mean to complain. Everyone's so sad now. Fanny's lost her second husband, and there's the baby coming and money matters to think about. Caleb doesn't know what to do, now that Dat won't be opening that shop. There are folks so much worse off than me. I don't know why I can't just be strong and take control of the fear."

"But you can't, and that's okay." Haley touched Elsie's shoulder. "Sometimes we need a little help. That's normal after what you've been through. We need to hook you up with Dylan, pronto."

"No, that's kind of you, but no." Elsie shook her head. "Counseling isn't really something for the Amish. We have our family and our ministers to talk to."

"But this is a case where you definitely need something more." Haley put her hands together in a prayerful gesture. "Please, talk to Dylan. Promise me you'll give it a chance. Pretty please?"

Elsie hesitated. She could imagine the bishop's cold glare. Once he heard she had seen a psychologist, he would be suspicious of her entanglements with the Englisher world. "I'll talk to Dylan," she said. "No harm in simply talking."

Haley put one arm around her and gave her a hug. "And if that doesn't work, we'll find something else that does. I'm not giving up on you, my friend. I'm going to be like that persistent fly that keeps looping back into your kitchen for another taste of pie."

A smile crept across Elsie's face. "You're always welcome in my kitchen, little fly."

26

When the girls rapped on the door at the Kraybills', Marta Kraybill offered much more than a phone.

"If it's the battery, we have jumper cables," she said. "But I can't offer you a jump until the morning. Mitch is working tonight, and he's got the car."

Haley learned that Mitch Kraybill drove a milk truck in the area, and sometimes he was required to pick up milk from local Amish farms at night, so that the milk made it to the larger dairies within a certain window of freshness.

"You should stay at our house tonight," Elsie suggested. "That way you can get a big jump in the morning. And I'd like you to stay."

"It would save my father having to drive out here tonight." Haley knew her parents would not be happy about that. "If it's okay, I'll stay the night."

Elsie nodded. "I would like that."

Haley called home, grateful that she didn't have to inconvenience her parents with her most recent mistake. When she got the voice mail instead of an answer, she left a quick message for them. She thanked Marta, and told her she would see her in the morning, bright and early.

By the time they returned to the Lapp house, horse-drawn buggies were making their way down the lane, their lights and fluorescent orange triangles standing out in the dim night. The last of the Amish visitors climbed into their buggy in front of the house, and Elsie called good-bye to Rose and Ira Lapp.

"That's Zed's parents," Elsie explained. "They're taking care of the household for us until after the funeral. It's a custom among the Amish, and I admit, it's nice to not have to worry about making beds and doing dishes for a bit."

Inside, the family was settled at the kitchen table, setting up the Game of Life. When Elsie explained that Haley would be staying the night, Will clapped.

"More players!" he exclaimed.

As Haley joined in the family's activities, she interjected a few positive comments, though she tried to take a backseat and absorb their conversations. This was a rare opportunity, to sit with Amish people at their family table, especially during such a critical time for them.

There were worries and jokes and questions about the future. But through it all, the underpinning of love came through. Through thick or thin, this family would be okay because they knew what mattered: faith, hope, and love.

Would a visitor find the same undercurrent of love in her home? Haley wasn't so sure about that, but she did love her parents. From now on, she would make sure they knew that.

Upstairs in Elsie's attic room, the two girls sat huddled on the dou-ble bed, their backs against the wall, a blanket over their legs.

In a borrowed flannel nightgown and her own fluffy socks, Haley felt cozy, despite the nip in the air. Elsie had explained that the house didn't have central heating, so they left the upstairs doors open all day, knowing that most of the hot air would rise to the attic level.

It wasn't even eight o'clock, but weariness tugged at Haley. "I'm usually up way later than this," she said, stifling a yawn. "I don't know what's come over me."

"Nighttime is sleeping time. That's what my dat used to say."

"It's not a bad idea. That way we can get up bright and early. I'll get my battery boosted, then drive you into town to meet with Dylan."

"Counseling." Elsie winced. "No, I don't like the sound of that."

"Believe me, the alternative is worse."

"I don't like talking about my problems to strangers. What do I say? I cry like a baby every night when darkness comes."

"That's better than admitting that, at twenty-two, I can't manage to take care of my own car." Haley brought her knees up to her chin and tucked the nightgown. "Or I could admit that I have a crush on the therapist."

"You and Dylan? Dr. Monroe." Elsie covered her mouth. "Does he know?"

"Probably. But he's not interested."

"Oh. I have a tiny crush, too, but nothing will come of it."

"Ruben?"

"How did you know?"

"You can sort of feel that love is in the air when you two are together."

"Not love. Just . . . a crush. Like Orange Crush. Sweet and sim-ple."

"And what's keeping you guys from becoming a couple?"

"I can't ever marry. It's my genetic disorder. Did you know that it might be passed on to my children?"

Haley nodded. She had done some research on EVC after she met Elsie.

"Well, I can't let it be passed on. And our faith is strict about marriage and children. Once you marry, it's expected that you have a family. So . . . I can never marry."

"Really? Does that upset you? I mean, I'm not one of those people who needs to define herself with a man." *At least, not anymore,* Haley thought. "But I do know that somewhere down the road, I want to have a husband and a family. It's important to me. Sort of tops on my bucket list."

Elsie squinted. "What's a bucket list?"

"A list of things you want to do before you kick the bucket . . . before you die."

"Oh." Elsie frowned, considering that. "I think that, for us Amish, we let Gott take care of our bucket list. He's got a plan for us all."

"But what about having children? Being a mother? Having a husband to come home to at the end of the day? A best friend to share your troubles."

"Oh, that would be right nice, but I can't be dreaming about things that I can't have in this life."

Haley sneaked a glance at her friend, who sat with her head bowed. Her kapp now hung on a hook on the wall, and her long dark hair hung in a braid down her back. Wisps of hair fell over her forehead, and the dim glow from the kerosene lamp backlit the profile of her face.

"Right now, when I look at you, I see a beautiful young woman with a graceful smile and impossibly long eyelashes that most fashion models dream of. You don't look so different from the rest of the world, and your community doesn't single out your differences. Or does it? Is there something I'm missing?"

"Amish folk are pretty accepting of little people," Elsie said. "We're taught that Gott created us in His image, so we're to love His creation."

"And do Plain folk follow that rule?"

"Most do. Others, I don't think they realize they're wooed by physical beauty. A lovely smile like Emma's. A tall, strong body like Caleb's. Folks just can't help but be drawn toward the things that please them."

"I hear you." Haley's experience was from the opposite end of the spectrum, with men deciding that they liked her solely based on her physical appearance. "There's no denying that looks do matter. But the wiser person, the more evolved person knows that it's what's inside that counts. And inside, you rock, Elsie. You're a shining star."

"You're making me blush." Elsie pressed her palms to her cheeks, endearing herself to Haley even more. "But denki. That's sweet of you."

"It's all true."

"Too bad not every man is a wise man."

"And too bad American society rewards people for their physical appearance. Do you ever feel harassed by Englishers?"

"People stare at me. Sometimes it even happens at the Country Store. Visitors seem to be taking me apart with their eyes. Or they'll ask me if I'm a midget. But I just tell them the truth, and the subject drops. The store has become a second home to me, and answering the questions of curious customers is just part of the business."

"Sounds like you're pretty strong," Haley teased, "under that sweet-as-pie exterior."

"I'm a tough cookie," Elsie said with a smile.

Haley wanted to get back to the baby thing, but they were burning the midnight oil . . . literally. "I could talk to you all night, but we both have stuff in the morning. Cars to fix, therapy, wonderful guys we can't fall in love with. We're some pair, aren't we?"

"A couple of silly geese." She turned to Haley. "I'm sorry I turned you away when you arrived today. That was unkind, I know. But I was so upset. I wasn't myself."

"You don't need to be sorry. Just promise me you'll try to talk to me when it gets bad again, and I'll do the same for you." Haley stuck out her small finger and wiggled it. "Pinky promise."

A grin overtook Elsie's face as she held her pinky out for Haley to hook. "Piggy promise? You Englishers have the oddest customs."

27

Elsie had very low expectations when she and Haley set out on Saturday morning. She didn't believe a stranger could help her.

But by the end of the session with Dylan, she felt a soft sense of renewal. Springtime in her own heart.

That night, Elsie slid into one of the twin beds in Emma's room, a whole person once again.

"Dylan Monroe is a very good doctor, helping you that way," Emma said, lowering the lantern light. Since Dat had died, Elsie occasionally joined her sister in the other attic room, reassured by the steady sound of Emma's breathing at night. "Tell me what he did, once again. The box with the flashing lights?"

"It was just a row of lights that blinked, and he asked me to follow them with my eyes."

"And that made you feel better?"

"It did, because I had to keep telling him what happened . . . about the accident. That was really hard to talk about at first. But then by the third or fourth time I went through the story, my heart wasn't aching so much."

"Praise be to Gott in heaven." Emma let out a sigh as she settled in bed. "You were in such a bad way, honey girl. Caleb and I were wracking our brains, trying to think of some way to make you feel better, but we couldn't come up with a single thing."

"Dylan knew just the thing to do. That's what psychology is for, I guess. I never put much stock in all that stuff, but now I've changed my mind. Dylan's a doctor who wants to help people. He says he's going to give a big session, and he hopes that everyone who was in the van will attend."

"Now, that'll be a tough one, getting old Jacob Fisher to go to a meeting like that."

"Ruben and I are planning to go. We're going to do our best to get the others to come along."

"That Ruben Zook has been a real surprise, running the Country Store for us. I never thought he was the sort of person to come through in a crisis." Emma yawned. "He's always been such a joker. I think the accident brought out his serious side."

"I think the accident brought out the real Ruben," Elsie said. She had been thinking about the large young man who towered over her. A gentle giant. How had he kept his wonderful kindness hidden all this time?

And his faith in Gott . . .

He had told her that Gott sent angels in surprising ways. "I think Dr. Monroe is your angel," he'd said. "Just listen to what he has to say and let Gott work through him."

It had sounded like so much verhuddelt medicine at first. But Elsie had been in such a bad way, she'd decided to try it.

And Gott had eased her pain. Praise Gott! It was a miracle to have peace in her heart again. It was a miracle that Dr. Monroe had even been there, in that back room of the library. Such a lovely twist, the way things happened, but Gott did work in wondrous ways.

Her relief was so sweet, she wanted to share it with Emma.

"You know, Em, you're welcome to come to the group session, too. It might ease your heart."

"Mmm." Emma seemed to be dropping off to sleep. "I'll think about it, after the funeral."

On Monday, Dat would be buried in a coffin made by Caleb and Adam King. Dat's body lay downstairs in the back room, lovingly dressed in a white shirt and trousers sewn by Elsie and Emma. Helping to dress the body had made it very clear to Elsie that he was gone.

"Remember, man, that you are dust, and unto dust you shall return."

It was the natural ending to life, but knowing that did not quench the sorrow that still flamed in her heart when she thought of losing Dat. Dylan had warned her that he had no magical cure for grief over a loved one.

But he had rid her mind of panic and confusion.

The horrible images of the accident.

Those angry white lights, like giant eyes.

Elsie still remembered every detail, but somehow the memories were not sharp enough to wound her anymore.

She huddled under the covers for warmth. Her bed felt deliciously soft and welcoming. Her heart still ached for Dat, and she asked that Gott bless Fanny, Caleb and Emma, Will and Beth, during this sad time. Elsie missed him already, and dear Fanny . . . she would have to raise her new baby without a father.

So much grief, and yet now Elsie felt ready to handle it.

That night when she closed her eyes, blessed sleep seeped in, warming her from head to toe like a fat mug of comfort. In this sleep, there was peace, calm, and a glimmer of joy.

That familiar joy that Elsie knew so well, the ability to find delight in a delicate snowflake or the smile of a child.

❦

With her terrible burden lifted, Elsie turned her attention to her dear family. By day, many visitors filled their home as folks stopped in to pay final respects to Thomas. As was the custom, the funeral was being handled by family and friends.

Although there was much activity during the day, there was plenty of quiet time in the evening, and the family turned to knitting or working puzzles to busy the mind while they talked of Dat.

"I'm sorry he didn't get to see any of us marry," Emma said.

Elsie kept her eyes on her knitting, not wanting to admit the truth: It wasn't a disappointment for her, since she would not be getting married.

"Is this your way of telling us you're engaged to Gabe King?" Caleb asked.

Elsie blinked in wonder that her brother would mention such a thing. Emma and Gabe had kept their romance a secret for years, and though Emma had confided a few details to Elsie, she wasn't one to talk about it much.

Emma shot Caleb a disapproving look. Though she had just turned twenty, she was wise for her years. "How can I be engaged, when Gabe isn't even a member of our church?"

"I reckon he'll be going to the bishop in May to prepare for baptism in the fall." Caleb sat back in the rocker, stretching his long legs out before him. "Everyone knows that he favors you, Emma. He doesn't keep a lid on the pot, the way you do."

"I've always liked Gabe King," Fanny said. "Look at all his family's been through, with his parents getting killed. They pulled together, the older ones raising the young ones."

It was Sunday night. A large bowl of popcorn was set out in the middle of the table—their light snack since the church meal had taken up their afternoon. Beth had a prominent purple mustache from drinking grape juice, and Will kept spilling popcorn on the puzzle he and Fanny were putting together.

Elsie put her knitting down to get a wet cloth. "Kumm, dear one." She beckoned Beth, who squirmed a bit when Elsie wiped her upper lip. "That's much better."

Fanny turned a puzzle piece around in her hands, watching the exchange. "All that I just said about the King family? It's going to be the same around here, I reckon. With Thomas gone, I'm going to need help with the baby. And you three already help with the housework and the little ones."

"We're old enough to take on the chores, and the little ones will learn soon enough." Elsie's needles clicked as she spoke, such a reassuring little sound.

Fanny paused to make eye contact with each of them: Caleb, Emma, and then Elsie. "I know I'm not your real mother. I'm not even old enough to be Caleb's mother. But I feel blessed that Gott brought us together as a family. Even when money is tight and the days are full of work and disappointment, I thank the Almighty Father for our family."

Caleb nodded, the knob on his throat moving as he swallowed.

"We will always look to you as the head of this family," Emma said. "And I'm grateful Dat had so much love in his life."

"You brought the light back into his eyes," Elsie added. "Our family was heartbroken after Mamm died, but you came along and made us whole again."

"Oh, honey girl, it's Gott's love that makes a family whole," Fanny said. "It's Gott's love that has us here today. Heartbroken again; I know that. But still, we are a family."

It dawned on Elsie that Fanny had been through this before;

she'd lost her first husband not long after they married. And after all that, to lose Tom! Elsie marveled at the strength of her faith. Fanny was a tall tree, able to bend in the wind, but still standing tall.

Elsie put her knitting aside and went over to put her arms around Fanny. "Don't you worry about the little ones. Or the baby. Or the household finances. We're all here to help."

Fanny blinked back tears and took a deep breath. "Denki."

Will looked up from the puzzle. "Now can we stop talking and finish this border, Mamm?"

Everyone chuckled.

"It's good that you're a hard worker, my boy," Fanny said. "Just like your father."

⊗⊙

It was a Plain funeral. The partitions had been removed from the house so that the ministers could be seen from any of the three main rooms. When Elsie saw the crowd of guests seated on the benches, she guessed that there were two hundred people, maybe more. There were ministers visiting from nearby communities, and the town mayor, Nancy Briggs. Rachel sat with her family, but Elsie knew that James would not be here, as he was still in the hospital. George Dornbecker stood at the back beside a woman who Elsie guessed was his wife. Haley was on a bench next to Dylan Monroe, and for a glimmer of a moment Elsie thought what a fine couple they would make. Maybe there was some matchmaking to be done in the future.

The bishop removed his hat—a cue for all the other men to do the same. The solemn mood of the room was comforting somehow. It was as if all the people here cushioned Elsie and her family from the bumpy road ahead of them.

"Our departed brother Thomas left us very suddenly." Samuel's eyes appeared owlish behind his glasses. "His bed is empty. His voice will not be heard in this house. He was needed here in our community, but Gott needs good men, too. We cannot wish him back. Instead, we must prepare to follow him."

As the bishop began to talk about the sin of Adam and Eve, Elsie thought of Mamm. Had Dat joined her in heaven? It hadn't occurred to her before, but somehow it eased her heart to think of her parents together once again, at least in spirit.

That was the last time this house had seen a funeral—when Mamm died. *And we sat in this same spot,* Elsie thought. Back then, Bishop Samuel had frightened her, but then she had been only a six-year-old girl, who kept thinking that she would wake up and find Mamm back in the kitchen again. Ya, in her six-year-old way, she had wanted it all to be a bad dream.

But Samuel didn't scare her anymore. Truly, now that she had gotten back on balance with some good sleep and a calm heart, the fear was fading from her heart.

"Fear not, for I am with thee." Gott's promise from the Bible brought her peace. As long as she had faith, she had nothing to fear.

PART TWO

❦

The
Long Way Home

Ye shall be sorrowful,
But your sorrow shall be turned into joy.

—JOHN 16:20

28

In the days and weeks that followed the accident, Haley's skills blossomed like a winter lily. Maybe it was just a matter of repetition mixed with confidence inspired by the accident, but when Haley was working at the hospital, things fell into place. She learned to balance therapeutic communication with clinical care. She figured out a way to stay on top of her scut work and get her reports done. And Swanson had given her extra credit for using her nursing skills in a trauma situation.

"I've seen a marked improvement in the quality and volume of work that you've done," Dr. Swanson had told her during her most recent evaluation. "Honestly, I didn't think you had it in you, but you've brought your grade up to an A."

"I'm thrilled about the grade," Haley had told her instructor. "But mostly, I'm excited that I realized nursing is where I want to be. Where I belong." She rapped a fist against her chest. "I know it in here, and it's a strong feeling. Did you ever feel that way, Dr. Swanson?"

The older woman touched her chin, eyeing Haley with a look of regret. "Honestly, I still feel that way."

"Really?"

"Every day." Dr. Swanson rose from the table and gathered her clipboard. "When that feeling goes away, I'm taking my retirement and moving to Palm Springs. Till then, it's good to know I'm in the right profession. And I'm happy for you, Haley. That gem of self-discovery is something that can't be taught by an instructor. Be grateful for it, and enjoy every moment."

At home, Haley had made peace with her parents, whose patience had worn thin with their daughter's pattern of switching from one interest to another since high school.

"I'm really proud of the way you took care of those people in the van accident," her father told her one evening. "From the way everyone's talking about it, it sounds like triage, like they do on the battlefield in the army."

Haley shrugged. "It wasn't quite that intense."

"But you're a hero, honey. Way to go."

Haley looked over at her mother, who nodded over the steaming pot of potatoes she was mashing. "That's right."

"Thanks. It's nice to be appreciated. Seems like I've been persona non grata around here for the past few years."

"I'm sorry if we haven't given you the support you needed with nursing school," her dad said, "but really, Haley, we've been behind you on so many things that you ended up walking away from. First, you wanted to be a veterinarian. Then there was the cleaning service. And after that, the cooking school, which cost us a lot of money."

"And don't forget the wedding," Mom said. "I know you're sick of hearing it, but we really did like Graham."

"Wendy, stop." Patrick Donovan held a hand up to his wife. "You're a broken record. Did you like Graham more than you love your own daughter?"

"No, but there was the wedding that we put money—"

"'Nuff said about that. The thing is, honey, we want you to succeed like your older sisters. But right now we're not going to get too excited about any one thing until we can be sure it's gonna stick. You know what I mean?"

"I get it, Dad. But this is different. It's where I'm meant to be. You'll see."

Her father slid his shoulders back and straightened to his full height. "Honey, I'm seeing it already, and I'm proud of you."

"Thanks."

The conversation stayed with her for a few days.

I'm proud of you, Dad had said.

The words resonated in her mind as she drove from class to the hospital, or to Halfway for group sessions led by Dylan. In her dealings with the Amish, she had learned that they believed pride was a bad thing—in the same vein as vanity. Still, she understood her father's message, but at the same time she realized how her sense of people and culture was expanding through her new bonds with the Amish community.

ↆↄ

There was a light dusting of snow on the ground as Haley headed off for group therapy. "Take it slow out there," her father had advised, and although the dry flakes didn't seem to be sticking, Haley proceeded with caution. The accident had made her a much more careful driver.

Her radio was tuned in to a popular station, and the deejays kept making jokes about the worst dates they had ever had. In the next segment they interviewed the winners of their Sweetheart Sweep-stakes, and Haley realized that it was Valentine's Day. January had flown by quickly, and now here she was on the most romantic day of the year, and without a sweetheart.

You could have had one. You could have had Graham, she reminded herself, glad that she'd dodged that bullet. What would she be doing now if she had gone through with the wedding? Maybe sitting in a bathrobe and staring at the snow and trying to decide what to make for dinner? Or maybe she would have been sitting in a nail salon, waiting for her pedicure to dry while wondering if she could squeeze a matinee in before Graham got home.

Tall, handsome Graham. That killer smile used to make her go weak in the knees. After the attraction had faded, she had to stop herself from wincing when he smiled. Now . . . she didn't think it would bother her anymore, because Graham no longer had power over her.

And life was too short to waste energy on old issues.

Dylan was walking down Halfway's Main Street as she pulled into the library parking lot. Now there was a man who was attractive, inside and out. Wispy snowflakes clung to the broad shoulders of his jacket and his cheeks were bright from the cold.

In his down jacket and boots, he could have stepped right out of the LL Bean catalog. At the hospital, his good looks still stirred many a heart. Last week, one patient in the ER asked what sort of ailment she had to have to be treated by *that* doctor.

He paused in front of her car, waiting as she popped open the door. "Hey, you."

"I just found out that it's Valentine's Day," Haley told him. In their time spent together in group sessions, they had developed an easy banter, but nothing too deep. Whenever she pushed for more information, Dylan had a gentle way of pushing back. "Did you know that?"

"I do have a calendar." He fished his keys out and opened the back entrance to the library that was used for private sessions. "How could a woman your age not be aware of every girl's favorite holiday?"

"That's what happens when it's all work and no play." She unzipped her jacket. "But it's not just a *girl's* holiday."

"As a therapist, I don't like the emphasis on romance. Valentine's Day makes people feel like losers if they're not hooked up with someone."

"Really?" She considered that as she circled around the big round table to the coffeemaker. "I never felt like a loser. I'm always just . . . hopeful."

Dylan nodded. "That's because you're a glass-half-full kind of girl."

She smiled, wondering if that glint in his blue eyes was just the library lights or his version of flirting. "Do you think the Amish celebrate it?"

"I hear that they do, complete with homemade valentines and boxes of chocolates."

Haley smiled at the thought of a young Amish woman like Rachel gluing a red fabric heart onto a card. "And how about you? Did you send someone a valentine?" She tossed off the question in a cavalier manner, though so much hinged on his response.

"Of course."

The pace of her heartbeat quickened, until he added, "I mailed one to my mother."

She grinned and started to measure coffee grounds into the basket. "That's sweet." She was tempted to tell him that he was the subject of speculation and longing among the majority of the female staff at work. He probably knew already. But that was the sort of thing a buddy would say, and she didn't want to be his "buddy." She wasn't ready to rule out other levels of attraction between them, although he wasn't exactly sending out signals that he was into her.

Their conversation shifted when George Dornbecker entered with a silent nod. In private, Elsie had confided that George normally had a very outgoing personality with a great sense of humor. But since the accident, he'd become quiet and withdrawn.

"At least he's coming to the sessions," Dylan had said. "That's a start."

Today would be their fourth session together as a group, and in some ways it seemed like a miracle that they'd made it through that long.

The first two sessions had been fraught with emotion. Haley's eyes misted over when she thought of those early meetings. Dylan had guided them each to talk through their memories of the accident, and the anguish had been difficult to take. Still, it had helped to talk through the horrible details. It was similar to Haley's experience with the light box; every time the awful story was told, it seemed more distant. It had lost the power to overwhelm them.

In their last session, Dylan had asked them to talk about anything but the accident. That had changed the tone of things, making it more positive when people in the group began looking toward the future. Haley had joined the group out of curiosity and a desire to spend some time with the people she had bonded with, but now she found that she looked forward to these meetings.

By the time Haley had coffee dripping into the pot, Ruben and Elsie had arrived. This location was a quick walk from the Country Store, where they were both working now. Seeing them together, Haley found it hard to believe that they hadn't been friends all their lives. Ruben was very protective of Elsie, and she obviously respected his opinion and valued his friendship.

"Did you see the snow?" Elsie asked, her face awash in delight.

Of all the passengers in the van, Elsie had earned a special place in Haley's heart. She was a generous, upbeat young woman with an indomitable spirit ten times the size of her small body. The accident and the death of her father had thrown her into post-traumatic stress, but thank goodness Dylan had helped her find relief in private counseling. Of course, Dylan never mentioned his sessions with individuals, but whenever Haley came to town, she spent an hour or so hanging out in the Country Store, catching up with Elsie and Ruben. In some ways, those two had become her new best friends—she trusted them so completely. She had begun to see that the clothing and cultural differences that separated them were easy to surmount, now that she was getting to know them better.

"I've been waiting all winter for a big snowstorm," Elsie said. "I love the way snow covers everything with a pure coat of white."

"Is it supposed to stick?" Dylan asked.

"I heard that we might get an inch or two," George said. "You have to be careful out there. The roads get slippery."

"How's the van shopping going?" Dylan asked. "Is your business back on the road?"

"Not yet. Can't find a vehicle that works for me. But then I'm not too eager to get back out there."

Haley didn't want to stare, but she'd noticed that George's hands were still shaking when he went to pour coffee. She wished he would take Dylan up on his offer for private therapy sessions. The man was obviously still suffering emotional pain.

While they were talking Zed Miller slipped in and quietly took a seat. She asked Zed how his job search was going, and he said he had found some temporary work helping out at the Stoltzfus farm. He also added that he was "talking with the bishop" about joining the congregation now—which meant getting baptized. The way Haley understood it, Zed was welcome to return to the flock, though some in the community were a bit leery of him after his long absence. "I feel like I have to earn my way back," he'd told the group.

Haley poured herself a cup of hot water for tea and took a seat, studying the faces of the people who had become like a second family to her. These sessions weren't always lighthearted, but they had become the highlight of her week.

The door opened wide and Rachel King came in with her father.

"Good afternoon." Nate King took off his hat. "Dr. Monroe, can I have a word with you?"

Dylan was on his feet immediately. "Of course, Nate."

The others continued talking as Nate asked Dylan if he knew anyone with a truck or van. Haley listened in, hearing something about the rising medical costs for James Lapp. "Getting an ambulance to take him home would cost hundreds of dollars."

"I have a friend with a van," Dylan said. "He'd loan it to us for a day or two. Let me know when James needs it, okay?"

Soon after Nate left, everyone took a seat around the table and Dylan got things started. "I'm glad you all came back. I guess last week wasn't too painful."

"I thought the part at the end was good," Ruben said. "That part when you did all the talking, nice and calm."

"The guided imagery." Dylan checked the faces of the others. "What was the general feeling about that?"

There were murmurs of approval.

"I think it got everyone thinking more positive thoughts," Elsie said.

"Good. We'll do that again at the end of our session. Does anyone have progress they want to report?"

"I've got some progress to share." Elsie folded her hands under her chin. "Remember I told you about those bad feelings I got every day at sundown? And Dylan thought that I was connecting it to the time of day when the accident happened. Well, yesterday, I went outside the shop just before closing and I found a spot facing the west and I stood there, real stern. Like I wasn't going to back down. And when the sky got all rosy and pink and then purple, I was still standing there and I was smiling. I made myself smile at the sunset. And you know what? It didn't get me down at all."

Ruben smiled. "Ya. You came back inside to close the store, and it was like a normal day."

"Except that a few customers saw me out in the cold without my coat, glaring off at nothing. They must think I'm verhuddelt." Elsie grinned.

Haley smiled, and some of the men chuckled.

"What does 'verhuddelt' mean?" Dylan asked.

"Crazy," Zed offered. "But not in a good way, like Englishers think."

"Well, I don't think you're crazy, Elsie, but that's a wonderful story." Dylan's lips curved in a rare smile. "Good work."

"I got some news about James," Rachel said. "You know already," she told Dylan, "because you've been visiting him at the rehab center. But the doctors are sending him home. He'll have to keep doing his exercises and all, but he's a strong man and he's learned a lot really fast. He can get himself out of bed and all dressed, and he can move himself from the bed to the wheelchair."

Haley gave her a thumbs-up.

"That's wonderful good news," Elsie said. "James must be excited to be coming home."

Rachel's lips puckered as sadness clouded her face. "James isn't excited about anything these days. He's downright mad. Like a bull that's been teased."

Haley bit her lower lip, not wanting to point to the elephant in the room. James was having trouble dealing with his paralysis. The doctors did not completely rule out the chance that he would regain the use of his legs, but they had hoped for more progress at this point.

"James came away from the accident with an injury the rest of us did not suffer," Dylan said. "I'm sure you can understand his anger over his loss."

"But the bishop says it's Gott's will," Rachel insisted. "It's not ours to question."

"And we won't go against the bishop in this room," Dylan said. "That's not what we're about. We're here to be constructive, not destructive. I hope that James will join our sessions after he returns home. I'm heading over to the rehab center to see him tonight. I'll try to help him arrange some transportation to get him to our sessions if he's interested. Right now he needs to be in a wheelchair. That's the reality."

"But I pray that Gott will let him walk again," Elsie said. Sweet, ever-hopeful Elsie.

"We'll all pray for him," George offered.

Rachel nodded. "I'll tell him that."

"James is going through a difficult time," Dylan said. "After the physical and emotional trauma he's gone through, that's not unusual. Everyone here survived a traumatic accident that has the potential to leave lasting emotional scars. You're here because you want to recover. And the guided imagery exercise that we'll finish with is a powerful tool for alleviating that suffering."

"I've got something good to report." The love and acceptance on their faces made Haley appreciate the rare bond in this room. "I found out this week that my nursing grade is up to an A now. Before the accident, I was in danger of failing."

"That's wonderful good," Rachel said. "But hard to believe a good nurse like you could be failing."

"That part is a long story," Haley said. "But I've always struggled in school. Dyslexia and ADD. And after high school, I didn't know what to do with myself. I tried a dozen different jobs, all failures. The thing is, I wasn't sure what to do or where I belonged; but now I know. I belong in nursing." She sighed. "After a lifetime of searching, I'm finally in the right place."

"Another account of monumental progress," Dylan said. "Wow. Some folks in this room had a very good week." He talked about the effects of trauma on family members, and extended an invitation to family or friends who were still suffering post-traumatic stress.

Ruben shifted in his chair. "Can we do the guided imagery now?"

Dylan checked his watch. "Yes, we'd better get to that before everyone has to leave." Dylan asked everyone to get comfortable in their chairs. "You may want to lean forward and rest your head and arms on the table. Let the chair and table support you gently, and then let your eyes glide closed.

"Now focus on your body. Take a full, deep breath, deep into your belly, and let the energy and comfort fill your lungs and abdomen. Then, as you breathe out, imagine that you're releasing your pain and discomfort. Let it drift out through your nose and leave your body cleansed and refreshed."

With a deep exhale, Haley imagined little barbs of tension and negative feelings rushing from the corners of her body and soaring out and rising high to blend with the deep blue of outer space, where they would not be a bother to any living thing.

Lulled by the sound of Dylan's voice, she surrendered to the warm, loving light.

29

"*F*rom above you, thick, bold white clouds part and a shaft of light shines down on you. It is God's love," Dylan said, watching the body language of the group gathered around the table with their eyes closed. Generally, in that part of the session, he called the light "gentle energy" or a "positive glow"; but as far as he knew, everyone in this group was a believer, a Christian, and so he had changed the words to speak personally to this audience.

"God's gentle light spills over your shoulders, warming and caressing you. Its glow enters your chest, illuminating your lungs and ribs, gently easing any tension around your heart."

As he spoke, his gaze paused on George, whose gray pallor and trembling hands were warning signs. The man was in crisis. As soon as the session ended, Dylan was going to make a date to visit George at home, hoping to enlist his wife's help in getting George into treatment. If the man didn't want to be treated by Dylan, they could work together to find another therapist who would take the case without charging. One way or another, Dylan was going to push George Dornbecker to get help.

The other unknown in the group was Haley. Was she a Christian? Dylan wasn't sure, but so far she had not objected to his reference to God in the guided imagery. Ordinarily, as a therapist, he would ask her about her religious orientation. However, Dylan didn't want to think of himself as her therapist.

That would preclude him from any personal involvement with her, and he wanted to be involved with her. In some ways, he already was. When he and Haley went to see James at the rehab center, when they shared a sandwich at the hospital or worked together with a patient, things clicked.

To be honest with himself, he was still working on his own issues, but he had spent years trying to lay his own ghosts to rest, and maybe it was time to man up and move on. That's what Patrick had told him in his last few sessions, and his therapist was an intuitive guy.

And since Dylan had met Haley, he really wanted to move on. For the first time since he'd lost Kris, he had found another person who brought magic into his life. Haley could light up a room with a pop of brilliant color and honesty. He liked the way she put her personal stuff aside when someone else needed her. She was a helper. He appreciated the obstacles she had overcome to get into the nursing program. He loved the sound of her laugh, and sometimes he hated the fact that they worked together. If they were just friends, he could act on his impulse and kiss her. But as long as they were working together . . . that kind of relationship would be complicated.

When she had asked him about Valentine's Day, he had wanted to laugh out loud. He'd thought of her that morning, when he'd noted the date. He'd even been tempted to send her flowers or candy . . . but he would have had to do it in secret, since they weren't a couple. And that had led him to ponder the ethics of having her in this group session. If he wanted to be her boyfriend, he could not be her therapist.

That was a mess he would have to sort out later. ·

Right now he pushed his thoughts away so that he could give his all to guiding the group through the healing exercise. Long ago he had memorized the cues for the exercise so they could spill from his tongue, but he believed it was better when he put his heart and soul into it. Although he tried to come across as warm and professional in leading this group, in truth he was nervous and deeply honored to have been chosen by God to lead them in this healing process. It was a painful blessing, as his mom used to say, because the thing that had brought them here was terrible and tragic.

Still, accepting that bad things happened to good people, he was grateful to be an agent of God's peace. A healer.

❧ 30 ❧

*R*uben pressed the blue chalk to the clean blackboard.

BENEFIT AUCTION
TO PAY MEDICAL BILLS FOR JAMES LAPP
MARCH 4TH AT ZOOK'S BARN
FINE AMISH GOODS & CRAFTS

Long ago, he had mastered writing the square block letters that everyone could read. He propped the chalkboard on an easel near the barn entrance and reached for his hat on a hook.

"I've got to get to the meeting," he told his father. "And then I'm going back to the Country Store."

His father's eyes were stern as he looked over the sign. "How much money do the Lapps need?"

"They got medical bills for almost twenty thousand dollars.

James had two surgeries, and then he had to stay in that rehab center."

Joseph Zook grunted. "That's crazy. More money than any good family could afford, but what can you do? I thank Gott every day that my family has good health."

A bitter memory stung the back of Ruben's throat, and he looked away so that his father would not see his annoyance. Their family hadn't always been blessed with good health. They'd lost Mamm and Paul, and there'd been that terrible year when Ruben had been stuck on the daybed in the kitchen. A year of blinding pain and so many setbacks.

And though the pain had faded, there were the scars . . . knots of flesh across his back and belly that made him look stout. And the limp that slowed him when he was tired. The awkward gait that sometimes made Englisher people stare and giggle..

Ya, that terrible time had forced him to turn to the angels, and he might never have discovered them without the pain. But Dat didn't know any of that.

Although Ruben didn't dwell on the pain of the past, it struck him that Dat forgot it all too easily.

His dat clapped a hand on his shoulder. "You'd better get going." In a society of waiting, Dat could not abide a person who was late. No excuse for that.

"So I'm going to tell Elsie I can stay on for another few weeks, until after the auction."

Joe tugged gently at his beard. "I reckon. But the bookkeeping is going to fall behind."

"I'll catch up on paperwork at night," Ruben promised.

He had pretended to stop in at the family's market for lunch—and he'd eaten a wurst on a roll—but really he had come to straighten a few things out with Dat. Ruben wanted to stay on at

Elsie's store, even after things were back to normal, but Dat didn't think the business could spare Ruben.

At least I got some more time out of him, Ruben thought as he threaded his way through the customers in the aisle.

Zook's barn was buzzing with conversation—chatty vendors and curious tourists. Everyone was caught up in the enduring cold of winter, trying to look forward to the thaw to come, those spring days when the pale gray sky burned blue and sad winter grass began to green. Folks spent so much time talking about the weather and crops. Ruben hadn't realized that until recently, until he had met people who dared to talk about personal matters, like their hopes and fears.

In the weeks since the accident, something had changed between Ruben and the other young people in the van. Like a group of lone trees that had grown together into a forest, a bond had formed among the young passengers.

Not so much the elders, who took their concerns to the ministers and to their own wives. But the younger folk—Rachel and Zed, even Market Joe and Lizzy—they were becoming like family to him, too. Good family.

And then there was Elsie.

Ruben knew he could count on her as a friend. His initial instinct to protect her had grown into something more, something he had never encountered before.

Working side by side with her, he had come to rely on Elsie's smile, the light in her eyes, the kind words she had for everyone. Every day with Elsie felt like Christmas Day. She was a little person, but she had a very big heart—a heart full of love.

Elsie had all the qualities that had been missing from Ruben's life, and for every moment spent basking in her light, he wanted more. He wanted to wake up with her by his side in the morning, to sit with her for breakfast, lunch, and dinner. And right now, the only way he knew to stay close to her was to keep helping her out at the Country Store.

As he walked down Halfway's Main Street, he whistled a song.

It used to be that Ruben sprang pranks on people who tried to get too close. People who looked too long at him, or those who gossiped about him behind his back, as if he didn't hear the words that could cut him to ribbons.

But he hadn't pulled any lousy pranks since the accident. Oh, his sense of humor was still intact, but he hadn't felt the need to push anyone away. These sessions were turning him inside out, in a good way.

☙❧

"I shouldn't have been in that van," Rachel said. "I know it's done, and I can't change what happened, but the bad thoughts keep going through my head. I shouldn't have gone to the city at all. I was only there to make a deal with a gallery to sell my paintings. So selfish of me."

"I wouldn't call that selfish," Dylan said. "And you weren't violating any rules. George had room in the van, and you paid for your seat, like everyone else."

"But I didn't have to go," Rachel said. "Don't you see? If I had stayed home, maybe James would have been just fine." She pointed toward the door. "He'd be walking around out there in his family's orchard, hauling things around and singing to himself and . . ." Her voice failed her, and she pressed a fist to her mouth.

It hurt Ruben to see her in such a dark place, blaming herself.

"Dear Rachel." Elsie reached over and took her hand. "It's not your fault. What happened to James was terrible, but it's Gott's will."

Rachel shook her head, tears glittering in her eyes. "It was my fault, and I don't know how to stop thinking about it. I don't think I'll ever get over this. It will never end."

For the second time that day, Ruben pictured himself on the daybed in the kitchen. His six-year-old self, moaning in anguish. Alone and desperate for relief.

"I thought it would never end," he said aloud.

"What was that?" Dylan asked.

When Ruben looked up, everyone was watching him. Everyone except Rachel, who whimpered into a handkerchief.

"I didn't mean to say that out loud." Ruben rubbed his chin.

"That's okay." Dylan held his hand out, palm up. "Tell us more. If you've had a similar experience, it might help Rachel to hear about it."

Ruben let his eyes sweep round the table, afraid of the disapproval that he encountered so often.

Instead, he saw understanding. Compassion. Sorrow. These folks had been through a lot with him. They didn't care that his father had given up farming for a more profitable trade.

"I was thinking of something that happened to me when I was a boy. A terrible thing. I was in pain for a long time, and I wanted to give up. I thought it would never end."

"So you were experiencing feelings similar to what Rachel is going through now." Dylan's eyes tracked Ruben, as if he were a deer in the forest. "But it did end, didn't it. The pain ended."

"It did."

"How did you cope? Was it your faith that got you through those difficult times?"

"It was my faith . . . in a funny sort of way."

Dylan nodded encouragingly, and the others watched expectantly. Even Zed had uncrossed his arms and leaned in toward the table.

Ruben took a deep breath and sighed. He didn't want to give

voice to the miracle, but right now Rachel needed a miracle of her own. "Don't laugh," he said. "It's angels who help me get through."

Silence filled the room, soft and respectful.

Elsie's eyes were round as quarters, full of awe and wonder.

"It's not that I'm saying I'm blessed more than anyone else. It's just that, when I was a boy, I was in a terrible accident. That was when the angels started coming."

Dylan pushed back the sleeves of his sweater. "Please . . . tell us more."

Ruben shifted in his chair. He didn't like talking about himself, but he wasn't afraid of the people here at the table. "Some of you know about what happened to me when I was a young boy. It was a terrible thing that left scars, inside and out. I was in physical pain, and after it happened many people thought it was my fault. Ya, I was just a kid, but around here a good Amish boy knows his way around a plow. I wasn't experienced, and sometimes when things go wrong folks are quick to pin the blame."

Zed swallowed hard, his eyes softening. Rachel and Elsie watched him quietly. He knew they had heard the story.

"It was back in the days when my father was still farming the land. Everyone in the family worked at it one way or another. Dat didn't have a love for farming in his heart, but he was born into it like his brother, and so that was what they did. One day, I was out helping my uncle. He was going to let me steer the plow, and I was pretty happy about that. I was six years old, and I wanted to show that I could do a man's work."

Ruben paused as he slid into that sunny spring day. He remembered the sheer joy of being able to ride the plow with Paul. It was a bumpy ride, but his uncle made a joke of it, just as he did of every small problem. Always joking. Paul was telling a funny story and Ruben was looking down, watching the ground pass below them: rich, dark dirt unearthed by the blade of the plow.

"I looked up, and Paul was swatting at the air and . . . I thought someone had sprinkled pepper on us. The air was thick with black specks. Paul got frantic, slapping at his neck and arms. And then there was a burning on my neck, and I realized it was bees in the air. We had plowed through a nest of bees." The fear of that moment was a fist in his gut.

"Ach!" Rachel balled the handkerchief up in her hands. "What a terrible thing!"

Ruben closed his eyes a moment, imagining Paul here beside him, Paul smiling and clapping him on the back. Paul telling him to let the bad memory go.

"Are you allergic to bees?" Haley asked.

"I'm not allergic, but it turned out Paul was. He lost control of the plow and it went off-track. I think the horses panicked, and we both fell off and got run over by the equipment."

"Was Paul okay?" Elsie asked, the pure love in her eyes causing his throat to grow thick. She was too young to know the details.

Ruben shook his head. "He died. Between his allergic reaction and a bump on the head, it killed him."

Had he ever spoken these words aloud? Ruben didn't think so. He didn't know that he had the courage to tell his story, but now that he had started the words flowed like an endless river.

"I woke up in a hospital, all stitched up across my belly and my back and my leg. The doctors thought it was a miracle that I didn't get killed, too. But there were problems, serious infections. The wounds were painful and they kept me in bed for a whole year. At one point, I thought I'd never get out and see the blue sky again." Ruben pressed his eyes closed, as Paul's voice whispered in his ear.

You're fine now. That bad spell is over.

That was Paul; vigilant, always by his side.

"I'm fine now, but back then . . . then I was in pain all the time. I couldn't sleep, and when I did, my dreams took me to a dark, terrible place. The doctors said I would be fine again, but the recovery was so slow. It didn't seem to be getting any better, and I couldn't take it. I wanted to get away from myself. I felt like I had lost myself. I started praying that Gott would take me to be with Paul, and then, sort of blurry-eyed and tired, I imagined that Paul was coming to me. He seemed to be there, right by my side, kind and good. He protected me and helped me look away from the pain. I was six. I thought he was an angel."

"An angel." Elsie smiled. "Praise be to Gott!"

"That's beautiful," Haley said. "It gives me goose bumps."

"Do you still see Paul?" Rachel asked. "Does he still visit you?"

"He does. Along with other angels. Some of them, I can't see their faces, but I know they visit. I feel them beside me, patting my back. Some of them are people I knew. My doddy. A dog we used to have named Booboo. A boy I met at the hospital who had cancer."

"And after these angels visit you, do you feel better?" Dylan asked.

"I do. They bring me comfort, but it's not always easy. I used to cry with them. All the sadness wells up inside me and . . ." Ruben felt that familiar sorrow burn the back of his throat. "The angels surround me with comfort and I cry. Then, I feel better."

"Light is most precious when it comes after darkness." The old proverb was probably the first thing Zed had said all day, but he hit the nail on the head.

"That's right." Ruben looked around at the folks he had come to care about. "We've all learned that, haven't we?" He looked directly at Rachel. Was she ready to let herself step out of the pool of misery?

Silently, Rachel nodded.

"This would be a good time for our guided imagery exercise," Dylan said in his authoritative but calm "therapist" voice. "Today, we'll focus on healing, both in body and soul. Healing from physical wounds, and healing a broken heart." As Dylan helped them relax, one muscle at a time, Ruben felt a flash of insecurity. Had he just admitted that he cried with angels? He had told the girls that he cried. That alone was something no self-respecting man would admit. But, well, it was out now, and his friends seemed to understand.

Rachel seemed to have calmed down, at least for now.

Ruben hoped that his angel story had helped.

It was a good thing, said a familiar voice. Paul? Or his doddy? Or simply his conscience? Ruben wasn't sure, but it didn't matter. He settled into the chair and fell into Dr. Monroe's tale of being guided through a tunnel of golden light by friends, angels, teachers, favorite animals, loved ones who had passed.

🐝 31 🐝

"This will look so perfect in my house." The customer wearing the necklace of brightly colored stones chatted as Elsie began to wrap the wooden baby cradle. "It's an old Victorian, and there's a nook beside the stairs that's just crying out for something like this."

Elsie wondered what a crying nook would sound like. She thought to make a joke, but simply smiled as she kept wrapping the item.

"I think I might put one of those fake fat candles beside it." The customer—Gwen Slavin, from the check she had written—didn't seem to care at all about the cradle's high price. "You know those fake candles that run on batteries? That'll be quaint, don't you think?"

"Ya." Elsie nodded for Ruben to lift the cradle so that she could properly wrap it. Her hand brushed his as she slid bubble wrap under the runners, and she smiled to herself at the tingle of warmth that passed between them. Ruben was such a big help. She was grateful his father had said that he could spare him from managing Zook's barn until the busy season came in the late spring.

She glanced up at him, admiring his square jaw, his wide and thoughtful eyes. But then he caught her looking and she lowered her head once again. Whenever their eyes met, she was sure he could see what she was feeling, and she wasn't ready to share that. Truth be told, she wanted him here because she wanted to be near him. His daily presence filled her heart with laughter, and there was nothing like his honesty.

And at last week's session, when he had told the group about his angels, that was the moment. That was when Elsie knew there was no one in the world quite as wonderful as Ruben Zook.

"You must think I'm verhuddelt," he had said after last week's counseling session. "A grown man, talking about angels."

"Your story took my breath away," Elsie had told him. "It's such a beautiful thing, Ruben, having angels to comfort you. Gott has truly blessed you."

"I'm thankful for it—but I don't want anyone thinking that I'm special. I wasn't bragging about it."

She had assured him that no one thought he was bragging, and the conversation had fallen off. But in her mind, she was thrilled to imagine Ruben and the angels. In some ways her heart ached to think of six-year-old Ruben, so alone and in such pain! But then Gott in His Mercy had sent Ruben the comfort he'd needed. It was nothing short of a miracle.

"There we go," Elsie said as she finished wrapping the wooden cradle. "That should keep anything from scratching it on the way home."

"And there's a card taped to the bottom of the cradle," Ruben added. "It tells you a little about Adam King, the Amish man who made it."

"Perfect. You have a delightful shop, Elsie. I know I haven't been here before, but it seems so familiar."

"Maybe you're thinking of another country store. There are many in Lancaster County."

"Oh, sure, but there's something about yours . . . I don't know."

Elsie had to tamp down the surge of delight over Gwen's comments. She didn't want to be proud, and she wasn't taking credit for the store's success. The truth was, with Halfway right smack between Lancaster and Philadelphia, in the heart of Amish country, it was a great location for a store with Amish goods. She had always thought of the town as a sort of crossroads for the Amish, but since the accident she had come to see that their little town was a crossroads for Englishers, too.

"Halfway is a good location for our shop," Elsie said. "And whether you choose to go north, south, east, or west from here, I say a prayer that Gott will bless each person who passes through here."

Gwen smiled. "That's such a lovely sentiment."

The bells at the shop door jangled and Haley came in, dressed in her nursing scrubs and clogs. "Long time, no see," she joked. Ruben and Elsie had seen her thirty minutes ago at a counseling session down the street. "I hope you don't mind. Got some time to kill before I head over to the hospital."

"You're always welcome here." It wasn't unusual for Haley to hang around the store. In the month or so since the accident, Elsie had gotten attached to the Englisher girl who spoke her mind and always seemed on the lookout to help other folks.

"Are you a doctor?" the customer asked.

"Just a nursing student. But I live right outside Halfway."

Gwen Slavin looked from Haley to Elsie to Ruben. "Wait a minute. Are you the nursing student in the newspaper? The one who came across the accident on the highway a while back?"

"That was me," Haley answered slowly.

Elsie licked her suddenly dry lips.

"And you're Elsie Lapp and . . ." She covered her mouth with one hand. "You were in the van. Of course! That's why the name of your store rings a bell. I read all about it. I'm so sorry. It must be hard for you. I wouldn't have brought it up, except that I just pieced it all together right now."

"It's okay," Elsie said softly. "It doesn't bother me to talk about it so much anymore." For that, she was grateful to Dylan Monroe. Counseling had taken the sharp edge from the terrible memories of the crash, allowing her to talk about it without breaking into tears. The crash and losing Dat . . . it still hurt her to remember that difficult time.

These days Elsie's heart ached more for the losses that clung to their lives. James stuck in a wheelchair. Rachel suffering from guilt. Fanny about to have a baby that would never know their father. Dear Fanny, so strong on the outside, but delicate as a rose on the inside.

Gwen pressed a hand to her chest. "I am sorry."

"No reason to be," Elsie said. "Everyone has some healing to do; it's a part of life."

"You're a sweet young lady, and I'm happy to have met you and found your shop. I'm sure I'll be sending my friends here. The town is really charming, but what an odd name. How did that happen?"

"I've always wondered about that, too," Haley agreed.

Elsie looked up at Ruben, whose blue eyes twinkled. "Do you want to tell them?"

"No one knows for sure, but my family's marketplace—you know Zook's barn?" When Gwen nodded, Ruben went on. "That was built many, many years ago by a man named Jeremiah Stoltzfus. Jeremiah lived in a settlement in Christiana, but he had brothers he was always visiting in Strasburg. Being Amish, he was always traveling to Strasburg by horse and buggy, and that's a very long trip. Jeremiah got tired of so much traveling. So one day, he bought some land halfway between Christiana and Strasburg. He built a house and a barn, and other people started building and it became a town. And that's how Halfway got its name."

"Fascinating." Gwen put her checkbook away in her purse. "Well, I guess that's it for me. Unless you want to sell me that beautiful box in the window."

"The box with the cherries painted on it?" Haley asked. "I like that one, too."

"But it's a family treasure, made by my great-great-grandmother in 1933." Elsie recalled how her dat had told Caleb and Emma and her that it was something to pass down to the next generation. "I want to keep it in our family."

"I can understand that." Gwen tapped the check on the counter. "But you've got my phone number. Promise me you'll call me first if you decide to sell."

"Ya. I promise." But she knew that day would never come.

While Ruben carried the cradle out to Gwen's car, Haley moved closer to the sales counter.

"Now that we're alone, I wanted to ask you about Dylan's suggestion today," Haley said. "About Graciana."

At today's session, Dylan had told the group that he wanted to invite Graciana Estevez to join in future sessions. He knew it might be difficult, but he thought that in the end it could help everyone heal, including Graciana.

"What is it?"

"Is it really okay with you if she attends a meeting? I mean, I know everyone said yes, that all is forgiven, but you lost more than anyone in our group. If it would bother you in the least, I'll talk to Dylan about calling it off. He could say it didn't work with her schedule or whatever."

Running a feather duster over one of the shelves, Elsie tried to measure the reaction deep inside her. "When I think of Graciana, I remember the love in her eyes when she talked about her daughter. And then the sorrow . . . the pain of losing Clara."

Haley nodded. "I'll never forget that. When she said the angels came to carry Clara to heaven."

"It was so very sad. And that's my feeling for Graciana. Sorrow and sympathy."

"Really?" Haley put one hand on her hip and cocked her head to the side. "It doesn't bother you that her daughter made a stupid mistake that killed two people and put one in a wheelchair? Because I can go there, too."

"I have no bad feelings for Graciana," Elsie said firmly.

"Okay, good. Just wanted to make sure that was the case." Haley squinted at her. "Because you're way too nice to say anything hurtful. I just want to make sure someone's watching out for you."

"There is always someone watching over me." Elsie was thinking of the Almighty Father and His angels when the bells jangled and Ruben came in the door.

Haley looked toward the door, then leaned forward to whisper, "That's right; you have Ruben. And that stuff you said about just being friends? You're not slipping that one past me."

Elsie squinted up at her. "What do you mean?"

"Gotta go!" Haley raised one hand in a wave. "Bye, guys. Catch you next week."

She blew out of the store like a winter wind, leaving Elsie to wonder just what folks were thinking about Ruben and her.

"We got a customer for life, I think," Ruben said.

Elsie had to admit she liked the way he said "we." Ruben had slipped into her routine in the store so smoothly, the way that winter slowly melted into spring.

He came closer and then stopped at the display of baby items and rearranged the two remaining cradles to fill the space. "Gwen Slavin said she'll be back with all her friends."

"I hope you'll still be working here when she returns."

"I'm going to have to talk Dat into getting one of my brothers to manage the summer market." He folded his arms across his chest, casually smiling. "Who would have thought I'd be so good at working for the competition?"

"We don't really compete with the market," Elsie said, moving the feather duster over jars of pie filling that had been put up by Annie Stoltzfus. "But it would be great if you could stay on here."

"I know it started off with me helping you out and all." Ruben paused. "But now I'm thinking I'm more than just a helper."

"Of course you are!" She looked up at him. When he looked at her that way, his eyes were as blue as the sky.

"Good. I was thinking I would come by your house on Saturday night?"

Saturday night? Elsie couldn't imagine what was going on that night . . . and then it dawned on her. That was the night when a young man visited after dark to see his girl.

He wanted to court her.

Her palms felt suddenly moist and her heart was beating in double time. How odd to be a bundle of joy and disappointment at the same time! Of course, she had become accustomed to having Ruben by her side. She couldn't imagine this little shop without him humming in the background, joking with customers, helping with all the heavy lifting and inventory. Over the past weeks he had become like a kind brother to her. Well, maybe more than a brother. There was something different about the excitement buzzing in her chest like a hummingbird at the sight of his towering form waiting at the shop door each morning. And the times in the store when she and Ruben accidentally brushed past each other or touched as they handed something off. . . . Oh! She had to admit that a certain excitement swirled between them.

But she couldn't let him court her. She couldn't let anything come of their relationship.

"I'll flash a light on your bedroom window, and you'll let me in," Ruben was saying.

Elsie pulled herself clear of her cascading thoughts. "How do you know which window is mine?" she asked.

He gave a laugh. "I know. Are you a heavy sleeper? I don't want to have to chuck any stones up there to wake you."

"Ruben . . ." She paused to compose a careful explanation of why his plan was not a good idea. In that moment, the bells at the door gave a merry jingle and they both turned to see a line of customers streaming in from a van parked in front of the shop window.

This was not a good time. For all his jokes and pranks, she knew that Ruben was not so calloused inside. He had shown her a tenderness in his heart that most folks never got to see, and right now, she didn't dare wound him.

"I am a heavy sleeper," she said quickly as a customer approached the counter. "But for you, I'll stay awake."

His smile melted her heart. He really was a good man. Just not for her.

೦ಞ 32 ೩೦

"What's with the van? What happened to your sporty car?" Haley asked. Usually Dylan drove a Volkswagen Jetta, but today he had picked her up in a red minivan, which he handled like a bus driver. She loved the manly way he kept the steering wheel low to his lap as he steered through brown winter fields. In his plaid shirt and jeans, he was handsome and accessible. It would be so easy to reach out and touch the soft flannel of his sleeve.

"This thing is a loaner," he said, bringing her back to the conversation. "James Lapp needed a way to get around."

Haley smoothed one hand over the gleaming dashboard. "Someone keeps their van in good shape." Her eyes flicked over to a sticker in the corner of the window. HERTZ. What? He had rented the van.

"Oh, I get it," she said. "Your friend Hertz likes to keep his van clean."

"What are you, a detective?"

"I have eyes, Dr. Monroe."

"Okay, you caught me. But I got a great rate for a monthly rental, and you and I know the Lapp family is already into the hospital for nearly twenty grand. They needed a little help, and I was in a position to give it. But I'd appreciate it if you don't mention anything to the family."

"It's very generous of you. I mean, you're really going out of your way for a family you didn't even know two months ago."

"Don't be so quick to put me on a pedestal, because I'm getting something out of it, too. It's my opportunity to become involved with the Amish community."

"I won't say a word." His modesty and kindness struck a chord deep inside her. Every time she was with Dylan, she liked him more. Actually, "like" was a lame word for the emotions coursing through her. Somewhere along the way she had fallen in love with him. She knew he cared for her, too, but she could tell that he was holding back, and she wasn't sure why.

She stared ahead at the gray buggy they were approaching and ran her hand along the seat belt. "I'm a little nervous about this." Today was her first physical therapy session with James Lapp, and she was a little worried about what to expect. "How is James doing?" she asked. "Any better? The last time I visited him in the rehab center with Rachel, he was withdrawn and uncommunicative."

"I'd say his mental state is about the same. As the oldest son, James is expecting to take over the family farm, which is really a series of orchards. I've heard that many of the apples, peaches, and cherries in this area come from the Lapp farm. Anyway, James feels the pressure to get back on his feet and back to work. The Amish aren't materialistic people, but I think he feels as if he's losing everything he's spent his life working for."

"And there's still no word from the doctors whether he will be able to walk again." It wasn't really a question; as part of his physical therapy team, Haley had been fully updated on his medical condition.

"He's struggling with that," Dylan said. "I think he would be more accepting if the doctors told him it was physically impossible. But as it is, I see James trying to push himself to make it happen, and so far, it's not working. Add to that the advice of Bishop Samuel, who keeps telling James to accept his handicap as God's will."

One of the fields they passed had rows of bare trees—apple or peach? She wasn't sure. The narrow lanes between trees seemed to open and close quickly as they passed.

Dylan's hands slid easily over the steering wheel. Blue jeans and flannel really suited him, she thought. In that getup, she could imagine him out chopping wood, roping a calf, or snuggling by the fire.

Whoa, girl. That fantasy was going way too far.

She let her hand glide over the edge of her seat belt, floating back down to the seat. "Thanks for making this whole thing happen."

"I'm glad you were interested. The other nursing students weren't exactly chomping at the bit to get the position."

Haley held back a grin as she turned toward the window. The other nursing students had been chomping at the bit to work side by side with Dr. Dreamy, but when they had heard the words "Amish" and "farm," the allure had fizzled.

Dylan had gone to Dr. Swanson requesting a nursing student to work with him in a home healthcare capacity, and once she heard about the situation with James Lapp, Swanson rattled some cages to make the program come together quickly. Most of the nursing students rolled their eyes at the prospect of patient care at an Amish farm, but Haley had a personal tie to James, albeit slight, and somehow every time she worked with someone who had been in the accident, it lightened the trauma in her mind.

Another mile or so down the road, Dylan turned down the lane to a two-story house set away from a barn with two silos and a cluster of smaller buildings.

The Lapp farm.

The house was tidy from the outside, but certainly plain, painted white with no shutters. Smoke rose from the chimney, and the front door opened as soon as Dylan parked beside a gray horseless buggy.

"You met James's mother, Edna?" he asked.

"Briefly. She's the person who will oversee his PT."

With that, he was out of the car, calling a greeting to Edna and introducing Haley.

The Amish woman with tawny brown hair and a wriggly scar on her chin welcomed Haley and directed them both into the back room, where James sat in his wheelchair.

"I brought you someone new," Dylan announced. "And she comes with her own brand of torture called physical therapy."

Haley bumped Dylan on the shoulder, trying to keep things playful. "That's no way to introduce me. Really, James, I'm here to help."

James nodded, his face expressionless but his gaze lifting to her face.

Haley sat on the neatly made bed so that she could be level with James. "I'm not a licensed physical therapist, but I know you were drilled on your exercises in the hospital."

"That's right," Edna chimed in from the doorway. "And they taught me the routine, too."

"Perfect. So that will make my job really easy. I'll mostly be watching to make sure you're doing the exercises properly, and over the next few weeks we may introduce some more challenging things once you master your routine."

James rubbed his clean-shaven chin with the knuckles of one hand. "More challenging. Like walking?"

"Don't go putting the cart before the horse," Edna warned her son.

Haley threw up her hands. "Who knows? That would be great, wouldn't it?"

James's expression was flat as he bounced his fists on his thighs. "Did they tell you I have some feeling in my legs?"

"So I've been told," Haley said. "But we're not going to work on walking so soon. As I understand it, there's still some healing going on in your spine. We don't want to jeopardize that. Now, I see you're dressed and you've made the transfer from the bed to the wheelchair. Did you do that alone?"

"He did it all," Edna said. "He probably would have cooked his own eggs if he knew how."

"Wow. They told me you were a hard worker in occupational therapy. Looks like you're going to make my job really easy."

Although Haley's praise did nothing to melt the wall of indifference surrounding James, she maintained a positive attitude as she directed him to start his daily exercises. Technically, Haley's task wasn't difficult, and Edna and Verena, James's sister, were attentive students. It was James who concerned her. Despite the many little jokes she added or stories she told about herself, James's demeanor remained flat. When she asked questions, his answers were terse, though never impolite.

As the exercises were winding down, she glanced over at Dylan, who had been standing off to the side, observing and occasionally joining in the conversation. She wondered if he had used guided imagery with James, but there was no way she could ask here in the Lapp home. Besides, maybe that therapy didn't work with everyone. Maybe it didn't work with depression, which was what James seemed to be suffering.

As she finished, Edna and Verena summoned her to the main room to have a hot drink while Dr. Monroe worked with James.

The baking smells made the kitchen cozy, but the desperate plea in James's eyes haunted her as she sat on a bench at the kitchen table. James was reaching out to her without words. And his message?

Help me.

∞ 33 ∞

$\mathcal{H}$aley traced a cheerful daisy in the vinyl tablecloth and took in the comfortable great room off the kitchen. The linoleum floor was shiny and clean, and there was a tidiness that made the home comforting. Everything had its place. A wide butcher-block counter separated the kitchen from the living area, where three easy chairs sat under an embroidered cross surrounded by words. Haley squinted to make out the saying done in blue thread:

> Now I lay me down to sleep.
> I pray thee, Lord, my soul to keep.

It was the bedtime prayer she had learned as a child.

A warm glow emanated from a freestanding stove between the kitchen and great room, and the sweet smell of baking bread filled the air. Why had she been worried about coming here? It was yet another lesson in the universal qualities all humans shared. An Amish home was simply a home.

Over at the kitchen counter, Edna took the kettle off the stove.

"Here's your tea." Edna brought over a steaming mug. "Do you take milk or sugar?"

"Milk and one sugar, please."

When Verena returned, there were roses on her cheeks as she placed a bin near the freestanding stove. She was a quiet girl of twelve or thirteen, with creamy white skin and hair the color of tobacco. "The coal in the cellar is getting low. When's the next delivery?"

"We'll wait till after the auction for it," Edna called from the counter. "It's been mighty expensive this year. All the prices seem to have gone up."

"No kidding," Haley said, hoping to make conversation. "I can barely afford to breathe these days."

Verena squinted at Haley, then began to smile as she opened the stove. "I never thought to be grateful for air."

"Ya," Edna chimed in. "The Almighty gives the air around us for free."

Watching Verena add more coal to the stove, Haley wondered if the Lapps had suspended their coal delivery because of their medical bills. Was Verena putting extra coal in the stove to keep the house warm for her? She hoped that she wasn't causing the family any inconvenience.

"How are the plans for the auction going?" Haley asked. She had heard talk of the fund-raiser from the others at group therapy.

"Gut. We're not in charge, but two young women in our church, Mary Beiler and Remy King, are putting it all together. They've been doing quilting bees, hoping to make three quilts. Lots of folks have donated things. And Dr. Monroe talked to some doctors at the hospital, and they're donating, too. Can you imagine that? Most of them have never even met our James."

"That's very generous." Haley knew that most doctors had disposable income, but it was Dylan's lobbying that had gotten them on board.

Edna opened the stove and peeked inside. "Verena. Kumm, and I'll show you how to check the bread." She slipped on oven mitts and pulled out a rack.

The sight and smell of three golden loaves made Haley's mouth water. "That's a lot of bread."

"It goes fast when you have a family our size," Edna said. "We'll probably go through two loaves tonight."

"There's ten of us," Verena offered. "And some nights Mammi and Doddy come for dinner."

"That's quite a crew."

"Now get a little closer and tap the bread," Edna instructed. "Just tap it with the tip of your finger. Hear that? When you hear that hollow sound, it's done with baking."

"Can I take them out?" Verena asked.

Edna handed over the oven mitts. "Ya, but mind you don't get burned."

Watching them, Haley recalled her own adventures in baking with her older sisters. There was the time her sister Jessie had mismeasured the salt, making a batch of inedible oatmeal cookies. And no one in the family would let Haley forget the time she had cracked open a half pound of chocolate chips, sending them rolling and scurrying over the floor, under stools, behind the fridge, and through the slats of the floor vent. As the baby of the family, Haley had gained a reputation as chief mischief-maker, though she'd never tried to be so notorious.

"The kitchen always smells good after you bake bread, Mamm."

Verena set the third pan on the rack to cool, then slipped off the mitts.

"It does smell wonderful," Haley said, still thinking of her siblings.

"Verena will cut you a slice, soon as it sets up."

"Thank you. Is James particularly close with any of his siblings? He has brothers close in age, right?"

"Peter and Luke. They're twins, a year younger than James."

Just then there was a knock on the door, and Verena went off to answer it.

"I was wondering if one of your other sons might want to learn James's exercise routine, so they could help him," Haley suggested. "That would give you a break, Edna."

The Amish woman's lips were pursed as she slid one of the pans of bread onto the stove burners. "I don't think so. Peter and Luke are needed out in the orchards, especially now that James can't work."

Animated voices flowed from the main room, and Haley turned to see two young Amish women shuffling a pair of small children through the door.

"We won't stay long." The woman with dark brown hair carried a covered dish into the kitchen and placed it on the counter. "That's a casserole for your dinner. Remy has another so you don't have to stretch it out. Saves you two nights of cooking, though I see you've been baking."

"Denki, Mary."

"Something smells good, and I'm hungry." The boy looked eagerly around the kitchen for signs of baking. He seemed to be five or six, and Haley thought he looked adorable in a mini version of the Amish dress she'd seen on the men: black pants, suspenders, blue shirt, and a black wide-brimmed hat.

"Such an appetite!" Mary took off the boy's hat and handed it to him. "Didn't you just eat, Sam?"

Sam shrugged. "But I wasn't so hungry then."

"Verena and I just made some bread. Sit and have some tea."

"Tea would be perfect," said the woman with fiery red hair. She placed a second casserole dish on the counter and helped the little girl shrug out of her coat. "You can warm up by the stove, Katie. It's so cold out there, I'm surprised that my mouth isn't frozen shut."

Verena paused, kettle in hand. "I don't think that can really happen."

"I hope not." The women chuckled, and Edna nodded at Haley. "This here's Haley. She came to help James with his physical therapy."

The young women murmured a greeting as Edna introduced Mary Beiler and Remy King, the two auction organizers. Haley felt warmed by their approval and appreciation for what she was doing.

"It's good of you to come out and help James," Mary said as she laid her coat on a rocking chair and took a seat on the bench opposite Haley. She had wise brown eyes that matched her dark hair.

"I'm just glad that he can have home healthcare now." Remy had a professional demeanor about her that belied her Amish clothing and white kapp. "All that time in the rehab facility had to be lonely for a guy who'd never spent even a week away from home."

"That's a good point," Haley agreed. "When you're not feeling well, there's no place like home."

Everyone took a place at the table, where Verena served tea and Edna put out slices of fresh-baked bread with butter, honey, and jam. A certain coziness surrounded them, with the fragrance of baking and the warmth of the glowing stove. Haley sensed contentment here, and she felt honored to be included in this little gathering.

"Now, mind you don't ruin your appetite," Edna told the children.

"I can eat and eat and eat some more," Sam said. "I'm always hungry."

The women laughed.

"But it's true," Remy said, with a fond look at the boy. "I think he's going through a growth spurt."

Haley learned through conversation that Remy was an Englisher who had joined the Anabaptist Church and married an Amish man. That was an unusual twist, and it certainly explained the shock of red hair that stood out under her kapp.

"I didn't know that a person could marry into the Amish faith," Haley said, giving voice to her thoughts.

"It's hardly ever done," Mary explained.

"The bishop did discourage me for a while." Remy held her mug aloft, her green eyes thoughtful. "The Amish are not looking for people to join the faith. I guess I was the anomaly."

What had it been like for Remy to have a faith so strong that she would give up all the conveniences of modern life—cell phones and dishwashers and cars—to become Amish?

"I hope I don't sound nosy," Haley said. "But what drove you to do what you did? Was it a matter of faith?"

Remy wiped a dab of milk from the table in front of Katie. "I'll admit, it was love that first hooked me. I fell for my husband, Adam, but I fell in love with his family, too."

"Which is a very good thing, because Adam came with a large family. Eleven of us in all," Mary said.

"But in the end, it all boiled down to faith. I had to do some soul-searching to be sure it was the right choice for me." Remy recalled how she had met with the bishop, who had told her that if she got baptized, there was no going back. He said that joining the Anabaptist Church was not like having an ice-cream cone. "He told me that I couldn't make vanilla my favorite one month and then move on to chocolate or strawberry." Remy smiled. "That conversation still sticks with me. I told him: 'Vanilla it is,' and we laughed. So now I'm vanilla for life."

Although the women chuckled, Haley was intrigued by a certain reverence in what Remy was saying. It made her take a look inward at her own faith, meager though it was. She believed in God and she attended a Christian church. She had taught Sunday school and always hoped to go on a ministry overseas, but that was motivated more by the desire to travel than by faith.

So where did she stand with God?

She believed in Him. Definitely. But beyond that . . . was she chocolate or vanilla or chocolate chip cookie dough? She didn't have a clue.

Together, Remy and her new husband, Adam, were raising his siblings, of whom Sam and Katie were the youngest. Haley had to keep herself from staring as Remy talked about putting together the charity auction. It was odd to hear a young woman in Amish apparel sounding a bit like a Madison Avenue ad executive.

As the women talked, the underlying love and support came through clearly. Haley looked toward the door, wondering if James was aware of all the people banding together out of concern for him. Did he notice?

☙❧

That afternoon, as Dylan drove her home, Haley asked how James's treatment was progressing. "I know you can't tell me specifics, with doctor-patient confidentiality and everything. It's just that I feel like he was reaching out to me. He feels trapped, doesn't he?"

"You've got that part right."

"Did you try the guided imagery with him . . . or are you allowed to tell me?"

"I can tell you that it doesn't work in every case. Some patients are not receptive to it. There needs to be a certain level of trust between the therapist and patient."

"And you're not there with James yet." There was no mistaking James's desire to withdraw; the lack of eye contact and conversation was evidence of his emotional distance.

Dylan gave her a quick look. "You're pretty insightful for a nursing student."

"Yeah, well, I'm a little older than the norm. Older and wiser."

"Gimme a break. You're a creaky old twenty-two."

"Sometimes I feel like I'm a hundred and three." The warm interior of the car held a certain intimacy. She had slipped off her clogs and sat with one leg folded under her. "Especially when I see a young man stuck in a wheelchair with little hope of ever walking again."

"This job you chose, it's not always pretty."

"I know that. But it's the only job for me." She looked up and realized that they were at the curb outside her parents' house. "Do you want to come in?" she asked, not ready to lose his company.

"I should go. We both have things to do. But I wanted to thank you for taking on James. His family appreciates your help, and I'm glad we'll be working together."

"Me, too." She removed her seat belt, leaned toward him, and squeezed his lower arm. "Flannel works for you. Maybe you should go casual at the hospital."

"Maybe."

Her fingers were still grazing his arm, and she realized she'd broken through that wall by touching him. Now they were connected, intimately attached. Her face was inches from his, so close she could see a tiny scar on his chin. She reached up and pressed her fingertip to the small half-moon.

"You have a scar," she said softly.

"I have a lot of scars. That's one of the few you can see."

"I can make it better." Her finger slipped away and she leaned closer to place a kiss on his chin. "See?"

He tipped his face down and suddenly the air between them sparked with electricity as she pressed her lips against his.

The kiss made her pulse thrum happily, a murmur of pleasure that surged from head to toe. She shifted and reached out to him, finding support in soft flannel and strong shoulders. When the kiss deepened, she opened her lips to his gentle pressure. He tasted of coffee and mint gum, bitter and sweet, and she sighed against him, warmed by comfort and joy.

"Mmm." He ended the kiss, and they both took a breath. "You do have a gift for healing."

"Are you sure you don't want to come in?" she offered. "I think my dad is here. We could watch a game with him." Haley did not want to let him go.

"Maybe next time."

"Okay." She leaned back. "I'll let you put me off again. But I want you to know that I'm on to you."

"Really? So I guess you're familiar with those bad clichés about not fishing off the company pier? Don't get your honey where you get your money."

She winced. "That sounds like something teenage boys would laugh about in a locker room."

"Still . . . we work together. I'm in a position of authority over you."

"Hold on, there. You're not my boss."

"No, but . . . I am a good deal older than you. And I'm a loner. A hermit. You wouldn't like me if you really got to know me."

She pressed her lips together and took a deep breath. "I see where this is going. You're going to make a million excuses and I'm going to knock them all down."

"I just don't think it's a good idea."

"I hear you, but . . . I don't agree." Her hand lingered on the door handle. "And I'm not going to take it personally, because I know there's something between us. You just haven't admitted it yet." She hoped that her voice sounded confident, unlike the quivering in her soul. She opened the door to the bracing cold. "Call me when you decide to come back to the human race."

She stormed into the house. Half an hour later, while crying in the shower, she pressed a fingertip to her swollen lips and wondered about Dylan's scars. Who had hurt him so much that he had closed himself to love?

He needed healing. She sniffed. So did she.

Dear God, please heal our hearts.

34

*A*ll day Saturday, Elsie wondered if he had meant what he said. Would Ruben really shine a light on her window tonight, after everyone else in the house was asleep?

It was a normal courtship ritual for Amish youth, but not having had a boyfriend, Elsie felt a bit out of sorts. Should she warn Fanny, or keep to herself? What about Emma and Caleb? Would they be worried if they heard something stirring in the frozen bushes outside?

Embarrassment flared under her skin, making her blush at the dinner table as Caleb remarked that he wanted a good night's sleep after working all day on the carriage house.

Oh, if you want to sleep, you'd best pull the covers tight over your eyes, Elsie worried.

"Elsie?" Caleb prodded her, trying to pass the pickled beets. "What's come over you? Your face is red as these beets."

"I'm fine." She passed the bowl on to Fanny and touched the

neckline of her dress. It did seem warm in here, especially for a cold February night.

Finally, when she was elbow-deep in the suds of the dinner dishes, she could no longer hold her secret from dear Emma. "I'm just saying, if you hear a strange voice in the house tonight, it's just Ruben, coming to see me."

"Ruben? Why's he coming so late . . . and on a Saturday?" Emma's jaw dropped as she cradled a teacup and towel to her breast. "Ruben's courting you? Why didn't you tell me?"

Elsie closed her eyes, glad that she was facing away from her sister. "We're not courting. I mean . . . we haven't been."

"Ya, on account of it being so soon after losing Dat." Emma's hand was soft and soothing on Elsie's shoulder. "I understand, dear one."

Dat . . .

Thoughts of Dat and courtship and Ruben flowed over Elsie like rain, mixing and melding into a waterfall of memory. Dat would have been thrilled to think that a young man was coming here to see his Elsie. What had he said that last day, before they'd left Philadelphia?

You need to find a good Amish man and marry. . . .

Elsie had found a wonderful good Amish man, but that did not change the fact that she could not marry. Not now, not ever.

"I shouldn't be surprised," Emma was saying, "with him working side by side with you at the shop every day. The real wonder is that he didn't take a liking to you sooner."

"I don't know what to do." Elsie slid a plate into the rinse water and looked over her shoulder to make sure Caleb and Fanny weren't nearby. "I've never had a young man come to the house. What if Fanny wakes up?"

"She'll just roll over and go back to sleep." Emma gave her shoulder a gentle squeeze. "Trust me. Parents look the other way during rumspringa. Well, for things like this."

"And where should we go? What will we say?"

"You could go for a walk under the moonlight, but since it's so cold you should probably have him come in. Bring him up to your room to talk."

Elsie couldn't imagine leading Ruben up the narrow staircase to the attic. "In my room?"

"Why do you think Dat finished the attic into two separate rooms for us? When young folks reach rumspringa age, parents want them to have a bit of private space."

"I don't feel so good about this." Elsie shook her head, not ready to spill the details about her feelings for Ruben or her decision to not marry. It was all too much for one night, and it didn't seem fair to share so many private details with her sister before she talked with Ruben himself.

"Trust me, it will be fine." Emma rubbed a plate dry. "You and Ruben talk all day long in the store. You told me he's become a very good friend."

"That's true." She had come to rely on Ruben for his sense of humor, his determination, his gift for reading people, his fierce loyalty. . . .

"That's how Gabe and I were . . . friends first." A gentle smile lit Emma's face as the memory carried her off. "It was a sad time for him that first brought us close, with his parents getting killed. Everyone thought Gabe was a real quiet guy, but that boy could talk a blue streak. We'd talk about anything and everything. Our families, my scholars, his cows." She put the plate away and took another. "It's good to have a beau who was your friend first. That way you can be friends for life."

Elsie drew in a worried breath. Emma was so smart and wise, but unfortunately all the wisdom in the world could not save Elsie from her dilemma.

Wind whistled through the hole in the windowpane as Elsie climbed the stool once again to peer outside. Still no sign of him.

She wrapped her black shawl closer around her and yawned. Most nights she was asleep by this time, tucked into her bed under layers of blankets. Although the attic rooms held on to some of the warm air of the day, on windy nights like this, the bedrooms cooled down quickly.

Maybe he wasn't coming, and she had gotten herself all worked up over nothing. She was thinking about taking off her kapp and unpinning her apron and crawling into bed when she heard the clap of horse's hooves on the road. The dim lights of a buggy came closer and pulled into their short driveway.

Ruben's horse and buggy.

His hands were probably frozen on the reins in the open buggy. She pressed closer to the frosted glass, wanting to make sure it was him and not Gabe come to court Emma. She could barely make out the dark figure walking over the frozen lawn. Then, a yellow beam of light bounced on her window, filling her with exhilaration.

Even if courting was not for her, it was a joyous, silly game.

She dashed down the stairs, forgetting to keep her footsteps light in the excitement of it all. Ruben was waiting on the front porch when she threw open the door.

"What took you so long?" he teased.

"I could ask you the same question." Their words were puffs of steam in the cold night air. "Do you want to come in?"

"I was thinking we could take a ride." He turned toward the night. "It's a bit cold, but I have bottles of hot water in the buggy. They do the trick."

A buggy ride so late at night seemed dangerous and silly and romantic. Elsie liked the idea, and it would save her the odd embarrassment of ushering Ruben into her bedroom. "Let me get a coat and scarf."

As soon as she stepped outside, cold air swirled around her, seeping through her clothes. Ruben didn't have a crate for her to use to step into the buggy, but he laced his fingers together and she placed her boot in his palms and he boosted her up, one-two-three, as if she were light as a feather.

Ruben adjusted two fat bottles to warm her legs, then handed her a smaller one to tuck under the lap blanket. "How's that?"

"Much better. I'm not shivering so much now."

He chuckled as he took the reins. "Not so much? You never do have the heart to say anything negative. That's one of the things I like about you. You do see the rainbow in every shower."

Pleasure washed over her at the thought of Ruben counting the things he liked about her. She had never expected that a young man would ever show her this sort of attention, and despite her resolve, she had to admit that being with Ruben warmed her heart.

"Does your horse mind the cold?" Elsie asked. Living so close to town and not being a farming family, the Lapps had only one horse, which they used for transportation.

"He has a thick coat, and he gets to keep moving. Rascal is fine." Ruben took a deep breath and tipped his head back. "One of the good things about a cold clear night is that you can see the stars."

Elsie let her head roll back, and her jaw dropped at the twinkling gems that were scattered through the inky blue sky. "So beautiful."

Ruben pointed out the North Star, then showed her how to find the Big Dipper and the Little Dipper. Together they searched for a river of stars that might be the Milky Way, but neither of them was sure.

The steady clip-clop of Rascal's hooves lulled Elsie into an easy peace. When Ruben turned to her, his face just inches away, the spark in his eyes nearly took her breath away.

"You must know I like you, Elsie. I knew you before the accident, but when I saw you trying to take care of your dat, the way you let Market Joe and his Lizzy ride to the hospital instead of you, it just opened my eyes to you."

Her heart thrummed so loud in her ears, she was sure farmers could hear it for miles around.

"I know it's soon after losing your dat. You're still wearing black and mourning his loss, and I respect that. But when it's over, I want to court you, Elsie. I want to be your fella."

Love and fear and disappointment welled up inside her, causing her eyes to sting with tears. "Oh, Ruben, you deserve a gal so much better than me."

"There's no one in the world better than you, Elsie. And we're right for each other. We belong together."

"No . . . I'm sorry, but . . . Ruben, I'm sure you've noticed that I'm not a normal girl."

He nodded. "That's right. You're special."

"I'm a little person. I have a genetic condition that made me short. It made my teeth different . . . and a few other things."

"But that doesn't change who you are inside, Elsie."

She squeezed his beefy hand, knowing he spoke the truth that so many in the world did not understand. "That's true, but many people never know the person inside because they get caught up on what they see."

"You're just right the way you are," he said fervently. "And you being a little person, I think it's made you look straight through to the heart of other people. You're one of the few people who was willing to look past my wide girth and practical jokes to see the person inside."

"Maybe I was one of the first, but I won't be the last." A wind kicked up, and she began to shiver again. "You have a good heart, Ruben. Another girl is going to see that and snatch you up."

He snorted. "I don't want another girl. You're the girl of my heart."

"But nothing could ever come of us two." Elsie pinched the blanket at her chest, trying to find the right words. "You need to know that I can never have children. I've talked to Doc Trueherz about it, and there's a genetic link with EVC. If I have children, I could pass the little people gene on to them, and that's something I can't allow to happen."

Confusion glimmered in Ruben's eyes. "But that's not the Amish way, the way we were raised. You and I were born to find a husband or wife and start families. That's the rule for everyone."

Elsie nearly choked on the words. "Not for me."

"Other little people have families. There's a lot of them over in the settlement in Paradise. Some of their children have EVC, some don't. It's Gott's will."

"I know that, but it doesn't change my decision." Elsie knew she was coming close to disobeying the rules of their church, but she was adamant. "This is not just a whim; I've thought and prayed about it long and hard. It can't happen. I won't do it to a little child."

"Don't get mad at me if I say it's not such a terrible thing to have children. The world would be a better place with a little girl or boy like you, Elsie."

She shook her head, tears forming in her eyes from the icy wind. Ya, it was from the wind. "I won't let it happen. That's the truth."

"Then I'll have to change your mind. Just give me some time."

A shiver rippled through Elsie as she fumbled to pull the lap blanket higher. "You can have all the time in the world, Ruben. It won't change my decision."

Suddenly, the heat of the bottles was no match for the brisk wind that whipped over them. Elsie heard a rattling sound; it was her own teeth chattering gently.

"Look at you, shivering like a leaf in the wind. Let me warm you." He lifted his arm so that she could scoot over beside him. "I won't change your decision tonight, but at least I can keep you warm. Kumm."

Without thinking she moved close and snuggled against him, pressing her face into his coat. His arms folded over her, enclosing her in a warm cocoon.

The glow of love and comfort held her in a daze for a moment. The great wall of his chest smelled of soap and wood smoke, and she allowed herself to nuzzle into the safety there, just for a minute.

Oh, if only this could be the way she ended every evening, wrapped in Ruben's strong arms. She stayed there, warm and protected from the wind until the gentle patter of the horse's hooves faded and the buggy stopped rocking over the road.

Dragging herself from his embrace, she blinked into the night and saw that they had arrived back at her home.

"Home again, and I'm not even cold anymore. Denki."

"You'll think about what I said . . . about us courting."

Elsie sighed, knowing she would think of nothing but Ruben for the rest of the night . . . maybe for the rest of the week. "I won't be changing my mind," she said. "But I will think about you."

She turned to jump out of the buggy, but he hopped out first and held his arms out to her. She moved to the edge of the seat and went to take his hands, but instead he held her at the waist and lifted her down.

Her boots landed softly on the ground, but her heart was still floating. Oh, how could her heart go to a place where she could never stay?

His hands moved up to her shoulders, and she could feel his gaze upon her.

Facing him, she had to crane her neck up to see his face.

"Hold on." He dropped down on one knee so that they were eye to eye. "That's better. I want to leave you with something to remember me."

She cocked her head to one side, hoping that he hadn't bought her a gift. "What's that?"

"One kiss," he said. "There's no harm in it. And it will give you something to think about."

"Who thinks about a kiss?" she asked.

"When Gott blesses a man and a woman with love, folks think about a lot more than kissing."

Her face grew warm at the thought that Ruben wanted to be with her, and that she truly was a woman. Of course, it was true, but with her small stature and her denial of any romance in her life, she had thought of herself as a perennial girl. Like the flowers that tucked themselves away each winter and bloomed each spring, that was the way Elsie imagined her life would be.

But the solid wall of man before her told her that she had definitely crossed the threshold into womanhood. And there was no denying the yearning to blossom in the arms of the man before her.

"One kiss," she whispered.

Gently, tenderly, he cupped her face with his big hands. When he leaned forward and brushed his lips gently over hers, she felt as if a spark had jumped between them, setting her senses on fire. He deepened the kiss, and suddenly she was alive with wonder at the feel of his body against hers, the smell of him, the taste of him.

The rest of the world blurred into the night as she melted against him.

One kiss.

One kiss to last a lifetime.

⚭ 35 ⚭

One kiss.

One kiss, and now Ruben knew for sure that Elsie Lapp was the love of his life. They were meant to be together. It was one of those things you didn't question, like the sun rising in the east and the leaves turning red and gold each October.

That kiss had let him know that his heart was in the right place, though with Elsie determined never to marry, winning her wasn't going to be easy.

He wondered about that the next day at church, as he turned to look across the open room to the benches on the other side where the women sat.

There she was, holding Beth in her lap. She held the plate of gmay cookies for the little girl to take one, then passed them down the row. Beth smiled as Elsie whispered something and tucked a stray lock of hair behind the little girl's ear.

Ruben didn't want to stare, but for a moment he studied her, recalling the way his hands had cupped her smooth cheeks. The way he'd kissed the plump lips that were whispering now. He'd tried to memorize every sensation, the taste of her, the lavender scent of her hair. He remembered it all so well, and yet, he wanted more.

One kiss would never be enough.

Elsie wasn't baptized yet, so she hadn't promised to follow all the rules of the Ordnung. But she'd told him she would always live among the Plain folk.

And Plain folk married and started a family. It was the Amish way of life . . . though not in Elsie's thinking. Her worries about having a baby that looked like her must have been keeping her from thinking straight.

Ruben hadn't realized that it bothered her, being a little person. Her sweet smile, the sparkle in her eyes, the way she saw the good in people . . . Elsie seemed to be happy with life. Looking at her, you'd never know that she felt bad about the way she was.

Ruben understood how it felt to be trapped inside a body that wasn't right. He had learned that lesson very painfully as a child. But he'd come around. His body still wasn't right, but he'd had help accepting it as it was. He prayed that Elsie would meet her own angels to help her find the way.

     ∽

Monday morning, the Country Store was bursting with women, Amish and Englisher alike. With the auction coming up on Saturday, Mary and her younger sister Susie had come by to pick up donations from the store, and as luck would have it they had arrived at the same time as a minibus full of white-haired Englisher ladies. Ruben and Elsie did their best to juggle customers and the collection of items that were to go into the auction.

"Yesterday after church I got a chance to talk to every Amish person who sells crafts in the store, and everyone wants to donate." Because the Country Store sold things on consignment, Elsie could not donate anything without permission from the person who made it. She gathered up items in a small basket as she walked up one aisle. "We decided that some of the smaller items, like lavender, soaps, honey, and jam, can go together in a gift basket. More expensive things, like one of Rachel's paintings, can be auctioned off on their own."

"That makes good sense," Mary said. "Do you want us to put the baskets together at home?"

"You can do it here." Elsie pointed to the bolts of cloth. "We've got baskets and fabric and ribbon."

"Can I do a basket?" Susie King clasped her hands together under her chin. "That sounds like fun."

"The baskets are in the storeroom," Elsie said, sending Susie skipping toward the back of the store.

For the first time, Ruben realized that he was surrounded by women in this shop, and while he could hold his own in conversation, he didn't favor the giggles and skipping. He came to the register to make the sale for an older woman with bold black eyeglasses. He'd seen her here before.

She sniffed a bar of soap and sighed. "Ah, lavender. Did you know it eases stress?"

"Then maybe I need a sniff this morning." Ruben picked up a satchel of lavender and brought it to his nose. "Ya. That's better."

"Oh, you're a fresh one." The woman waved at him. "What's this auction about? I was here last month and didn't hear a peep about it."

"That's because we hadn't thought it up yet," he said as he punched keys on the old mechanical register. "The auction is for James Lapp, a friend of ours who was injured in an accident. His family needs money to pay his medical bills."

The woman squinted. "Is this the young man who was paralyzed when that van got hit?"

Ruben didn't like hearing the word "paralyzed." It sounded too final. "It is."

"And is this auction open to the public?" The woman nodded toward the back of the store. "I'm sure our group would love to attend."

"It's open to everyone, and we're hoping for a good turnout to help the Lapps. There'll be everything from quilts and paintings to pincushions and seedlings."

"That sounds marvelous. Make sure you put one of those flyers in when you wrap my purchases."

Ruben stayed at the register and handled four more transactions. When he held the door open for a customer, a growing mound of items sat on the counter, waiting to be loaded into Mary's buggy.

"I'll get going with these." He carried out Rachel King's watercolor of a Diamond quilt on a fence by a garden. Rachel's painting looked so real, Ruben could almost smell the honeysuckle meandering up over the fence. On his second trip, there was a birdhouse, and then a heavy pine chest made by Adam King. He loaded it all into the back of the buggy, making sure nothing got scraped or cracked. When he returned to the shop, Mary held the wooden box that was always on display in the window—the one that had been in Elsie's family for so many years.

"Would you mind taking this out?" Mary smoothed her palm over the top of the box. "And mind, it's very delicate."

Ruben took it from her, wariness prickling the back of his neck. "But, Mary, this is not for sale. Elsie wants to keep it in her family."

Mary touched her chin and turned to Elsie. "Did I take the wrong box?"

Elsie peeked out from behind the display of birdhouses. "That's the right one." She smiled up at Ruben, but he sensed the undercurrent of uneasiness. "You know, I've been thinking and praying about it. I checked with Emma and Caleb, and they thought it was a good idea. We're donating the box."

"Elsie . . . no." Ruben shook his head.

"All these wonderful good things in the store, and none of them are ours to give. But the box, that's something we can donate. And it would ease my heart to see something good come of that old box."

That old box had been cherished by her father . . . and by Elsie, too. Not for the wood chest itself, but for the long line of family members who had kept it in their homes and lovingly passed it on.

"Are you sure, Elsie?" Ruben stood tall, holding the painted box as if it were made of glass. "Do you think it's right to give it up? This is something that's always been in your family. Something you could pass down to your kids."

Elsie closed the distance between them and took the small wood chest from Ruben. "I want to help James, and this box is the only thing I can give that will make money for him."

"You're helping in other ways," he said softly. "By rounding up all these donations from your store. I didn't have anything to donate, but I got Dat to let us use the barn for the auction."

"And that's a huge contribution." Elsie smoothed her fingertips over the cherries painted on the outside. "I know this was made by my great-great-grandmother, but it's only wood and paint and some glue. It's so very pretty, but now it can be useful, too."

A knot was growing in Ruben's throat. He didn't want Elsie to make this mistake, but he couldn't stop her.

"Take it, Ruben. Load it along with the other things."

He opened his hands to take the box, wishing that instead he could take her into his arms and kiss her over and over again until she changed her mind.

Verhuddelt. He was a crazy man now. A crazy man in love. "I'll put it in the buggy, then."

He was halfway to the door when he remembered. "What about that customer who wanted to buy the box? Gwen something."

"Gwen Slavin," Elsie called from behind the bolts of fabric. "She was in yesterday while you were running errands and I told her about it. She's coming to the auction."

Ruben frowned as he plodded out to the buggy with the box. This was not right. Gott loved a generous heart, but a person did not have to sacrifice the small possessions that traced a family's history.

It reminded him of Elsie's decision not to have children.

Selling the box was a strike at her family's past. Not having children would end her own future, cutting the family tree short.

Gott willing, he was going to turn Elsie Lapp around. Stubborn as she was, he would melt her resolve with the strongest measure the Ordnung allowed.

He would wear her down with love.

⊷⊶ 36 ⊷⊶

"Are you comfortable?" The familiar, steady voice on the phone comforted Dylan, closing the distance between him and his therapist of four years. "Because I can feel your anxiety, Dylan."

"I'm pacing," Dylan told Patrick. "I'm walking from one window to another, looking out over a frozen field that I'm told will contain some massive beets come the summer. Sweet beets and stinking fertilizer." That had been what the upstairs tenants, the Dawsons, had told him the day he'd moved into this apartment just outside Halfway. Funny, but his landlady had failed to mention the free aromatherapy that came along with the spring thaw.

"You really are out in the sticks. So you're kicking back in farm country. I take it all this pastoral scenery has brought you great peace."

"Sometimes. Other times, I'm just the hermit of the beet fields."

"So that's why you haven't checked in for a session since I saw you in December."

"Honestly?"

"Honest is the only way to be in therapy," Patrick said wryly.

"I've been busy, but good." He told Patrick how his outreach program had barely been in place before crisis had swept through the community, bringing more than half a dozen traumatized Amish clients in for therapy sessions. The accident had brought him acceptance into Amish homes, and he was grateful for the chance to visit people who needed help but weren't comfortable with group therapy. Fanny Lapp. Jacob Fisher. George and Cookie Dornbecker. John Beiler.

"You were right about the change of venue getting me out of that rut." Dylan pressed one palm to the window glass; even through the double pane, the cold bruised his skin. "When I go to work, when I come home here, I'm not facing constant reminders of Kristin and Angela." It felt strange to say their names after all these months of consciously keeping them hovering at the back of his consciousness, bringing them out only in occasional quiet moments of grief and reflection.

Like Ruben's angels.

"Of course I was right," Patrick said. "I'm glad you're finally seeing it my way." A pause. "But enough about me. You called to arrange this session, so I know something's on your mind. Some distant memory rising to the surface?"

Dylan paused in front of the large picture window, staring at a magnificent sunrise. A swath of light cast a golden hue over the land. How could a barren field be so beautiful?

He'd thought of this apartment as a sort of hermitage, a place to hole up and escape most vestiges of civilization. Aside from the occasional wave to the tenants upstairs and the monthly rent check, nothing was expected of him in this residence. He'd taken this place to crash, to be alone, to escape from a life as cold, empty, and barren as the fields that stretched from here to the hills.

But suddenly, those fields were an intricate study in contrasts between darkness and light, color and negative space. Not so bleak, after all.

"Dylan? You need to talk, buddy. Tell me what's going on and I'll listen with the occasional brilliant guiding question."

"It's about a woman."

"Go on."

"A young woman I work with. She's a student nurse at the hospital and, well, there's always been chemistry between us." Dylan raked back his hair as he paced to the kitchen. He poured another cup of coffee but left it on the counter as he shuffled back to the window still in sweats and a T-shirt. His first appointment this morning was two hours off, and that was with James Lapp.

James Lapp, and his sparkling nursing assistant, Haley Donovan.

"This student nurse," Patrick said. "How old is she?"

"Just a kid. She's twenty-two."

"That's old enough to be a contender."

"But I'm not looking for a relationship. I came here to get away from the ghosts of trauma. I need to heal before I get involved with anyone."

"You've been healing for more than four years, Dylan. And I gotta give you a lot of credit on that because you worked on it all that time. And as you know, there comes a point when a person is ready to be in a relationship again. I'm not pushing, and I'm not saying you're there. I'm just saying it's not beyond the realm of possibility."

"I don't know, Patrick." Dylan perched on the arm of the sofa. "Sounds to me like you're pushing."

"Maybe I am. What's this young woman's name?"

"Haley."

"Tell me about her."

"She has eyes the color of warm honey and an impetuous manner that always sneaks up on me."

"Nice. Sounds like poetry."

"She's a beautiful girl with true compassion for people. She's not afraid to get involved with the Amish. In fact, I think she's as intrigued by their culture as I am."

"And you work with her at the hospital?"

"And in the field." He explained how Haley was making house calls on James Lapp with him. "She was sort of my entrée into the local Amish community. Haley was the first person to come upon that accident. She has helped me connect with the passengers. Without her, I don't know if I would have gotten any of them to agree to group therapy. But they come, every week. There's a core group of four young Amish people who are there like clockwork."

"So, essentially, Haley is a key factor in your practice there."

"Well, no, but . . ." He thought about it a moment. "Yes. Maybe not at the hospital, but here in Halfway, yes. She's the center of my universe."

The realization hit him like a blow to the chest.

"Dylan? Was that a joke?"

"Sort of."

Patrick whistled through his teeth. "You weren't joking. So you realize she's a special person. She's important to you. And you're holding back from involvement . . . why?"

"She's too young, we work together, and I'm not ready."

"She's old enough, you work at the same hospital, and it's been more than four years."

Dylan pushed away from the sofa and went back to the window.

"You're pacing again," Patrick said.

Dylan paused and threw out one arm. "How do you know that from seventy miles away?"

The low rumble of Patrick's laugh was somehow reassuring. "I know you well, my friend. So what's going on with this relationship? Is she pressuring you? Trying to get a commitment?"

"She asked me out for coffee or lunch a few times."

"And you're not willing to spring for a latte?"

Dylan took a sip of his coffee. Cold coffee. "Look, I'd love to have a glass of wine and some dinner with her. But it's not that simple."

"It never is. But you can move in baby steps. A coffee date is not a proposal of marriage."

"Whose side are you on?"

"I'm here for you, buddy. I'm just looking out for your best interests, and I think it might be a good idea to pursue someone who you seem to think is worth pursuing. Here's the best way to start. You should share your story with her. Tell her about Kris and Angela."

"I can't do that. I came here to get away from those memories."

"And you've had a good break. A fresh start. But you know the drill. It's time to face your fears."

Dylan rubbed the bristle on his jaw, thinking it was time to shave and get going. He could face his fears in a few weeks . . . or a few years.

"I hear your hesitation," Patrick said. "So just think about it, okay?"

"I will." Dylan looked at the clock over the stove. "I have to go."

"Just one more question. Do you feel guilty because of your attraction to Haley?"

Guilt: It was the monkey on his back. "I don't know. I thought I'd worked through all that."

"But saying that you don't blame yourself is different from actually allowing yourself to have another romantic relationship."

Dylan bristled. "I've got my hands full now, between the hospital and the field work. I'm helping half a dozen patients through post-traumatic stress. That's my focus right now. That's why God brought me here."

"The work you're doing sounds great. But maybe God has a greater plan for you than even you can see right now. Maybe there is a relationship in your future. Just think about it," Patrick insisted. "Be open to it. Everyone needs to love and be loved."

I've already had my share of love, Dylan thought as he got off the phone and headed to the shower. Kris had been his perfect match, something he'd known since the day they'd met in a class at Temple. English majors, both of them, they had debated the merits and myths of love at first sight and the way it had played out in literature.

Romeo and Juliet.

Antony and Cleopatra.

Dylan and Kristin.

Kris had been the one who'd argued that the most classic love affairs in history had ended tragically, while Dylan had insisted that millions of couples enjoyed fulfilled love but didn't advertise it.

Now, if he were to debate the matter again, he would argue that Kris had been right: True love was destined to tangle itself into a tragic ending.

As he lathered up shampoo in his hair, he thought about his morning appointment with James Lapp, who still suffered from a depression that kept him from communicating much with anyone, including his longtime girlfriend, Rachel.

Talk about a romance on the rocks.

Dylan had counseled Rachel, too, without compromising his relationship with James. Truth be told, James had shared so little with him that there wasn't much of a relationship to compromise, anyway.

At the moment, Rachel seemed determined to stick by James, but she was hurt by his withdrawal. As was his mother, Edna. But the family wasn't interested in treating James's depression through drug therapy, and James was not open to guided imagery. For the time being, they would stick to talk therapy.

∞ 37 ∞

"How's that?" Edna Lapp asked, hovering over the table with pitcher in hand. "Can I get you more milk?"

Dylan waved her off. "I'm good, thanks." When he arrived to find Haley already working with James, Edna had insisted that Dylan have a slice of fresh-baked chocolate chip pie while he was waiting. "And this is one amazing pie. It reminds me of my wife's chocolate chip cookies." The mention of Kris slipped out unfiltered, as if he talked about her every day.

"That's what makes it popular for young and old."

"You're a fabulous cook, Edna."

"Oh, I don't know about that. The Fishers, now, there's a family that knows how to bake. They're donating bread and cookies for the auction."

"That's this week, right?" He took out his cell phone to check the date. "Let me make sure I have it on my calendar."

"It's the day after tomorrow, and Mary says that we've already got more than six thousand dollars in donations." Edna looked down, almost embarrassed as she folded a dish towel. "A few big checks came from your doctor friends at the hospital. They couldn't come to the auction, but they sent the money anyway."

"Good. I'm glad they did the right thing."

"Please, tell them we're ever so grateful."

"I'll spread the word." He rose as Haley appeared, her backpack slung casually over one shoulder, her long blond hair cascading over the other shoulder. She really could be a model. One shot of that pose, and thousands of young people would buy that simple black backpack.

"We're all finished," she said with a slight smile. He noticed that she didn't look him in the eye, and he wondered if there was going to be awkwardness over the date that could never be.

"Please, Haley. Sit." Edna pulled out a chair and hurried to the counter. "You can't go without having some pie."

"Best chocolate chip pie I ever tasted," Dylan said from the doorway, hesitating. "And if you don't mind, I'm going to bring James out here to talk. We're not digging into anything too personal, and I think a more social environment would oil the hinges a little."

Haley hung her backpack on the kitchen chair. "Fine with me."

"Oil away," Edna said with an amused grin.

A minute later, James was wheeling himself out the wide bedroom door into the kitchen. Dylan moved the chair at the end so that James could roll up to the table.

"Do you want a piece of pie?" his mother offered.

He waved her off, but gruffly agreed to a cup of tea.

Keep things casual, Dylan told himself. James seemed to close down when questioned directly, so it was worth trying a more relaxed atmosphere.

"This morning as I was driving down the lane to your house, I realized I don't know beans about what goes into taking care of an orchard." Dylan eyed a stray chocolate chip that had fallen from Haley's plate. He shot her a look, then swiped it in one swift move.

"Stop," Haley teased, sliding her plate away.

Edna smiled as she placed a mug of tea in front of her son. "Do you want another piece, Dr. Monroe?"

"No, thanks. I just couldn't bear to see that morsel go to waste."

James didn't react, but at least he'd been watching.

"Anyway, what does it take to manage an orchard? I'm guessing there's not a lot going on this time of year, since there's no fruit to be harvested or protected."

"Winter's the time for pruning," James said. "And you've got to watch that the trees don't go without water."

James explained how the average rainfall and snowmelt provided the orchards with plenty of water for the winter. However, a few years ago, there had been a dry winter "that just about did our trees in." James and his brothers had devised watering systems to keep the fruit trees alive.

Listening, Dylan could imagine James and his brothers out in the orchards, winter, spring, summer, and fall. He could also sense James's strong connection to this farm, his feel for the land, his ingenuity and experience tending to the trees. James talked about learning to climb the trees as a young boy, eating a fresh-picked apple as he straddled a thick bough. This orchard was the fabric of his life.

At last, he had hit on James's passion, evoking more than a string of five or six words at one time.

Haley kept quiet as she nibbled on her pie, but occasionally, he caught a glimpse of recognition in her eyes. She, too, was intrigued by this new facet of James.

"So it's pruning time." Dylan nodded toward the windows. "Are all those trees going to be okay without you?"

"We got most of the pruning done before the accident. My dat and brothers have been working on the rest."

"A good thing, because you've got a lot of trees out there. I've noticed how you can go a mile down the road and you're still passing Lapp orchards."

"We've got some acres," James said modestly, "but it's not so much work at pruning time. If you take care of your trees every year, there's just some trimming to do. It's just a few trees that have a mind of their own and need to be reshaped. The centers have to be opened up to allow light to reach all parts of the tree."

Dylan could picture that . . . a few clipped branches falling to the ground so that sunlight could reach the fruit growing at the heart of the tree.

It felt great to hear James's voice. "Before today I never thought much about what went into growing a peach or an apple."

As James rubbed his clean-shaven chin, Dylan thought he detected a trace of a smile. "It's not so much," James said. "You do a little pruning, and the Almighty Father takes care of the rest."

Dylan cocked his head to one side. "Remember what you just said about pruning the branches, that sunlight could reach all parts of the tree?"

James nodded.

"It's a good image. I'm just wondering if that's true of a man's faith. Sometimes we have to prune away our fear and anger so that the power of God can reach our hearts."

Edna closed the door of the fridge. "How do you prune away anger?"

"Maybe it's just a crazy thought," Dylan said. "A verhuddelt thought," he added, trying to incorporate the Pennsylvania Dutch word he'd learned.

James stared at him, as if the answer were forming in the air between them.

"It's just some food for thought," Dylan said.

James nodded, a silent promise that he would think about it.

As Dylan followed Haley out to their cars, a chill wind swept over the winter grasses.

"Ooh!" Haley squealed, struggling to zip up her jacket. "I'm ka-frizzling."

The instinct to sweep her into his arms and warm her with a kiss burned strong inside him. As they came around the barn, out of sight of the house, he reached over for her hand. "Come here."

Her eyes registered surprise, but she did not hesitate to face him and give him her hands. "Your hands are like ice cubes," he said as he rubbed warmth into them.

"It was cold in there. Did you know they're running out of coal?"

He frowned. "I guess that auction can't come soon enough." He pressed her hands to his flannel shirt as two rosy patches appeared on her cheeks. "I know it's cold. I just . . . I think I owe you some explanation, and I've got to do it now before I lose my nerve."

Her golden eyes opened wide, so warm and receptive. He wanted to kick himself for not being honest with Haley long before this.

"So here it is, for your ears only. You probably realize there's a reason I'm not jumping into a relationship with you." The truth sat on his tongue, painfully bitter. "The thing is, I have a past that I'm struggling to reconcile. I was married, very happily married."

"Oh, Dylan . . ." Haley stood motionless, her sweet lips pressed into a frown as she nodded. "Tell me."

"There isn't much to tell." That was a lie. There were plenty of stories, but it hurt him to go there. He swallowed back the knot of emotion growing in his throat. "Kris and I had a wonderful life in

Philadelphia. We did the DINK thing in the city, then our daughter came along. Angie. And our lives changed in a way I'd never expected. We were . . ." His voice was suddenly strained, and he paused. If he told Haley every blessed detail about his baby girl, they would be here forever. "You don't need the long version. In a nutshell, I lost them both in a car accident a few years ago."

"Oh, no." Reflexively, she put her arms around him and pulled him into a hug. "I'm so sorry."

He stared straight ahead, aware of the pain but also relieved to have the truth out.

"If you don't already know . . ." Haley said with a note of levity. "The nursing students have been dreaming up scenarios about your past, but I don't think anyone imagined this. How long has it been since . . . since the accident?"

"Four years . . . a little more than that. After it happened I quit my teaching job and went back to school for my master's in social work. I think I needed the whole psychology thing to keep my own fluctuating emotions in check."

"That's understandable. And, boy, did you make the right choice. Being a therapist . . . I think it's a great fit for you."

"Well . . . thanks for that." He gave her a squeeze, then leaned back so that he could decipher her golden eyes. "Though I wasn't fishing for compliments. I just wanted to share these things with you because I value our relationship. I really do."

His voice was low and hoarse, threaded with emotion. He put his hands on her shoulders, as if to hold on to her. "I don't want to lose you, Haley, but I don't know if I can get involved yet. I'm not sure about a commitment." He screwed his mouth to the side, annoyed with himself. "Bottom line, I'm not very good boyfriend material, and I don't know if that's ever going to change. I might wind up a wizened old hermit and you . . . you deserve to have love in your life. I'm afraid you need to move on."

Haley gripped the lapels of his jacket and pulled him close. "Look and listen. I'm not going anywhere, Dylan. You're not going to shake me loose that easily."

"But this is so unfair to you." He raked back his hair with one hand. "You deserve better than me. You don't need some ghost of a man in your life."

"You are flesh and bones, Dylan." She gripped his arms for emphasis. "And I value every minute we have together."

He took in a breath. "I'm crazy about you, kid. I may be a beet field hermit now, but if there's ever anyone I'd like to share the beets with, it would be you."

The sincerity in his blue eyes, crisp and clear as a summer lake, evoked a visceral reaction deep inside her. How could she work so closely with this man and not fall in love with him? He needed her support, and she was going to be a friend to him. "Tell me what you need and I'll be there," she said. "I think you know that patience is not one of my personal virtues, but I'll do my best. I'll pray on it and give it up to God and try to cool my jets."

He laughed. "You have such a poetic way of putting it."

"But I mean it. I—" She wanted to tell him that she loved him—the feeling was so pure and strong in her heart, she was sure he could see it in her eyes. But she didn't want to rush him. "You know, I've been praying for healing, for both of us," she said. "And God is answering. This is an answered prayer."

"You seem surprised at that."

"Not surprised. Just hopeful." After years of gray skies, the clouds were breaking apart and sunlight was streaming through. After years of sorrow, she saw hope streaming through, and it was a beautiful sight.

38

$\mathcal{F}$or the past hour, Elsie had peered out the shop window, watching the traffic on Main Street swell into a slow crawl. She had prayed that everyone was headed toward Zook's barn, where Ruben had been working since before dawn, preparing for the big event. Once Caleb had replaced her at the shop, she had hustled up the street, grinning as soon as she saw the cars and people surrounding the barn.

Her prayers had been answered!

She nodded to Zed, who was busy outside the big red barn, directing cars and buggies to parking areas. With a glorious swarm of Englishers and a full staff of Amish helpers, the benefit auction was off to a good start. Young boys in black hats and dark jackets waited near the doors for customers who needed help carrying their purchases to their cars.

As Elsie passed through the wide barn doors, her feet felt surprisingly light. Her usual discomfort in large public places wasn't pressing on her so much today. Maybe because she knew it was worth coming out for this cause. In any case, she avoided the crowd gathering near the auction stage to weave through the stragglers at the back of the barn.

A long line of booths was set up for Amish merchants to sell items like the Fishers' baked goods and hot coffee and tea, courtesy of Ye Olde Tea Shop. Market Joe and Lizzy were in charge of the Kings' booth, where they were selling a variety of cheeses. Lizzy wore a bigger gown with more room at the waist for her growing belly, and her cheeks were rosy with good health, thank the Lord. Remy King waved at her from the same booth, and Elsie waved back, smiling at the sight of little Sam grinning up at a customer with his missing front teeth.

Taking in the many familiar faces from her community, Elsie took a breath of pure joy. She thanked Gott for these generous Plain folk who were quick to come to the aid of those in need.

At the far end of the barn was a banner that read: THANK YOU FROM THE LAPP FAMILY. Nearby was a table where the Lapps sold pie fillings from their orchards: peaches and cherries, apples and apricots. Fanny also canned fruits when they were in season, and Elsie knew there was nothing quite as mouthwatering as a pie made from ingredients that were put up in the peak of freshness.

"Elsie!"

Hearing her name, she turned to see Rachel waving at her with James beside her, wheeling himself over the dirt floor of the barn.

Elsie smiled and hurried over to meet them, relieved that James had decided to come to the auction after all. There'd been some doubt, when he told his family that he didn't want to be wheeled out "like a wounded pet," just to make people empty their pockets.

But here he was, looking healthy and strong, with Rachel beaming by his side.

"Such a turnout!" Elsie said, hands on her hips. "I don't think I've ever seen so many visitors here in Halfway at one time."

"I don't know where all these people came from," Rachel said, "but I'm sure glad they're here."

James scanned the crowd, his eyes dark and serious, but without the anger that had burned there so recently. "Is that Dylan Monroe, just coming in?"

The girls followed his gaze to the area by the main entrance. "Ya. Dylan and Haley." Elsie gave a wave to bring them over, but James rolled one wheel around to turn his chair. Then with a brisk shove of his arms, he rolled the chair over toward them.

"James, wait. . . ." Elsie called, knowing it wouldn't be easy to navigate through the thick crowd.

Rachel pressed gently on her arm. "There's no holding him back, and maybe that's a good thing. I'm just glad he agreed to come today, with all these people going out of their way to help him."

Elsie lifted her chin, but she could no longer see James beyond the crowd of families and couples, tourists and Amish. "At least he's out and about." She turned to Rachel. "And you're looking a little pale. Have you been chasing James around all morning?"

"Oh, Elsie, I would gladly chase him if I thought he'd have a word for me once I caught up with him."

Elsie's heart ached for her friend. "I know it's hard to take. But like Dylan says, healing takes time, and everyone responds to trauma differently. It's different for James. We got to walk away from the accident. He didn't."

"I know that. It's just that sometimes I get so worked up, it makes me grit my teeth to think that I would do anything to help him, and he can barely spare two words for me."

"He's not talking much to anyone." Elsie hated seeing Rachel so upset. "And here I thought you were nervous about having your painting auctioned off today."

Rachel's hands flew to her face. "That, too! I can barely look at it on display at that end of the barn, with people walking by all with big eyes and talking about it. It's like having a piece of me out there on display, and that feels wrong." She touched Elsie's shoulder. "Promise me you'll take a turn at a quilting table with me when the time comes to auction it off. I can't be here to watch."

"I'm happy to do some quilting with you. I was planning on it." With a store to run, Elsie didn't spend a lot of time quilting, but from the time she was a young girl she had been taught how to make neat, tiny stitches.

At that moment a large group moved off and Elsie saw James heading their way, with Haley and Dylan walking alongside him.

"Good morning, ladies." Dylan nodded, asking Elsie how her family was doing. She explained that Emma was here with the little ones, while Fanny had stayed home for some needed rest.

"These two have never been to an auction before," James said.

"It's true, and I didn't know what to expect, but this is really cool," Haley said, looking around. She wore a quilted jacket with a hood trimmed in fake fur—Elsie had heard customers discussing the fuzzy white fabric—and worn-out blue jeans, and as she spoke, she caught everyone's attention. So bubbly and outspoken, Haley was always good to have around. "I didn't realize you'd have all these booths in the back of the barn. I thought it would be just the auctioneer guy shouting out at us."

"There are plenty of other things for sale," Elsie said. "Like coffee. I was just thinking of getting a cup."

"That sounds good." Haley took two dollars from her purse. "I'll go with."

"I can get it for you," James said.

Haley cocked her head to one side. "Aren't you the guest of honor here?"

"I've got nothing else to do, and I'm sick of being waited on."

"That's what I like to hear from my PT patients." Haley handed him the money. "Go for it, James."

Watching the exchange, Dylan shrugged. "I'll go along. I could use a cup, too, and I don't like being waited on either."

The women watched as the two men disappeared in the throng.

"You're good with him," Rachel said. "He talks to you."

"Only because I just about knock it out of him," Haley said. "And Dylan and I have been visiting him a few times a week for more than two weeks. We've logged in some time together."

Rachel shook her head, a pout shadowing her face. "I visit him nearly every day, but he still won't talk to me."

Haley winced. "I'm sorry, honey. I don't know what to tell you besides the fact that trauma can put a huge strain on a relationship. But I think you're feeling that firsthand."

"Give it time, honey girl." Elsie couldn't imagine the hurt Rachel was feeling, being turned away by someone she cared for. "It takes a century for Gott to make a sturdy oak tree. Relationships don't grow overnight."

"I know that in my head," Rachel said. "But my heart just isn't listening."

Elsie understood how it was to have a wayward heart that didn't obey orders from the brain. She tried to keep her own heart in check every day, when it warmed at the sight of Ruben, when laughter filled the store, when his gentle care cloaked her in a feeling of love.

Such a wonderful thing, to be loved by a good, kind man!

But Elsie kept reminding herself that it would not last forever. In a matter of days, Ruben would have to return here to help his father run Zook's barn during the busy season. He would be gone from the store, eventually gone from her life, as it was meant to be.

She swallowed past a knot in her throat as she imagined that he would move on and find another girl. Ya . . . and he would marry and have babies and make a family with someone else.

The thought of Ruben's bright, happy future weighed her down with regret, and she quickly swung away from the other girls only to come face-to-face with the object of her sadness.

Ruben.

He was walking toward them with an older man beside him.

"Jacob Fisher!" Haley's golden eyes gleamed as her voice bubbled up over the noise of the crowd. "Look at you, walking strong. You look great!"

She was right. His first week back at church, old Jacob could walk only with help from his sons. But now, he had a spring in his step again, and his skin had the warm hue of a sun-kissed peach.

Jacob tipped his hat to her. "I'm better now. A heart at peace gives life to the body."

"I guess so. The last time I saw you, you were hooked up to oxygen in the hospital."

"I've been back on my feet a few weeks now, thanks to the merciful Father in heaven." He patted his torso and grinned, winking at Haley. "The ribs are better, and no more problem breathing."

"You are a model of recovery," Haley said. "Are you still doing physical therapy?"

"I do the exercises at home, everything they told me to do. The doctors got me breathing again and the Almighty took care of the rest."

"I'm happy to see you back on your feet, Jacob," Haley said. "Often, patients your age are laid up for a long time."

"Ya. I never felt such pain in my eighty-two years. But it's all behind me now, thanks to your quick thinking." Jacob touched his gray beard, his weathered hand quivering ever so slightly. "My family is grateful that you were there that day, Haley."

"We're all grateful," Ruben said.

"Thanks, but I didn't really do anything that any normal Good Samaritan wouldn't have done."

"That's the important thing, Haley." Jacob squinted, looking around the group to be sure everyone was listening. "We must all be like the Good Samaritan."

"And that's why so many folks are here today," Elsie said, still overjoyed by the great turnout. "People want to help."

"Ya," Jacob said, turning back toward the door. "I'd better check on my cart. The boys were unloading more trays of cookies and whoopie pies. We almost sold out."

Ruben offered to help, but Jacob assured him he had it in hand. As the older man made his way toward the door, Haley asked Ruben a few questions about the auction.

While they chatted, Elsie was glad to have the excuse to remain quiet and simply gaze up at the young man who'd earned a special place in her heart.

Sometimes she imagined that her lips still tingled from the kiss they had shared last Saturday night. A wonderful kiss, but forbidden fruit, all the same.

It would be hard to let him go . . . but that moment was down the road apiece, and she wouldn't let the shadows of a future storm ruin her current joy. She needed to live each moment, each day. As Dat used to say, savor each drop you can squeeze from life.

James and Dylan returned with the coffee, and they were followed by George Dornbecker, who introduced his wife, Cookie. Elsie was glad to see George back to his old self, joking with a twinkle in his eyes. He told James that he was buying a new van with wheelchair access to help the young man get around. Cookie explained that their son Tyler was going to be driving part-time so that George could cut down his hours.

"It'll be good to have another Dornbecker driving us," Elsie said. Being Amish, she understood the custom of passing a business on to a family member. "But I hope you teach him some of your jokes."

Emma came over to tell Elsie and Rachel that they were needed at the quilting tables, and they said their good-byes and headed over to the area sectioned off from the auction. Behind her, Elsie heard the announcements that the auction would begin shortly, and she thought of all the wonderful items people had donated in a sweep of generosity.

Somewhere on one of the auction tables was the box that had been in her family for generations. In her mind she could picture the box, with cherries painted on its sides, the metal hasp, the message painted inside from her great-great-grandmother.

It worried her a bit to think that she was the one responsible for letting it go, but she reminded herself that it was a material possession. It wasn't helping anyone by sitting around in the window of the shop.

Dat used to say that generosity tasted much better than stinginess.

And so, the box would soon belong to someone else.

39

Elsie followed Rachel around the partition and paused at the sight of Amish women seated at the edge of a large table. From here she saw the backs of four white kapps with heads bent intently over work. On the other side of the table, four Amish women were similarly lost in their stitching, their right hands working the top of the quilt as they chatted.

Such a lovely sight—like daisies growing together in a field, all stretching in the same direction toward the sun.

Elsie wondered why she had avoided quilting bees in the past few years. Quilting was an important part of social life for Amish women. How had she forgotten the sweet serenity that came from so many hands and hearts working together?

Today, three tables were set up with quilt tops ready for the fine, even stitches from loving hands. If one woman was working on a quilt top alone, it would take weeks of steady work to finish it off. But here, with so many skilled hands stitching away, the three quilts would be done by the end of the day. Elsie knew that each quilt would fetch at least four hundred dollars, and if the bidding got going, a single quilt might bring in thousands. She was happy to pitch in for James.

"Girls?" One of the older women motioned Rachel and her over to a far table. "Kumm. There are two empty seats here."

Elsie put her coat over the back of a chair and sat down at the finished quilt top held in place by clamps at the edges of the table. She pushed back her sleeves. Someone had left needles, a thimble, and scissors atop the quilt, and she slipped the thimble onto her finger and threaded one of the needles from the pack. It had been a while since she'd held a needle, but her hands seemed to recall what to do. Before long, she found a steady rhythm.

Sitting beside her, Rachel asked about Fanny.

"She wanted to come, but you know she's got to stay off her feet. Emma brought Will and Beth, and our neighbor Marta Kraybill is keeping Fanny company."

Just then Elsie spotted her older sister coming toward the table. Emma's pretty face was lit with a sweet smile as she came around the table and leaned close to Elsie.

"Guess what just happened? I just saw the box get auctioned off."

The little wooden box. The air went still around her as Elsie pictured it. "Did someone buy it?"

"Ya, and for a pretty penny. It sold for five thousand dollars. Isn't that amazing? Think of all the medical bills that'll pay for."

Elsie nodded, trying to tamp down the bitter taste rising up in her throat. Probably just indigestion. Too much coffee. She should have known better.

"I just wanted to let you know, since it was your good idea to donate it," Emma said, squeezing Elsie's shoulder. "I'll get back to the little ones. Verena's minding them, but they can be a handful."

Elsie thanked her sister, keeping her head bent over her stitches because she knew Emma would be able to read her consternation with one glimpse of her face.

"That's good news," Lois Mast, the bishop's wife, said from beside Rachel. "So many good deeds to help Jimmy Lapp and his family."

Other women chimed in, but Elsie stayed on task.

"How's the Country Store going?" Rachel asked. "You don't seem to mind having Ruben helping out there."

"Why would I mind, when more hands make light work?" Elsie asked, glancing past Rachel to Lois Mast, whose head was bent to her task, her eyes unreadable beyond the glare of her glasses. "Ruben has been a big help." She wanted to say more, but her feelings for Ruben could not ever be known by folks like Lois Mast, the bishop's wife, or Candy Eicher, who kept lifting her eyes from the quilt to peer across at Elsie. No, it was best to stick to a safe topic.

"Have you done any new paintings lately?" Elsie asked.

"None at all. My paint box has been dry since the accident."

"Dear Rachel. That's not like you. I don't know how many times I've run into you and you have paint smeared on your hands from fitting in some painting here and there."

"My days are full, with helping out at home and going to visit James."

"And James needs you now. I was just thinking of that lady at the gallery in the city. Remember Claudia Stein?"

"I know." Rachel sighed. "I got a note from her, after she heard about the accident. She's still interested, but she's going to have to wait till summer if she wants a collection of paintings from me."

"Harvest comes not every day," Elsie said. "I'm sure Claudia will understand that. Your pretty paintings are certainly worth waiting for."

Just then a short Englisher woman with silver-streaked hair came up to the quilters' table and paused. "There you are, Elsie."

Glancing up, Elsie recognized Nancy Briggs, the mayor of Halfway. A woman in her fifties, she wore her hair in a pretty cloud around her face, though that was her one "fancy" feature. Her quilted down coat, boots, and denim jeans were very practical, well suited to her down-to-earth nature.

"I've been looking for you. Got a call from your neighbor Marta, and it looks like Fanny is having the baby."

"Dear Gott in heaven." Elsie flushed at the mention of such news in public. She stuck the needle into the fabric and rose from the table. "But it's too soon . . . and the doctors wanted her to go to the hospital."

"Sounds like there isn't time." Nancy pointed a thumb toward the auction. "About ten minutes ago I sent Anna Beiler over to your place with a driver, and Marta told me Doc Trueherz was already on his way. I'm sure they'll call an ambulance if they need to get her to the hospital."

Elsie pressed a hand to her mouth as fear knotted inside her. She couldn't let anything happen to Fanny.

"I've got to get home." Her heartbeat drummed in her ears.

Rachel was immediately on her feet beside her. "I'll help you find Emma."

Outside in the main area of the barn, the crowd that had brought her joy minutes before now seemed like a maddening throng.

"There's Emma." Rachel moved around two boys pushing a desk on a handcart and disappeared into the crowd.

But they needed a driver, too. Caleb had the family's single horse and buggy over at the store, and even if he were already hitched up, it was an agonizing slow way to travel in an emergency.

Calm down. Take a breath, Elsie told herself. No one had said it was an emergency, but most folks didn't know about Fanny's medical problems through this pregnancy.

Biting her lower lip, Elsie scanned the crowd, searching for

George Dornbecker. Instead, the first face that emerged was her friend Haley.

"What's wrong?" Haley reached out to touch her shoulder. "Are you okay?"

"Fanny's gone into labor, and . . ."

"She has that blood pressure issue. . . ." Haley's amber eyes flashed as she made the immediate connection. "Where is she?"

"At home. Emma and I need to get home. And Will and Beth, too."

"I'll take you there." Haley tossed her coffee cup into a trash bin and put an arm around Elsie's shoulders. "Come on, honey. We are outtie."

〜 40 〜

The tiny thing mewed as Anna placed him firmly in Elsie's arms.

"Oh, little baby boy! What do you have to whimper about?" Elsie asked softly as she swayed gently back and forth. "You have a mamm who loves you so, and two big brothers to show you the way to be a man. And three big sisters to tease you and sneak cook-ies for you. Once you get teeth, of course."

Elsie's comment evoked soft chuckles from the others in the room. Doc Trueherz and Anna Beiler, the midwife, were still here, and Haley had stayed, just in case the doctor needed extra assis-tance.

The baby mewled again, and Elsie felt a tender tug of affection for him. He was sunshine and joy and tender new life, and he was ever so welcome in this house that had known so much sadness lately.

"What's his name, Mamm?" Will asked.

"Ya." Beth climbed up on the couch and perched beside her mother. "What his name, Mamm?"

"I was thinking of Thomas," Fanny said. "And we could call him Tom." She seemed so relaxed on the couch, so content and happy, that Elsie had trouble believing that she had given birth to this beautiful little baby less than an hour ago.

"Tom?" Elsie folded the blanket away so that she could see his face. "What do you think? Are you a Tom?"

He moved his peachy head so that he could stare up at her. "Such eyes you have." A deep, warm brown, they were soulful and wise, as if he already understood that this world he was coming into wasn't perfect, but that he would find his own right good place.

"Does he like his name?" Will asked.

"I would say he's thinking about it," Emma responded, holding out her arms for a chance to hold him. He kicked his tiny legs as they made the switch. "Such a feisty one, you are!" Emma cooed.

"He's got spirit," Anna agreed. "Just like his mamm." She leaned in closer to Emma and Elsie to click her tongue at the baby. "This one was a challenge, preeclampsia and all," she said, in a quiet, women-only voice.

Tom let out another cry, and everyone looked toward Emma.

"The kid's got a good pair of lungs," Haley said.

"What a day! Delivering babies is one of the highlights of my job," Henry Trueherz said, as he pumped up the cuff on Fanny's arm to check her blood pressure. "But I don't get to do it too often because of competent midwives like you, Anna."

"Ach!" Anna waved a withered hand at him. "I should know what I'm doing. Been doing it nearly forty years. I'd say that's right good practice."

"Can't argue with that." Dr. Trueherz checked the monitor and wrote the numbers down in his notebook.

"How is her blood pressure now?" Haley asked. She had been helpful in explaining preeclampsia for the family.

"It looks good. Fanny, I'd say we're through the worst of it without complications."

"Thank the Heavenly Father," Elsie said. If the blood pressure had gotten too high during labor, there was a chance that Fanny could have begun having seizures, which would have been dangerous for mother and baby.

Fanny sighed. "I'm grateful to be home. I have no love for the hospital, but I would have gone if you told me so, Doc."

"You've got the blood pressure of a marathon runner now," the doctor said. "Your prayers worked, young lady."

It seemed funny to hear Fanny being called a young lady when she was the mamm in their house. But truth be told, she was only twenty-nine, just eight years older than Caleb.

The doctor packed his things in a brown leather satchel. "Looks like my work is done here. Anna, do you want a ride home?"

"I'm going to stay on a bit." Anna handed Fanny a glass of water. "I like to dote on the newborns."

Dr. Trueherz said his good-byes, and the family settled in once again, a semicircle of rocking chairs facing the blue sofa.

"Is it all right if I get up?" Fanny asked the midwife. "There's a little cap that I knit for Tom, and I want to try it on him."

Anna pressed a finger to her chin. "You're looking fit, but you best stay put for now."

"I'll fetch it," Elsie offered.

"It's yellow and white," Fanny said. "I think it's in the bedroom, on the chest of drawers."

Elsie went into the bedroom that had been shared by Dat and Fanny for many years. Although she had avoided entering it since Dat passed, she now stepped inside with a new vision of the room now that the baby had been born in here. It was time to let go of the shadow of grief and clear the way for the new life Gott had blessed them with.

She found the hat sitting right on the dresser as Fanny had said. As she stepped in to get it, she saw a flurry of white outside the window.

Snow.

Already it was beginning to stick to the ground, mottling the dirt trail and fence and golden grass with white specks. Caleb would have an interesting trip home from the store.

"Elsie?" Haley poked her head into the doorway. "Did you find it?"

"I did, but look. It's snowing."

"Wow." Haley stepped up to the window. "It's really coming down. I should probably go soon."

"Will you be okay driving in it?"

"No worries. The Geo has all-wheel drive, and I'll take it slow."

"It's such a beautiful sight. A blanket of white. It's as if Gott is making everything fresh and clean for Tom's arrival."

Haley's smile eased the strain on her face. "That's one of the many things I love about you, Els. You find the good in everything."

"It's a wonderful good day. Tom's birth is a new start for our family."

"And a small miracle, I think. To have everything go off without a hitch, without complications. God had His angels watching over Fanny today."

"We have so much to be thankful for." Elsie picked up the knit cap. "You know, I was worried about how I'd feel when the baby came. I was afraid I would fall back into despair over Dat. It's such a sad thing for a child not to have a father. But now that Tom is here, something inside of me has shifted. Like a flower has blossomed inside of me. I'm going to love that baby as if he were my own."

"He is so precious. Doesn't it make you want a baby, Els? A child of your own? When I see a tiny infant like Tom, it just pushes all my buttons."

Elsie knew the tug of longing her friend was experiencing. She had begun to feel that way when she saw Amish mamms with their infants and toddlers. A baby grasping for the string of her mother's prayer kapp, a toddler hiding behind the skirt of his mother's dress. The sight of mother and child awakened that yearning that she had put to rest so many years ago.

But Tom would be the child she would never have. "I'll just have to shower Tom with the same love I would give my own baby," Elsie said.

"Everyone is already falling for him," Haley said. "He's lucky to be surrounded by so much love."

"He's a child of winter. A cold, dark time . . . but it's cozy, too. And spring is just around the corner."

Haley's amber eyes flickered as she put her hands on Elsie's shoulders. "You are the master of finding the silver lining in every cloud, and after everything you've been through. You're my hero, Elsie."

"Oh, it's not a big deal . . . I just look for the little glimmer of light in the darkness. For a time, I couldn't find it, but I can now. Little Tom has brought light into our house again."

"I'm so happy for you." They hugged, and in the moment of quiet came the sound of snow crystals tapping the window in the blustery wind.

"I guess it's time to get my snow leopard on the road," Haley said.

As Elsie followed her into the main room with the little cap in hand, she couldn't help but smile. That was who she was, deep in the core of her heart. The one who could see good in everyone. The person who saw the silver lining in a dark storm cloud.

She gave a happy sigh, so relieved that her sunny disposition was coming back. Ya. If little Tom was still fussing, she would find a way to turn his frown upside down.

⊙⊙

That night, after everyone else had gone to bed, Elsie added one last batch of coal to the stove as Fanny finished nursing the baby.

"Now it's time to sleep, little one." Fanny ran a hand over her baby's downy head.

"Gott has blessed us today." Elsie had stayed up to keep Fanny company, and to hold the baby one last time before going off to bed. If Tom was going to be the only babe in her life, the child of her heart, she wanted to make the day of his birth last long in her memory.

Fanny let out a yawn as Tom's little rosebud mouth sucked at the air, then settled.

"Can I hold him a bit?" Elsie asked.

"Sure." Fanny placed her warm bundle in Elsie's arm. "I'm off to bed. You can bring him in to the cradle in my room when you've had enough cuddling."

Elsie looked down at the sleeping baby, his perfectly formed nose shining in the dim light. "I don't know that I'll ever get enough of this little one."

With a chuckle, Fanny headed off to the washroom.

As Elsie settled into a slow, steady rocking pattern, she began to hum. Before long, she realized it was a song she had loved since she was a child, called "I Have Found a Hiding Place." As a small girl, skilled in the game of hide-and-seek, she had thought the song was written for her.

> "I have found a hiding place when sore distressed,
>   Jesus, Rock of Ages, strong and true . . ."

She sang softly as her mind painted a warm, happy future for the little baby in her arms. Outside, something rattled against the front window. The wind must have been kicking up the snow, but they were safe and warm inside.

> "I have found a lovely star that shines on high,
> Jesus, Bright and Morning Star to me;
> In the night of sorrow He is ever nigh,
> He drives the darkest shadows away . . ."

A clatter outside the window caused her to abruptly stop singing.

"Don't worry, Tom," she whispered to the sleeping baby. "It's probably just a branch blowing in the snow." It was hard to see anything with the curtains drawn over the window to keep the draft out. But as she rose and crossed the room, baby in her arms, a bouncing light made her heartbeat quicken.

That was not the wind.

With Tom cradled in her arms, she parted the curtains and peered out. Someone was out there with a flashlight; a young man who'd come courting, despite the snow. For a moment she expected it to be Gabe King, here for Emma, but as she made out the dark silhouette, it was too large to be Gabe.

"Ruben?" she called through the glass.

With one hand he turned the flashlight on himself, hitting the snow from his hat with the other hand.

She tapped on the glass, then pointed toward the side of the house. "Go round to the mud porch. I'll meet you there."

Had he really come all this way in the snow? She hadn't heard his horse and buggy come down the lane, but then snow tended to muffle noises in the night.

She checked the sleeping baby in her arms, then walked through the kitchen. A cold draft swept in as she opened the door to the mud porch, where rows of socks hung from a line like sleeping bats. She cradled the baby closer for warmth, but he breathed quietly, unfazed by the cold.

Ruben was huddled over by the hat rack, knocking snow from the shoulders of his coat.

"What are you doing out in the deepest snow of the winter?" she asked.

"I hope it's all right. I wanted to tell you how the auction went, and besides that, it's Saturday night."

The night when young men courted their girls . . . was that what he meant?

As she looked up at his broad, kind face, she couldn't deny that she was overjoyed to see him on this night of all nights. In the past few months, Ruben had been at her side for nearly every important moment, sharing in the sadness and healing. She wanted him to be here, to have a peek at Tom, to tell her about the auction and keep her company by the warm stove.

And there was still the matter of that wonderful kiss from last week. That spark that still lingered in the air between them.

Just the thought of it set tender emotions trembling through her.

But there would be no kissing tonight . . . not with little Tom nestled in her arms. Tonight was a night to celebrate a gift from Gott. A night for celebration and friendship.

He looked up as he stepped out of a boot. "Is that the new baby you're holding?"

"It is. Tom Lapp."

"Praise be to Gott. But shouldn't he be asleep?"

She chuckled softly. "He is asleep. That's the joy of being a baby. You get passed from one set of loving arms to the next, and you settle in and go back to sleep.

"Kumm," she said, leading him inside after he had left his wet things on the mud porch. "You can warm up by the stove."

"Denki." He followed her inside, stepping right up to fold down the blanket at Tom's chin and study his little face. "*Wilkommen,* little man. You're a lucky one to be in Elsie's arms."

His words, his presence, the twinkle in his blue eyes—everything conspired to warm her from within. "Do you want some hot cocoa?"

"That would hit the spot. The snow is already thick out there. Like slogging through a bucket of flour."

Elsie turned to the kitchen to prepare the hot drink, then paused. She didn't want to jostle the baby too much. "I need to put you back in your cradle."

"Here." Ruben motioned her closer. "Give him to me." Without a moment's hesitation he reached out and gently lifted little Tom from her arms. In Ruben's large hands, Tom looked like a tiny little doll, but from the way Ruben cradled the baby in the crook of one arm, Elsie could see he had experience with babies.

"You've been around little ones," she said.

"Ya. Our family is still growing. Little Perry is only a few months old."

Ruben didn't talk about his family often, and she had forgotten that his father, like her dat, had taken a younger bride after being widowed.

She watched as he lowered himself into a rocker by the stove and gently shifted the baby, supporting his head. Oh, he was good with babies. The sight of him talking softly to Tom tugged at something deep inside her, something that had been long buried, tucked into a secret hiding place.

There's no reason to doubt that Elsie will be able to have healthy babies of her own, Doc Trueherz had told her and Fanny years ago, when she had gone into the clinic for a throat infection that had turned into a physical exam.

And Fanny's smile had cast a gentle shower of grace over Elsie. "That's good news. There's nothing more important in this world than having a family of your own."

A baby of her own . . . that would be heavenly. A toddler tugging on her skirt. A little Ruben tracking mud into their house. Although she didn't want to admit it, she had fallen for Ruben . . . fallen hard. And the thought that he might one day be her husband, sitting beside her at the family table, sharing a bed . . . oh, that would truly be a life of happiness.

Another glimpse of Ruben rocking the baby, and Elsie wanted to cry out for the terrible unfairness of it all.

It could never be . . . not for her.

She turned away quickly and tugged the refrigerator open, trying to push such thoughts from her mind.

As she heated milk on the stove, he told her about the fruitful day at Zook's barn. "You saw the turnout. There were a lot more Englishers than we usually see in Halfway this time of year."

"Such a crowd." She stirred the milk, careful not to stare at the lovely sight of the big, sweet man holding her little Tom.

Ruben explained that some of the handmade and rare items had fetched high bids—including her family's wooden box. But there had been other creative donations. The Fishers had auctioned off a day of baking, and Dave Zook agreed to give a tour of his buggy shop, along with a ride in a real Amish buggy. By the end of the day, Mary and Remy had counted receipts of more than twenty-three thousand dollars.

"That's wonderful for James and his family." Goose bumps tickled the back of her neck at the wonder of it all. That daunting mountain of debt would be gone! When Gott took a family in His loving arms, He truly did move mountains.

"I knew our Plain folk would pull it together for Jimmy Lapp and his family." Ruben lowered his head, as if speaking directly to Tom. "This is how we do it, little man. You must follow the Golden Rule and love your neighbor as yourself."

"That's a good lesson." With a tender smile, Elsie brought the warm mug of cocoa over to them. "But it might be a little early for Tom, being just a few hours old."

"It's never too early to learn Gott's goodness." Ruben spoke directly to the sleeping baby. "Am I right?"

Tom simply turned his head and nuzzled his little nose into the soft blanket.

Every little movement the baby made stole Elsie's breath away. She put the mug down and held her arms out. "I'll take him while you drink your hot chocolate."

"Back to Elsie you go," Ruben told the sleeping baby.

As she dipped her hands into the warm crook of his arms, her skin tingled from brushing against his sleeves. Such a wild, warm sensation! It happened every time he touched her.

Suddenly warm and content, she settled onto the sofa across from Ruben and thought what a pretty picture they made, the three of them warming together by the stove. Soft light playing on Ruben's face. His words falling over her like gentle snowflakes.

The only thing that could have made things more perfect would have been if the baby were theirs.

41

The glow that surrounded Elsie tonight, like an angel's halo, was an answer to Ruben's prayers. Every night, he'd been getting down on his knees, praying that Gott would give him the words to convince her that she had made the wrong decision, that she had to give him a chance to be in her life, beside her, forever and for always.

The need to persuade her had consumed him for most of the week, distracting him when customers were telling him stories or during those stretches when he was alone in his buggy, letting his horse take him down the open road.

It wasn't the sort of thing he could bring up at home with any of his brothers, who would laugh at him or tease him for liking a girl. And he'd thought about telling Amos at church last week, but the young man who shared his place on the outside of the Amish youth group had been sick with the flu.

Oddly, the only person Ruben had been able to talk with was

the last person Elsie would want him spilling the beans to. But Preacher Dave was the easiest member of the clergy to talk with. He wasn't so quick to pass judgment like the bishop. Besides that, he was Ruben's uncle, so Dave and his family were often over at the house, visiting.

And Friday night, when Dave had stopped over to drop off a rug Lydia had hooked for the auction, he got to teasing Ruben.

"This auction is a good-size event for a fella like yourself to be managing," Dave said. "Pretty soon you'll figure out that it takes two to pull things like this together. For a charity like this, you need a wife."

"Lots of folks are chipping in for James," Ruben said. "But what makes you think there isn't a young woman working with me?"

"Oops!" Dave clapped him on the back. "I guess I spoke too soon. So you have been courting a girl?"

Ruben shrugged, thinking that maybe he shouldn't have spoken up. He wasn't really ready to talk about Elsie, but with the pressure on him to find a suitable Amish girl to marry, he thought that talk of a girlfriend might take some of the heat off. "I'm working on it."

Dave leaned forward and rested his elbows on his knees. "It shouldn't be so much work. Have you been to visit her?"

"Ya. And I see a lot of her." Ruben didn't want Dave to know it was Elsie he was talking about. Not yet. "But there's a twist in the road between us."

"What's that?"

"She doesn't want to marry. Ever."

"Not ever?" Dave stroked his beard. "Is this an Amish girl?"

"Ya. She's lived Plain all her life."

"Then she'll change her mind." Dave nodded knowingly as he straightened up. "All Amish girls do."

"I don't know. She's different from most girls."

"Every young man feels that way when he's falling in love. But any road worth taking has its challenges. Don't give up on her because it's not easy. You can tell when you're on the right track even if it's going uphill."

Giving up on Elsie was out of the question, but now, sitting across from her as she held little Tom close to her heart, he could see that Gott had given her a change of heart. She loved this baby. Watching her, Ruben had no doubt that she would be a wonderful mother. Motherhood was what Gott intended for her, and now it seemed that she was beginning to see that.

"That's good cocoa," he said, holding the mug in one hand. "It warms from the inside."

"I reckon you need it, traveling here through all that snow. Did you put your horse in the carriage house?"

"I left him in there to get him out of the snow. It's only about a foot high, but the drifts—you don't know what you're stepping into under those snow mounds."

"Well, it was brave and kind of you to make the trip, but I don't want to mislead you, Ruben. You know I can't court you."

"Whoa." He held up one hand to stop her and made a gesture to pretend that he was sewing his mouth shut. "Here we are, sitting by a warm fire with a newborn miracle. Snow is falling past the window, but we're cozy in here. Why would you want to go and ruin it all by saying something like that?"

There was a mixture of amusement and regret in her eyes. "Because it's true. There's a special place for you in my heart. There always will be."

He wanted her to stop there so that he could bask in her words like a dog in a pool of sunshine. There was a place in her heart for him. He wasn't alone in this love.

"But we can't court like other Amish couples because . . ." She turned away. "Because I'm not normal."

"Ach, there you go again with silly talk. Do you think I haven't noticed that you're a little person? I know it, Elsie, and I love the Gott who made you in a different mold from other Amish girls." He shifted in the rocking chair, letting his long legs stretch out before him. Since the accident on the plow, one was shorter than the other.

"I don't mean to spoil anything, so I'll toss my words out into the snow if you agree to keep this a social call and not a courtship."

"Mmm. I shined the light on your bedroom window first. I didn't figure you'd still be down here so late."

"I couldn't sleep. I'm just so relieved that Fanny is all right, and so excited to have a new baby in the house. It's a new life, Ruben."

"My mamm used to say that every baby is a miracle, and no one was more excited than her when there was a new baby in the house."

"She was right." Elsie shifted the baby so that he rested firmly on her legs, facing her. "Do you still miss her, Ruben?"

"I do." Kate Zook had died of cancer when Ruben was fifteen. "It's been five years, and sometimes I still think I hear her voice calling me from the kitchen, or I come home expecting to smell the peanut butter cookies she baked for us."

"The same thing happens to me with Dat. I think I hear his footsteps down here, first thing in the morning, to start the fire, but it turns out to be Caleb. Or sometimes at the store, when the door bells jingle, I think it's Dat dropping in to check on things."

"I think he'd be mighty satisfied with the way things are going in the Country Store," Ruben said.

"I hope so."

The gleam in her eyes, the light of grace and peace, reminded him of one of his mamm's expressions. Maybe that was one of the reasons he wanted to be near her. "Seeing you sitting there with Tom in your lap reminds me of my mamm. She was the light in our house. Sunshine and light. Like you, she always saw the good side of things. The good in people. The good in her children. After the accident on the plow, people didn't think I'd ever get back to normal. Some of them gave up on me, but Mamm, she was always there, always with a smile and a peanut butter cookie."

"I'd better figure out a recipe for peanut butter cookies," she teased.

A smile welled up from deep inside Ruben. She did love him. She didn't want to say the word because she was afraid of what it might mean down the road, but in her heart, she knew it was true.

She loved him, and oh, he loved every little thing about her.

He put his mug down. "Look at you, so happy with this baby in your arms. Doesn't it feel right? The way he fits in the bend of your arm. The wonders of hearing him breathe or watching his little mouth twitch while he's sleeping. Doesn't this tell you what Gott wants for you, Elsie? You're meant to have a family. A baby in your arms. Little ones tugging on your skirts." He leaned forward, elbows on his knees, as he lowered his voice. "A husband who loves you."

Her eyes opened, round as quarters. "Now who's the one who should be sewing the mouth closed?" Despite her teasing tone, he could see the flicker of longing in her eyes.

Elsie, darling, why can't you see what's best for us both?

The clock struck one A.M. "I'd better get going, or else I'll turn into a snowman."

"We can't let that happen," she said in a teasing voice as he rose.

Ruben was wondering if it would be wise to swoop down for a kiss when he remembered the auction. "Ach! I almost forgot. I've got a small gift for you." He went to the mud porch and retrieved the satchel he had carried inside his coat, to keep it dry.

Back inside, he held the satchel to his chest as he took a seat beside Elsie and the baby on the couch. "At the auction today, I got a gift for you."

When he removed the wooden box, she gasped.

"Ruben! How did you get that? They told me it was sold to make money for James."

"It was. The money went to the Lapps."

"But how?"

"That nice customer from the Country Store, Gwen Slavin, she bought it. But she was acting as an agent for me. Dat wanted to give a good donation to the Lapps, but, well, he wanted to be anonymous, knowing how some folks feel about his leasing out his land."

When Joe Zook had decided to lease his share of the family land out and give up farming, some people in the community had been disgruntled. By tradition, the Amish had farmed any land they could get access to. Some people thought it was wrong for an Amish man to make a deliberate choice to separate from the land and start a business.

"Oh, Ruben." She handed him the baby so that she could hold the box in her lap. Her eyes glistened as she ran her hands over the smooth wood painted with red borders and decorative cherries. She turned the latch and opened it.

"From Grandmother Elizabeth Lapp to Sammy Lapp," she said, reading the message stenciled on the inside lid of the box. "I can still see Dat showing it to us when we were children. He would always throw in a story about his father or his grandparents. I know it's a material thing, just a wooden box, but it's special because it's been in the Lapp family for so many years."

"I know that. That's why I wanted to buy it back for you."

"It's the nicest thing anyone has ever done for me." She shook her head. "I still can't get over it. But I don't think it would be right for me to accept it, especially coming from you."

Ruben squinted, not sure what she was driving at.

"I mean . . ." She cocked her head to one side, her voice going so soft, he could barely hear. "Is it an engagement gift?"

"No. I wasn't thinking that." Although he would be walking on air to know that he and Elsie were committed to each other, it was too soon to press for that. Especially since she wasn't even baptized yet. "It's a gift, plain and simple." Tom gave a squeak as he squirmed in Ruben's arms. "Right, *Liewi*?" he asked, calling the baby by the name his mother had used for her children. *Darling.*

Elsie put the box aside, watching as Ruben shushed Tom back to sleep.

"For a man, you're good with babies," she said.

"That's what happens when you have little ones underfoot." His father and Mary had added three to the family in as many years, and Ruben liked the noise and contentment of young children.

With Tom settled again, he passed the delicate bundle back to Elsie, and then rose. It was hard to leave them, especially for a trek through the snow. But someday, Gott willing, he would spend every night with Elsie Lapp.

"Good night, liewi," he said.

Good night, darling.

As he pulled on his outerwear in the mudroom, he hoped that Elsie knew that his farewell was meant for her.

Ҩҩ 42 Ҩҩ

Although Dylan had been inviting her to join them since the accident occurred, Graciana Estevez didn't finally agree to attend the Halfway group therapy session until the second week of March. As the regulars trickled into the back room of the library, Dylan had asked the group to make Graciana feel welcome, but he knew that was an unnecessary request. Support and kindness swept through this group like a wildfire in the forest.

If she was intent on healing, Graciana had come to the right place.

Already Rachel had made sure that the older woman tried some of the snickerdoodles she had brought. Ruben had told her about the charity auction for James. George had told a joke about the origin of the word "snickerdoodle," and Haley had explained the nursing program at LanCo General. Even the usually reserved Zed had stepped up for a few words about the weather.

This was a very functional group. Dylan would have been proud, if he thought he had earned any of the credit. In essence, he'd deduced that the Amish made excellent patients.

After Dylan's brief introduction and welcome to Graciana, Rachel started off the meeting with her "good news" report.

"Last week I picked up my paintbrush again, and I'm painting." Rachel's index finger drew tiny loops on the table as she spoke. "Fast and wild. I guess all the ideas that I was saving in my mind are eager to fly out."

"That's wonderful good." Elsie's smile was encouraging. "When do you find the time, with your chores and visiting James?"

"I decided not to visit James so much anymore. He needs some time to recuperate, and I've got to give it to him." She turned to Dylan, her eyes clear with resolve. "I fought that. I didn't want to stay away. But now I've learned to accept the things I can't change."

Dylan nodded his approval, glad that she had embraced a difficult life lesson.

"Will you be sending the paintings to the gallery in Philadelphia?" Elsie asked. Then she explained to the group that a dealer in the city had offered to represent Rachel.

"That's my plan for now," Rachel said. "Claudia Stein, that's the dealer, she thinks my paintings will fetch a very good price."

"The one you donated for the auction brought in a lot of money," Ruben pointed out.

"If everything works out, if the paintings do sell, I'm hoping that I might eventually make enough to live on. If I can do that, if I can save some money, I'd like to move to a house in town. The chores of the farm are too distracting for me, and I never was one for milking the cows and mucking the stalls. A house in Halfway would be very nice."

"That is good news." Dylan felt grateful to Rachel for starting them off on a positive note. "Who else wants to share?"

"There's baby Tom, born on Saturday." Elsie positively glowed, as if he were her own newborn. "Most everyone here has heard the news, but I'm bursting with happiness over the change in our house. Mother and baby are both doing fine. Fanny had high blood pressure when she was pregnant, but that's gone now, so that worry is over. Gott has truly blessed us."

"Congratulations." It was one of the first times Dylan had seen smiles from everyone in the group. Even Graciana, who had joined them today with a heavy heart, managed a wistful smile. "There's nothing like a newborn baby to remind us what really matters, is there?"

Elsie nodded. "We take turns holding him and rocking him. There's something wonderful about being needed. Even the little ones enjoy caring for him. Beth is learning how to change diapers."

At that, Graciana winced, blinking back tears. Dylan turned to her, his voice gentle. "Graciana, does it bring back memories for you?"

"When Clara was a baby . . ." She nodded, swiping one hand over her eyes. "She was my only one."

Haley pushed the box of tissues across the table to her.

"Please, don't be offended by my tears," Graciana told Elsie. "I'm truly happy for you, and I wish your family many blessings."

"It's okay to cry." Elsie reached across the table and touched her arm. "We've learned that here."

"I guess I'm a little late to the game." Graciana pressed a tissue to her eyes, and then took a deep, calming breath. "You might be wondering why I'm here, since I wasn't even close to the scene of the accident. I wasn't, but my daughter caused it."

She pressed two fingers to her forehead, taking another pronounced breath. "It's unforgivable, what she did. I'm angry with her, blazing mad, and at the same time I wish I could give her a big hug and smell the shampoo in her hair and remind her to go take her senior photos for graduation. I want to ask her what she was doing that day on that highway so far from our home, when it was strictly forbidden. What was she doing texting on her phone when it was supposed to be put away in her purse until she turned off the car?

"These are all questions I have for my daughter. Things I want to ask her. But my Clara can't answer, because she's never coming home again. My Clara is gone. Forever. And this is one mistake her mom can't undo for her."

"Your anger is certainly justified," Dylan said. "I'm wondering if you would feel differently if you learned that the accident was caused by something beyond Clara's control. Say that the brakes failed, or there was ice on the road. Would you blame Clara then?"

Graciana's lips puckered as she considered the question. "I guess I wouldn't. No."

"But the tragic circumstances would remain. Clara would be gone. One person dead in George's van. Two seriously injured. You would be grieving the loss of your daughter and the other injuries caused by the crash. Can you separate your anger and simply allow yourself to grieve?"

"No," she said quickly. "No, I can't forgive her for doing something so stupid, so selfish. It's unforgivable."

"In our faith, there is always room for forgiveness." Zed's voice was even but firm, holding no judgment. "Gott wants us to forgive others because He forgives us. His love for us is great. It knows no boundaries . . . like the sky above. That's how I think of His forgiveness. A big, blue sky that goes on forever."

"That's a beautiful image, but I think it's different when your own child does something horrific like this. It's an extension of you." She looked around the table. "Does anyone here even have children?"

George lifted his hand. "Three sons, and I know what you mean. They do shame a parent when they do the wrong thing. But I think you're being hard on Clara. Hard on yourself, too."

"I feel like I could have changed all this if I'd done the right thing. If I'd been more strict with her, a better parent . . ."

"We can't change the past, Graciana." Dylan stepped in, wanting to keep the conversation moving forward. "As Rachel said, we have to let go of the things beyond our control."

"I know it's not always easy to forgive," Elsie said. "But it's Gott's will. And if we don't forgive, the bad feelings eat away at the soul. Anger is a heavy burden to carry around."

"I can vouch for that." Haley held up her hands, as if surrendering. "I've been walking around with a lot of anger and blame for people in my life. I've been mad at my parents for thinking that I was a failure. I was mad at my ex-fiancé for not being the right man for me. I was mad at my sisters for being the type of daughters my parents wanted, and . . ." She let out a sigh. "I've just been mad, mad, mad, and I blamed other people for the things that went wrong in my life."

Dylan had to keep himself from smiling at her animated admission. There was something so lovable about Haley. She was human and fallible and quick to admit it all and laugh it off. She was sunshine and laughter and . . . He swallowed, reminding himself to stay on track. He was the therapist for this group.

"Somehow, the accident released me from the anger that was festering inside me. Not that I don't still get mad now and then, but now I won't let it stew. I'll never forget that terrible night, or the way it shook my life up. But I've come away from it seeing how precious life is. I realized that I'd been wasting mine, spending too much energy worrying about qualities in myself that I couldn't fix instead of focusing on the gifts God gave me. It's been a hard road, but I'm making my way. And now I'm glad the circumstances of my life have forced me to move on."

Moving on . . .

As if looking at a timeline, Dylan saw the various stages of Haley's progress over the past few months. She was thriving, despite all adversity.

And what about you, pal?

He was stuck in the muck, right around the same spot he'd been in three years ago when the wounds were still fresh and life choices could be put off until he'd had a chance to heal.

How many years had it been? How many years could a man coddle himself in healing mode?

Oh, he'd made a few halfhearted attempts to connect with people who weren't his clients. There were all those movie dates set up by mutual friends who'd thought that he and the hapless female would be great together. He'd gone ice skating with a woman whose name he couldn't remember. He'd attended holiday parties and Super Bowl gatherings and church picnics. But through it all, he'd maintained a safe emotional distance, watching the world from behind a wall of glass.

"You've all been very kind, but I'm not ready to move on." Graciana stared down at the table. "And honestly, I don't think I'll ever be able to forgive my baby for being so stupid. I still have a lot of anger for Clara . . . and for the genius who invented cell phones in the first place."

"If you will, I'd like to step out of my role of facilitator for just a moment and share something with you." Dylan's throat was tight and he felt a strong desire to crawl under the table and hide. But the voice inside him persisted. "Most of you don't know my background, but I moved here from Philadelphia, where I used to live with my wife and daughter. They were killed a few years ago in a collision on the interstate. It was the Tuesday before Thanksgiving, and they were headed up to Boston to be with my wife's parents. I planned to fly up Thursday morning, so I could finish teaching my classes. I was a schoolteacher at the time."

He swallowed, sensing their curious stares but not wanting to lose his courage. "For years, I blamed myself for not being there ... for not taking the time to drive them that long distance. Our daughter, Angela, she was still a baby, pretty demanding, and Kris was the one who lost sleep to attend to her. Up late, out of bed early. Feeding her in the middle of the night. I kept thinking of the many ways that I could have saved them. I could have taken off from work to drive with them. We could have all flown up together. If Kris had the sleep she needed, if she'd been alert enough to have a better reaction time." He rubbed his jaw. "The mind is good at coming up with a million ways to punish yourself."

Tears sparkled in Graciana's eyes as she nodded. "I can relate to that."

"For myself, I have to admit that I'm still working my way through the healing process." Dylan's throat felt raw. Was his pain leaching into his voice? He had wanted to share his story as a lesson in healing, but in this moment he felt like the client, tapping the gusher of pain, fumbling to stanch the flow as the session began to wind down. "But I want to underline what Haley said today, because it's a valuable message. Anger and blame and guilt will suck the life out of a person. When we learn to let go of those things, we can begin to heal."

Elsie and Rachel were nodding in agreement.

"I know that sometimes healing doesn't happen overnight. Letting go and moving on can be a process, and that's why we're here. To help each other."

Graciana's face hardened into a stoic frown. "I'm sorry, but I don't think it's possible."

"Don't give up." Elsie's dark eyes glimmered with hope. "Gott's love is as sure as the sun rising in the morning."

"Elsie's right." Dylan caught Graciana with a firm look. "You need to have faith that healing is possible."

The older woman turned pleading eyes toward Dylan. "I'll do whatever you say, Doc. I do trust you."

I hope your trust is not misplaced, Dylan thought, knowing it was time to wrap up their session. "Here's something we can try. For our next meeting, I would like everyone here to bring in photos or small objects that remind you of someone you lost. Graciana, it would help if you brought pictures of Clara and some things that she loved so that everyone here can get to know what she was like."

It would also serve to get Graciana talking about her daughter's positive qualities. Maybe it would help her own the compassion she felt toward Clara.

And maybe it was selfish, but the exercise would help him, too. Maybe it was time to start talking more about the past to free up the future.

〜 43 〜

When the therapy session ended, Haley walked out with Elsie and Ruben, who said good-bye and headed off in different directions. Ruben's father had ordered him back to Zook's barn, and though no one had mentioned it, it was clear that Ruben and Elsie were not happy with the new situation.

Left on her own with a lump in her throat, Haley crossed the parking lot to the picnic tables behind the ice-cream parlor. Someone had cleared the snow from the wooden tables, and she climbed up and took a seat atop one. In the summer, this parking lot would be abuzz with cars and buggies. Couples and families would sit back here, enjoying the sweet frozen treats advertised by giant photos in the building's windows.

Banana Split!

Hot Fudge Sundae!

Strawberry Parfait!

When she was a little kid, Haley had imagined herself sitting back here as an adult, finally able to order the big ice-cream treats. Finally, a big girl. A teenager. A woman.

But independence wasn't nearly as sweet as a sundae. In fact, the more she learned, the more she tasted the bittersweet in situations. Life was a contrast of sweet and sour, darkness and light.

The miracle of Fanny's newborn baby against the tragic reality that he would never know his father.

The beautiful connection between Ruben and Elsie against the sad fact that Elsie could not allow herself to be his wife.

The glory of finally falling in love against the irony that the man who held her heart was haunted by another life.

A chill wind snapped around her, but she had left her jacket inside and she wasn't going to go in there until Dylan was gone. She hunkered down and squeezed her eyes shut against tears.

The meeting had been cathartic for her. Articulating her journey since the accident had helped to gel her own issues.

But then . . . then came the rain. To hear Dylan's heartbreak, to visualize his life with Kris and Angela, a young happy family living in the city, and to think that it all had ended with one random event.

Just like a fat SUV swerving into your lane.

So now Dylan was on the fringes of two highway collisions that had sent lives spinning out of control. Had God chosen him to be here for the Amish because of his own experience with sudden loss and trauma?

She had to believe that was true. The Amish talked about "Gott's will" often, and she was beginning to understand the incredible grace that could be had in accepting the things beyond your reach.

Cupping her hands and blowing into them to warm up, she thought of the prayer her grandmother used to have hanging on the kitchen wall.

The serenity prayer.

God, grant me the serenity to accept the things I cannot change; courage to change the things I can; and wisdom to know the difference.

Haley had always had the courage to bulldoze ahead with change, but she wasn't so strong in the serenity and wisdom departments.

A motion at the corner of the parking lot caught her eye. Dylan was headed her way, carrying her coat. *Oh, great.*

"I'd say that you were going to get a cold being out here without this, but I know that's not clinically true." He held up her jacket. "But you will get sore muscles from bracing against the wind." He climbed onto the table beside her and held her jacket so that she could slip her arms into the sleeves.

The brief touch of his hands sent a different kind of shiver through her body, and she winced, annoyed with herself for wanting him so much when he was obviously out of reach.

She had been wrong, thinking that she could simply win him over.

She couldn't compete with the ghost of a beautiful marriage. She did not have the power to heal him, and he wasn't going to move forward until he was whole again.

"So . . . what's the deal?" he asked. "Are you feeling feverish, or was the session so intense that we drove you out into the cold?"

"I had an epiphany, I guess." She leaned back so that she could zip her jacket up.

"That's good." He turned to look at her. "Do you want to talk about it?"

"I think . . ." She started to say she was sorry, so sorry for every-thing he had gone through, but before the words came her throat closed up and a tear slid down her cheek.

There was a pause. The flash of compassion in his eyes. And then he put an arm around her and rubbed her back, as if summoning warmth.

"We don't have to talk about it right now."

"I'm sorry. I'm just so sorry. You have a much better reason to cry than I do."

"I've cried myself a river or two. I'm all dried out. And I hope that's not pity I hear in your voice, because that's why I stopped telling people what happened. I couldn't stand to see that sad-sack look in their eyes."

"No pity. Just compassion."

"I'm okay with that. We can never have enough compassion in the world."

Sitting in the cold, quietly crying with Dylan by her side, Haley vowed to be here for him as a friend. That was all he wanted, all he could handle right now, and she wanted to respect his limits.

But oh, how she wished she could wrap her arms around him and kiss away the pain, soothe away the scars, whisper away the past.

She wished she had the power to heal him, to make him whole again, but she didn't. A tough lesson, but a valuable one.

True healing and grace came only from God.

It was time to harness the power of prayer.

⊷ 44 ⊷

$\mathcal{R}$uben unlatched the back of his horse cart and let his gaze sweep up to the top of the red barn that had been in his family for many generations. The building, now used to house an indoor farmer's market and emporium, was showing some signs of wear, with paint blistering on the wood panels.

It was time to get the painters there, he thought, taking a moment to walk the length of the back of the building. From a distance, the barn looked like a quaint roadside stand, but once you took on a task like sweeping the floors or cleaning horse droppings from the parking lot, you got a sense of the length and breadth of the place.

Having been away from Zook's barn, working at the Country Store, he now saw the place with a new eye. Just outside of town, right on the main road, the barn made a good stop for tourists looking for everything from a quick snack of a pretzel to a piece of furniture for their home.

He saw the value of Zook's barn as a business.

But he missed the cozy, quieter surroundings of Elsie's shop. The birdhouses with their tiled roofs. The scented soaps and lavender sachets. Rachel's paintings, like windows to moments of Amish life. The candy aisle of homemade taffy, candy apples, and butterscotch fudge. The furniture made by an Amish craftsman, particularly the cradles.

He had imagined a child of theirs rocking in one of those cradles, a tiny, murmuring baby like little Tom. Why was it so hard for Elsie to see her way to having a little one like that? A brood of babies to love and nurture, the way she was looking after Tom?

He returned to the cart and hoisted a bale of hay, shifting it to a wheelbarrow. The bales were stored in a small shed at the back of the barn, kept dry and ready for visiting horses, which needed food and water while they waited out the day in the parking lot.

It was heavy work, keeping the hay stocked and the parking lot clean—just one of the many chores that had to be done to keep Zook's barn running smoothly. Dry chaff and straw fluttered in the wind as he transferred a bale into the shed. The wind held the last gust of winter, raw and icy, but Ruben kept warm from the fire inside. He was bound and determined to find someone else in the family to take on these chores for him. Not that he minded the work, but every day away from Elsie was like a day without food and drink. The hunger was curling inside him and his throat was parched. He couldn't go on this way, day after day.

From behind him came the clack of a horse's hooves on pavement. It was his dat's buggy, and someone else rode in front beside him. Ruben brushed straw from his coat as he took a closer look and recognized the broad, friendly face of his uncle.

"Dave." He nodded, glad to see his uncle. While Joe Zook tended to be hard on his sons, never quite satisfied that their work was good enough, his brother Dave had a cheerful, easy manner that made room for people to be people.

"Ruben." Dave stepped down from the gray buggy. "I'm glad to see you back to work here."

"Not for long," Ruben said, looking tentatively at his father. "I'm going back to the Country Store as soon as I can find someone to take over here. Elsie still needs the help."

"Tell Elsie Lapp to bring Caleb in." Dat's voice was full of gravel and vinegar. "He can't be looking to open a business of his own with his dat gone."

"He's right," Dave said. "Why isn't Caleb helping out with the store?"

"He's better working with his hands. I've heard that his manner scared a few customers away."

"A lesson to be learned there. If they need someone to help run the store, Caleb needs to learn how to handle the Englishers," Dave said, folding his arms across his chest and tucking his hands in to keep warm.

Dat tied off his horse and headed into the barn. "I'll just be a minute."

As Dave stepped forward to help Ruben transfer the bales, Ruben remembered a message he was supposed to give one of the ministers. "Dylan and Haley are going to be attending church this Sunday. They were happy for the invitation."

When Dylan had expressed an interest in observing their Sunday service, Jimmy and Edna Lapp, who were hosting this week, had cleared it with the ministers. At first Deacon Moses had asked if they were "secure in their faith," as the Amish weren't in the business of trying to convert Englishers. But the bishop, having met both Dylan and Haley, thought it was okay.

"Dylan offered to bring some food," Ruben added, "but I told him the women would put out more than enough."

"Good. Dr. Dylan has helped ease the mind of many Amish. So we'll see them Sunday."

"Ya." Ruben bent his knees as he reached down to help Dave offload the last bale. "This is a task anyone could do. I'm thinking that Caleb Lapp should take my place here and I'll go back to the Country Store."

"You are bound and determined to get back there, aren't you?" Dave rubbed his hands together, his eyes narrowed in thought. "I've never seen you with such ants in your pants. What's got into you?"

Ruben was about to brush off the question, but he couldn't lie, and Dave wasn't one to judge a man. "Truth is, I want to work with Elsie Lapp."

"Elsie?" Dave's brows lifted in interest. "Ach, Elsie." Dave rolled his eyes toward the heavens. "How could I not see the one thing right before my eyes? So Elsie is the girl you favor."

"Ya." Ruben rolled the wheelbarrow back into place and closed the door of the shed. "She's the one." He wasn't ashamed of that.

"And she's the girl who has said she'll never marry?"

An image of Elsie popped into Ruben's mind—Elsie sitting by the warm fire, cuddling the baby in her arms. It made his knees go weak at the thought that she refused to let herself have a family, that she would throw away so much happiness for the two of them. "Here's the thing," he said, and in the gentlest way possible, he explained about Elsie's vow to remain chaste so that she would not bring a child with EVC into the world.

"Mmm." Dave listened to the explanation, his eyes somber, his breath steaming in the cold. "What she's thinking . . . what she's planning, it's not in keeping with the Ordnung."

Ruben had suspected as much. "I'm working on changing her mind. She wants to have a family. She wants to do the right thing."

"Ya, but it's not really her choice. If she gets baptized, she'll be making a promise to follow the Ordnung. There's no picking and choosing which rule you want to follow."

Dave's words gave Ruben hope that Elsie would come around.

She was just seventeen. Maybe this was something that would pass. "I reckon she'll come around then. She's still in her rumspringa, and you know how that goes."

"I do. Our Becky is not seventeen yet and by the time she gets baptized, I don't know if I'll have a single hair left on my head."

Ruben grinned. Dave had a knack for lightening a man's load.

"Elsie will come around," Ruben said. With one matter resolved, he looked toward the barn, where his father had emerged from the door. Now . . . if he could just come up with a way to free himself from running Zook's barn so that he could return to the Country Store.

Every day without Elsie was a day without sunshine.

As Dave and Dat headed down the road in the buggy, Ruben stamped his feet on the frozen ground and lifted his gaze to the pearl winter sky. He'd never realized how cold it got in the shadows.

ᘓᕽ 45 ᘏᕽ

The sight of her car parked amid rows of gray horseless buggies brought a nervous smile to Haley's face as she and Dylan made their way to the farmhouse. She paused, turned on the camera in her cell phone, and snapped a shot, careful not to include any of the young Amish men who were parking buggies.

"A fish out of water," she said, showing Dylan the photo.

As he leaned in close enough for her to breathe in that clean, tangy smell that clung to him, she told herself to keep it slow and steady.

You're his friend, nothing more, she reminded herself, tamping down the desire to hold his hand as they walked along together. The parameters of their relationship were still clear in her mind; it was her heart that kept pushing the boundaries.

"And now I'm turning my cell phone off," she said, trying to keep the conversation going to avoid her wayward thoughts. "I can't imagine anything ruder than interrupting an Amish church service with a ringing phone."

"Good point. I left mine at home. Didn't want to be bothered with it." Dylan smoothed down his white shirt and buttoned his black suit jacket. Looking handsome in his dark suit, he had captured the color combination to mix in among the Amish today.

Wanting to dress modestly, Haley had borrowed a long pleated skirt from her mother. Although it was far from fashionable, it was a solid navy blue and covered her legs to the top of her ankles—a tad longer than the dresses worn by most Amish women in Halfway. Her mother told her she looked like an escaped nun, but now as Haley smoothed down her skirt, she relied on the more conservative outfit to help ease her anxiety about being the only Englisher woman present today.

All around them were fields swept with last week's blanket of snow, framed by the distant purple hills. Closer in were the Lapp orchards, rows of fruit trees, now dormant in the winter lull. As they climbed the slope from the parking field, the sight of half a dozen gray buggies slowly edging down the lane stirred something from deep in Haley's soul. The air was still and cool and full of a sense of community, of mutual respect and rock-solid faith. She felt honored to be a part of such a gathering, even if only for one day.

On the gravel run between the house and barn, people congregated, talking in small groups. Women and children filed into the kitchen, and a handful of children chased off the Lapps' dogs. In the distance a rooster pealed a greeting, and two large cows stood at a nearby fence, as if they wanted to see what all the commotion was about.

"I understand we won't be sitting together for the service," Dylan said as they approached the barn, where groups of men lingered beyond the wide-open door.

"Elsie told me I could sit with her. I'm supposed to go in with the unbaptized single women and girls."

"I think these guys right here are my guides," Dylan said as Haley recognized Ruben, Caleb, and Zed among the young men gathered in a group.

James was there, too, hands on the wheels of his chair. He was the first to recognize Haley and Dylan.

"There's the good nurse," he said, nodding up at her. "Haley watches over my exercises."

"Hey, there." Haley smiled at the other young men in the group. "It's a wonder you're even speaking to me in public, considering the torture of physical therapy."

James lifted his chin, sitting taller in the chair. "It's not so bad."

When James introduced Dylan as the doctor for the "verhuddelt," the guys laughed.

"I also work with the not-so-verhuddelt," Dylan said with a deadpan expression. "Basically, I'll talk to anyone who has an interesting story."

"You'll find lots of good stories from the fellas here," said a young man with honey blond hair that flipped out under the brim of his hat. "Everybody has a story."

"Ain't that the truth," Dylan said, eliciting more chuckles.

He's a hit, Haley reflected, pleased by Dylan's ability to find a niche among the Amish men. He really was an all-around guy, able to make conversation with anyone.

Ruben directed her into the kitchen, telling her that Elsie was waiting in there. Probably with other women and children, Haley thought, noticing that most of the assembling groups were divided by gender. With a quick nod, she headed for the side door of the house she had come to know well from her visits here to work with James.

At the kitchen entry, Haley was greeted by Edna Lapp, who seemed genuinely glad to see her.

"Come in, come in. Elsie's been looking for you. She's here somewhere."

The large kitchen was crowded with women, many of them with infants in their arms. Haley recognized Fanny Lapp. She was still dressed in black to mourn her husband, but the glow of motherhood on her face belied her mourning clothes. Motherhood agreed with her.

Looking beyond, she found Elsie guiding Will toward the door. "Go on out and find Caleb. You're to sit with him," Elsie said. Her dark hair was scraped back, every hair smoothed into place, and her kapp was crisp and neat as a pin.

"I just saw Caleb over by the barn," Haley said, catching Elsie's attention.

"You made it!" She squeezed Haley's arm. "I'm so glad. Come along. We need to walk in at a certain time and sit with our group. It's how we do it every week. But don't worry. I'll help you."

"Denki." Haley smiled down at her Amish friend, no longer nervous.

⬡

It was a morning steeped in tradition. The doors had been opened up off the living area and all the main rooms were now filled with benches, lined up neatly to face the area where the ministers sat. Hymns that reminded her of Gregorian chants, sermons and Bible readings in High German. Haley understood none of it on a literal level, but her heart knew the language of fellowship, love, and faith.

The service itself, which started promptly at nine, did not end until well after noon. Truly an accomplishment for toddlers, children, and old folks. Without a clue as to what was being said, Haley let herself relax and enjoy the view of this gracious community that had always been "just down the road" from her home. In some ways it was a marvel that a service for more than one hundred and fifty members could be staged in a different home every two weeks. But . . . here they were, sitting in someone's living room, listening intently as the bishop spoke.

Haley was happy to stick close to Elsie and follow her cues. When a pan of cookies was passed down their bench around ten-thirty, Haley perked up. They smelled sweet and delicious. Then Elsie explained that the cookies were not for the adults, but for the little ones, who found it hard to make it through the service without a snack. Haley made a sad face as she passed the cookies on, and Elsie bit her lower lip as they both suppressed a chuckle.

After the service ended, the congregation filed out with the youngest leaving first, followed by the older members. The cool air was refreshing as they stepped outside to wait as young men carried in tables to transform the downstairs room into a dining hall.

The sun was high in a crisp blue sky dotted with cotton-ball clouds. Haley took in the golden light that illuminated the red of the barn, dozens of black hats and coats gathered in clusters, the crisscrossing patchwork of fields below them. Despite the lingering snow, the still March day held a tender promise of spring, with purple and yellow crocuses peeking up through the snow here and there.

The atmosphere was festive, with children cutting loose on the lawn. One group was already into a snowball fight with the melting remnants of the last storm, while younger kids bent their heads over some sort of game atop a picnic table.

"We'll go back inside to eat when they've set everything up," Elsie said as they meandered away from the house, heading over to a secluded area by the fenced-off pasture. "We'll be in one of the later shifts."

"What sort of things do they serve?"

"A simple meal. Bean soup and pickled beets. And bread with sandwich spread. Have you ever had that? Peanut butter and marshmallow cream?" When Haley shook her head, Elsie nodded. "It's very good."

"Haley?" Rachel called, the strings of her kapp undulating in the breeze as she headed over. "I wanted to sit with you, but I was tending to my younger sisters, and they're a handful."

"Can we sit together at the meal?" Haley asked.

"Ya. It's my sister Rose's turn to keep an eye on the little ones."

A plaintive groan from the other side of the fence interrupted, and the three girls looked up to see a fat brown cow trotting over.

"That is one large beast." Haley stood back with some trepidation. "How do you get it to stop coming at us?" If the creature barreled into the fence, it would shatter into toothpicks.

"It'll stop at the fence." Rachel shot a look at the cow, then rolled her eyes to the heavens. "Why do cows follow me everywhere I go? My mamm doesn't want to hear it anymore, but I keep telling her I'm not a farm girl. Up in the morning to milk and back at it in the afternoon . . . some folks like that schedule, but it's not for me. I'd rather scrub the kitchen from top to bottom than have to deal with the likes of that heifer."

"Sounds like you're not cut out to be a country girl," Haley said.

"Ya. That's not what my parents want to hear. A good Amish girl lives the life she was born to."

"We never had a milk cow, but I always thought that mooing sound they make sounds so sad." Elsie climbed up on the bottom rung of the pillar-and-post fence and faced the cow. "Why so glum today?" she asked. "Don't you know this is the day that the Lord has made?"

Haley and Rachel chuckled over Elsie's soft words. The cow turned one inquisitive eye toward her, intrigued.

"Look at that, Elsie, you have another friend." Rachel smiled. "The cows love you, just like everyone else."

Leaning against the fence, Haley basked in the sunshine and scanned the scattered group. Sunlight slanted over the red planking of the barn and its whitewashed trim. Her gaze landed on Dylan, and her heartbeat quickened slightly. She took a deep breath, noting that he sat on a hay bale, talking with Ruben and James.

"Don't look now, but our guys are over by the barn door." Haley tried to observe without staring.

Rachel turned around and held a hand to her forehead to block the sun as she scrutinized the congregation.

Haley grabbed her sleeve playfully. "I said, don't look!"

"I'm trying to see who your beau is." Rachel turned back to her, hands on her hips. "Dylan Monroe? The doctor is your beau?"

"Well, that's a long story. I would like him to be, but right now he just wants to be friends."

"Oh, that's too bad. I might be in the same boat with James now. He doesn't seem so happy to see me anymore, but then, he's not so happy about anything these days."

"I know." Haley cocked her head to one side, sympathetic to her friend's feelings of rejection. "He's still in a rough patch."

Elsie turned away from the fence, and let her gaze sweep casually across the farmyard. "Hmm. What do you think they're talking about?"

Rachel's hands smoothed down her apron, fumbling over the pins. "If I know James, he's talking about fertilizing the peach trees."

Haley chuckled. "I think they're talking about how crazy they are about us. That we're the most amazing women in the universe, and they can't imagine living without us."

Elsie giggled, pressing a hand to her mouth. "Is that what they're saying?"

"Crazy about us?" Rachel frowned. "More likely they're thinking *we're* crazy. At least, that's what James is thinking about me these days. He says I'm putting too much stock in my paintings. He doesn't believe that anyone would want to pay for a picture of a 'bunch of clothes blowing in the wind on the line.' That's how he sees my pictures." She folded her arms. "That hurts."

They were interrupted when an older Amish woman called to Rachel. It was her mother, Betsy King, who asked her to come inside and help serve up the pie.

"Save me a seat," she said, heading inside.

Turning back to Elsie, Haley found her friend staring across the farmyard, her dark eyes round and laden with sorrow. "Els, you look sadder than our friend the cow. What's the matter?"

"It's Ruben." Elsie lowered her voice. "He loves me. He hasn't said the word yet, but I see it in his eyes. In the things he does, the way he tries to protect me."

Haley nodded, alarmed by her friend's quiet intensity. "And you don't love him?"

"Oh, I do. I really do. Now that he's gone from the shop, I think about him day and night. But I can't ever marry him. I'm wasting his time, letting him think he's courting me. It's unfair to him. He deserves a good wife, a kind and loving woman who will give him children."

"Oh, Elsie, I know we've talked about your fears of passing on the EVC. I understand. But we all have weak genes and bad qualities that might be passed on to our children, and most people in the world trust it up to God and take that chance. It's so rare to find someone you love . . . someone you really love. . . ." Haley's voice cracked as tears flooded her eyes.

"Haley?" Elsie stepped onto the middle rung of the fence to be eye to eye with her. "Liewi, please don't cry for me. There's nothing you can do to mend the hole in my life."

"I'm crying for myself." Haley swiped at her eyes, facing the chewing cow so that no one would see her in tears. How embarrassing! "I'm sorry. It's so selfish of me, but I'm thinking of Dylan and me. I love him, Els. I really do, but there's nothing I can do to win his heart."

"That's not selfish. That's your heart crying out for love," Elsie said tenderly.

"And I do love him. But you heard him at the session, talking about his wife and daughter. He's still grieving, still so much in love. I know he cares about me, and we're a great team, but I can't compete with a ghost. His love is just something in life that I can't have and . . . and it's killing me."

A mournful sigh came from Elsie as they leaned into each other, both facing the pasture. Haley felt Elsie's hand gently patting her back, such a sweet gesture. She stared past the giant cow to the distant purple hills, ignoring the tears that slid down her cheeks.

"I'm sorry. I don't mean to be disrespectful, falling apart at your church luncheon."

"It's okay. Gott gives us our sorrows for a reason, and there's no law against crying on a Sunday."

Haley sniffed. "My heart breaks every time he smiles. My pulse races every time he just looks at me."

"I know how that feels. When Ruben first came to the store, he was a good friend to me, but as the days went on my heart opened to him in every way. Like a flower blooming in the sun—that was me in the light of his love."

"But he loves you, Elsie! Let yourself love him back. You two can be together."

"No." Elsie drew in a ragged breath. "I won't do that to Ruben or to a child. Do you know I was born with a sixth finger on each hand? Surgeons removed them when I was a year old. I don't remember that, but I do remember a later surgery, to fix my legs. There was pain when I was in the hospital, ya. But the true pain came from simply traveling to the hospital with my mother. We took a series of buses, starting at Lancaster, and some of the Englishers were cruel. They scared me. A midget, they called me. I was barely six years old. One man asked me if I escaped from the . . . the circus." Elsie's voice cracked, and she sniffed.

Now it was Haley's turn to rub her friend's back and try to soothe. "I'm sorry. People can be so cruel."

"I've forgiven them . . . it's all nearly forgotten, but for my vow to keep that pain for myself. I won't be the one to burden a child with it. And as soon as Ruben understands that, I'm sure he'll . . . he'll move on."

"But look at how he loves you, Elsie."

"I know," she said sadly. "I know, and my heart is breaking because I love him, too. But we are not meant to be together. In my heart, I know it's not what Gott intends, so I must push him away."

Haley squeezed Elsie's shoulder. "Are you sure about this? To be honest, it sounds to me like you're making a mistake."

"Gott makes no mistakes." When Elsie turned to her, there was a glint of wisdom in her dark eyes. "I know it's upsetting that Gott doesn't make things work out the way we planned, but it's also reassuring to know that whatever happens is meant to be. The way Gott planned it. If we can accept the events of our lives, then we are living Gott's will. 'Thy will be done.'"

Recognizing the words from the "Our Father," Haley nodded solemnly.

Of course, she wanted God's will to be done in her own life. She just wished it didn't hurt quite so much.

ɕʘɕ

By the time it was their turn to eat, both Elsie and Haley had managed to recover from their intensely emotional moment and pull themselves together. Inside, they ran into Rachel's family—and

Haley was glad to have a chance to talk with Remy King, who seemed to glow with happiness.

"I haven't seen you since the auction," Haley said.

"Mm-hmm." Remy's smile was secretive, her green eyes glimmering with a hint of mischief. "We've been sticking close to home."

"Really? Is everything okay?"

Remy looked over her shoulder and lowered her voice. "Umm, we Amish women don't really discuss it in public but . . ." She leaned forward and squeezed Haley's arm as she whispered, "Mary and I are pregnant."

Haley gripped Remy's hand. "Congratulations. That *is* news."

"I used to think it would never happen for me. Meeting the love of my life and starting a family. But now . . . now I have this enormous, loving family in a community that cares. I feel so blessed."

"I'm so happy for you." Haley smiled wistfully. Mary and Remy were in their twenties—her age.

Her mother's voice sounded in her mind, unbidden: *If you're going to have kids, you'd better get going.*

Well, it was sort of hard to get going when there wasn't a willing husband in the picture.

Being involved in the church service today, seeing the way these Amish families worshipped and worked together, Haley saw the importance of family. She definitely wanted children, but that would have to wait.

Steeling herself against disappointment, she repeated Elsie's advice: *God makes no mistakes.*

○○

Haley and Dylan were saying good-bye to their friends when a boy stopped in front of Dylan and tipped his black hat back. "Mister, can I have my slingshot back?"

All eyes turned to Dylan, who pursed his lips.

Normally stoic, Zed was fighting a grin. So much so that he had to turn away.

Haley stepped in, enjoying the controversy. "Did this man take your slingshot?" she asked the boy, who, cute as a jack-o'-lantern, was missing two of his front teeth.

The kid looked up at the other men, frowning at Ruben. "Don't tell Dat."

"Don't tell him what?" Ruben put his hands on his hips, standing his ground. "That you were fiddling with your slingshot during the prayers?"

"It was actually during one of the hymns." Dylan reached into his pants pocket and extracted a forked branch made into a slingshot with a piece of a rubber band. "And I borrowed it before anyone got hurt." He bent down to be level with the kid. "What's your name?"

Ruben stepped forward and clamped a hand on the boy's shoulder. "This is my brother Eli, and I can't believe a little angel like this would have a toy at church."

Eli shrugged out of his brother's grip. "It's not a toy. You could use it for hunting."

Dylan held the slingshot out to Eli. "Promise me you won't shoot anyone with this. Not your sister or your teacher or a crow scrounging for seeds in the snow."

Eli nodded. "We just try for rocks and cans on top of the fence."

"Good. You'd better keep it that way."

Eli snatched the slingshot and pivoted to make a quick exit.

"And, Eli. Hold on." Dylan dug in his other pocket. This time, he had a fistful of jacks and a small rubber ball. "Do me a favor and return these to your friend."

Eli turned back and cupped the jacks in his hand. "Simon said you would never give these back."

"I'm feeling generous after all those sermons. I didn't understand a word, but I have to believe some saving grace soaked in." Dylan grinned. "You're welcome."

"Thank you!" Eli chirped, then ran off.

Haley turned to him. "You are a character, Dr. Monroe. Were you going to leave with that poor boy's slingshot in your pocket?"

Ruben stepped in. "Believe me, Eli deserved to have it taken away."

"I planned to give it back," Dylan said. "I just forgot about it."

"Um-hmm," Haley teased.

"I would never steal. Especially from a child." Dylan patted down his pockets to make sure they were empty now. "But that was a very cool slingshot."

The group laughed as Dylan waved, and he and Haley started down the hill toward her car.

46

The next day, Elsie was washing the windows on the outside of the shop, straining to reach from the top of the stepladder, when a breeze made the strings of her kapp flicker.

A spring breeze. A cool wind, but no longer the biting tendrils of winter.

She rubbed until the cloth squeaked against the glass, then climbed down the ladder. The glass was clean, but Ruben had done a better job getting the dirt all around the edges at the top.

She missed him. He'd been a great worker and a good friend. He'd come to her rescue when she'd needed someone to hold her up, and now . . . now she didn't know how she was going to stand without him.

Folding up the ladder, she gazed up Main Street in the direction of Zook's barn. Of course, she couldn't see it from here, but it was reassuring to know he was there, just up the road a piece.

A few customers came along, and she greeted them and brought the ladder inside.

One lady wanted six caramel apples for her grandchildren. Her friend purchased a birdhouse, which would have been easier to wrap with Ruben's help.

Please, bring him back to me, she prayed silently. Then she wondered if that was selfish. She wanted him by her side, but she could not be his girl. Was that selfish?

The bells at the door jangled, and Preacher Dave came in with a fat folded afghan in his arms.

"Lydia asked me to bring you this," he said. "She's been working on it steadily for two weeks."

"This is coming in the nick of time." Elsie put the blanket on the counter to admire the variegated edges of blue, green, and yellow wool. "I only have one left in the store, and folks will like these cheerful colors for spring."

"Good." Dave nodded, but instead of saying good-bye, he took his hat off and turned it in his hands. "And I wanted to talk with you, Elsie."

She lifted her chin with a somber smile, thinking he was going to counsel her about grieving for her dat.

"This could be putting the cart before the horse, 'cause I know you're not baptized, but here goes. I hear you've decided that you're never getting married, because you don't want to have children. Is that so?"

Stumped, Elsie felt her mouth drop open. Who had told the preacher of her plan? Her private, innermost fears and plans . . .

Ruben.

Something akin to disappointment trembled through her as she fumbled for words. "It's not that I don't want to have children," she said quietly. "I don't want to have children because they might be born like me, with EVC. Little people."

"I see." Dave squinted, following every word. "And why is that a problem? Do you not feel that Gott loves you because you're shorter than most folk?"

"I know the Heavenly Father loves me. It's the people in the world who stare and say hurtful things. Some of the Englishers, they're very cruel toward anyone who looks different." She closed her eyes against the pain of the past, not wanting to dredge up the stories that brought her to tears. "Hurtful. It's not something any parent would wish on their little ones. And I can't consider having a child who will face that pain."

"Hmm." Dave's blue eyes sparkled with concern. "It would be nice if we could all protect our children from harm, don't you think?"

Elsie nodded.

"But we can't do that." Dave's blue eyes glimmered with understanding. "A toddler learning to walk will fall and get bruises. It can't be helped. So your children, if they are born to be small, with EVC, they must learn to fall and get up on their own."

Elsie shook her head. "There won't be any little ones for me, Dave. It's not Gott's will for me."

"It is if you're going to live Amish." The lines in his forehead told her that he was serious. This was not something that the clergy would make an exception on.

Her throat felt tight—too thick to swallow.

"Don't be steered wrong," the preacher went on. "If you're going to live Plain, this is not your choice to make. Amish folk marry and have children. We don't pick and choose our future like an Englisher person walking down the line at a salad bar."

"I don't mean to be picky."

"You and I know that, Elsie. But all the best intentions melt away to nothing when the rules are broken."

"But I'm not going to break any rules. I'm hoping to get baptized in the fall, and I won't break any rules." She would simply not marry. Although marriage was encouraged, no one ever shunned a woman when she became an old maid.

Just then the bells jangled and in came a gaggle of customers. What poor timing.

Dave put his hat back on his head. "Well. You've got some time to think on it. The classes for baptism start in May, if that's what you choose."

How could Ruben betray her like this? To have to face one of the ministers, not being prepared at all. She probably hadn't explained herself well, but her chance was lost.

She thanked Dave for bringing in the crocheted blanket and attended to her customers, trying to tamp down the worries that kept rising up to taunt her. The disapproval of the ministers cast a dark shadow over a person in the community. How could Ruben do this to her?

∽∾

"Since we met last week, one mystery has been solved for me," Graciana told the group the next day at their regular meeting in the back room of the library.

Elsie kept her eyes on the older woman, refusing to look across the table at Ruben, no matter how appealing his sparkling blue eyes and wide, friendly smile. Her mind was still reeling from Dave's unexpected visit yesterday, and despite her sister Emma's attempts to calm her, anger still simmered inside her.

If I were a teapot, I'd be whistling now, loud and shrill.

She bit her lip, trying to focus on what Graciana was saying.

"I got this letter from Cross College. It's in Lancaster." Graciana unfolded a crisp white sheet of paper. "It's from a dean of admissions, and she was writing to thank my daughter for attending the interview that day. This letter says my Clara is accepted to Cross College with a scholarship . . . and I didn't even know she applied."

"So she drove in to Lancaster for a college interview?" Dylan's voice was firm and steady. Always calm, that Dylan.

"That was it. After the letter came, I did some snooping in Clara's journals. After the accident, I wasn't able to look. It felt wrong, and I . . . I just couldn't do it. But my sister-in-law and niece sat down with me, and we read things aloud when they seemed important." Graciana closed her eyes and sniffed back tears. "We laughed and we cried. And by the time we were finished, I remembered my Clara. I remembered her good qualities, like you said, Dr. Monroe." She reached into the fat envelope and removed a photograph. "This is my Clara."

Elsie bit back a pang of sadness at the sight of the young girl who had died back in January. Her sparkling eyes, her happy smile.

"She was a beautiful girl," Haley said.

Zed nodded. "She had your eyes, Graciana."

The older woman nodded, sucking in her lips to keep from crying. "I also brought this." She took a round stuffed animal from her purse and held it in front of her for everyone to see. "Pooh Bear. She used to read to him when she was a little girl. Before she could even read, she would sit with a book on her lap and tell him a story. And she slept with him in her bed every night. Even as a teenager. She said he brought her comfort."

Elsie thought of her little sister and her threadbare doll. Beth never would settle in until her dolly was beside her. Sometimes, when she said her prayers out loud before bed, Beth asked Gott to bless her dolly, as if she were one of the family.

"That's just like my sister Beth with her dolly," Elsie said, giving voice to her thoughts. "Some things are the same, Amish or Englisher."

Graciana gave Elsie's hand a trembling squeeze as Dylan called for a break.

"Oh." The older woman let out a breath as the others at the table rose and stretched. "This is so difficult to talk about. But it feels good, too."

Elsie nodded. Now that everyone was relaxing, her worries came rushing back like a cold wind.

"You're quiet today," Graciana told Elsie.

Elsie darted a heated glance at Ruben, who was pouring coffee as if he didn't have a care in the world. "Something's weighing on my mind. I'm sorry. It's got my head spinning so that it's hard to think of anything else."

"Are you going to share it with the group?" Graciana asked, her voice quiet with sympathy.

Elsie sucked in a breath. "Oh, no." The thought of even more people knowing her most private pain cut her deep inside.

She scooted her chair back from the table. "Excuse me," she told Graciana, not wanting to be rude. She admired the woman and wanted to hear more about Clara, but suddenly the air in the conference room was thick with regret, the walls much too close. She was already at the door when Ruben called her name.

When she turned back for a quick look, tears stung her eyes.

Oh, no. Don't cry in front of everyone.

She didn't want to upset the people here, folks who cared about her. It was best to leave.

Outside the cool air did little to ease the warm flush of her skin. She was in the parking lot when she heard the footsteps behind her, followed by his voice.

"Elsie? Are you leaving so soon?"

Caught, she braced herself and turned to him . . . his glimmering blue eyes, warm with concern, the lines over his brows that she longed to trace with her fingertips.

Oh, why did she love him so, after all this? The betrayal. The reality that they could not be together. Why did her heart yearn for his kisses when her head knew that she must keep him at arm's length?

"I can't stay." Her lower lip quivered, revealing her sorrow. "I need to go."

"What is it, Elsie? Are you sick?" He moved closer, holding a cup out to her. "I poured you some coffee, and when I turned around, you were flying out the door."

She pressed her balled-up fists to her belly. "I'm sick with worry about what you told Preacher Dave about me. Do you know that I'm in trouble now?"

His face went pale as his smile slid away. "But . . . you're not truly in trouble. You're not baptized yet. You're in your rumspringa, and just because you're thinking—"

"Dave came to see me. He wanted to set things right." She winced, swallowing over the knot in her throat. "Those things I told you, about not having children? That was personal, Ruben. My own private thoughts. How could you go and tell a minister everything?"

"I didn't mean to. It wasn't like I planned it. You know Dave is my uncle, and we talk all the time. He can tell when something's on my mind. He asked a few questions and the story spilled out."

"But don't you understand? It's spilled milk. Once it's out of the pitcher, there's no putting it back in."

Ruben frowned. He seemed to notice the cups of hot coffee in his hands. In one motion he pitched the hot liquid from both of them into the melting snow at the side of the road. He stacked the cups and looked down at them, his face shadowed with regret. "I never meant to hurt you, Elsie. You've got to believe that. I told Dave what was on my mind because I couldn't stop thinking about you . . . about us. No matter what you say, I know we're meant to be together."

She shook her head. "I wish it were so."

"It's the truth. You're one of the few people in all the community who know me—the real me. You aren't put off by the way I look. By my big size or the limping. And I've gotten to know you, too, Elsie. And I have to say you're the most beautiful girl I've ever known. Maybe even more beautiful because you don't think of yourself that way."

She squeezed her eyes shut. How could he say these things—to think she was pretty when she had spent a lifetime trying to hide her ugly teeth. Born bowlegged, with six fingers on each hand. "I have been called a circus freak, Ruben. I know that the Almighty created me. My family has always loved me and my community has supported me. But I was always sure the goodwill ended there. I never expected to meet a man who truly loved me."

"But I do," Ruben said softly. "I love the small hands that have organized the Country Store into a marketplace that helps Amish folk sell their crafts. I love the voice that offers words of encouragement to everyone. I love the way you bring sunshine into a room with your smile and your bright enthusiasm."

Elsie blinked back tears. *I love you, too,* she wanted to whisper. She wanted to call it from the highest hilltop . . . but she couldn't. It would be wrong to promise something that was not meant to be.

"If you look different from other folks, that's only because Gott changed the mold for you," Ruben went on. "That's what my mamm used to say, after I got scarred from the accident. Lots of folks fit the mold. It's a special few that Gott stepped in and crafted by hand."

Elsie bent her head down, unable to look at him anymore. He was kind and loving, and he deserved to find a girl who could be a good wife to him. "You are a good man, Ruben." She would always love him, but right now, the loving thing to do was let him go.

"I'd better get back to the store." She turned away from him, her best friend in the world, her only love.

"Elsie, wait. . . ."

"Good-bye, Ruben." Her heart ached as she trudged across the parking lot, knowing that their wonderful time together was over.

It was the end of Ruben's easy laugh and his strong, protective arms.

The end of a beautiful love.

*H*aley had been so intent on watching Elsie and Ruben through the window, she had nearly lost focus on the very important conversation going on in the therapy session. And apparently, she wasn't alone. When Elsie and Ruben didn't return to the session, the members were concerned.

"Give them some space," Dylan had told the group, sweeping one hand toward the door. "We're going to move forward with the people who are here."

Haley had stayed in her seat, despite the desire to bolt from her chair and inch closer to hear what was going on outside in the parking lot of the ice-cream shop. Elsie and Ruben had faced each other, talking, but from their body language, Haley had known it was not happy talk. Ruben had tossed away the coffee, then Elsie had started to cry. After a few minutes, Elsie had turned and walked across the parking lot, leaving Ruben to stare after her.

When he limped away, his uneven gait more pronounced than ever, Haley was overcome by a chilling sadness.

Two people who loved each other that much ought to be together. Dylan had warned her not to be a matchmaker, especially among the Amish. "You don't understand the restrictions and mores of the culture yet," he had told her.

But Haley knew that something had to be done. She couldn't stand to see her friends stuck in misery.

As soon as the session ended, she snatched up Elsie's forgotten coat and hurried over to the Country Store, where Elsie had a full house.

"I brought your coat." Haley lifted her arm, where the coat was draped. "I'll just put it in the back room."

"Denki. Caleb is back there, organizing. I have trouble getting to the higher shelves now that . . ." Elsie's voice faded. "Now that Ruben's gone."

In the back room, Haley found Elsie's older brother on a ladder, sliding a plastic bin onto a high shelf. "Hey, there," she said. "How's it going?"

"Good." Caleb shared Elsie's dark eyes and heart-shaped face, though he was probably twice her height.

Haley hung Elsie's coat on a hook, beside Caleb's wide-brimmed black hat. "I guess you'll be spending more time here now that Ruben had to go back to his job at Zook's barn."

"For now. But I'll probably begin work at a real job soon."

"You're not going to open that shop in the old carriage house?"

"Nay. That was my father's dream, but I'm not so good with wheels and buggies. I might work at the Stoltzfuses' sheep farm. Or Deacon Moses says he'll teach me carpentry. He has an Amish crew that builds houses."

"Sounds like some good opportunities."

"Much better than running a store."

"I don't know. I guess there's something for everyone."

"For me, I need to be outside, in the fresh air."

On a day like today, with gray snowmelt fringing the sidewalks and the damp clutch of winter still in the air, Haley couldn't imagine wanting to be outside. "Like I said, something for everyone."

She left Caleb to his task and joined her friend. Although Elsie wasn't her usual cheerful self, she didn't let her mood affect her service to customers. A gaggle of ladies from a church group had descended on the store in search of items that would make this Easter more "quaint."

"Do you have any snow globes with Easter bunnies inside?" one woman asked.

"We try to stock crafts from our Amish community," Elsie said, showing them a few hand-painted wall plaques that said things like SPRING IS JUST AROUND THE CORNER! "We also have a good variety of pie fillings, all put up when the fruit was at its peak." She led some of the ladies over to Edna Lapp's jars of peaches, strawberries, cherries, and strawberry-rhubarb. "And I can give you a simple pie crust recipe if you like. There's nothing like the smell of fresh-baked pie on an Easter Sunday."

"That's a splendid idea," one customer said.

Elsie gave them a few minutes to decide on pie fillings as she rang up two other customers, wrapping each purchase in a swatch of cloth with a ribbon.

"If you don't mind, we would like your pie crust recipe," one woman called from down the aisle.

"I'll write it down while I talk with my friend Haley."

"Hello, friend." Haley moved up to the counter. "We were all worried when you and Ruben left the meeting."

"Don't you worry about me." Elsie sat down on her stool behind the counter and began to write in neat, uniform letters: Pat-a-Pan Crust. She seemed relieved for the activity so that she wouldn't have to face Haley.

"Of course I'm going to worry. I hate to see you unhappy, Els." From close up, Haley could see that Elsie's eyes were still red and puffy from crying.

"It's hard to give up the one you love most, but it had to be. I don't know how I got myself in this situation." Speaking quietly so that no one else would hear, Elsie explained about the preacher's visit and his warning. Elsie had been upset with Ruben for sharing something so personal with Dave. "I was angry and I let Ruben know it," she admitted. "And now I've hurt Ruben, and I have only myself to blame."

"He'll forgive you," Haley said, knowing it was true. "Can't you tell him you're sorry?"

"I can do that, but I can't let things go back to the way they were." She looked up from the notepad, making sure no one was listening. "I can't lead him on anymore. I do love him, but I can never marry. It's up to me to let Ruben go so he can find someone else."

Haley was about to say that Ruben didn't belong with someone else, but they were interrupted by the customers approaching the register with their purchases. As Haley waited, she ventured up one aisle, past colorful pincushions and hooked rugs to a shelf of soaps and lavender. She sniffed a pretty sachet, wishing for the calming effect lavender was supposed to have. She was feeling her friend's tension, and though empathy was a good thing, she wanted to stay objective so that she could help Elsie.

It seemed to her that Elsie and Ruben's problems would be solved if Elsie could see herself in a new light. Haley suspected that Elsie's self-image was at the heart of the matter. Considering Elsie's experiences, her feelings of inadequacy were understandable. But if she truly believed that God loved her the way she was, would she be so adamantly against having children who might be like her?

Replacing the lavender, Haley picked up a birdhouse with nine holes cut in the side, nine windows lined up like neat portholes. Elsie had told her that her favorite bird was the blue jay. Apparently, it was rather bossy toward other birds, but it was fiercely loyal to other blue jays. "Haven't you ever noticed," Elsie had said, "you never see just one blue jay; there are always two or three nearby. They have very close family bonds."

Family was so dear to Elsie's heart—her family and her faith.

Dear God—if you're still listening—please help me find a way to help my friend. Elsie deserves to be with the man she loves. They both deserve to have a big Amish family of their own. Please, God. I know I haven't been the most loyal follower, but I do believe in you. And I believe you can light Elsie's path with your love.

A few minutes later, after the big push of customers left, two women ventured in—a mother and daughter. The older woman walked with the support of a cane, but her eyes were bright as she strode right up to the counter.

"Well, if it isn't Rachel Lapp," she said, squinting at Elsie. "Have you been drinking from the fountain of youth? You don't look a day older than when I used to come in here some twenty years ago."

Elsie blinked. "I'm not Rachel."

"Mom, I told you times have changed," said the younger woman. "My mother was sure everything in your store would be exactly the way it was years and years ago when she lived in the area. She lives in Michigan now. She's just back for a short visit."

"But it is the same," the older woman said. "The Country Store hasn't changed a bit." She picked up a jar of preserves. "Didn't I tell you? Amish strawberry jam. And Rachel's sitting right in the same spot."

"But my name is Elsie. Rachel was my mother. She's been gone now for more than ten years."

"I'm sorry to hear that, but you're the spitting image of her."

Elsie chuckled. "Oh, but we're so different! She did have dark hair, I remember that. But I'm a lot shorter, and my teeth aren't so good."

"Just like Mamm," Caleb said, putting a box on the counter.

"No, silly." Elsie smiled at her brother. "Mamm didn't have EVC."

Caleb frowned. "But she did. Mamm was a little person, and she did look a lot like you. Don't you remember, Elsie?"

"I was six when she died," Elsie said. "I remember that she had brown hair, like me. . . ."

"You were so young," Haley said. "And you don't have a photo of her."

"Don't you remember how little she was?" Caleb asked. "She was the one who knew you had to have the surgeries and all that. She knew because she'd been through it herself."

"Are you sure about that, Caleb?" Elsie rubbed the back of her neck, baffled. "People would have talked about it. Dat would have told me."

"There was nothing to talk about. It was the way she was, and everyone loved her just the same. Just the way folks love you." He moved the carton down one aisle and began restocking jars. "If you don't believe me, ask around. Edna and Jimmy will tell you, or any of the ministers."

"Well." The older woman put a jar of pie filling on the counter, beaming with satisfaction. "It's a day for discoveries, isn't it? I'm so glad to have rediscovered your store."

"Oh, Mom." Her daughter appeared holding a box of fudge. "You can be so dramatic."

"I'm glad, too." Elsie smiled at the woman, looking beyond her to Haley. The detail about her mother seemed to lighten her heart.

It was an answered prayer.

Of course, Elsie wasn't transformed. In their brief conversation before Haley headed off to the hospital, she could tell that her friend still stood by her plan to live a solitary life.

But Elsie was definitely warmed by the news. With a few days to sink in, that new connection to her mother could shift Elsie's perspective. Haley was still praying for it.

&C;

That afternoon, Haley stood at the nurses' station taking notes as heavy footsteps sounded in the corridor.

A handful of uniformed life-flight personnel and medical technicians were headed down the hall, walking with a purpose. At first she thought they were on their way to respond to an emergency. Then she noticed the coolers they carried.

The bright orange coolers were distinctly marked; they were organs on their way to various hospitals, where surgical teams waited to transplant them to recipients.

A patient had died here at the hospital.

But so many lives were about to be saved, due to a family's generosity.

An idea sprang into her head. Maybe it was crazy, but it was worth a shot. She fished her cell phone out of her pocket and searched for Graciana's number.

❦ 48 ❦

Such a long week it's been, Elsie thought as she headed toward the library for the regular group session. The air smelled of spring— the tang of manure in the distance, where fields were being turned. She closed her sweater tighter around her, still cold despite the sunshine.

Chilled by the loneliness inside her.

She missed Ruben. Every day, every moment.

Since their terrible parting at last week's session, she had lain in bed every single night, trying to think of a way that she could be with him without abandoning the vow she had made. What a wonderful world it would be to wake up to his kind smile every day, instead of this heavy burden of sorrow.

To add to her misery, she knew that she had hurt him. She had hurt the kindest, most loving person she had ever known. *Please, Gott, forgive me,* she whispered as she walked past the ice-cream shop and turned into the parking lot.

It would be so hard to face her wonderful Ruben today. She had planned to skip the meeting until Haley had stopped in to the shop and persuaded her to come.

"You have to come! There's a special surprise that I've been working on all week," Haley had said. "Promise me you'll be there."

Elsie had agreed, and a promise was a promise.

Inside the conference room, Elsie tucked her sweater tighter around her and took her seat. She returned the greetings of the others and refused coffee from Haley. Graciana patted her hand encouragingly—such a motherly gesture—and Elsie had to bite her lower lip to keep from crying. And when Dylan started the meeting, she dared to look at Ruben's empty seat.

So he wasn't coming today. All her worry had been in vain, though that was little relief. Even if she couldn't allow herself to love him completely, just being near him was a lift to her spirits.

Dylan started the meeting by saying that this would be an unusual session. "Last week Haley called me with a proposal, and I thought it would be a good idea if she could make it all come together." He turned to give Haley a quiet smile. "So . . . I'm going to hand it all over to her now."

"Okay." Haley clasped her hands together, a pretty pink tint on her cheeks. "After last week I was wracking my brain, trying to think of examples of positive things that come from tragedy." Her amber eyes were steady as she looked from one member to another. "We've all suffered. We've been through terror and sorrow, shame and guilt, fury and numbness. But I think we're also beginning to see that when you work through those things you can emerge on the other side with a greater ability to experience joy and happiness, a new view of the wonders of life. The beauty of each precious moment."

Across the table, Rachel smiled and George nodded.

"Yes, this accident tore our hearts open. But it opened us up to a level of compassion and understanding we didn't have before."

Haley turned to Elsie. "Sometimes healing is painful, but if we let ourselves dig deep, if we open up and share our fears and scars, the healing can transform our lives."

Elsie pressed her lips together in disagreement. Haley was wrong. Amish girls like Elsie and Rachel were not to be transformed. They were to grow up and become Amish women.

"So . . . I'm not sure how to really introduce this, but we have some special guests waiting outside. I think it's safe to say that they're alive today because of Graciana's generosity, as well as her immeasurable loss."

Everyone looked up as Haley pushed away from the table and went to the door. "These people are organ recipients. The donor was Clara Estevez."

In came a woman leading two toddlers. "This is Maria Giordano. You're a kidney recipient, right?"

"That's right." A shiny lock of Maria's dark hair slid over her cheek as she lowered her head. "And these are my children, Laurel and Wylie. Their dad would have liked to come along, but he had to work." She glanced over at the table. "Is Mrs. Estevez here?"

Graciana rose and went over to the woman. "Please, call me Graciana. Your children are so . . . so beautiful. Thank you for the lovely letter."

"No . . . thank *you*. You gave me my life back. I'm sorry for your loss, but when Haley contacted me I wanted to meet you so you could see how your daughter has given new life to our family."

The little girl, Laurel, stretched away from her mother toward the coffeemaker, where a box of pastries sat.

"Doughnuts, Mommy." Her voice was breathless with wonder.

"Would you like one?" Graciana asked. "Come in and sit down. Is that okay?"

"Maybe she can split one with her brother," Maria said as she helped the children settle into chairs.

"And that's not all." Haley leaned out the door, motioning to someone down the library hall. "There's another special guest. She's sixteen, and her name is Aubrey."

A tall, lean young teen with flashing eyes and a sprinkle of freckles on her nose appeared in the doorway. "Am I late?" she asked.

"It's never too late," Graciana said, welcoming Aubrey and her mother.

༠༠

Unlike their other sessions, this meeting was festive, with conversation breaking off into smaller groups and then unifying again as Maria or Aubrey shared their experiences with their illnesses and recovery after the transplant.

Elsie listened intently, not wanting to miss a single detail of their fascinating stories. Aubrey had been near death, and Maria had been so sick that she'd needed dialysis, which meant she had to spend long hours in the hospital hooked up to a machine that cleaned her blood.

The room was aglow with love and so much hope, Elsie felt as if a heavy cape had been lifted from her shoulders. She wished Ruben had been here to hear the wonderful stories and see the living, breathing examples of Gott's miracles.

As she listened to Aubrey's mother describe the worries she'd had for her daughter, and then Aubrey talk of how she was happy to be back at school now, hoping to run with her cross-country team next year, Haley came over and took the chair beside her.

"What do you think of our guests?" Haley asked quietly.

"I think you found two wonderful good examples of Gott's power to heal." Elsie nodded. Haley had brought hope to Graciana, and to every member of the group. "It's a wonderful thing you've done for Graciana, bringing these women here."

"It wasn't Graciana I was thinking of." Haley paused, biting her lower lip. "I did it for you."

"For me?" Elsie blinked.

"I wanted you to see the power of God's healing. These women had major medical issues. Their bodies weren't perfect, but God loved them all the same. Maybe the transplants were a miracle, maybe it's just a new twist in science. In any case, these women saw their lives transformed, their bodies healed."

"It is a wondrous thing," Elsie agreed. "But I'm not sick, thank the Lord."

"Sometimes there are things deep inside that need to be healed. The way we see ourselves. The way we think the world sees us."

Elsie's face grew warm. "You're talking about me and my EVC."

"I am." Haley leaned closer until her face was just inches from Elsie's. "A wise woman once told me that God makes no mistakes."

Elsie rolled her eyes. "Maybe not so wise."

"But it's true, Els. The Almighty didn't make a mistake when He created you. And it wouldn't be a mistake if you had a child. It says in the Bible that God created man in His own image. That's you and me, just as we are."

Elsie shook her head. "You are a hard person to argue with."

There was a glimmer of hope in Haley's golden eyes. "And you don't like to argue, anyway."

"I don't. Especially now, with my heart feeling so light. I don't think an Amish person would ever be allowed to do such a thing—donating organs. We believe the body must be in one piece for Judgment Day. But this transplant thing is wonderful. Graciana did a wonderful thing when she signed those papers."

As the meeting broke up, Elsie felt drawn to Zook's barn, where she knew Ruben was working. She had to be getting back to the store to take over for Caleb, but it would only take a few minutes to walk down the road and talk to Ruben.

The air was ripe with spring, and Halfway seemed to be coming alive, like an animal emerging from its winter home. Kate and Hannah Fisher waved to her through the window of the Sweet 'N' Simple Bakery. A group of fire department volunteers were testing a hydrant by the library, and a handful of children too young for school marveled at the fountain of water running down Main Street. Marta Kraybill was outside Molly's Restaurant, chatting with the mayor and the bishop's wife. Elsie passed Preacher Dave, who was inspecting a buggy outside his shop, and Leah King, who hummed as she cheerfully swept the patio outside the tea shop.

Halfway was a wonderful town, and Elsie thanked Gott that He had put her here with so many good people. A caring community, a loving family, and Ruben.

She would start by asking his forgiveness. After that, she would tell him about the two miracles who had walked into their group session. How she hoped he would understand the windows that had opened in her soul today.

As she approached the big red roadside barn, she recognized the familiar gait of the young Amish man cleaning up the part of the parking lot reserved for buggies.

That was the man she loved, maneuvering a broom and pan around parked buggies, sweeping manure into the bin.

"Ruben? I've come to ask your forgiveness," she called.

He shifted the broom aside, blinking. "Am I seeing an angel, or is that Elsie Lapp coming to see me after a dry spell?"

"It's been a long week." She didn't stop until she was close enough to see the slight bristle on his chin. How she longed to reach up and touch it . . . to soothe his brow . . . to press her lips to his. "I'm sorry I was cross with you last week. It wasn't your fault, your talking to Dave."

He squinted. "Maybe I am seeing an angel."

"No, I'm a real girl, but it is a day for angels. Haley brought two of them to our meeting."

"Ya?" His face softened with a crooked grin. "The one day I miss and angels show up."

She put her hands on her hips, stretching her neck to smile up at him. "Do you think you're the only one seeing angels?"

He pushed his hat back. "I never said that. So tell me about these angels."

She did. She told him how Haley had tracked down two people who had received organs from the body of Clara Estevez. She told him of the new lives they enjoyed now that they had healed. She shared what Haley had said about healing the wounds inside.

"I've been thinking of myself like I was a broken doll, being born like this," she said. "And all along, Gott had made me just the way He wanted me to be."

"Meine kleine Liewi." His eyes glimmered like diamonds of light on a summer lake. "You are Gott's wonderful creation and I love you just the way you are."

"I love you, too." Joy brimmed inside her, a cup overflowing. "Do you want to kiss me?" she asked giddily.

He leaned the shovel against the fence, placed his hands on her waist, and lifted her onto a hay bale so that they were face-to-face.

His hands stayed on her waist, making her feel secure and warm as he leaned forward and brushed his lips against hers—a sweet, short kiss. "My first kiss in a parking lot," he said.

"My first kiss out in front of the whole town." She looked around. "Tongues are going to be wagging."

"Let them talk. We've been through worse together, haven't we?

We've seen each other through some bad times. I want to be with you for the good and bad times that are to come. Will you marry me and have a big Amish family with me?"

"That would be such a blessing." She held his face in her hands for another quick kiss that tugged at a longing so deep, her toes curled in her boots. "But first I need to be baptized. That will give us time for a proper courtship."

"Ya, and we will be able to tell our children about this romantic proposal, in a parking lot, while shoveling manure."

Elsie laughed. "At least you took a minute to put the shovel down."

"I'll always put the shovel aside for you, Elsie. Always."

49

$\mathcal{D}$ylan couldn't stop smiling.

It had been a long time since he'd felt this way, but a silly, goofy grin had risen from his soul, and he didn't even try to suppress it.

The glacier inside was melting, easing, shifting, and it felt good to be able to take in a full breath after years of being crushed by memories.

When Haley had asked if she could bring a handful of guests to the session, he had consented, but the transplant recipients had been a surprise to him, too. Their words had been a renewal of life and faith, a reminder that life went on and that the Lord wanted every person on the planet to celebrate it . . . not muddle through as he had been doing.

After the session, when the guests had congregated with Haley and Graciana out in the parking lot, Dylan had gotten a distinct sense that they were doing that female bonding ritual of endless gab. Really, he hadn't been able to get a single word in, and ultimately he realized that they did not need his presence or expect him to stay.

That had been oddly liberating, to know his group could survive without him. Just like the session during which Haley had stepped up and acted as the mediator. And she'd done a good job. A great job. Once again, she had proven herself to be the Good Samaritan.

She was an amazing woman, and he'd been a fool to push her away.

His grin held as he braked at the stop sign by Zook's barn. Ruben had missed today's meeting. What was going on with him?

It was worth checking out.

Besides, in a mood this good, he had no desire to return to his apartment and reclaim his throne as hermit of the beet fields. He pulled into the lot beside a large bakery truck, and headed over to the wide double doors.

A horse-drawn cart was backed up to the entrance, and Bishop Samuel reached into it to slide a crate full of jars closer to the edge.

"Samuel." Dylan nodded. "Beautiful day, isn't it?"

The bishop straightened. "Ya. Spring is in today. Everyone is ready for longer days and warmer weather. Time to turn the soil."

Dylan smiled, thinking of the sight from his apartment. "I've been watching the Amish farmers near my place. The plowshare is so silent as it cuts through the soil. It's a peaceful sight to watch."

"Something about working the soil soothes the soul."

"Can I help you haul this stuff inside?" Dylan offered.

"James is taking care of that." He looked toward the barn, where James came, wheeling his chair over. "We're restocking the Lapps' stand. I'm just the buggy driver."

Dylan greeted James and observed the way the bishop stacked the case of jars atop James's wheelchair. The young man had developed massively strong arms during his rehabilitation. As James propelled the chair back into the barn, laden with a heavy case of pie filling, Dylan hoped that the chair would hold up under the wear and tear of farm life.

"So you're the helper today," Dylan asked.

"I am."

It was surprising that a man of status like the bishop would give up an afternoon to do such menial work, but then, the Amish didn't really look down on any sort of work, as long as it was in keeping with their rules, their Ordnung.

"A helper, just like you." Samuel's gray eyes glinted with interest behind his glasses. "I hear you have a way of talking folks into a calm mood during your meetings."

"Guided imagery. It's an effective form of counseling." Dylan nodded toward the barn. "James hasn't been willing to try it yet, but I've found that most Amish are very open to it. People find it soothing."

"Because they trust you."

"And I'm grateful for that." He turned back to Samuel, whose piercing gray eyes weren't as cold as he'd remembered. "Would you like to try it sometime?"

"Nay. When I need soothing, I turn to the Almighty Father. You can't stumble when you're already on your knees."

Dylan nodded. "Prayer is a great counselor."

"I keep reminding young James of that. We need to remember that it's the Almighty who heals." The bishop dragged another case to the edge of the cart and turned back to Dylan. "Sometimes the healing doesn't match our plans. It's hard to understand what Gott has in mind for us. I don't know. James doesn't, and neither do you."

Dylan slid his fingertips into the pockets of his jeans as he let the bishop's words wash over him. He'd had so many plans foiled and ruined. A major change, of course. A crossroads. "I hear you, Bishop."

"I'm sorry about your wife and daughter." The glint of compassion in the bishop's silvery eyes touched a chord deep inside Dylan.

"These things break our hearts, and we can never understand why they happen."

"I spent a lot of time looking for a reason," Dylan admitted, "but it's a waste of time."

The bishop nodded. "That's right. It's fruitless to try and understand Gott's plan for us. But He put us on this earth to live a Christ-like life. Not to sit around trying to figure out why this and that happened. I keep saying this to James, but I'm not sure he hears me."

"It's one thing to hear words of wisdom. It's another thing to take them to heart," Dylan said.

"Ach!" The bishop smiled, clapping Dylan on the back. "You do get it. Gut."

He got it all right. It had taken more than four years, but now he got it, and the message was a kick in the pants. It was time to move on.

After James and the bishop left in the cart, Dylan bought a bottle of Reading Draft sarsaparilla soda and straddled the bench of a picnic table outside as the sun cut through two clouds. The shafts of light streaming through the clouds were pretty as a postcard. God's touch—that was what Kris had called the sight.

The soda was sweet on his tongue. It reminded him of happier days. Carefree bike rides with the kids in the neighborhood. Swimming pools and Battleship games and airsoft gun wars. Sunny mornings when he'd had the courage to bite into life as if it were a crisp, sweet apple.

Those days would come again, if he would let them.

He had made the break from Philadelphia. He'd given up his practice there and moved to Lancaster County—all a good effort on his part. But when it came to moving on, all progress had stopped.

All for Kris and Angela.

He loved them, he always would, but today's revelation had brought home the fact that they were gone from his life. And when he got honest with himself, he knew that Kris would have smacked his shoulder if she knew that he was carrying a torch for her. With her frank disposition, Kris wasn't one for drawn-out ceremonies or long good-byes.

And yet, he had drawn out his farewell to her over the past four years.

His bad.

Meeting Aubrey and Maria had reminded him of the letter in his wallet. He shifted to remove the leather billfold from his back pocket. There, behind a photo of Kris holding the baby, the light of love in her eyes, was the worn letter, folded into small segments.

> *Dear Mr. Monroe,*
> *I can't imagine your grief at losing your child at this difficult time, but I had to write to thank you. Thank you, from the bottom of our hearts. I'm sure we never met, since my family lives on the Eastern Shore of Maryland, but our three-year-old son Milo received a kidney from your daughter. . . .*

Milo would be seven years old by now. Seven and in school and probably reading on his own. Dylan raked back his hair and smiled at the image of a kid that age, probably riding bikes and playing Battleship himself.

Life went on. God willing, life would go on.

❦ 50 ❦

$\mathcal{H}$aley had been saying good-bye to Graciana when the text came from Dylan.

Meet me at Zook's barn for a sarsaparilla?

She had grinned and responded: *Sarsaparilla? Are you a cowboy?*

Reviving my youth, he'd answered, with uncharacteristic levity.

Well, this is going to be interesting, she thought as she put her car in gear and headed toward Zook's barn.

She found him sitting on a table outside, the only patron daring enough to brave the spring chill. Hands on her hips, she paused beside the table. "Cozy?"

"Hey, the sun was just out a minute ago. Have a seat and I'll get you a soda." His smile brought a light to his eyes, a glimmer she'd never seen there before. Hope? Joy? Whatever it was, it made something ticklish bubble up inside her.

"How about a cup of tea? I'm not quite as warm-blooded as you."

"Got it."

While he ducked inside, she sat and studied the red wall of the old barn. How many years had it been standing? How many stories had it witnessed as people passed through here? So many lives coming to a crossroads in Halfway.

Haley felt like she had navigated a turning point herself earlier today. By inviting Maria and Aubrey to the meeting, she had pushed strangers together in the interest of healing. Fortunately, her move had been successful, and it had solidified something in her heart.

She was in the right place now. God wanted her here, working with the Amish and the English alike. She still didn't know how that would look in five years, but for now, she was happy to finish her nursing training at LanCo General.

Dylan returned, smiling, with a steaming cup in hand. That smile . . . dazzling and effervescent and so unusual. Dylan almost never smiled.

"Tea with milk and one sugar," he said, putting the cup on the table before her.

"How did you know how I take my tea?"

"Uh, we've only had tea and pie in the Lapps' kitchen a dozen or so times."

"Thank you." She wrapped her palms around the paper cup, grateful for the warmth. "I thought that went well today, right?"

"It was off the charts. That was brilliant, bringing in Maria and Aubrey. I don't know how you managed to cut through the red tape and find them and coerce them to come to the meeting all in one week, but you did it. It bonded all of us together in a very natural way. I'm utterly impressed and a little jealous that I didn't think of it myself."

Haley blinked. "Well, thanks. You were so quiet during the session, I wasn't really sure what you were thinking."

"I was swept up in it all. To be honest, it was a moment of personal healing for me."

"Oh." Haley took a sip of tea and tried to quiet the pulse that was thrumming in her ears. The women had reached Dylan, too. It really had been a blessed moment. And right now it took every ounce of restraint to keep from reaching out and squeezing him in a big hug. "That's good."

He laughed, a low, sexy rumble. "Are you underwhelmed?"

She let out a nervous breath. "I'm not sure whether I should do a happy dance on the table or throw myself into your arms and beg you to reconsider being my boyfriend."

"Let's spare the table and make a date." The air froze in her lungs as he reached over and wrapped his arms around her, pulling her hips against his on the weathered bench. Her last impression was of strong arms and a warm solid chest and sunshine glazing the tips of his hair before his lips descended on hers in a kiss.

He smelled of soap and tasted of mint and salt and, yes . . . sarsaparilla. Her fingers clutched the edges of his down vest as the kiss deepened and her heart soared. No happy dance on the table, but her pulse was making up for that. She was kissing the man she loved, wrapped in his arms!

When he ended the kiss and leaned back, she blinked up at him in wonder. "That was nice."

"That was great. I should have gotten back into dating years ago."

She gave him a tap on the shoulder. "You didn't know me years ago."

"You're right. It wouldn't have packed such a wallop without you."

"What's happened, Dylan? What's changed since you told me you'd be a hermit the rest of your life?"

"I know you were aiming today's meeting to be therapeutic for the clients, but you were treating the therapist, too. *I* had an epiphany today." He explained that his wife and daughter had been organ donors, too. He had signed the papers and hadn't thought much about it until today.

"Today you made me realize that life goes on. It has to go on, or else we're wasting it."

"Such a wise man." Haley rubbed the warm flannel of his sleeves, knowing that she'd come to the same conclusion sometime over the past few months. She was ready to try another kiss when two figures moved into her peripheral vision.

"Dylan?" Elsie called.

"Mmm?" Dylan turned as the small girl appeared with Ruben by her side. "Hey, guys."

"You two lovebirds look like tourists," Ruben teased. "Zook's barn is a family place, you know."

"You're right." Dylan bit back a grin as Haley sidled away from him. "I apologize. We just lost our senses for a minute. Spring fever, I guess."

Elsie's bright smile told Haley that she understood, and Elsie was glad to see her friend side by side with the man she loved. If they hadn't worked things out, Haley was confident that they would find their way together sometime soon. With the blessing of God's love, Elsie and Ruben would marry and have a large brood of children.

Just like us, Haley thought, smiling up at the man she loved. *All with God's blessing.*

ACKNOWLEDGMENTS

It is a true joy to write about the kind, caring people of Halfway, and I'm grateful to the people who help me make that happen.

Abundant thanks to Dr. Violet Dutcher, who helps me keep the details and spirit of the Amish culture authentic. Your anecdotes touch my heart, and it makes my day when you tell me I got it right!

It's rare to find an editor who worries about my characters as much as I do, but Junessa Viloria is a master at squeezing the dramatic potential from every character, every moment. Many thanks to Junessa and the fabulous staff at Ballantine.

To my agent Robin Rue, who is always bringing me brand-new seeds to sow, it's all good. Isn't it fun to watch them grow?

Read on for an exciting preview of

A Simple Hope

THE NEXT LANCASTER CROSSROADS NOVEL

BY ROSALIND LAUER

1

The gentle spring breeze sent cherry blossoms floating through the air, pink petals settling over Rachel King and James Lapp as they walked hand in hand through the orchard.

Rachel stepped away from James and held her arms out, wanting to breathe in the beauty of the blossom shower. "It's like falling snow!"

James planted his legs apart and tipped back his hat. A slight smile appeared as he watched her reach out to catch falling petals. "That's the difference between us, Rachel. You see a shower of flowers. I see early blooms that'll wither if we get a late frost."

"So practical."

"That's what I like about living off the land. It keeps a man down to earth."

"I know you're used to this wonderful sight, working in the orchard every day, but there's something about blossoming trees that makes the heart burst with joy."

"Ya, if you don't have to prune them." The warmth in his dark eyes told her he was teasing.

"Is it a chore when you love what you do? You've told me yourself that your dat used to call you a tree monkey. When it was time to pick peaches, he couldn't get you to use the ladder."

James chuckled. "That was me." He took a flying leap and grabbed on to an overhead branch and hung there a moment, before doing an easy chin-up.

"You're still a tree monkey!" she said, glorying in the cascade of petals loosened by the jolt to the tree limb.

With dark hair that framed his handsome face and smoky eyes that warmed for Rachel, James was solid and well-grounded. His steady calm was one of the things that had won Rachel over a year ago when he'd started driving her home from singings and youth gatherings. At a time when other Amish fellas were putting boom boxes in their buggies and tossing back beers, James followed a simple path, choosing baptism and the management of the Lapp family orchards. Rachel liked to picture him as the root system that anchored her to the earth.

James dropped to the ground and leaned down to pick up a fallen bud. "Here's one for you."

Rachel held her breath as he came close, brushing back the edge of her prayer kapp to tuck the pale pink bud over her left ear. His touch sent shimmers rippling down her spine even as the gesture warmed her from head to toe. Ya, he kept her feet on the ground, but he let her heart soar.

"There." His dark eyes held her as his broad hands dropped to her shoulders. "You're the finest blossom in the Lapp orchards." His arms encircled her, and she melted in his embrace. Rachel loved the way he made her feel small and delicate against his strong, solid body.

"We should go to the sugar shack," she murmured. "Out here in the orchard . . . people can see. Your parents might be watching."

"With these trees in full bloom? I think we're well hidden." He caught her in his dark gaze. The flicker in his eyes let her know that he was feeling the same love that stirred her heart. Could he feel the quiet tremble of her limbs? Or the wooziness that overtook her when his lips nuzzled her jaw, leaving a trail of tingling sensation that became heated by his warm breath?

"Besides," he whispered, "I don't care if they see us. I don't care if they know that I love you, Rachel."

I love you, Rachel.

His words swelled and blossomed inside her, filling her heart with goodness and light. But just when they were about to kiss, the sweet moment faded, slipping away like sugar sifting between her fingers.

A dream . . . it was all a dream.

In the pink light of early morning, Rachel opened her eyes to blots of color that made up the large bedroom shared by the King girls.

Just a dream.

Rachel closed her eyes and clung to the sweetness, holding tight to the scent of cherry blossoms and the sureness of love. James loved her! And James was strong, standing and walking and swinging from a tree, as healthy and hearty as ever!

She tried to hold on to the goodness of the dream, but reality tapped on her mind like falling raindrops.

The reality of the accident was just as vivid, with the sickening screech of tires on the road, the grind of metal. Although Rachel had been able to walk away from the wrecked van, James had not. He was still recovering from spinal injuries, confined to a wheelchair for now. Maybe forever.

Sighing, she rolled over to see her younger sisters asleep in the double bed. Twelve-year-old Bethany's bare foot hung out from under the quilt, and nine-year-old Molly's sweet lips were pursed like a rosebud. Sleep was the only time Molly's lips were still, but Rachel didn't mind her chatterbox little sister. In fact, her sister's gabbing was just the sort of reassuring company Rachel had sought when she had given up her room in the attic to move down here with the younger girls. Rachel had hoped to spend more time with her sister Rose, too, but Rose, now sixteen, had other notions. Eager to leap into rumspringa, Rose had missed the point of companionship and moved up to Rachel's room, sure that a young man would soon come courting at her window. Oh, Rose, so full of dreams!

Still, Rachel was grateful for the chance to talk more with the other girls, whose steady breathing in the bed across from her was reassuring. Let Rose have the room upstairs; no young man would be calling for Rachel anytime soon, not with James still unable to walk.

Rachel closed her eyes in the hopes of recapturing the sweet dream—reliving the time when James had moved freely and managed the family orchard without fail. With a deep breath, she tried to bring back the scent of blossoms and the warm strength of James's arms around her.

But the dream was gone, and so was the James she had fallen in love with. The accident had pulled him away from her . . . so far away. Many things changed when a vehicle had hit the van Rachel and James had been riding in back in January. The other driver, a young Englisher girl, had been killed, and James's uncle Tom Lapp had died later in the hospital. So much heartbreak for two families,

Englisher and Amish alike. The accident had sent old Jacob Fisher into a fit of terrible breathing, but he seemed to be recovering, thank the good Lord. And James, her James, had hurt his back, really bad.

The golden wash of light told Rachel that it would be time to get out of bed soon. Time to wake her sisters and roust them from bed. There would be the morning chores to do, breakfast to prepare. Cows to milk, and a house and barns to clean. All tasks that went against Rachel's grain. But now, she would do the stinkiest chores gladly if it meant that James could get better.

She slid out of bed, pulled the quilt over her shoulders and padded barefoot to the window seat Dat had built. Outside, sunshine shot over the green and purple hills in the distance. The morning air was cold, but the sun promised a warmth to the day—Gott's promise of springtime and light and hope. Rachel thought of the colors in the paint kit her Englisher friend Haley had given her and wished she had time to paint right now. How she would enjoy mixing colors to come up with spring-green field, daffodil yellow, crocus purple, and the rich blots of pink and purple and orange and red that made up a sunrise. But these days, she didn't have time to paint if she wanted to see James and attend counseling sessions with the other accident victims.

She kneeled beside the window seat and clasped her hands together for a silent prayer. *Dear Gott, please heal James. Teach him to walk again. Please, don't let my selfish dreams get in his way.*

Long before the terrible accident, Rachel had thought of marrying James, and their relationship had been moving in that direction. But Rachel had secretly dreamed of a life away from the work of a farm or orchard. Her paintings sold well at the Country Store in Halfway—so well that she had been invited to sell them in a gallery in Philadelphia. In the back of her mind, she had always wanted to leave farm life behind and live in a small house in Halfway. With her love of peace and quiet and her yearning to paint all day and all night, Rachel longed to break free of the bonds of milking cows twice a day, tending to the chickens, and weeding the family vegetable garden.

Plenty of Amish had moved away from tending the land. Her cousin Market Joe traveled to Philadelphia six days a week to run the family cheese shop in the city's market. James's cousin Elsie Lapp ran their family's store in Halfway. Why couldn't she be among those who left the farm behind for a job or craft? She knew the bishop would allow it. The only fly in the ointment had been James. He loved working the orchard, a life of sunshine, he said. Before the accident, he would not have considered living in town.

And now? She wasn't sure what James was planning for the future. The James she loved, the man in her dream, was so hard to reach these days. And how she missed him! Without his sure, steady footing, she felt unsure and scared, like a seed blowing in the wind with no say in its direction, no idea where she might land.

Dear Gott, please bring James back to me.

"Rachel?" Molly's voice chirped from the bed. "Are you praying for James?"

"Ya, always."

"Me, too. Every morning and every night, and sometimes in between, I pray for Gott to heal his legs so that he can walk again. Bethany says I shouldn't tell Gott what to do, but Bishop Sam says we can pray for anything. Bishop says that Gott always listens, but he doesn't always give us the answer we want."

"I've heard Bishop Samuel say that, too." Rachel turned back toward the bed, where her little sister was sitting up, twisting one of her long blond braids around one hand. Little sprigs of Molly's wheat-gold hair had worked loose along her hairline, and the fluffy hair and shiny eyes made her resemble a baby chick.

"Thank you for praying, Molly," Rachel said. "Right now, I think James needs every prayer he can get."

"Do his legs hurt him really bad?" the younger girl asked.

"I don't think it's pain that's the problem." Although James had not offered to discuss his medical condition with Rachel, from what she'd overheard during her visits, it was the lack of sensation in James's legs that left him unable to walk. A few times a week, therapists visited the Lapp house to help James through his exercises so that his muscles wouldn't weaken and atrophy. The doctors were still not sure about his future—about whether or not he would walk again. No, pain wasn't what was bothering James. It was fear that he wouldn't recover.

Pulling the blanket up on her shoulders, Rachel went over to the double bed and sat down facing Molly. "You have a big heart, liewe." Too big to take on worries about James.

"I pray for everyone who was in that van," Molly said. "It must have been a terrible thing, being in a crash. Ben says two cars can crack each other in half, just like eggshells."

"Don't let Ben scare you. He's full of stories these days, and he wasn't there." At seventeen, their brother Ben was feeling his oats, as Dat said. Although rumspringa was meant to be a time for parents to look the other way while their teenaged son or daughter found a mate in the Amish community, some young people pushed the walls out way too far. Rachel had heard talk of Ben learning to drive a car and racing motorbikes. But mostly, he seemed to collect tidbits of Englisher culture, gobbling up stories about the Englisher world as if they were candy.

"Are you still scared to ride in a car?" Molly asked.

"A little," Rachel admitted. "But I don't get that tight feeling inside anymore. The meetings with Dylan have helped me a lot." Dylan Monroe was an Englisher counselor who had offered free

sessions to help the passengers deal with the aftermath of the accident. Post-traumatic stress, he called it.

"You're so brave."

"Not really." As Rachel smoothed back her sister's hair, she
thought of the story shared by Ruben Zook, one of the other passengers. The notion of angels had come up when the group members were questioning why they were spared while Tom Lapp was
taken by Gott and James was seriously injured. "Ruben says that we
had angels with us that afternoon. Gott's angels, watching over us."

Molly flung her arms around Rachel and hugged her close. "I
love that story. Sometimes when I can't sleep at night, I pretend that
an angel just slipped into bed beside me. And that helps me sleep."

"That's a wonderful good way to doze off." Rachel yawned.
"But now it's time to get up."

"Time to greet the day!" Molly pushed back the covers, slipped
out of bed, then turned back to Rachel. "I'm so glad you moved
back down with us. I missed you."

Rachel smiled. "I'm glad, too."

Molly prodded Bethany, whose face was pressed into her pillow.
"Now it's time to get up, sleepyhead."

"I'm up," Bethany groaned. "How could I sleep with you two
yacking?"

"Rise and shine," Rachel said as she began to pin her long hair
back. "It's the early bird that gets the worm."

"I want to sleep." Bethany rolled over and groaned. "I don't need
any worms."

Chuckling softly, Rachel was glad to be back down here sharing
a room with her sisters. Gott did work in wondrous ways.

ABOUT THE AUTHOR

ROSALIND LAUER grew up in a large family in Maryland and began visiting Lancaster County's Amish community as a child. She attended Wagner College in New York City and worked as an editor for Simon & Schuster and Harlequin Books. She currently lives with her family in Oregon, where she writes in the shade of some towering two-hundred-year-old Douglas fir trees.